D0477565

Cold Blood

Other books by Denise Ryan

The Hit
Dead Keen
Betrayed
Backlash
Blood Knot

Cold Blood

Denise Ryan

PIATKUS

Visit the Piatkus website!

Piatkus publishes a wide range of best-selling fiction and non-fiction, including books on health, mind, body & spirit, sex, self-help, cookery, biography and the paranormal.

If you want to:
- read descriptions of our popular titles
- buy our books over the Internet
- take advantage of our special offers
- enter our monthly competition
- learn more about your favourite Piatkus authors

VISIT OUR WEBSITE AT: www.piatkus.co.uk

All the characters in this book are fictitious and any resemblance to real persons, living or dead, is entirely coincidental.

Copyright © 2005 by Denise Ryan

First published in Great Britain in 2005 by
Piatkus Books Ltd of
5 Windmill Street, London W1T 2JA
email: info@piatkus.co.uk

The moral right of the author has been asserted

A catalogue record for this book is available from the British Library

ISBN 0 7499 0721 5

Set in Times by
Phoenix Photosetting, Chatham, Kent

Printed and bound in Great Britain by
William Clowes Ltd. Beccles, Suffolk

To the people I love
(they know who they are!)

MORAY COUNCIL LIBRARIES & INFO.SERVICES	
2O 15 11 O7	
Askews	
MF	

Prologue

'I'm sick of telling clients the legal system isn't perfect but it's the best we've got when I think it stinks. I wish I hadn't let my ex-husband persuade me to take his name when we got married, because a year on from the divorce I still can't face the hassle of changing it back. And I'm sick of other patronising lawyers with posh accents—'

'What, posher than yours?'

'—telling me there's no class system any more.'

'But apart from all that you're deliriously happy?'

'*Deliriously.*'

One woman had long, curly blonde hair, the other's was straight silky black. Two dolls, a perfect contrast; light and dark, lemon chiffon ice cream and espresso. They came laughing out of the club, their arms around one another's shoulders. They were not falling down drunk, but it was obvious they had had a good night. They teetered over the cobblestones and paused to gaze at the new autumn moon shining on the calm river, their breath forming clouds in the frosty air.

'And now you've got someone else who'd love you to take his name.'

'Hmm, yeah, lucky old me, eh? I'll walk home,' the blonde announced.

'Joking, aren't you? If you get raped on the way you'll be accused of contributing negligently to your fate worse than death.'

'Yes, what's a poor, unevolved rapist to think when he clocks a solitary woman walking late at night? That he should leave her alone? Right, do you want to get a cab or doss at my gaff?'

'Get a cab – if I can find one. God, it's freezing.'

'That was a great night. We should do it again soon.'

'How about tomorrow?'

They laughed again and the blonde hugged her friend. 'I love you. I'll call you soon. Take care, okay?'

'Can we live together when we're old and any men we had have croaked it?'

'We might croak it first. We drink, we've got careers and executive stress; our testosterone levels must be right up there with the guys.' The blonde put on a deep voice. 'I blame feminism, by God.' She slapped her friend on the back. 'But yes, deal. You pay for the stair lift.'

They carried on teetering over cobblestones designed for hobnailed boots, horses' hooves and iron-wheeled wagons, not black satin, spike-heeled pumps. The voices and thump of music from the club faded, and moonlight washed out colour. They turned a corner, hugged one last time and parted.

Light? The natural agent that stimulates things and makes them visible. Light is electromagnetic radiation whose wavelength falls within the range to which the human retina responds, and it consists of energy quanta called photons. Photons behave partly like waves and partly like particles.

Or dark? Little or no light. Hidden from knowledge. Mysterious, a dark secret. A period of time characterised by unhappiness or tragedy. Angry, threatening, suggestive of or arising from evil characteristics or sinister forces.

Which to choose? Dark, of course.

Every time.

The old man started shouting at him as he let himself out of the house, leaving Mariam and the baby asleep upstairs. Jevko could not understand all the words, but it was obvious the man did not want to be best mates. His features were twisted with rage, shadowed by dark hollows. He was always up early, on the lookout for the milkman or the paper boy who brought the grimy, densely-printed tabloid in which he could read more lies and bullshit. Jevko's father had always said that reading a newspaper was a terrible way to start the day.

'Get stuffed, you old bastard.' He shivered in the icy darkness and felt in his jacket pocket for the van keys.

'Don't you talk to me like that, you fuzzy-wuzzy scum! Get back to the plains of the Hindu Kush where you belong.'

Not an option. He would never return to Afghanistan. Jevko glanced up beyond the orange street lights and frosted roofs of the ugly new houses built too close together, and stared at the moon. Several stars glittered on the dark-blue horizon. New city, new country. New dangers. He thought of his father's severed head lying on the Persian carpet in the back of the lorry, surrounded by swirling dust and jostling mourners. The scars on Jevko's back itched and ached in the cold; he wondered if they would ache for the rest of his life, never let him forget who and what had caused them.

A train roared along the embankment, startling him. He got into the dirty white van and turned the key in the ignition; the engine choked and croaked, so he tried again. There was no sign of the gang of teenage thugs who terrorised this street and several others in the neighbourhood. It was too early for them, hours yet before they would emerge red-eyed and ashen-faced from rumpled beds. Like vampires. Mariam took the baby out in the mornings to try and avoid them. She only went to the shops these days because she was too frightened to go to the park any more.

Jevko needed to make money to get himself and his wife and child out of this place. And after fleeing Afghanistan, trailing around various European countries for years and finally ending up in Britain, it seemed he had found a way. He had become a gangmaster, a boss who hired people and formed them into labour gangs which he then hired out to farmers and agricultural packing plants. Nothing wrong with that, except that Jevko was the illegal and unlicensed kind of gangmaster, one of those who gave the trade a bad name. His labour gangs consisted of illegal immigrants like himself, who lived in debt, squalor, misery and sometimes danger, depending on the kind of work they did. There had been some unwelcome publicity about illegal gangmasters, and the police were starting to crack down on them; Jevko did not know how much longer he could continue. A pity, because the money was good. His dead parents would have been desperately ashamed of their only son exploiting vulnerable people in this way. But what choice did he have? To be oppressor or victim. Jevko did not intend to be a victim, not any more.

He drove down the street and under the railway bridge. The pre-dawn city was quiet with few people about, not many lights on in the houses and tower blocks. He headed down London Road and turned left into Lime Street. The paws and manes of the stone Landseer lions outside St George's Hall sparkled with frost. His father had once been a student at the university here in Liverpool, studying medicine. He had liked the city and its people, which was why Jevko had decided to come here.

He had to drive through town to reach the run-down estate where his workers lived, then drive them out of the city to the plant where that day they would be packing vegetables for a supermarket chain. As gangmaster he needed to keep tight control over them. The men were more trouble than the women – women were used to hard work for little pay. If any man wanted to leave and try to survive without getting swept up by the police and Home Office and deported, good luck to him. He would need it.

Jevko glanced at his watch. Time to grab a coffee. He yawned until his jaw clicked, and closed his eyes for a second. The bitter cold had not cleared his head. He longed to be back beneath the warm quilt, Mariam's body snuggled against his. He opened his eyes to find himself blinded by headlights. A horn blared.

'What the ...?'

He gripped the wheel and swerved to the right. The van mounted the pavement, missing a lamp post by centimetres. Thank God no one was walking here. He jammed his foot on

4

the brakes, gasping in panic as he felt the vehicle skid out of control down the wide pavement. It crashed through a chain strung between low stone posts and came to a stop by the war memorial. Jevko jumped out, slipped on the icy flags and fell, arms flailing. Swearing and trembling, he got up and inspected the damage. The front of the van was damaged, one headlight smashed. But that was nothing. He had started to fall asleep and veered across the road into the path of oncoming traffic. He could have been killed. He glared up at a stone lion lounging on its plinth.

'What are you looking at, you bastard?'

He could not drive again before he'd had that coffee. Jevko locked the van, crossed the road and walked past the old Northwestern Hotel, now converted to student accommodation. He entered Lime Street station, gulped some hot, sweet coffee that was not strong enough for his liking – it never was in this country – and headed back. The sky was starting to lighten, clouds massing on the violet horizon. He reached the van and was about to unlock it when something – he did not know what – made him pause and turn round.

Why? Did he think the stone lion was going to come alive and cuff him with one gigantic, frosted paw? From behind its big, square plinth Jevko glimpsed part of a foot – a human foot. Female, he presumed, given that the toenails were painted. Poking through ripped stockings, they looked like tiny spots of black in the dim light.

He gasped and started to tremble again. Jevko knew he should ignore whatever this was, get back in the van right now and drive. The day had started badly enough already. Knowing what you should do was one thing, doing it another. He glanced around and moved slowly forward, his heart thudding.

On the other side of the plinth, concealed from the road and pavement, lay a woman. Jevko's first thought was that she must be freezing in that short dress. One high-heeled shoe lay nearby, the other a few metres away. He could not see a handbag or any other belongings. He wondered if she had staggered here and collapsed while drunk. A coat was flung over her face.

5

Jevko realised this was stupid and he did not understand why he was doing it, but he stepped closer, reached down and flipped the coat away. The woman was dead. He had seen bodies before, but not like this. Never like this. His stomach lurched and he turned away and spat several times. He realised he was not standing in slushy water, but blood.

'Ahhh, no. *No.*' He was shivering violently now, his breath coming in gasps. He caught a sudden movement some distance away, up the steps behind one of the building's huge columns. Somebody was watching him. Who? Was it the murderer?

Panic seized him and he turned to run. But first Jevko had to lose his meagre breakfast. He stumbled back to the van, climbed in and drove off at speed.

Not his business.

Chapter One

'*Escaped*?'

Shannon Flinder stared in horrified dismay at the embarrassed detective inspector who sat across the paper-strewn desk from her. 'I can't believe it. You hate lawyers, so this is a wind-up. Right?'

DI John Casey sighed and shook his head. 'I wish.'

She got up, walked to the window and looked out into the rain-drenched alley at the brick wall of the old warehouse, then up at goddess Minerva on her golden throne above Liverpool's Town Hall. Shannon tried to give herself a moment. Bad news never seemed to make sense.

'What is it about me?' she wondered. 'Maybe I try too hard to avoid trouble and that's why I keep getting it.'

Shannon had not wanted to suffer a marriage breakdown and traumatic divorce, fall in love with a suspected criminal, be pursued by a murderer and end up getting accused of murder herself. The past two years had been the worst of her life. Now more danger threatened. She turned back to DI Casey, sitting there with his hands bunched in the pockets of his black leather jacket. He had tired eyes, a pale complexion, dark hair threaded with silver.

'Okay. So you've let that murdering rapist escape from a hospital. And you think I'm at risk?'

'It's possible. Croft blames you for getting him caught. When he was sentenced he screamed that he'd kill you. Shortly before his arrest he'd phoned your office and home and told you to drop Julie as your client. You refused. He also made more threatening phone calls to you from prison until he was stopped. And there was a drawing he did ... I believe somebody showed it to you?'

'Yes.' Shannon tried to force from her mind the crude pencil sketch of the kneeling naked woman with a noose around her neck, her own name scrawled beneath by the artist himself. 'All right, I helped get Richard Croft arrested and he swore he'd kill me. But what makes you think he meant it? Threats and verbal abuse go with a Criminal Law solicitor's territory, and they're hardly ever serious. If I'd been paid a tenner every time someone called me a bitch or—' she paused '—the *C* word, or said they'd kill me I would have had the youngest retirement age on record.'

She thought back to the Richard Croft case. Croft had assaulted a young girl named Julie Ferris, the daughter of the woman he was living with. Julie had come to Shannon for help when her mother and the police refused to believe that Croft had sexually assaulted her. Shannon remembered being struck by Julie's fear and sense of helplessness and isolation, her shock and heartbreak at being let down by the one person she had thought she could always depend on – her mother.

'You went round to the Ferris house that day, didn't you?' DI Casey prompted. 'When Julie didn't turn up for an appointment with you?'

'That's right. I was worried about her. Especially after Croft had threatened me.' Shannon touched cold hands to her flushed face. 'Julie didn't answer the door so I called through the letter box. She screamed my name, screamed that Croft had raped her and murdered her mother when she'd come home unexpectedly and caught him in the act. She begged me to help her, said Croft had a gun.' Shannon paused. 'I phoned the police, and the armed response team did the rest. I still can't believe Croft survived that bullet wound to the head. What about Julie?' she asked. 'Won't she be his priority now, rather than me? Have you warned her?'

'That's the first thing we did.'

8

'She must be terrified. This, after all she's been through.'

Casey nodded glumly. 'Our news didn't make her day.'

'This could be wishful thinking, but—' Shannon thought. 'Croft might not plan to hurt me or Julie. Won't he have enough trouble trying to survive on the run? He's got no family, no friends – he can't go back to his old haunts. What's he going to do?'

'Exactly. That's why we hope to recapture him within the next twenty-four hours. Most escaped cons are recaptured within twenty-four to forty-eight hours.'

'He could do a lot of damage in that time. To me or Julie. Or someone else. If that's what he wants.'

Casey shrugged. 'Who knows how Croft's warped mind works? The bullet wound to his brain could have made him even more warped.' He looked at Shannon's frightened dark-blue eyes, mass of blonde corkscrew curls, her slender figure in the tight black suit, and realised with dismay that she was arousing his protective instincts. Not to mention other more base instincts. 'Maybe Croft blames you because you were the most ... I don't know ... visible.' Shannon Flinder was certainly that. 'Or believes that if you hadn't turned up at the house when you did, he would have got away with assault, rape and murder – double murder, probably. He wouldn't have let Julie go after he'd killed her mother.'

'Well, whatever he believes, I suppose it'd be mad to hope it was based on reason and logic.' Shannon took a long breath. 'Croft's been in prison for more than a year. How the hell did he escape?'

DI Casey sniffed the odour of fresh ground coffee that drifted into Shannon's office and regretted that Ms Flinder was too freaked to think of offering him a cup. He had gone without breakfast and would not have said no to a chocolate biscuit either. He could smell Shannon's warm, sensuous perfume which he bet cost a fortune. A little tube of palest pink lipgloss lay on top of some weighty legal volume.

'Croft had a hospital appointment yesterday,' he explained, feeling like a moron, even though Croft's escape was not his

9

fault. Shannon Flinder must despise him. 'For a brain scan. He's had them before and he was on his best behaviour as usual. He and the two guards—'

'Two? That was enough?' Shannon had turned pale now.

'Not for me to judge.' He shrugged again. 'They had to hang around the Neurology Unit. Croft said he felt exhausted and complained of a headache. Anyone who sustains a head or brain injury can suffer from fatigue and headaches for a long time afterwards.'

'I know.' Shannon glanced away.

She would know, DI Casey realised, because her ex-husband Rob, a former CID detective, had held her hostage in his parents' house one cold dark night. Rumour was that Rob Flinder had flipped after his sister Melanie's death and the discovery that his father was a paedophile who had murdered several young girls. Rob had strangled his pregnant girlfriend before taking Shannon hostage, then shot himself in the head after she managed to escape. Rob had survived his self-inflicted injury and was now just nine months into a terminal stretch. Casey noticed that Shannon's hands were trembling slightly.

She walked back to her desk, looked down at the open file in front of her and mechanically re-read a sentence from her sixteen-year-old client's statement: '*He gave me two mini brandy bottles which I opened and drank, then offered me Cola from a can. I said I wasn't drinking that in case he'd pissed in it. Then he dragged me down an alley and told me to get 'em off*'. Another less than magical night out in clubland. She looked at Casey again.

'Let me guess. Model prisoner turned nasty.'

'Right.' Casey flushed. 'They took the cuffs off, something they'd done on previous occasions without any problem. Croft requested that he be given some food—'

'Please.' Shannon raised one hand; she felt like snapping at him to get on with it. 'You don't have to report this as though you were in court.'

'Sorry. Force of habit, I'm afraid. One guard went to the canteen,' Casey continued, 'and Croft asked to use the toilet.

Once in there he lashed out at the other guard, punched him a few times and knocked him out. It was a vicious assault.'

'Vicious, what, him? You don't say.' This had to happen just when she'd thought her life was coming together again. Shannon could only hope and maybe pray that Casey was right and Croft would be recaptured fast. She wondered if she and Julie Ferris were the only people on his hit list, if he had one.

'He ran out of the hospital and carjacked a gynaecologist getting into his Merc,' Casey said. 'Stole the guy's wallet, which contained credit cards and a couple of hundred in cash. The car was found abandoned near Manchester Victoria. There's been no sign of Croft since.'

'Terrific.' Shannon sank into her chair. 'So what do I do now? Take a fast-track self-defence course? Get myself a Magnum forty-five and go blasting around downtown Liverpool while I quote Dirty Harry on how there's nothin' wrong with shootin' as long as the right people get shot?'

'Er – no.' DI Casey smiled for the first time. 'I definitely wouldn't recommend the Magnum forty-five.'

'Well, yes, I've heard it's heavy and difficult to use. D'you think I should *Czech* out a Glöck because that's more of a lay-dee's gun?'

He laughed. 'Take the self-defence course by all means. But Croft will probably be back inside before you've registered or had your first lesson.'

'Hmm. That word – *probably*.'

'We've put out a warning, a description. There's a lot of people working on this. Croft won't get far, he can't. And while we can't be certain he intends to harm you, Julie Ferris or anyone else, there's a strong possibility he might, and we have to...'

'Warn me,' Shannon sighed. 'Thanks for warning me.' She picked up a pencil and tapped it against the desk edge.

DI Casey felt sorry for her as he sensed her vulnerability and fear. She must be having a difficult enough time trying to put her troubles behind her, and she didn't need this. Rob Flinder might have been driven to the edge and that was tragic. But his

11

ex-wife hadn't flipped or murdered anyone. She had just tried to get her life back on track.

'I'm sorry about all this,' he muttered. 'I know it's the last thing you need now.'

Shannon gave him a sharp look. Of course he must know about her and Rob. She was practically a local celebrity these days, notorious as the solicitor who had been briefly suspected of murdering her paedophile father-in-law and whose ex had turned psycho and tried to murder her. Her notoriety was attracting more clients – some of them the kind she did not want.

'So what happens now?' she asked Casey. 'Do Julie and I get protection?'

'Yes. I can't discuss what Julie gets, but we'll provide you with a panic alarm or personal attack alarm, and establish a phone link from your home direct to the nearest police station. We'll have more police officers present at Dale Street Magistrates' Court, and the Crown Court. We'll also arrange for police patrols outside your home.'

'I'm not always at home in the evenings.' Shannon hesitated. 'I spend a lot of time at my partner's place.'

Her partner, yes. DI Casey had heard about him too. The Irish guy, Finbar Linnell, who seemed to be the model businessman these days, if there was such a thing, all rumours of drugs and arms dealing and organised crime connections long gone. Linnell was a smart bastard and had never been nicked for anything, much to the fury of some of his colleagues. Shannon Flinder's thing for Linnell was unfortunate, Casey thought. Still. None of his business.

'No problem.' He nodded. 'We can establish a phone link and arrange patrols from there as well. You can let us know where you'll be.' He had to suppress a smile, because he had a feeling that Linnell would not welcome police surveillance of his big, swish Albert Dock apartment, even if it was to protect his beloved girlfriend. 'And of course I don't need to remind you to be vigilant. If Croft should contact you – if you notice anything suspicious – give us a call immediately.' He pulled one of his cool new business cards from his wallet, reached across and handed it to her, feeling disappointed when Shannon dropped it on her desk without bothering to look at it.

'OK.' She stood up. 'I get panic alarms, phone links and patrols and generally watch my back until you've recaptured Croft. At least that's the theory.'

'And practice.' Casey stood up too. 'Call me,' he reminded her, 'if anything happens. Doesn't matter what time of day or night.'

'Right. Thank you.'

Why am I thanking him? Shannon wondered as he left. The people he represents just allowed a murderous con with a grudge to escape. Did Richard Croft plan to come after her? She sat down again and put her head in her hands. Someone tapped at the door.

'Go away,' she murmured. Leon Rossini, Kam Flinder Najeba's accredited representative, or clerk, as some people might call it, came in.

'An inspector calls,' he grinned. 'What did the officer of the law want?'

Shannon looked up. 'Remember Richard Croft?'

'Bloody hell. Yeah, why?'

'He's escaped from jail. Well, from—'

'*What?* You're—' Leon stared at her. 'No, not joking.'

Shannon told him the story. 'The inspector reassures me he'll be recaptured in a day or so. *Probably.*'

'What if he isn't? Some cons stay on the run for weeks or months. Years even.'

'Gee, thanks for that. Look, let's not even go there, Leon. Anyway, the police can't be certain Croft wants to harm Julie Ferris or me.'

'But you wouldn't be amazed if he did?'

'Well, no.'

'How could those morons let him escape?' Leon frowned. 'I don't believe this.'

'I wish I didn't. Unfortunately I've got no choice.' Shannon looked at him. 'Did you want something?'

'No. Just being nosey, wondering what the inspector wanted.'

'Now you know. Keep an eye out, will you, Leon? If you see Croft hanging around here – if anything weird happens – tell me straight away. Or just phone the police.' She showed him Casey's business card and Leon jotted down the numbers. 'I'll warn Mi-Hae and Khalida. And Helena, our charming receptionist.' She glanced at her watch. 'I'm about due at the Magistrates' Court. Just got time for a coffee.'

'I'll get it.' Leon straightened his tie and raked his fingers through his black hair. His brown eyes were troubled. 'The cops will give you protection, I hope?'

'Some, yes.' Shannon jumped as her phone rang. Leon gave her a sympathetic grimace and left her to take the call.

'You nipped off bloody early,' Finbar complained. 'I woke up to find nothing but a blonde hair and trace of perfume on my pillow. You blow in at three a.m., ravish my body and bugger off by seven. Makes me feel like a sex object.'

'I thought that was most full-blooded males' fantasy.'

'Yeah, well, when you've met the full-blooded female of your fantasies you tend to want more than a quick...'

'I had to go home and get changed. None of your sharp suits fit me.' A year now since she had moved out of Finbar's apartment because after what had happened with Rob, Shannon had felt the need to have her own space and take time to get over everything. It still only seemed like last week.

'You sound a bit —' Finbar paused. 'I don't know. Something wrong?'

She told him.

'Christ. So you're just supposed to try and stay out of this bastard's clutches – with a little help from the cops – until they've recaptured him?'

'Apparently.' Shannon smiled her thanks as Leon came back with a cup of coffee. He placed it on her desk and went out again. 'God, I hope they do get Croft soon.' She sniffed, found herself blinking back tears. 'This is such a shock. And bloody typical that it happens just when I was starting to feel safe again. After Rob and ...' her voice shook, '... and everything.'

14

'Yeah. I know.' Finbar's voice was gentle. 'Don't you think it'd be a good idea for you to stay with me for now? The cops can establish their bloody phone links and patrols from my place.'

'You wouldn't mind that?'

'Course not. Got nothing to hide now, have I? I promised you – no more secrets, no more dark deeds. I'm strictly legit these days, you know that. A right boring bastard.'

Shannon smiled. 'Boring is the last thing you are.'

'Thank you for that, darling. Look, I know I've been asking – well, all right, begging – you to move back in with me. But I'm not trying to take advantage of this situation. I wouldn't do that.'

'I know.' Shannon picked up her coffee and took a sip. 'I just don't want to be the frightened female.'

'This is about being sensible, not trying to prove how brave you are.'

'In that case it might be better if I stay away from your beautiful dockside apartment. Croft phoned me there, remember, just before I moved out? I still don't know how he got hold of that number. He might think I still live there. But he won't know my present address.'

'Are you sure?'

'As sure as I can be. He might turn up here at Exchange Street East, or hang around the Mags' or Crown courts. But there would be lots of people around and an increased police presence. He'd be crazy to do that.'

'He is crazy, last I heard. Can't you take some time off work?'

'I suppose – if it was absolutely necessary. But I don't fancy cowering around my apartment freakin' and trippin' every time the phone or door bell rings.'

'You don't have to do that. We could go to my house in Ireland.'

Shannon pictured Finbar's beautiful, isolated house set in acres of gardens, imagined taking walks along the nearby beach and looking out at the Atlantic breakers. Yes, she would feel safe there. 'Maybe at the weekend.'

'So how about if I come and stay with you for the next few days? Hopefully the cops will have recaptured their psycho by then.'

'Yes. That'd be good. OK.'

'I'll pick you up from work later. What are you going to do now?'

'Warn my partners, Mi-Hae and Khalida – if Leon hasn't already. And then I've got a couple of clients locked in the Bridewell who'd really like to get bail.'

'Right, I'll see you around six at your office. And don't walk to the Mags' Court, take a cab.'

'It's less than five minutes walk,' she protested. 'A cab would be—'

'Just humour me, Shannon, will you?'

'OK. I love you,' she whispered. 'Bye.'

Shannon hung up and dialled Jenny Fong's office, wondering if her friend had made it into work after drinking all those Manhattans at the Blue Bar last night. After the Blue Bar they had gone on to a club. Jenny had drunk more than usual because she was depressed about her ex – a married man who had just dumped her for his wife.

She thought of how Jenny had stuck by her as her marriage collapsed when Rob changed, following the nightmare revelations about his respected headmaster father and became a nightmare himself, callous, unpredictable and violent. Shannon had been the one to discover the truth about Rob's father, Bernard Flinder, who had tried to silence her. Shannon had survived Bernard Flinder's attempt on her life and fought back: it was either kill or be killed. It was during that terrible time that she had met Finbar Linnell. Shannon still feared that what she had done to Bernard Flinder would one day somehow return to haunt her.

'Jenny didn't come in this morning,' Anita, the receptionist at Shannon's old firm informed her in a hushed voice. 'She hasn't phoned either. Gavin's ballistic – she was supposed to go with him to court.'

'Hmm. Weird.' Shannon was not of course going to tell Anita about her and Jenny's wild night out. She said goodbye and called Jenny's apartment. No answer. Had Jenny switched off her phone in order to peacefully sleep away her hangover? But surely she would have first phoned work to lie about period pain or some mystery virus? Shannon was about to give up when she heard a click.

'At last. The frightful fiend rises from its pit,' she laughed. 'Hey lady, you'd better get a triple espresso down your neck right now.'

'Who's speaking, please?' a male voice inquired.

'What? Who's *this*?' Shannon was astonished. She must have the wrong number, but how was that possible when she had programmed Jenny's number into her phone? This man did not sound like Chris, Jenny's ex. And what would Chris be doing there anyway? From what Jenny had told her of his insultingly casual indifference and downright nastiness, Shannon could not see any miraculous romantic reunion happening.

'Who are you?' the mystery man asked. 'Identify yourself, please.'

'I think not.' Shannon hung up and dialled the entire number slowly and carefully. He answered again, and she started to feel nervous. 'Look, I must have the wrong number, although I can't imagine how. I want to speak to someone named Jenny Fong.'

'This is Ms Fong's home. She isn't here. I'm a police officer.'

'A *police*...?' Shannon wondered if this was some sort of sick joke. But there was not the faintest trace of amusement in this calm, serious voice. Her nervousness increased.

'What's your name, please?'

'Shannon Flinder.' Her heart beat faster. 'I'm Jenny's best friend.'

'All right. Thank you. We'll want to talk to you as soon as—'

'Just a second.' Shannon forgot Richard Croft. 'What's going on there? Is Jenny all right?' But no, she couldn't be. If you were all right you did not need a police officer to answer your phone for you.

17

'I'm very sorry.' His voice softened. 'It's bad news, I'm afraid. Ms Fong is dead. Her body was discovered early this morning.'

Shannon went cold. She stood up, gripping the phone, and stared around her office as if there was something she could do, somewhere she could go. She could not believe his words, take them in. This had to be a terrible mistake. 'You're telling me Jenny's *dead*?'

'I'm afraid so, yes. I'm very sorry,' he repeated.

'No. No, she can't be.' Hot tears stung Shannon's eyes and spilled over. 'I mean, I only saw her last night,' she stammered. 'Are you …?'

She wanted to ask him if he was sure. At the same time she knew it was true, it had to be, even though she was too stunned right now to take in the horror of it, wanted with all her heart not to believe this.

'I'm sure,' he said gently, obviously familiar with grim scenarios. 'There's no doubt. She's been formally identified.'

'But what *happened*?' The tears rolled down Shannon's face. 'Did Jenny have an accident? Get hit by a car, or …?'

'Her death wasn't an accident.' He paused. 'Ms Fong was murdered.'

Chapter Two

'I'd prefer the bastard dead, not recaptured,' Finbar Linnell muttered to himself. 'Break out another bloody armed response team and let them finish the job this time.'

The cops first had to find Richard Croft. And where the hell could he be? This might be all over by tonight or tomorrow. But what if it wasn't?

Finbar tossed his mobile on the sofa and got up to stare out at the River Mersey, the double glazing and central heating protecting him from the chill drizzle of the October morning. The huge apartment was silent except for a whispering voice on the television. Dark clouds bunched low over the river, almost seeming to touch the grey water. A ferry disappeared into the mist. Finbar remembered the old man in the pub the other night, laughing over the excuse he and his mates had always given as boys when they were late for school: '*Fog on the river, sir.*'

He picked up the phone again and dialled his India Buildings office. 'Paula, hi.'

'Oh my God, it's the big boss man. I'm working dead hard, I swear. Absolutely run off me Jimmy Choo's.'

'Yeah, right, I believe you. Listen, I won't be in until after lunch. I've got some stuff to take care of at the airport. Everything OK there?'

'Fine. Quiet. Except ...' His office manager's voice was wary. 'There's a letter come for you. From the insurance company.'

'Oh great. What does it say? Like I can't guess.'

'I haven't opened it – it's marked *Private and Confidential*.'

'Overcome your delicate sensibilities and take a look.'

'OK, hang on.' He waited while Paula ripped open the envelope and scanned the letter's contents, her slight breathing audible down the line. 'They refuse to pay out on the claim you made for your bombed club,' she said at last.

'That figures.' Finbar felt pissed off nonetheless.

'It says the police investigation proved inconclusive, but they can't rule out foul play. A copy of the letter has been sent to your accountant, Mr Nick Forth, and your lawyer ... there's a bit more.' She paused. 'Want the gory details?'

'I'm usually a sucker for them, but no thanks. They'll keep.'

Finbar knew who had blown up his club – the terrorist group who had wanted to demonstrate their power of life and death over him. They had followed up the bombing with a threat to murder Shannon if he did not help them with their plan to destroy a shopping mall and everyone in it. They had not succeeded and their leader was dead now, the others in jail.

'I don't know why it took almost a year for them to tell me this bullshit.'

'Insurance companies move in slow and mysterious ways.'

'Got that right.'

Of course the police investigation was inconclusive; they did not give a damn about him once he had risked his life to help them with their sting operation. He and Shannon could have been murdered, and Shannon had also narrowly escaped being killed by her psycho ex. Now this Richard Croft was on the loose. Would it never end?

'Cheer up,' Paula urged, getting the wrong idea from his silence. 'This doesn't matter too much. You've still got the air cargo business. That'll keep me in designer gear and you in bog roll, Armani suits and Assam teabags. Plus you're tall, dark and handsome, so some model agency might take you on if you get desperate.'

'Isn't thirty-eight knocking on a bit for that?'

'Maybe. Never mind. I'm sure Shannon will invite you over for a meal and lend you a tenner now and then.'

'Sounds great, I'm cheering up already. I'll see you later, OK?'

'Yeah. 'Bye, Finbar.'

He felt too restless to work. This was a bad day. A year on from the terrifying events which had gripped him and Shannon, Finbar still felt depressed at times. And vulnerable, something he never admitted to anyone, not even Shannon. She knew though, because she felt the same. That was the trouble with life – once you did something, once something happened, you had to live with it. Endure whatever comes, as the Bible said. He paced the sitting room, paused to stare out at the river again, then went into the kitchen and poured himself more coffee.

He hoped to God Richard bloody Croft would get picked up soon. Where was he now? Shannon must be wondering the same thing as she worked her way through her morning's case-load at court. This would freak her out. Finbar stirred sugar into his coffee, took one sip and poured the rest down the sink. Of course Croft wanted to hurt her. It was what bastards like him did. He remembered the threatening phone calls Shannon had told him about. And that drawing which he had never seen and would not have wanted to see.

All this would make Shannon think about Rob again, about that terrible night when he had held her hostage. Finbar had a feeling she thought more about Rob than she let on. She had been through so much, and he did not blame her for being inse-cure now, wanting her own space and feeling unable to link her fate to his again by moving back in with him, getting re-engaged and maybe even marrying him. Not that that was likely at present. He recalled Shannon's response the last time he had tentatively sounded her out on the dreaded M-word.

'Holy deadlock? Don't even go there. Did you know marriage was defined as a friendship recognised by the police? I read that in *Brewer's Dictionary of Phrase and Fable*.' He had laughed – or pretended to – poured them both more wine and transferred the unopened box containing thirty grand's

21

worth of gold and glittering diamond from his jeans pocket to the back of the safe where it still sat now, three months later.

Most people, if they considered it any of their business, might think he and Shannon had the perfect relationship, living apart and seeing as much or as little of one another as they liked. It was not enough for him, but Finbar supposed he would go on putting up with it. To pressure her now would be a mistake.

He strolled into the bathroom and saw her toothbrush lying in the sink where she had dropped it, a small pot of night cream and a white tube of eye balm on the glass shelf above. He thought about last night – or rather, this morning. His shock at the bad news about Croft faded as he started to get angry. There was no way he would let Croft – or anyone else – hurt Shannon. Ever again. He would do whatever it took. Shannon could take care of herself, or so she thought, but everyone needed a helping hand now and then.

He went back into the sitting room and slipped on his jacket. He would go to the airport to check on that cargo of engine parts, then take the rest of the day off. Think what to do. The police might just prove startlingly efficient and recapture Croft before he could do any damage. If not, he would have to sort something. Finbar thought how Rob Flinder might be released one day. Not for many years, of course, but the shadow was there, hovering over Shannon. And himself. All these demons that needed to be locked away. His mobile rang.

'It's Paula again. That guy, Feico something, called back. Says he's got a great deal for you.'

'I'm sure he has.' Finbar frowned. 'I've already told him I'm not interested. I've heard about him, and it wouldn't be helicopter parts he's interested in moving.'

'Oh? What then?'

'Illegal things.' Arms, actually, but Finbar did not want to say that over the phone.

'My God. You mean he's a criminal?'

'The gentleman in question has had several major brushes with the law.'

22

As had he himself. These days everything had to be legit. Finbar did not mind, as he had had more than enough unwelcome police attention. And now there was Shannon to consider. It wouldn't be a great idea for a criminal law solicitor to be seen having a thing with someone known to be engaging in criminal activity. She took enough flak for being involved with someone who was rumoured to have engaged in it.

'He seemed really nice. Sexy.' Paula sounded shocked. 'He asked me out.'

'Well, go for it if you think a slap in the mouth is sexy.'

'Jesus. No thanks, I'll pass.'

'Sensible girl. Now get back to all that work you're supposed to be doing.'

He put the mobile on the coffee table and picked up the remote control. About to switch off the television, he paused and stared at the screen. He turned up the volume and moved closer.

The local news item was about the renovation of docklands. Some people approved, others complained that it was destroying much of the city's historical character and asked how many more leisure developments and how much more weird new architecture could Liverpool withstand? Finbar flinched as he recognised the clock tower, collapsing wooden huts and low brick buildings of the old Clarence Dock.

What was going on? The normally deserted spot swarmed with people, onlookers standing in groups watching builders in dirty yellow hard hats striding around shouting at one another. The rotting wooden dock gates were flung open, vans and lorries parked on the mossy cobblestones. A huge crane loomed into view. Fronting the busy scene was a smiling regional TV presenter, rain droplets and mist frizzing the ends of her smooth, blonde up-do.

'Renovation work has finally begun on this abandoned stretch of dockland.' Pause for turn and excited wave of arm. 'A new shopping mall is planned as well as a multi-storey car park, but the developers have undertaken to protect various historical features on the site, such as this Victorian clock tower behind me.' Another turn and wave of arm.

23

'Shit,' Finbar breathed. How come he had not heard anything about this before?

'The Clarence Dock tower was built after an earlier building on the spot was demolished. There is an old local rumour of an ancient dungeon beneath the tower which once formed part of a demolished fort, and that captured French soldiers from the Napoleonic Wars were imprisoned there.'

As was somebody from a much more recent era. Finbar felt sick. He watched the rest of the report, but there was nothing else of interest. The project was expected to take approximately eighteen months.

He clicked off the television and threw the remote on a sofa. The room seemed to get darker, the rain clouds over the grey river more gloomy and threatening. He glanced at the stone pillars that rose up through the floors of the old building which had formerly been a spice warehouse.

Like Shannon, he knew what it meant to take a life. Alone, thinking she had no one to turn to, she had hired a hit man to save herself from Bernard Flinder. Finbar had been trapped here in his own home by someone who wanted to kill him. He remembered Shannon creeping in and smashing a glass against that pillar to distract the moron with the gun. Blood on the shiny wood floor mingling with water from a fractured radiator pipe. Finbar recalled the fear and rage, the revulsion and horror that had gripped him on realising he had shot and killed another human being, even if it was in self-defence. Declan Dowd, intent on avenging big brother Lenny, not knowing that Lenny Dowd had murdered Finbar's wife and child when they had stumbled across an arms dump outside an Irish village, refusing to believe his hero brother had also tried to kill Finbar when he discovered that Lenny, and not trigger-happy British soldiers, had caused their deaths. That day Finbar had thought the Dowd family would finish him off. Shannon had saved him.

He remembered the terror in Shannon's eyes. He told her he would sort it, and he had. He had dumped Dowd's body in the dungeon beneath the clock tower, thinking it would stay hidden there for good. It had seemed the best option at the time. He

24

recalled the sickening thud of the wrapped body as it hit the dungeon's damp stone floor. Finbar knew prisoners had once been kept there because there were rusted chains hanging from the slimy walls, and a skeleton on the floor, as well as other human bones.

Dowd's corpse would not yet be a skeleton. How decomposed would it be exactly, after a year? There were two bullets lodged in the decaying flesh. Finbar sat down heavily on the sofa, swallowed hard and took several slow, deep breaths. He had not told Shannon what he had done with the body, and she had not asked because she did not want to know. He did not want her to know either.

He had made sure no personal effects – passport, credit cards, tickets to some concert in Dublin – had been left on the body. If it was discovered though, forensics people would be able to identify it sooner or later. The police might be able to trace the gun from which the two bullets had been fired. There would be nothing he could do then.

Finbar considered going back to the dock at night, getting into the clock tower and trying to retrieve the body from its resting place, but quickly abandoned the idea. Apart from feeling sick at the thought of handling the decomposing corpse of a man he had killed, he knew the idea was mad. He had seen from the news report that the site was cordoned off, guarded at all times. Even if he could bring himself to retrieve the body and get away without being caught, where the hell else could he dump it? That would mean more risk and danger. No, there was zero chance of pulling such a stunt.

Maybe there was no need to worry. The body might not be discovered. If the developers intended to preserve the structural integrity of the clock tower, surely they would simply seal it up and not investigate further? Or would local historians and archaeologists, intrigued by rumours of dungeons and Napoleonic war prisoners, try to get in on the act? He had to hope they would not be allowed to. Developers worked to tight schedules, didn't they? There would be no time for archaeologists to mess about. He remembered a national news item about

25

some mediaeval graveyard in London which had been covered by the foundations of a new building before the archaeologists had barely had a chance to excavate any corpses.

Finbar's only chance was that this corpse remained in its stone tomb.

For ever.

Chapter Three

'You are one bloody useless solicitor.'

'I'm sorry that's your opinion, Mrs Brennan, but I don't know what more you think we can do for you. It's not common practice for the victim to have a solicitor.'

It struck Wanda Brennan that she was not frightened any more. She had been afraid of lifts, debts, deadlines, flying – not that she boarded any aircraft these days – allergic reactions to fish, kiwi fruit and hair dyes, crashing her car, and waking at night to find a masked intruder with a knife at the foot of her bed. Those nightmares, however, were nothing compared to the reality of her existence now.

It was a drastic kind of cure, Wanda supposed, although not one she would wish on her worst enemy. And being a hack on a local rag meant she had a few of those. Most people hated journalists. *City Enquirer* had to compete with a couple of major regional dailies, and circulation kept dropping. The next disaster could be a cut in salary or even the loss of her job – not that she could consider either of those a disaster, given what had gone before.

'My husband Alex is still in a coma after that thug kicked his head in.' She swallowed and blinked away tears, felt her throat tighten. Wanda sometimes thought all the misery, rage and powerlessness would literally choke her. 'That happened more than a year ago, and the police made no attempt to investigate the man who I think could have attacked him. And now that man's escaped from prison. He might go after Alex!'

'I very much doubt it. Mrs Brennan, I've heard about Richard Croft's escape and that's extremely unfortunate. But there was never the slightest bit of evidence to suggest he was the man who attacked your husband.'

'No evidence? But I've told you what happened. I went into a clothes shop with Alex late in the afternoon of the day he was attacked, and we saw a man who looked just like Croft hassling one of the sales assistants – it turned out later that she was the girl he raped and held hostage, and whose mother he murdered. Alex told him to leave her alone, and Croft started shouting, threatening him. We were scared. He followed us out of the shop and down the street, then disappeared. When he'd gone, Alex and I parted – I went to get the car and drive home, and Alex walked off to meet two friends for drinks and a meal. But I don't think Croft did go – I think he tailed Alex that evening and attacked him after Alex said goodnight to his friends. It's just the kind of thing a psycho like that would do. The man who attacked Alex fitted Croft's description as well.'

'Mrs Brennan, just how many dark-haired, scruffy, heavily built, middle-aged men with moustaches do you imagine are walking around Liverpool city centre on any given day or night of the year?'

'Don't get sarcastic with me.' Wanda trembled. 'And just because this Croft got sent to jail for other crimes didn't mean I'd think, oh, OK, fine. I wanted him to be charged with the attack on Alex, be tried for it, get a longer sentence. I wanted – I *want* – acknowledgement.'

'Mrs Brennan, I suggest you talk to the police about this.'

'I have, lots of times. I went to a police station this morning. They don't want to know – they say Alex isn't in any danger from Croft.'

'I'm sure they're right. And as to the other matter you came to us about – there's also no suggestion that the hospital wants to switch off your husband's life support.'

'But they might want to do it one day.' Wanda's eyes flooded with tears. 'I have to make sure they don't get the chance. Who's on my side? On Alex's? We've got nobody to help us.'

'Have you considered counselling, Mrs Brennan? Victim Support?'

'Fuck off.'

Wanda crashed the phone down and wiped her eyes on the back of her hand. She glanced around the busy office; her colleagues appeared mesmerised by their PC screens. They were so kind, patient and tactful with her these days that it made her sick. It also made her feel more isolated. She jumped as someone tapped her on the shoulder.

'Sorry, Wanda.' It was Jane, the secretary. 'I didn't mean to startle you. Anything wrong?' she whispered. 'Apart from ...'

'The police say Alex isn't in danger from that escaped con. I hope they're right. And I just dumped that firm of solicitors. Don't know why I bothered with them. Suppose I just got sick of taking it up the arse.'

Jane flinched then blushed. 'How's Alex doing?'

'Oh.' Wanda pursed her lips and shook her head. 'There's no change, well, that's what the doctors and nurses tell me. But yesterday evening I could have sworn he squeezed my hand a bit – I got this really strong feeling he knew I was there wit' him.' She shrugged. 'Wishful thinking, maybe. His mum and dad drove down from Edinburgh a couple of days ago and set off back this morning. Alex's brother's wife just had a baby. Next time they see Alex I'm sure they'll tell him all about his new baby niece. They've named her Alexandra.'

Jane stared at her, lost for words. Wanda was familiar with that reaction. 'Rod wants to see you,' Jane said at last.

'OK. Is this about me being late too often and going to visit Alex a few times during working hours?'

'I don't know. He didn't say.'

'Right. I'll just nip to the loo.' Wanda did not need to go, she just wanted a couple of minutes on her own. She got up and walked down the long, noisy room, feeling curious and sympathetic looks burn the spot between her shoulder blades. Why can't they act normal? she wondered. I'm still the same person. But that wasn't true, was it?

29

She avoided looking at her reflection as she rinsed her hands and massaged her temples and the nape of her neck, because she knew she would not love what she saw. Since when had bulky black or brown cardigans become an essential wardrobe item? Her jeans were so tight she could barely zip them up, and what had happened to the 24½-inch waist of which she had once been proud? Comfort eating, of course, and all those fat and salt-loaded ready meals she shoved in the microwave after long working hours and exhausting, traumatic hospital visits. The curl had dropped out of her hair, which was long, dry and dull, the rich Titian shade of a decade ago now streaked with grey.

Wanda was forty-one but felt decades older. Ancient even, as if she had fought her way through the whirling dustbowl of several existences. She went out of the washroom, got herself another coffee and tapped on Rod's office door.

'Wanda, hi. How yer diddlin'?' Rod Jakes, Ken Dodd fan and editor of *City Enquirer,* who liked to imagine himself as the harassed chief at the heart of a great news empire, did not want more than the most perfunctory of answers to that question. Wanda obliged.

'You know. The usual.' Rod had got coffee stains on his blue shirt, and she could not even be bothered to wonder why a balding man in his fifties used so much hair gel on the sparse follicles which remained. 'I finished the piece on Dale Street Magistrates' Court,' she said. 'It's funny ...' No. Nothing was funny. 'They were having discussions after the Second World War on how to improve the building's facilities, and that's still a hot topic even though we're into the twenty-first century.'

'Yeah. Hilarious. Listen, Wand. Quick warning. Do something about the lateness, OK? Pissing me off, and everyone around here knows they have to keep old Uncle Roddy happy. Don't they now?'

Wanda shuddered at the thought of Rod as an uncle. 'I won't be late again...'

'Good girl. Hey, have you heard about this escaped psycho? Richard Croft?'

30

'Yes. I can't believe the police let him escape. I'm frightened for Alex.'

'What? Why?'

'Don't you remember? I told you I thought Croft could have been the man who attacked Alex. Just before Croft got arrested for rape and murder.'

'Oh. Yeah. Right. But there was no proof he did it, was there, Wand? I mean, like, no DNA, witnesses who could I.D. him, absolutely nothing.'

He didn't take her any more seriously than the police. And of course she could be wrong about Croft, Wanda had often told herself that. But how could she ever find out the truth when no one would help her?

'I'm sure Alex isn't in danger, Wand. Don't worry. Anyway, listen, there's been another murder in the big bad city. Have you heard about it?'

She gave up. 'The Asian woman? Yes. I don't know much though.'

'Early this morning —' Rod grinned and broke into song '– *just as the sun was ri-i-sing*, some tourists found a woman's body dumped outside St George's Hall. That must have ruined their autumn city break, eh?'

Wanda nodded. 'Very much so.'

'Exceedingly graphic and gruesome knife work, my thrillingly secret sources give me to understand.'

God's sake, Wanda thought. 'What's – what was her name?'

'Jenny Fong. Chinese, legal exec at some prestigious city firm of which I can't for the life of me remember the name. But guess what? This is where it gets more interesting.' Rod's pale little rodent eyes gleamed. 'The murder victim was best mates with lovely local legal celeb Shannon Flinder. The pair of them were out clubbing last night, and Flinder must have been the last person to see Fong alive – apart from the killer. Talk to Flinder, OK? Find out all you can. Pronto.' Rod paused. 'I take it you have heard of Shannon Flinder, Wand? You seem to be on a different planet from the rest of us these days. OK, I realise you've got—' He glanced away.

'Problems?' She flushed. Different planet indeed. She wasn't that bad. Sometimes Wanda wished she was on a different planet.

'Yes, Rod,' she said. 'I have definitely heard of Shannon Flinder.'

'So we meet again.' Detective Inspector Cindy Nightingale flounced into the cheerless interview room and slapped a file on the desk. 'Amazing how you keep popping up in nearly every murder inquiry on Merseyside.'

Shannon looked at her in horror. 'Don't tell me *you're* heading the investigation into Jenny's murder?'

'That I am,' Cindy sighed. 'For my sins.'

Cindy Nightingale, the bitch cop with the grudge who had tried and failed to get her convicted of Bernard Flinder's murder. Would this woman be even remotely interested in finding out who had murdered Jenny? She must have kept quiet about their connection when she was put in charge of this case, Shannon thought, because Cindy Nightingale's obsessive pursuit of Shannon Flinder had not only started to gain her a reputation as a loony but had cost her a promotion, and when she had insisted on carrying on regardless of the fact that no evidence came to light she had narrowly escaped being disciplined.

Shannon had also decided to keep quiet about their connection; there was no way she wanted the dark past raked up, especially when the present was terrible enough. She wiped her eyes and her associate and friend, Khalida Najeba, squeezed her arm and gave her a sympathetic glance.

Cindy flipped open the file and pulled out two sheets of paper, trying to contain her anger. It wasn't as if she didn't have much more important things to be getting on with rather than have to try and nail whoever had stabbed this snot bitch lawyer's bestest fwendy to death, but she was stuck with it now and there was nothing she could do. She was longing to be really rude to Flinder, sitting there all red-eyed and devastated, but did not dare, not when Flinder had brought a little helper.

32

Of course she would expect urgent priority to be given to solving her mate's murder. La-di-bloody-da.

There was one murder Shannon Flinder did not want solved – dear old Bernie, her deceased paedo Daddy-in-law, his ageing, flabby bits and pieces minced all over the road by a car bomb. Cindy got that hollow, despairing sensation again, the feeling that she might never nail Flinder now, and her anger escalated.

'I hear Richard Croft's done a jump. That's bad news, isn't it?' She looked at Shannon and smiled. 'He can't have been as lame and tame as his keepers thought. God —' she grimaced '— you must be terrified.'

Shannon looked back at her. 'I wondered if Croft could have murdered Jenny.'

'Croft?' Cindy wanted to laugh.

'Well, he escaped yesterday morning. It's possible.'

'But why her and not you? I mean, you're the one he's supposed to hate.' Cindy tried not to lay too much emphasis on that last word. 'Did Croft even know Jenny Fong?'

'I don't think so. But suppose he tailed us last night? He would have realised she was a friend. I said goodnight to Jenny and she went off to look for a cab. Maybe he couldn't reach me before I got indoors, so decided to go after her. He might have murdered her to get to me. To warn me.' Shannon tried not to cry. She did not want to show weakness in front of DI Nightingale.

Cindy held up the two typed pages and shook them. Who was in charge of this bloody interview? 'Can we just slow down a minute, please, and go over your statement?' Minding her manners was almost choking her. She scanned the statement again. 'You said goodnight to Ms Fong after you both left the Angel Club at the Albert Dock. Which was at approximately 2.40 a.m. And that was the last time you saw her, right?'

'Right.' Shannon sniffed. 'I asked Jenny if she wanted to stay at my place, but she said she'd get a cab home. I wish I'd persuaded her to stay. She'd be alive now.'

'But you didn't go home, did you?' Cindy re-read more of the statement. 'You went to Finbar Linnell's apartment.' Nice, she thought. The perfect end to a perfect evening.

'Yes, I did go there – immediately after Jenny had gone off to find a cab. It was just a few yards. That's why I think maybe Richard Croft couldn't get to me in time.'

'And you spent the rest of the night at Finbar Linnell's apartment?'

'Yes. I took a cab back to my place at around six-thirty, quarter to seven. I had to go home and get ready for work.'

'I see.' So she had stayed long enough to ravish the guy's tasty, toned body and grab a few hours sleep before nipping home to change her knickers. A jealous pang went through Cindy. She had come across Finbar Linnell a few times over the past couple of years in the course of previous investigations, and there was only one way he would look at her – with contempt.

'Would you like to read this over and sign it?' She slid the statement across the table and waited, examining her pink pearl acrylic nails, wishing she'd washed her lank brown hair that morning, and fantasising about arresting Shannon Flinder for murder. Shannon signed the statement at last and slid it back.

'Thanks very much.' Cindy thought. 'Did you and Ms Fong have a lot to drink last night?'

'Well – quite a lot, yes.' Shannon felt angry. 'So what? Don't start judging the victim's behaviour.'

'Being a lawyer, you'd know all about judging victims' behaviour, wouldn't you?'

'Can we stick to what's relevant here, please?' Khalida Najeba's voice was sharp.

'Have you got any leads?' Shannon asked.

'Not yet, no.'

'Will you check Jenny's ... Jenny's body for DNA belonging to Richard Croft?'

Jesus, Cindy thought. Do my job for me, why don't you? She bared her teeth in a resemblance of a smile. 'We're doing everything we can.'

'I hope so.' Khalida got up.

'For the sake of your brilliant career,' Shannon added. She grabbed her bag and pushed back her chair.

'Excuse me?' Cindy felt furious again. And uneasy. 'Is that some kind of threat?'

'Scum lawyers have got friends in high places, isn't that what you always say?' Shannon's eyes filled with tears. 'I know you don't give a damn who murdered any friend of mine, but you'd better—'

'Shannon, come on.' Khalida put one arm around her shoulders. 'Leave it, you're very upset. Let's just go now, OK?'

Cindy closed the file, thinking the bloody thing could stay closed for ever as far as she was concerned. She supposed Flinder breaking down in front of her was a kind of victory, although it didn't feel particularly satisfying. 'I'll let you know if we need to talk to you again,' she called as Khalida escorted Shannon out of the interview room.

She went to the door and stared after the two women as they headed down the corridor. She hated to see Shannon Flinder walk out of a police station when she belonged on some A wing living in terror of what the big girls would do to her when they got her alone.

Cindy swore. Shannon knew damn well that she did not give a damn about finding out who murdered Fong, but she would go through the motions; she had her brilliant career to think about after all, and failing to show the appropriate enthusiasm in a murder investigation would not do wonders for it.

She glanced in the opposite direction and rolled her eyes as DC Eddie Merton lumbered towards her, gulping steaming, milky coffee which Cindy knew contained a ton of sugar, an unlit cigarette poised between banana fingers; the cliché, scruffball, loner cop beloved of crime novelists, who sank too many pints in the pub each night before drink-driving home to a microwave and telly. Cindy deliberately relaxed her twisted features and lounged against the door jamb. But Eddie Merton was not fooled.

'You look upset.' He smirked. 'Could that possibly have anything to do with the beautiful, peachy arse of my favourite solicitor that I can see is about to vanish into the distance, for ever out of reach?'

'Out of your reach for sure, sad old fat man.'

'That face,' Eddie drooled, ignoring her remark. 'The eyes, the hair, the body.' He looked at Cindy and laughed. 'Oh dear. I see you're no nearer to resolving the deep-seated personal issues which continue to plague you.'

'How many times do I have to remind you that you can't talk to me like you did *way* back when I was a DC? Piss off and get your nicotine fix. I hope it chokes you.'

'Don't overdo the charm, will you, DI Nightingale, ma'am?' Eddie walked on, shaking his head. He might still be a DC, but he didn't care. He was happy, he had a life. Unlike some people. She needs a shrink, he thought. Cindy looked back just in time to see Shannon turn the corner and disappear.

'She had Bernard Flinder murdered,' she whispered. 'I know she did.'

And Cindy would prove it. One day.

Chapter Four

Trash killed by trash.

The police had used a different word, one he had heard too often in prison: *Shite.* In prison and out of the foul mouth of the late Yvonne. She had been shite, no question about that. Richard Croft stared at the statue of the Virgin Mary, blonde and wearing white and blue robes. There was the whore in all of them. He would never again allow another woman to share his life.

'Go in peace to love and serve the Lord.'

He turned his head and looked at the banks of dripping, ivory candles at the side altar, each one lit to symbolise a prayer, a wish, a memory of a loved one. He had no loved ones, never had if the truth be told. The phrase – trash killed by trash – kept floating across the surface of his mind, the words dissolving and reforming.

He had not wanted to sit through Mass, but churches were locked outside service hours these days due to the threat of vandalism. He smelled the incense and tried not to breathe too deeply; someone had once told him that incense was forty times more toxic than cigarette smoke.

Mass over, the few people in the front rows got up and began to file out. Most of them were women in their sixties and seventies. One of them gave him a suspicious glance, or so he imagined. Why? Because he was male? Younger? He sat still as the church emptied, gazing at the altar and another statue of the Virgin Mary with Baby Jesus on her hip. There was also a statue of the adult Jesus, red robe open to display his bleeding heart. As a child, Richard had always felt scared of that bleeding heart. The altar lights went out and a shadow glided past the rows of candles, causing the tiny flames to flicker. He became aware of someone hovering at the end of the pew where he sat.

'Er ... excuse me? I have to lock up now, I'm afraid.'

The bearded young priest looked a bit like Jesus. He had already changed out of his ceremonial robes. He did not ask if anything was wrong or if he could help.

'Oh, sorry Father.' Richard smiled, smoothed his moustache and scratched his chin. 'I was miles away.' He stood up. His knees were stiff and the headache was getting worse. 'Mind if I light a candle before I go?'

'Of course not. Help yourself.' But the priest looked as though he did mind. 'Just drop the money in the box.'

'Right. It's for a very special intention, Father.'

'Is it?' The priest nodded. 'Well, good luck with that.'

He moved away back down the aisle and paused to genuflect and cross himself as he passed the altar again. Richard frowned. He had hoped for an invitation to a hot lunch in the presbytery, but obviously he could forget that. He needed to eat soon. Food would help the headache.

He walked down the aisle, stopped in front of the candles and stared into the flames, enjoying their warming glow in the chill darkness of the church. A shower of rain hit the stained-glass window to his left. His eye caught a sentence or prayer engraved in red on the window: *He is not dead. He is risen.* Richard did not hold with the tenets of the Catholic faith, or any other. He despised all organised religion, considered it a prop for the weak and simple-minded, people who were in denial about the state of the world.

When his father beat the crap out of his mother – while he watched from his vantage point beneath the dining table – she had gone crawling to the priest instead of the police. The priest had emphasised the great virtue of forbearance and reminded her that marriage was for life, no matter what. The night she

38

had lunged for the carving knife and stabbed his father through the heart, then killed herself when she realised what she had done, had proved a defining moment in the seven-year-old Richard's life. After that his life had taken what most people would describe as a wrong turn.

He stuck his face closer to the candles, and their warmth turned to heat. He thought of prison life, the noise and lack of privacy, the endless need to keep proving to morons that they couldn't mess with you. The monotony of making car mats, which another prisoner had described as the 21st-century equivalent of picking oakum. Richard asked him what that meant, and he said prisoners in Victorian times and before were made to untwist old rope from ships. Hence the expression, *Money for old rope*.

Richard had become a firefighter years ago, after his application to join the police force had been rejected. He had valuable skills, years of experience. All going to waste. How was that supposed to rehabilitate or reform anyone? Not that he needed reforming. Yvonne had got what she deserved, and so had her bloody daughter Julie. He thought back to the night he had met Yvonne in that pub – another defining moment! – and how he had liked her smile, her long, smooth, dark hair and the big brown eyes that regarded him with such respectful interest. The respect and interest had not lasted long. But that night had been magical. They seemed to have a lot in common – she liked reading too, thrillers mostly, and country music. It turned out that she was lying – she never picked up a newspaper, let alone a book. But he had believed her then. A few weeks later Yvonne had invited him to move in with her and he had accepted. Big mistake.

He was a peaceful man, everyone who had dealings with him knew that; he never looked for trouble. Although Richard would be the first to admit he wasn't always easy to get on with, live with, because he had his moods. Most people thought he was a laid-back type, if also something they could not quite define. The eternal optimist despite a string of failed relationships, Richard had thought – hoped –

Yvonne was different. But things had deteriorated from the first night he had laid his head on her pink polycotton pillow. Her demands and criticisms increased, a bad temper cracked the quiet, smiling veneer she had used to hook him, and the daughter wasn't the shy, frightened little thing Richard had taken her for either.

After a few months Yvonne had started seeing another bloke. She denied it, called him a paranoid bastard when he accused her of cheating. Her life consisted of lies, big and small. Then the daughter tried to cause trouble after he touched her up a few times, more for a laugh than anything. What did she expect, prancing around the house in her underwear, or wrapped in a towel after one of her baths or showers? She was hardly ever properly dressed, especially when Yvonne was out. She often skived off work, and Richard had got the distinct impression that Julie wanted to be alone with him. But that day he whipped the towel off her slim body and pushed her down on the bed, thinking he'd finally give her what she'd been wanting, the little bitch had screamed blue murder.

Julie had gone to the police then got herself a solicitor – Shannon Flinder – who had actually listened to her rubbish and tried to cause him big problems. He'd told her to back off, but she hadn't listened. Then that day had come, the day when he had ordered Julie to drop her crazy allegations and dump her solicitor, because neither the police nor her own mother believed her, and it was time she showed him some respect. Julie had reacted with screaming rage and one thing led to another – Richard still did not quite know how he had come to be pinning Julie to the sofa, her denim mini skirt and red cotton panties torn off and thrown on the carpet, one hand clamped over her mouth as she struggled beneath him, her eyes frantic. Yvonne was not supposed to come home unexpectedly from the factory.

He had not meant to kill Yvonne – had he? But Richard was not sorry. And he had not meant to keep Julie there in the house – or take her hostage, as the police described it. The truth was, he had not known what to do once Yvonne was dead. He had to admit though, he probably would have killed Julie. He would have had to. But he would have got away if Shannon Flinder had not come calling and phoned the cops on him. He would have been the number one suspect, of course. But he planned to get out of the city, out of the country, before the cops could arrest him.

At his trial he had been portrayed as a monster. He had Julie and Shannon bloody Flinder to thank for that. Especially Flinder. If she hadn't taken Julie's rubbish seriously, made a big fuss, then come nosing around the house that day, he might never have been arrested and charged. Or shot.

What right did the losers in prison have to judge him? Call him names, spit at him, throw hot curry sauce over him? What right did anybody have to judge him?

Richard's temples pulsed with pain and anger, and he wished he could lie down. The first dirty old diesel train he had jumped on at Manchester Victoria after reluctantly abandoning the doctor's Merc had brought him to this cold, windy, grey stone little Pennine town in the middle of bloody nowhere. It had a dark hill looming over it. He wouldn't stay here, of course. He would move on, get more money and a false passport, fly abroad to a new life, somewhere there was hot sun and no extradition treaties. He was not going back to jail. They could shoot him again and finish the job before he would let that happen. Enough was enough.

His breath made the candle flames waver. Human life was just as tenuous as these pretty little lights burning in the darkness. He was back in the world now. This was a new beginning. Richard picked a slender, ivory candle out of the wooden box, lit it and placed it in the centre of the row. He blew out the other candles.

'Er ... what are you doing?' He turned to find the priest standing there. 'You're supposed to pay for that candle. And why did you blow out the others?'

He went quiet as Richard stared at him without speaking. Richard knew the power of silence in this querulous, chattering world. He smiled as the priest took a step back.

'You know, Father, you should have a bit more time for people.' He stuck his hands in his jacket pockets. 'Oh, and don't blow out my candle. It's for a very special person. All right?'

The priest nodded and swallowed. Richard walked out of the church and slammed the heavy wooden door, the movement sending waves of pain undulating through his skull. Miserable bastard, he thought. He walked back down the dismal main street of the town, shivering in the sharp wind that cut right through his thin jacket.

He needed painkillers, but the only kind that did anything for this headache could not be obtained without a doctor's prescription. Could he find an understanding chemist? The chemist in the pharmacy by the railway station was not under-standing, so he bought a pack of the strongest painkillers he could get without a prescription and went into a nearby burger bar. He bought coffee, a large coke and a double cheeseburger, and swallowed three tablets. The food helped, if you could describe this as food. He remembered what a fundamentalist veggie inmate had told him one day at dinner: '*They shove the whole cow in the machine, mate, don't even bother to wipe its arse.*'

Richard thought of the solitary candle burning in the locked, silent church. Things would work out. They had to. This was an all-or-nothing situation. But first things first.

'Scores to settle,' he whispered to himself.

By the time that candle burned down somebody would be dead.

'I know you're busy, Shannon, but couldn't I just get your comments about your friend's murder?' Wanda asked, biro and notepad at the ready. 'Although what I'd really like is to have an in-depth talk with you about Jenny—'

'Sorry. I'm not prepared to talk to the press about Jenny.' Shannon Flinder's voice was polite but firm. She rushed down the stairs of the Magistrates' Court, Wanda struggling to stay with her. The security guard smiled and nodded at Shannon but frowned at Wanda and demanded to examine the contents of her bag.

'You know me,' she protested.

His frown deepened. 'Exactly.'

By the time she got out Shannon had disappeared. Wanda stopped and swore, glancing up and down busy Dale Street, then clocked Shannon in the midst of a group of people waiting to cross the road. A shaft of sunlight pierced the cloud layer, helpfully illuminating her blonde hair. The little man glowed green.

'I don't expect you to talk about the murder investigation,' she panted as she caught up with Shannon, who was obviously a lot fitter and at least a decade younger. 'Or what you know, what you've told the police. I just want to hear about your friend. What sort of person Jenny was. How you spent yesterday evening. Her last words to you before she—'

'Look. Just get lost, OK?' Shannon glared at her, then gripped her briefcase and bundle of blue folders and sprinted across the road. Wanda swore again, thinking of abandoned New Year diet resolutions and lapsed gym memberships. She ran after Shannon, everything bouncing and jigging, then had to stop for a coughing fit. That's it, she thought, I won't catch her now. But several folders slipped from under Shannon's arm and fell on the wet pavement, spilling papers.

'Oh, *shh* ...!'

'Let me help you,' Wanda called. She staggered forward and tried to get a look at the papers as she stooped, still coughing and spluttering, and grabbed a few. A passing boy trod on what appeared to be a photocopied witness statement, leaving a muddy trainer imprint. Wanda could not see Jenny Fong's name on anything. Damn.

'Don't touch those, I can manage.' Shannon gathered the rest of the papers and shoved them back into the damp folders. 'Look,' she repeated, her voice rising, 'I told you to get lost. I won't talk to the papers about Jenny Fong – or about anything or anyone else either, come to that. So goodbye.' She straightened up and resumed her jog.

'Can I be honest?' Wanda called, desperate.

'Does that mean you're not usually?'

'I'm not that bothered about – I mean, I'm not really interested in talking to you about Jenny Fong. OK, of course I am to some extent, because my editor wants this story. Your input could make Jenny appear more sympathetic.'

'More ...?' Shannon stopped and turned. 'What are you on about? What do you think this is?'

'Is it true Jenny was having an affair with a senior police officer who started stalking her when she dumped him?' It probably wasn't true because Wanda had just made it up, but she had to get Shannon Flinder's attention somehow and hey, you never could tell.

Shannon looked at her, stunned. 'That's absolute rubbish.' Her voice shook. She pointed a finger. 'I'm warning you. If you or your bloody editor even think about printing any such crap, I'll—'

'Oh, we wouldn't dream of it,' Wanda panted. 'It's just a rumour.'

'It's not even that. You won't get away with trashing her name, so don't try.'

'Again, wouldn't dream.' Wanda hoped she had not gone too far; Shannon looked furious now. But at least she had her attention. 'Please.' She pushed her damp, heavy hair off her broad, pale forehead. 'What I really want to talk to you about is my husband. I want you to take him on as a client.'

Shannon shook her head. 'I don't have time for this.'

They passed a sandwich shop and newsagent on the corner of Stanley Street and walked beneath scaffolding, something else Wanda had once been frightened of.

'He – that's Alex, my husband – is in a coma. He's been in it for over a year. A man kicked his head in, it was a totally unprovoked attack. And now the man who I think did it has escaped from prison – I heard about it on the news. His name's Richard Croft.'

Shannon stopped again. 'Richard *Croft*?' She frowned. 'What is this? Some kind of sick joke?'

Wanda's eyes filled with tears. 'Do I look like I'm joking?' She quickly told Shannon about Alex and why she thought Richard Croft could have been the man who attacked him. Shannon listened, a shocked expression on her face.

'I'm so sorry,' she said at last. 'That's terrible. But the description of the attacker could fit lots of men. And if there was no DNA – no evidence of any kind to indicate Croft was the perpetrator – how can you possibly be sure it was him?'

'Well, I can't, of course. I've just got this feeling. Alex getting attacked the same day he came across Croft is a hell of a coincidence. No one will help me find out the truth. I got a firm of solicitors to try and help me and Alex, protect his interests, but they've proved as useless as the police.'

Maybe she should not have said that. Lawyers would stick together and defend one another just like police officers and doctors did.

'What I mean is – this particular firm didn't seem to care. If Alex dies – he might die, you see – it'll be murder. Even if he regains consciousness he could be permanently brain-damaged. I'm also worried that the hospital might switch off his life support.'

'I'm sure they wouldn't do that.' Shannon's voice was gentle now, her eyes kind. 'They can't, anyway, not without a lot of—'

'I can't bear the thought that the man who did this to Alex will get away with it.' Wanda was gasping, choking back tears. 'I just can't.' She recalled the feel of Alex's limp, softened hand in hers, his terrible, heartbreaking helplessness. Her own powerlessness. 'It's not fair,' she whispered. 'Alex is a lovely person. He's kind, caring. I think the world of him. He didn't – he doesn't deserve this.' Hot tears rolled down her wind-chilled face.

'I'm so sorry,' Shannon repeated. She looked as if she was going to cry herself. 'But even if I thought I could do something for you – and I'm not convinced I could, because I'm not sure you really need a lawyer – there's no way I can take on any new clients at present. I'm overloaded with work as it is.'

45

'Well, if not you, how about one of your partners or associates? Mi-Hae Kam or Khalida Najeba?'

'They've also got more than enough work, I'm afraid. I could get you some recommendations.'

'I want you.' Wanda wiped her eyes. 'I like you. And we've got a connection – I think Richard Croft attacked Alex, and you helped get Croft arrested and put away for those other crimes he committed. Now that he's escaped, Alex could be in danger. You might be too. Have the police warned you?'

'I can't discuss that. Look, there's no proof Croft attacked your husband.'

'Please help me. Help me get justice for Alex. He deserves that much.'

Shannon hesitated, glancing up and down the cold, rainy street. 'It's not just impossible professionally. There's a lot of other stuff—' She stopped suddenly, horrified, obviously remembering this was a journalist she was talking to. 'Sorry. I've really got to go now. I can't help you, except to refer you to another firm. I hope your husband—'

'Wakes up?' Wanda prompted, sarcastic in her disappointment. 'Gets better?'

'Well, yes. I do. I hope he recovers.'

'Thank you. So do I.'

Shannon walked off and this time Wanda did not dare follow. It was a bad idea to have hassled her in the street; she should have made an appointment. But would she have got one? She doubted it. She watched as Shannon turned into a small, narrow street and went up the steps of a Victorian office building, pressed an intercom button and disappeared behind a solid, dark–blue, shiny door. She sighed and wiped her eyes again. She shouldn't have implied that Jenny Fong had been sleeping with a senior police officer. That was seriously stupid.

'Stupid, that's you, Wanda,' she whispered to herself. 'You're losing it big style.'

Wanda returned to the office and wrote some creative copy. After that she had to go out again to chase up a couple of boring stories about car crime on some housing estate. She kept thinking about Shannon Flinder – she still liked the woman, despite Shannon's refusal to help. When Shannon said she was sorry about Alex she had meant it, had been visibly upset. But not upset enough to do anything. And what did she mean when she said there was a lot of other stuff? Personal stuff?

Wanda knew Shannon had been the daughter-in-law of the paedophile headmaster Bernard Flinder, who had been murdered by a car bomb. No one had ever been arrested for that. She was divorced from her ex-CID husband Rob, who had flipped big style. But that was all in the past. What could be going on now?

Wanda got into her grubby white VW Polo and drove home, parking a quarter of a mile away from the flat because any nearer and the risk of the car being vandalised was too great. Exhaustion and sadness overwhelmed her, and she forgot about Shannon Flinder. Wanda felt her life was a grotesque parody of . . . what? Modern woman, average looking, not well paid enough to save her house from being repossessed, driving home to cheap wine, a microwaved dinner and an evening of crap telly. Except that Wanda usually spent the greater part of her evenings visiting her comatose husband in intensive care.

She got that horrible feeling again as she walked the cold, dark, wet streets, the sensation that she might not be able to catch her next breath. How would Alex be tonight? Would there be any change? She had not had time to pop in and see him at lunchtime. Wanda passed the chippie and off-licence, the Rising Sun pub and the row of boarded up shops. Two loitering teenage boys in baseball caps eyed her, but she wasn't scared. She knew one of them by sight; a neighbour had pointed him out and told her the little bastard had more than sixty convictions for criminal damage. She tightened her grip on her bag. If the boys tried anything with her they would get more than they'd bargained for. She walked on, turned into Rosewood Avenue and fitted her key into the front door of a big Victorian house which had been converted to flats during the 1960s.

The little witch from the ground-floor flat was in the dim, dingy hall playing with a doll. Wanda would be a good name for a doll, Wanda thought as she passed. The Princess Wanda doll would have limp hair which came out when you combed it, long, shapeless sweaters and baggy jeans to conceal her fat arse, plus cardigans with big pockets to hold tissues, cigarettes and the day's chocolate bar of choice. She would have supermarket, telly-watching and hospital-visiting outfits, and her plastic fingers would be nicotine stained, the nails bitten. But there would be a big toy house, powder blue limousine and glam wardrobe waiting for when Princess Wanda's prince miraculously woke up and she became happy and beautiful again. The doll would dominate the Christmas market. The smell of cigarette smoke and fried food drifted into the hall. A baby inside the flat screamed for attention. The little girl glanced up.

'It's unlucky to meet a red-haired person when you set out on a journey,' she announced, her light eyes hostile.

Wanda paused and stared at her. Where had she got that superstitious crap from? The tired-looking, bitchy mother, or the grey-haired man with the malevolent expression she sometimes saw and assumed was the brat's grandfather? Of course he could be her father. Lots of men in their fifties and upwards had young children.

'Well, I've just come back from my journey.' She carried on towards the stairs. 'And you don't look like you're going anywhere.' For the rest of your life, she added silently. She felt the child's gaze on her as she climbed the stairs.

In the tiny kitchen cluttered with last night's and this morning's dishes Wanda poured herself a glass of white wine and took several quick sips. She wanted more, felt like drinking the whole bottle, but that would have to wait until she got back from the hospital. Drink in hand, she went into the living room and drew the curtains on the long, dark, overgrown back garden below, its high brick wall topped with broken glass. She moved a pile of old newspapers and dirty clothes and collapsed on the sofa.

Alex had never seen this flat, and maybe he never would. Things had happened so fast; the horrific attack, her shock, terror and devastation. She had tried and failed to cope. It hardly seemed to matter that she had missed several mortgage payments. As joint earners she and Alex were fine, but having to live on her income alone was a very different story. Bills and all kinds of expenses piled up until she could not manage financially any longer, even with the sickness benefit and other payments Alex was entitled to. Wanda did not even want to think about the rest of it. There were so many things she could not let herself think about. Suffice to say, she had ended up in this dump.

Alex's clothes, books, papers and other belongings were in suitcases and boxes all over the flat, most of them piled in the tiny spare room. Wanda did not know whether or not to unpack his stuff and arrange it around the place, as if he lived here and might walk in any minute, or leave everything packed in the fading hope that she would get out of here soon and find a good, spacious house in a better area to which she would one day be able to bring Alex. If he recovered.

She squeezed her eyes shut in an effort to prevent a burst of tears then sniffed hard, took a big breath and went back to the kitchen. Better eat something before she left for the hospital. She pulled the cardboard wrapping off a pack of lasagne, stabbed at the foil with a dirty fork and placed the dish in the microwave. She opened the cutlery drawer and looked at the jumbled knives, the Sabatiers and Kitchen Devils, some of them still in their greasy plastic covers.

At home – her real home, the repossessed house – she had taken better care of things. She and Alex had cooked together most evenings and weekends. Casseroles, stir-fry, pasta dishes with tomatoes and basil, or creamy Gorgonzola. Roast dinners. Wanda could not imagine being bothered to cook proper meals now. She picked up the big Sabatier knife she had used for chopping vegetables and slicing meat, and ran one finger lightly along the blade. She thought of the happy dinners, sometimes with friends or with Alex's parents; she couldn't

49

picture her own parents, or just her mother now, sitting around a dining table making civilised conversation. The friends didn't phone or visit any more. They were decent people, but how much sympathy and support could you expect them to provide? How much misery and bad news to have to keep trying to rise above? Wanda did not blame them. She would have been the same herself, or thought she would. That didn't stop her feeling resentful and let down though.

The knife blade was clean and sharp enough but suddenly, for no apparent reason, she wanted it sharper. She reached into the drawer, found the steel and went to work. Go easy, not too much. When it was done she held up the knife and stared at the gleaming blade. Her heart was pounding, her breathing rapid. She felt the tension press down on her head and shoulders, close around her diaphragm and abdomen as if she were about to implode or suffocate. The microwave timer pinged in the silence.

Trembling, not knowing why she was doing this, Wanda tightened her grip on the knife handle and carved a deep, criss-cross cut along her forearm. She gasped and cried out in pain, dropped the knife on the floor.

Blood dripped down.

Chapter Five

'I can't believe she's *dead.*'

Finbar stood looking out of Shannon's living-room windows at the city lights and rain-washed rooftops that sloped down to the dark glimmer of river. A surreal day followed by a cold, nasty night. He turned back to Shannon, who sat curled in one corner of the sofa wrapped in her thick blue cotton bathrobe and clutching a gin-and-tonic, her personal attack alarm lying on the coffee table in front of her.

Jenny Fong's murder, Cindy bloody Nightingale being put in charge of the investigation, Richard Croft's escape, and those builders and television people messing around the Clock Tower. When things went wrong they did so with a vengeance. Finbar reminded himself that not *every-thing* had gone wrong. Dowd's body had not been discovered, and with any luck it never would be. But he was seriously worried.

'So you think Croft might have killed Jenny?' He thought again of Dowd's wrapped corpse in the damp chill dark of the dungeon, unable to force the image out of his head.

'I'm not saying he *did,* only that it's possible.' Shannon sighed and took another sip of her drink. 'Just trying to think of all the angles. Stabbing isn't his MO.' She thought of how he had strangled his partner Yvonne and drawn that picture of the woman with the noose around her neck. 'But the police will check Croft's DNA with that found at the crime scene, or at least I hope they will. You can imagine I don't trust

51

Nightingale.' She looked up at Finbar. 'She still wants to get me – she hates me. I could see it in her eyes. It almost killed her to stay polite in front of Khalida.'

'OK, but given the history between you two, don't you think she'll want to be seen to be doing a good job on this case?'

Shannon finished her drink and put the glass down. 'The only case that mad, vindictive bitch wants to do a job on is mine!'

'Come on, Shannon.' Finbar put his glass of single malt on the grey marble mantelpiece, crossed to the sofa and sat down beside her. 'From what I hear, she nearly got herself in big trouble by pursuing her vendetta against you, trying to prove you had the bastard father-in-law stiffed. She didn't succeed, and now she won't want the hassle any more than you do.'

Shannon frowned. 'Let's hope.'

He slid one arm around her shoulders. 'And I hope you don't still blame yourself for not being psychic and persuading Jenny to stay the night here?'

'Not blame. Wish.'

'I suppose it's OK to wish.' He shifted closer.

'They'll trawl through Jenny's life.' Shannon had tears in her eyes. 'It's so undignified, so invasive. She might be dead but she won't be left to rest in peace. Maybe not for a long time.'

'The police have to do their job.'

'They'd better damn well do it. If they don't find out who killed Jenny, I will.'

Finbar curled a strand of her hair around one finger and looked into her eyes, loving their depth and colour. 'I'm worried about you. All this shit that's going on.'

'If Croft didn't kill Jenny, who the hell did? And why? Was it her bad luck to be in the wrong place at the wrong time – or did she know her murderer? Most murderers are known to their victims.' She shook her head. 'I couldn't believe that journalist today, asking if Jenny had been having a thing with a senior police officer. Of all the bullshit.'

'Sure it's bullshit? Not to speak ill of the dead, but she did have a spectacular instinct for picking the wrong men.'

'Jenny didn't even know any senior police officers. I suppose it's possible she might not have told me about someone if she knew I'd disapprove. You don't always tell even close friends everything. But she was obsessed with Chris, really in love with him. I'm sure she wouldn't have wanted to bother with another man as well.'

'Could Chris have killed her?'

'No way. He's in the clear. After my delightful interview with DI Nightingale, Khalida and I bumped into a DS Gary Leitz we're friendly with. He's also working on Jenny's case. I had a talk with him. He said Chris wasn't even in Liverpool when the murder happened. He was in London – with his wife – to see some West End musical and have a couple of job interviews with record companies. There are loads of people to vouch for him. Anyway, he had no motive to murder Jenny. He dumped her, Jenny accepted that, she didn't give his wife any hassle. Why on earth would he want to harm her? He might have been a bastard, but he was never violent. And he's got no criminal record, unless you count speeding fines and possessing the odd bit of skunk.'

'Maybe the wife wanted to harm her.'

'Jenny said she didn't know about the affair. If she didn't, she does now. And like I said – like Gary said – she was in London with her husband at the time. OK, she could have —' Shannon paused '— hired someone. But there's nothing to indicate that.'

'So it could have been one of those rare stranger murders?'

'God only knows. At this stage, anyway. I still can't take it in,' she whispered. 'It all seems so senseless.'

Finbar pulled her close and they were silent, each with their own thoughts. They had both suffered losses: Finbar having to try and cope with the tragic deaths of his wife and child, Shannon losing Rob her husband. Rob might still be alive, but the man she had loved bore no resemblance to the

Rob who had committed murder, attacked her and was now in prison.

'What freaks me most – and you too, I think – is loss.' More tears filled her eyes. 'Of people we love. I nearly lost you.' She thought of Declan Dowd, the man who had tried to kill Finbar, seeking revenge for the death of older brother Lenny. It had been self-defence, but they had both known that the police would not have believed someone with Finbar's track record. Or rumoured track record.

'We nearly lost each other.' Finbar's arms tightened around her, his expression grim. 'We've both had more than our share of crap. But the police will get whoever murdered Jenny – and your Inspector Casey and his helpers are bound to pick up Croft soon.' He hugged Shannon and kissed her, wanting to reassure himself as much as her. 'What's happened is terrible,' he said gently, 'but Jenny's gone. You can't do anything for her any more. You're shocked, you're upset. Exhausted. You could be in danger. You've got to think of yourself now, Shannon.'

He smelled her hair, her perfume. She was naked beneath the robe. He wanted to pull it open, slip it off her smooth shoulders and slide his hands all over her warm, soft, just-showered skin.

She sighed. 'I suppose I have had, to put it mildly, an intense day.' She pulled away and looked at him. 'What about you? Are you all right?'

'It's me who should be asking you that.'

'You seem a bit ... I don't know.'

Worried? Freaked? Finbar's desire died and his heart pounded as he thought of Dowd again, the imminent threat of his body being discovered and how there was absolutely bloody nothing he could do to stop that happening if it was going to. He took Shannon's hand and squeezed it.

'Ow.' She winced. 'That hurts.'

'Sorry.' He stroked her hair, kissed her again. 'I love you.'

'And I love you.'

'How much out of ten?'

'Twenty.'

He had thought some day a developer would stick an apartment block or offices on top of that little bastard Dowd, with him forming part of the foundations. Finbar told himself again that if they were looking to preserve the bloody clock tower they would just brick up the door, tart the building up a bit and leave it, a quaint monument for people to briefly admire and comment on as they went about their business.

Shannon got up and walked to the mantelpiece, stared into the fire. Her bare feet felt chilled, in fact she was chilled all over despite Finbar's embrace and the warmth of the lamp-lit room. He came to her and she felt his arms go around her again.

'It's going to be all right,' he murmured.

'Is it?' She laid her head against his shoulder and closed her eyes.

'I think we've done enough agonising for one night, don't you? *"How much pain have cost us the evils that never happened?"*'

She twisted around and smiled up at him. 'Who said that?'

'Can't remember. Some smart bastard.'

'And Peter Pan told Wendy to just close her eyes and think lovely thoughts.'

'That's good,' he grinned. 'You're getting there.'

'I always want to think lovely thoughts, but reality keeps intruding.'

'Don't let it. I could do with another drink. How about you?'

'I'll have some wine.'

'I'll join you. And I think we should eat something. Don't tell me you're not hungry,' he warned.

'I wasn't going to.' Shannon yawned and stretched her arms above her head. 'I was about to say I hadn't done any shopping.'

'Don't worry, Gorgeous, I've taken care of that. How'd you fancy tortillas?'

'Great. Can I help?'

'You're too kind, but no. Just rest.'

'I'll never see Jenny again,' she said as she followed him into the kitchen. 'I'll never be able to talk to her again ... we'll never have another night out. I can't believe this has happened.'

'So don't try.' He grimaced. 'Disbelief ... denial ... it's a protection mechanism.'

'Jenny's only got – only *had* – her mother as family. And a couple of aunts and some cousins in London. I called her mother and said I'd do anything I could to help. She said she doesn't know when the police will release Jenny's body so that they can have the funeral. I don't know how the hell she's going to cope with losing her only daughter.'

'That's a tough one.' Finbar looked away. 'The toughest.'

'Oh my God!' She stared at him in horror. 'Roiseann ... Finbar, I'm so sorry!' Finbar's baby daughter, shot dead as she sat strapped in the back of the car.

'It's OK.' He kissed her. 'It's all right. Please, don't worry. Look, go and sit down and try to relax. Listen to some music, watch telly. I'll get dinner.'

'I'm sorry,' she repeated. Her voice trembled.

He gave her a look. 'It's *OK*.'

Shannon drifted back to the sitting room, stretched out on the sofa and shut her eyes. Me and my big stupid mouth, she thought. Her body was aching, heavy with exhaustion and sadness.

Had Jenny been in agony before she died? How long had it taken her to die? Had she lain on that icy ground soaking in her own blood, maybe praying for help that did not come? Or had the cold and massive trauma mercifully numbed her pain and terror? Shannon told herself to try and not think about that any more. Her breathing slowed as her body relaxed. Finbar had to wake her when dinner was ready.

They ate in the kitchen. She managed two tortillas before she pushed away her plate and sat back.

'That was great. I didn't realise how hungry I was.'

'There's a bit of chicken and salad left. Can you eat another?'

'You're joking. I'm stuffed now.' She patted her stomach and sighed. 'I know it's stupid, but I feel guilty at being hungry. As if having an appetite after what's happened is somehow disloyal to Jenny.'

'I wouldn't say stupid. It's understandable in the circumstances.' Finbar paused, watching her. 'I think we should stick to non-tragic subjects for the rest of this evening,' he said slowly. 'Don't you agree?'

'Yes.' Shannon nodded and stood up. 'Ready for some coffee?'

'Great. Use the French-Columbian stuff we got in Harrods.' He smiled, sensing a way to change the conversation to something light. 'That was a great weekend in London. The hotel in Mayfair was good. Funny how it was crammed with Scousers.'

'I wouldn't say *crammed*. There was the couple in the lift laden with Harrods bags, and that group having afternoon tea in the lounge.'

'And the other couple in that restaurant we went to for dinner. That guy who overheard you ordering the lemon tart and told you it was *sound*.'

'Shame, because he'd got the last piece and I had to have tarte tatin.' Shannon smiled back. 'You're stereotyping Scousers. Why shouldn't they be in Mayfair hotels and Michelin-star restaurants?'

'Absolutely no reason, darling. I should be more politically correct, shouldn't I? Me being Irish and all, you'd think I'd be hyper-feckin' aware of negative stereotyping.'

'Is there positive stereotyping?' Shannon laughed. She switched on the coffee machine and the filter started to hiss and gurgle. She went into the living room and looked out of the windows. The street of Georgian terraced houses was quiet and deserted. She wondered again where Richard Croft might be. 'God's sake,' she groaned as the phone rang. 'Who the hell is it now?'

Finbar came in. 'Don't you want to get that?'

'No. Whoever's calling can try getting a life.'

'But it might be the police. Or Jenny's mother. Want me to answer?'

She nodded. 'Thanks.' Maybe Richard Croft had been caught. She could do with some good news.

'Who was it?' she asked as he hung up.

'Your senior partner, Ms Kam. She just got a call from the police. The office alarm was triggered.'

Shannon looked at him, felt herself turn pale. 'So what's. . .?'

'She wants you to get down there now. There's been a break-in.'

Chapter Six

'Help!' Wanda shrieked into the corridor at a passing nurse. 'Get a doctor in here now. Quick!' She ran back into the room sobbing, and cringed in horror as Alex's body jerked in the bed again as if he was being given an electric shock. She gasped as his eyes opened, only to show slits of yellow-tinged white. She grabbed his hand again, his poor helpless hand, and held on. Blood trickled from his mouth.

'Alex!' she cried. Was this it, was he going to die? 'Keep on. Don't die. Please, Alex, don't die.'

Two nurses rushed in. 'Best if you wait outside, Mrs Brennan. You can come back when we've stabilised him.'

'But what's happening? Where's the bloody doctor?'

'We've paged her, she's on her way. Now please wait outside.'

'Your husband has had a seizure,' the languid blonde Russian doctor explained to Wanda about ten minutes later as she sat limp, drained and tearful in the visitors' room, clutching a cup of tea in her trembling hands. The doctor reminded Wanda of the prostitutes who had been hanging around the Moscow hotel she and Alex had stayed in a couple of years back, smiling, nodding at and ogling men in the bar, restaurant and lobby, regardless of whether or not they were accompanied by wives or partners. Alex had joked about them and ignored the unwanted attention, but Wanda had felt like giving the more persistent ones a smack in their hard, over made-up faces. It wasn't so much their pursuit of Alex that enraged her as their infuriating assumption that she, his wife, was a total bloody inconsequence. So what if they couldn't do anything but be prostitutes? It wasn't her problem. Some city break that had turned out to be.

'A seizure?' She wiped her eyes. 'What caused it? Will he have another?'

The doctor gave a huge shrug. 'We cannot know for sure.'

There seemed to be a lot that doctors didn't know for sure. Wanda knew she was probably overreacting, but she had the feeling that this woman had written Alex off. It was one trauma after the other. Every time she came to see him she dreaded what might happen next.

'Can I see Alex now?'

'Yes, of course.' The doctor nodded to her. 'Goodnight.' She walked off, hands in the pockets of her white coat. Wanda went back into the room. Alex was lying motionless again, hooked up to all the tubes and other equipment, his mouth wiped clean of blood. There was the usual nasty chemical smell. She shivered and almost burst into tears again, but controlled herself. Alex might be able to hear, and he wouldn't like her to be upset.

'All better now?' If only. Wanda tried to keep her voice light. She nodded towards the dark, uncurtained window. 'It's pouring out there. Did you enjoy your mum and dad's visit? You'll be able to see your new baby niece soon. I bet she's beautiful. Your parents stayed in a bed and breakfast. I would have invited them to stay at my ... at our place, but there just isn't the room. And it's still a hell of a mess, boxes everywhere. I'm hoping to get us a house again, once I've sorted the finances.' And so on. Wanda did not know how she kept up the chat. She had never been one for small talk.

Alex seemed to have shrunk. He had lost weight, of course, at least two stone, and his muscles had wasted with the lack of exercise. A physio worked on him, but it didn't seem to help much. His brow was smoother, the frown line gone, and his skin had softened and turned pale. The nurses dressed him in white gowns or sometimes blue ones. She wondered if they were as kind and caring to Alex when she wasn't around.

Wanda hoped to God they were. Alex had suffered enough. The sight of him lying there always pierced her with pity, fear and a visceral protectiveness.

Had the seizure hurt him, she wondered, given him a fright? Did he ever hear anything or anyone, recognise her voice, have any idea what was happening? She bent over him and kissed his cool, clammy cheek, stroked his brown hair.

'Alex,' she whispered, 'please talk to me, darling.'

She got a sudden surge of energy and willpower, despite her exhaustion. She willed Alex to open his eyes, those brown eyes that used to be so full of life and fun. The feeling was so strong that she could not believe he would not sense her power and respond. But nothing happened.

'I'm here. I love you so much. I'll never let you go.' She squeezed his hand and caressed it.

How much longer would they go on looking after Alex? People could remain in comas for a lot longer than a year. Wanda dreaded the doctors coming to her some day – perhaps that Russian bitch would be one of them – and telling her they wanted to switch off his life support. She did not know what she would do if that happened. Shout at them, fight them, start screaming. Who would help her? Alex's parents and younger brother were not much use; apart from the fact that they lived far away in Edinburgh, they remained stunned and completely bewildered by what had happened, and combined this passivity with a God-like respect for the medical profession. I was wrong, Wanda thought, there is still something I'm frightened off. They might decide to switch off Alex's life support and I might not be able to stop them. She wished again that she had someone on her side, even a lawyer like Shannon Flinder.

The cut she had carved into her forearm earlier stung and throbbed, and she hoped it wouldn't get infected. She would give it a wash and dab it with antiseptic once she got back to the flat. What on earth had possessed her to do such a thing? She was not, never had been, one of those self-harmers. Wanda was disturbed by her action, shocked, did not understand it. Then again, what the fuck? There were lots of things she didn't understand. Like why the only person in the world that she loved had to lie here while the bastard who had injured him went free. Did Croft, or whoever had hurt Alex, ever think about what they had done? Did they care? She thought not. Was the man out on the streets right now? Shouting, laughing, getting pissed, looking for someone else to hurt? Hatred rose in her, suffocating and choking. She broke out in a cold sweat. A nurse walked in and gave her a startled glance.

'All right, Wanda?'

She was never all right, not any more. Wanda tried to relax her features. 'Fine.'

'And don't worry, love, Alex is safe here. We keep the intensive care unit doors shut all the time, like I told you. No one gets in unless we know exactly who they are. I promise you. OK?'

She nodded. 'OK.'

'It's after ten. Why don't you drive home and get some sleep? You must be tired. We're going to settle Alex down for the night now.' She looked at him and smiled. 'Aren't we, love?'

The endearment brought a lump to Wanda's throat. 'I was just going.'

'Good. Get to bed, don't stay up watching telly. See you tomorrow.'

'Goodnight, Alex.' Wanda leaned over and kissed him again. 'Take care, I'll see you soon. I love you.' Settle him down for the night? She pushed away the thought that in Alex's world now it was always night.

In the corridor heading for the lift she wiped away more tears. Her mobile rang and she pulled the phone out of her bag, wondering who the caller could be. A friend? Sorry not to have been in touch, wondered how you were. I do give a toss after all.

'I got your birthday card,' her mother snapped. 'A day late, like last year.'

Wanda's heart sank. 'Sorry about that.' She reached the lift and pressed the button. 'I did post it well in advance, honestly, and stuck a first-class stamp on. You should have got it in time. But you know what the post can be like these days.'

'Any excuse. You just can't be bothered, can you? Never could.'

Wanda had always dreamed of a kind, loving mother to whom she could confide anything, a mother who would be proud of her and support her no matter what. But loving mothers, like good friends, were for other people, not her. Her mother made her think of hate, not love. All those years of bad temper and criticism, nothing and no one ever being good enough. She was never allowed to play out or have friends or, when she got older, boyfriends. Always being berated for thoughtlessness, stupidity, selfishness, lack of consideration for people who didn't deserve it anyway. It never seemed to occur to Wanda's mother that love and affection were not things you could demand, especially when you never gave any love yourself. People like that were all the same, she thought. Selfish people accused others of selfishness, cold indifferent people complained that no one loved them. Wanda's father had spent most of his time down the pub playing darts and pool, then had walked out one day and never returned. She had not fantasised about searching for her long-lost father and re-establishing a connection, because she knew there was zero point.

'Not much use when a card doesn't arrive on the right day, is it?' The whining voice went on. 'I know my only daughter has a very important job as a journalist in the big city and can't be bothered to drive up to Carnforth now and then to see her lonely, widowed mother ...'

Lonely for a good reason. I don't deserve to be lonely, Wanda thought.

'So how is he then?'

She got a shock. 'You mean Alex?'

'Who else? You know I didn't like you marrying him, but you went ahead and now it's for better for worse, et cetera.'

'Alex is the same,' Wanda said, her voice dull and flat. 'No change.'

'Oh.'

'Why didn't you want me to marry him?' She wondered why she bothered to ask. 'He's a lovely person, a good teacher. He made me happy. Was that it?' She jabbed the lift button again. 'You couldn't stand the thought of me being happy for once?'

Her mother lived in a terraced house in a street near the railway station where *Brief Encounter* had been filmed. Wanda thought it was one of the most irritating films she had ever seen. Her mother had even looked a bit like the film's soppy heroine when she was young. Now she was gnarled and twisted from decades of disappointment and bad temper, and Wanda always expected her to snap *'Don't you know there's a war on?'* in response to any question or comment.

'Don't you bite the head off me, Wanda Brennan. You're not the only one with problems, you know.'

'You fucking old cow!' Wanda screamed suddenly, startling herself. 'Why aren't *you* in a coma?'

'*What* did you say to me?'

'You heard. You should be happy. Give you something else to whinge about now, won't it?' Wanda switched off the phone. She was shaking. She had never spoken to her mother like that although, God knew, the woman had had it coming for decades. But it did not feel liberating, just shocking. She could hardly believe what she had done. Wanda also felt somehow diminished.

Back at the flat she washed the cut on her arm, adding some antiseptic to the hot water, biting her lip and gasping at the stinging pain it caused. The bloodied knife still lay on the kitchen floor; she picked it up, washed that too, and put it away. She poured herself a big glass of white wine, gulped it down and poured another, and opened a packet of crisps. She stretched out on the living-room sofa, switched on the television and tried to watch a documentary about Queen Anne Boleyn, but could not get interested in it. She had once loved history programmes, but these days her concentration was shot to hell.

Wanda went into the bedroom, took her fountain pen and little black diary out of the bedside drawer and flipped through the pages with various dates circled. What a week, what a month, what a disastrous year. She would have liked to believe things could not get any worse, but had a horrible feeling they still might. Wanda had a big box full of diaries somewhere in the spare room, all the nasty events of her life recorded in neat black ink. She always used black ink. Black was the colour of grief.

She returned to the kitchen to open more wine and poured herself another glass. The wine helped soothe the stinging pain of her arm. She settled herself on the sofa once more, picked up her pen and diary and glanced at the television – Queen Anne on the scaffold was telling her masked executioner that she had a little neck, so his job shouldn't be too difficult. Wanda pushed back her hair and wrote. The ink flowed over the smooth cream page.

My darling Alex had a seizure tonight. I can't take any more.

'Julie, do you really think it's a good idea to come down the pub tonight when the bastard who murdered your Mum and attacked you is on the loose?' Julie Ferris' mate Miranda darted another frightened glance around the crowded, smoky Star & Garter.

'I'm safer here than I would be at home.'

'How d'you make that out?'

'Richard Croft knows where I live.' Julie finished her second bottle of Becks. 'I couldn't believe it when that bloody cop turned up and told me some morons had let him escape from a hospital. What was he doing in a hospital? He shouldn't have been let out of jail, and he doesn't deserve medical treatment anyway.' She flushed with anger and tossed back her long, straight, highlighted hair. 'I was terrified – hysterical. I'm still terrified.'

'Of course you are. But even though he knows where you live, at least the cops are giving you protection. Croft won't dare go near your house anyway, will he? He must know they'd be expecting him if he did. Have you got that alarm thing with you?'

'Yeah.' Julie pulled it out of her pocket and held it up. 'And that patrol car's sitting outside here waiting while I get a few drinks down me neck. That reminds me – it's your round. Hey, fancy going on to a club after this?'

'Joking, aren't you?' Miranda stood up, adjusting her short black suede jacket. She rubbed at a lager spot on her jeans. 'You want to go out clubbing when there might be a psycho after you?'

'Why not?'

'Well ... *why*? No, Jule. I don't think it's a good idea. Anyway, I've got college in the morning.'

'And I've got work.'

'Yeah, you'll be on your heels all day flogging designer gear to tourists in Cavern Walks. You'll feel terrible if you've got a massive hangover that even a gallon of espresso and a Full English can't cure.'

'I'll take a sickie.'

'What, another one? Pushing it, aren't you?'

'I don't care.' Julie's pretty face was sulky. 'Every day's a bonus after what happened to me.'

Richard Croft had taken her mother away, first by alienating Yvonne Ferris from her daughter with his lies, then by murdering her while Julie lay bound and helpless. She missed her mother terribly, and did not think she would ever come to terms with the horror of her death. How could anyone come to terms with that? The only way Julie knew how to cope was by making a huge effort to try and not think about it every day, by trying to go forward, make a new life. She had thought she was doing pretty well in the circumstances. She had a job, some money, she could feed herself – and her dog! – and pay the bills. She had a few good mates, she managed to go out and even enjoy herself sometimes. She looked forward to a future in which she did not have to wake up every morning and *cope*. But now this had happened. Her eyes filled with tears.

'He would have killed me too, Mirrie. He wouldn't have let me go. I wanted to help Mum, but I couldn't. I couldn't stop him.'

66

'I know, love. I know.' Miranda sat down again and put one arm around her, ignoring the whistles and calls that her gesture attracted from a gang of lads at the bar. She thought for a moment. 'Have you told your dad that Croft's escaped?'

'Like he'd care.'

'Oh come on, Julie. Of course he would. He's your dad, isn't he?'

'I phoned his place a few times this afternoon, but he didn't answer. I left a message on his mobile. I haven't seen him for a couple of months, I don't even know if he's in Liverpool at the moment. He's a salesman, so he's away a lot. Last I heard he was on the road most days and shagging his new girlfriend at night. He's made up because she's eleven years younger than him, it's pathetic. God knows what that daft bint must be on to fancy him. Probably fancies his money.'

'Well, keep trying to reach him. Why don't you go and stay with him until Croft's back inside?'

'What's the point when he's away so much? He doesn't want me anyway, Mirrie, he's got his own life. I don't want to stay with him. Even if I did, I don't know how long all this will go on, do I? The cops said they might recapture Croft within twenty-four hours, but that hasn't happened. Suppose he stayed on the run for weeks or months? Some escaped cons do.' Julie felt frightened again. 'They might never get him.'

'Course they will. He's got nowhere to go, has he? No family. Who'd want to help him? Nobody.'

Julie thought. 'Yeah.' She nodded. 'You're right, who'd help *him*? When he lived with us he never seemed to have any mates. That's why he tried to dominate Mum's life – he didn't have one of his own.' She sighed. 'I need another drink.'

'And then we call it a night, okay? You can stay at my place, if you like,' Miranda offered. 'You never know, the cops might get him soon.'

'Thanks Mirrie, it's really sweet of you. But I'll be okay. Anyway, there's Dixie – I can't leave him. And you don't want him shedding hairs all over your silk cushions and giving you an allergic reaction.'

Miranda grimaced. 'Soppy hound.'

'I can't believe Croft will come anywhere near Liverpool,' Julie said, trying to look on the bright side. 'He might be a psycho but he's not thick. He must know it'd be mad to come anywhere near me.'

'So what do you think he'll do? Where d'you think he might go?'

'The cops asked me that.' Julie shrugged. 'I haven't got a clue. I just hope he's got better things to do than come after me.' Or Shannon Flinder, the solicitor who had been so kind to her, listened and helped when she had no one else to turn to. Julie wondered briefly if Shannon was at risk too. But for now she could only worry about herself.

'Let's go back to my place for tonight, anyway,' Miranda suggested. 'I've got a bottle of wine. We can get some chips and watch a DVD.'

'I'll have to go home first and feed Dixie his supper.'

Miranda looked irritated. 'Can't the hound go without a meal for once? You spoil him rotten, he eats too much as it is.' She thought of the time she had put the apple pie her mother had made for Julie on the table, gone into the kitchen with Julie and come back a couple of minutes later to find the greedy labrador had pawed off the wrapping and scoffed half of it.

'Don't you slag off my Dixie.' But Julie was smiling. 'I love him.'

'I know you do. All right, go and feed him. I'll come with you.'

'No, don't bother.' No sense in putting her friend at risk too, Julie thought. That's if there was any risk. 'The cops will give me a lift and keep an eye out. I'll be fine. Get one more round in and wait for me. I'll be ten minutes tops.'

'Won't those policemen get pissed off chauffering you all over the place?'

'They can bloody well lump it. It's the cops' fault I'm in this situation. Right?' Julie stood up. 'Back soon.'

She was off before Miranda could raise any more objections, flinging her dusky pink lambswool scarf around her neck and zipping her fleece-lined denim jacket. She recoiled in shock and disgust as some drunk, slobbering moron lunged at her and tried to grab her around the waist, his fetid breath hot in her face. He stopped being amused when Julie shoved him away, making her revulsion too obvious for his fragile ego.

'Bitch. Fuck you, bloody stuck-up cow.'

Julie hurried on, trembling. She gasped at the cold outside, ran to the waiting police patrol car and got in.

'Good night?' one of the officers asked, sounding sarcastic.

'Yeah.' Julie rubbed her cold hands together. 'And it's not over. Take me home,' she ordered. 'Then back here, so I can meet my mate – we're going to the chippie and then to her place. I'm staying the night there.'

'Right you are, Your Ladyship.'

'Bloody hell,' the other officer sighed. 'I'm starving. Wouldn't mind a few chips meself. And a beer.'

Whether he posed a risk or not, Richard Croft was controlling her life again. Julie hoped the cops would pick him up soon, tomorrow with any luck, and stick him back inside with all the other murdering psychos. She felt depressed as the car stopped outside the small terraced house – her mother wasn't there any more. She would never again be able to go home to her mother.

'Won't be a sec,' she said, scrambling out. 'Just got to feed my dog.'

'You did switch on the new alarm before you came out, didn't you, Julie?'

'Yeah, 'course. I'm not thick.'

She had a bit of trouble unlocking the front door because the shiny new locks the police had installed were stiff. When she got inside Julie snapped on the hall light and managed to remember and type the alarm code within the required thirty seconds. She wondered if the police would let her keep the alarm once Croft was put back in prison.

'Dixie?' she called, shutting the door behind her.

The labrador normally came bounding up to her, crazy with excitement. But there was no sight nor sound of him. Then from the kitchen she heard a whining, retching sound.

'Oh no,' she sighed. 'Have you been at that cake?' She should have remembered to put away the chocolate cake and those biscuits, but of course she'd had bigger things on her mind.

Fear gripped Julie again as she realised she did not believe any of the stuff she had tried to tell herself. Croft might well try to come after her. He did not have better things to do – the only thing he really liked to do was hurt people. She thought of her mother lying dead, purple-faced, her tongue protruding. Those tortured, final breaths.

'Stop it!' she said. 'Stop. Now.'

She ran to the kitchen and put the light on. The dog was in his basket, chocolate cake crumbs and the cake wrapper lying nearby in a pool of pale vomit.

'Oh, for...! Ugh. You silly animal. Why d'you have to eat stuff just because it's *there*?'

But it was her fault, of course, for leaving the damn cake out. Julie went to unlock the back door so she could get the mop and bucket from the yard, then suddenly remembered Miranda waiting in the pub and starting to worry, maybe getting hassled by creeps. Cleaning up this mess would take a few minutes, and Dixie might be sick again. She couldn't leave him now. Miranda had better come here instead. But was that a good idea? Well, whatever – she was in for the night now. Better tell those two cops. Julie ran out to the patrol car.

'I've changed me mind,' she told them. 'I'm staying in now.'

'Are you sure?'

'Yes. Me mate might come over, but I don't know yet. I'm just going to call her.'

'OK, love. Make sure you lock up. Night night.'

She went back inside, locked the front door, phoned Miranda and explained about the sick dog. Miranda said she was tired and would just go home, if that was OK. Julie said goodnight, hung up and went through to the kitchen. She put her mobile phone and the panic alarm on the table. The dog whined as she unlocked the back door.

70

'All right, Dix. Just got to get the mop and bucket and clean this up, Don't suppose you'll be wanting any supper now, will you, you naughty boy?'

There was a rush of freezing air as the back door crashed open. Julie was sent flying across the kitchen. A dark figure rushed at her, grabbed her and pinioned her arms, clamped a rough cold hand over her mouth. The dog started barking.

'Shut up, you.'

Julie struggled frantically, furiously. How had he got in? She always kept the yard door that led into the alley bolted and padlocked. He must have slipped down the alley and managed to climb the wall into her yard. But how? The wall was about six feet high, so he would have needed a ladder. The police kept checking the alley; he must have somehow evaded them.

A cloth was being stuffed in her mouth so that she could barely breathe, let alone scream for the two policemen who sat out the front in their car. Dixie's barks turned to terrified yelps.

'Hello, Julie,' Richard Croft whispered in her ear. 'Did you miss me?'

Chapter Seven

'Why won't you tell me what's wrong?'

'Because nothing *is* wrong.' Jevko turned away from the television and looked up at Mariam, hating the anxiety in her dark eyes.

'You're different. On edge. Is it your work?' she asked. 'The people? Did something happen today?'

Something had certainly happened today. But Jevko was not going to tell his wife about the horror he had witnessed in the dark dawn of this morning, the frozen woman lying stabbed to death in her own blood, sprawled like a broken doll, the victim of what had obviously been a frenzied attack. He knew her name now from watching the local news: Jenny Fong. She must have parents, a family. Jevko sighed and rubbed his eyes. He could imagine what they were going through.

He thought of his father, mother and two sisters, all murdered by the Taliban because their politics were the wrong kind. And because they were educated, possessed too many books. Books were dangerous. He himself had been arrested and thrown into that terrible prison, hung upside-down and beaten, half drowned in baths of icy water, given electric shocks. If it hadn't been for his brother-in-law bribing a couple of guards, he would have died in that place. And what had happened to his brother-in-law? He had never been able to find out. Was he dead too? Jevko flinched and gripped the arms of the chair. *Stop*.

'Is it work?' Mariam persisted, moving closer.

She knew he was a gangmaster who hired out labour to farmers and packing plants, but did not realise that he was illegal and unlicensed, not like the legitimate gangmasters who paid their workers a decent wage and adhered to health and safety regulations. He relaxed his hands, stretching them out and flexing the fingers.

'It's not work. It's nothing.' He shrugged. 'I'm tired, that's all. Tired of this life. I want something better for us. Before Shamila gets old enough to walk and talk.'

'We've been through the worst. Better times will come.' Mariam turned away. 'I'll make some tea. Then you can go to bed.'

Jevko turned back to the television. The national news had finished, and now the regional news would come on. Then another weather forecast. Always so much about the weather. That normally made him smile because it was so typically British. But nothing could make him smile tonight.

He had been unable to resist driving past the murder scene on his way home this evening; he was not sure why. Did he want to go back and check that everything was normal, in the hope that this morning had been nothing worse than one of the night-mares that tore him from his sleep gasping and sweat-drenched several times a month?

Unfortunately things were not normal. The crime scene near St George's Hall and the war memorial was cordoned off with red-and-white striped tape, and guarded by several police officers. Jevko had to park the van in Lime Street station and walk back. A group of onlookers stood watching a television crew pack up their equipment. The lion statues lounged on their plinths, contemptuously ignoring all the fuss. Bunches of cellophane-wrapped flowers lay at the foot of the plinth where the woman's body had been, splashes of bright colour in the chill, autumnal gloom. When Jevko saw the flowers he started to cry and shake. He was ashamed of having run off and left her lying there. But what could he have done?

One of the onlookers, an overweight, grey-haired man in a dark-red jacket, had noticed his tears and asked him if he'd known the dead girl. Jevko shook his head and mumbled no, not at all. The man had looked suspicious then, obviously wondering why he was so upset. Jevko had turned and walked away, conscious of the man's stare, knowing he was speculating as to what the scruffy, dark-eyed, tangle-haired foreigner might be up to. He had glanced back and seen to his horror that the man was talking to one of the police officers and pointing at him. He had started to run then. Not clever.

Jevko wished he had been in time to help this Jenny Fong, save her from her murderer. Of course he would still have run off before the police arrived. Who was that figure he had seen lurking at the top of the steps, trying to hide behind that column? Was it the murderer? Or someone else who had come across her body and not known what to do, someone else with good reason to avoid contact with the police? It amazed Jevko that many British people seemed to think the police were there to help and protect them. After his own experiences in Afghanistan, he could not imagine feeling anything for them except fear.

Mariam brought him a cup of hot, sweet tea. While they were drinking it Shamila woke and started to cry. Jevko went into her tiny, stuffy bedroom, lifted her out of her cot and cradled the baby in his arms. It felt comforting to hold her. He kissed her beautiful little face, smoothed her hot forehead and settled her against his shoulder, started to hum one of the old songs his grandmother had sung to him when he was a child. Mariam smiled at them from the doorway. The baby relaxed against him and was soon deeply asleep again. Jevko laid her back in her cot and kissed her one more time. My beautiful daughter, he thought, looking down at the sleeping child. She will grow up to be educated, independent, as free as any human can be in this world. She will know oppression exists, but she won't suffer it. And she must not know fear. That is the worst of all.

The warm, dimly lit room and the peace of the sleeping baby made him feel sleepy himself. He went back into the sitting room yawning. Mariam was stretched out on the sofa watching *North West Tonight*.

'Terrible.' She shook her head as she stared at the screen. 'That poor, stabbed woman. Why was she out alone at such a time? Women here have too much freedom.'

Jevko glanced at the television and recoiled. Another news crew was at the murder scene, another presenter appealing for any witnesses to come forward and contact the police. Fury rose in him at Mariam's words. He picked up the remote control and hurled it at the wall. It broke open, the two batteries tumbling out as it fell to the carpet.

'*Murderers* have too much freedom!' he shouted. 'Not women! Think of Shamila, think of her future. Do you want people to say she has too much freedom? Are you going to be stupid all your life, even after what has happened to us?'

Mariam gasped and sat up, her eyes filling with tears. Jevko felt guilty.

'I'm sorry.' He sat down and put his arms around her. 'Forgive me. I'm very tired. Let's finish our tea and go to bed.'

Tired as he was, he did not know if he would be able to sleep. Jevko supposed he would get over this horror, or at least learn to live with it. He never read newspapers and he would stop watching the news for the next few days. The murder would gradually recede from his already overburdened consciousness.

They got up. Mariam took the cups to the kitchen then came back, slid her arms around his waist and hugged him. She looked up at him, blinking away her tears.

'I love you,' she whispered. 'So does Shamila. And we are safe now. Well ...' She smiled. '*Safer*. We have a new life now. Don't be afraid.' She kissed him. 'Everything will be all right.'

'They've kicked the door in.' The police officer examined the splintered wood. 'Battered it. Must have used something.'

Brilliant deduction, Sherlock. Shannon glanced back at Finbar and rolled her eyes. Mi-Hae Kam stood nearby, wrapped in her big, black wool coat, her thin face pale and anxious.

'Any ideas about who might have done this?' The officer turned to Shannon. His mate was examining the barred, ground-floor windows.

'Well, I've told you about Richard Croft's escape. I'm not saying he's broken in here tonight, but it's an unfortunate coincidence that it happens while he's on the run.' So many unfortunate coincidences. 'Could you check inside before we have a look to see if anything's been stolen?'

'We're just about to do that very thing, love.'

'Although I can't think what there is to steal,' Shannon said, anticipating his next question. 'We don't keep cash on the premises – certainly not large amounts, anyway.'

He grinned. 'Or drugs?'

'Not unless you count caffeine.'

'Which is a drug,' his mate butted in, 'although not considered an illegal substance by the higher anarchies.'

Mi-Hae looked at him, stunned. 'Don't you mean the higher *authorities*?'

Shannon nudged her. Mi-Hae was not used to this kind of thing, as she spent most of her working hours reading hundreds of pages of complicated fraud case documents when she was not communing with barristers.

'Whoever broke in might still be here.' She pointed down the dark hall. They had never had a break-in before. The minute Mi-Hae had phoned to tell them about the alarm going off, Shannon had thought of Richard Croft. But surely he wouldn't be this stupid or arrogant? Why would he break in anyway? Shannon could not think of a reason. She had a bad feeling about this, but who wouldn't? She supposed she should give DI Casey a call, as this event could certainly be described as 'something weird'.

'You should think about getting CCTV. And a steel-lined front door.' The officer shone his torch down the hall, then stepped inside and switched on the lights. He walked in, his mate behind him. Shannon, Finbar and Mi-Hae followed.

'Everything seems normal.' Mi-Hae glanced nervously around the reception area. 'Tidy. Well, as tidy as we ever get it.' One of the officers turned.

'Stay back, please, while we check the rest of the premises.' He went into the reception area. 'Gordy,' he said to his mate. 'Check the upstairs, will you?'

76

'Right.'

'I locked my desk and office door, as usual.' For some reason Shannon felt she had to whisper. 'And my filing cabinets.'

'So did I,' Mi-Hae whispered back. 'Nothing seems to have been touched,' she said. Footsteps sounded overhead, going in and out of various rooms. Shannon watched as the policeman headed for her office and tried the door. It was still locked.

'Got the key?' he asked. Shannon gave it to him and he opened the door. She went inside and looked around. She tried her desk and the filing cabinets.

'Everything's locked.'

'Hmm.' The policeman looked puzzled. 'Maybe they legged it as soon as the alarm went off. Didn't have time to do anything.'

Shannon took a long breath. 'Was it opportunists, do you think?' But why would opportunist burglars be so determined to batter the door down? It was wrecked.

Mi-Hae came in frowning. 'The receptionist's desk seems to be in a bit of a mess,' she said to the police officer. 'Things moved around. Papers scattered on the floor. And I can't find the office address book. She usually keeps it in the top right-hand drawer. I don't know, maybe she took it home with her for some reason. I can't imagine any ordinary burglar stealing *that*.'

'Might have just grabbed an armful of stuff and legged it when the alarm sounded,' he said. 'That often happens. You'll probably find they dropped it somewhere outside.'

Shannon felt herself turn pale. 'Maybe this wasn't an ordinary burglar. If Croft took it ... my God!' she exclaimed. 'That book's got all our contact details, as well as those of other solicitors and barristers we deal with. Home addresses, phone numbers, e-mail. It's also got the names and phone numbers of stationers, computer people, cleaners.'

'I'll call Helena,' Mi-Hae said. 'Find out if she took it home for some reason.' She went out and came back a minute later. 'No. She said she thinks the address book was in that drawer, but she can't be certain. She hasn't used it for a while.'

'What if Richard Croft took it?' Shannon tried not to panic. Finbar stepped forward and put one arm around her.

'It might be here somewhere. Has anyone else used it?'

'Not that I know of.' Mi-Hae shook her head. 'Shannon?'

'No.' She turned to the officer. 'Maybe you're right, and whoever broke in grabbed it and then dumped it. Let's search here then look outside.'

They spent the next ten minutes searching the office and outside in the street, but could not find the book. Shannon's fear increased, even though she tried to tell herself this might be nothing to do with Croft. She phoned DI Casey and told him what had happened.

'We'll check this place for Croft's prints, DNA,' he said when he arrived.

Mi-Hae frowned. 'I suppose I'll have to call a locksmith before I can even think about going home and getting some sleep.' She glanced at her watch. 'They'll charge a fortune to come out at this time of night. I don't know anyone. Do you, Shannon?'

'I do,' Finbar said. 'And he won't charge a fortune. I'll give him a call, shall I?'

'Oh thanks, Finbar. That'd be great.'

They got back to Shannon's apartment after midnight. She was angry, exhausted. 'I don't believe that was some ordinary opportunist burglar who freaked and ran when the alarm went off.' She threw her jacket over the sofa. 'I just don't. It's too much of a coincidence.'

'Well, hopefully we'll know soon. Want a drink?' Finbar asked. 'Some tea?'

Shannon yawned. 'All I want now is *sleep*.'

He put his arms around her and kissed her. 'Come on then.'

It seemed as if she had only been asleep for about five minutes when she was woken by the repeated ringing of the doorbell. She looked at the bedside clock; it was ten-to-two in the morning.

'Bloody hell ... *what* ...? Don't answer it,' she gasped, as Finbar started to get out of bed. 'It might be ...!'

'I'm not going to let anyone in, am I? I'll find out who it is first. You stay here.' He pulled on his robe, went into the hall and picked up the intercom phone. Shannon switched on a lamp and sat up, rubbing her eyes. Finbar was back a second later. 'It's the police. DI Casey.'

'Oh God,' she groaned. He wouldn't turn up at this hour to tell her anything she'd be happy to hear.

'Sorry to bother you at this time of night.' Casey was grim-faced, and looked as exhausted as she felt. 'But it's bad news, I'm afraid.'

Shannon shivered, pulling her robe tighter around her. 'So I gather.'

'Croft – at least we presume it was Croft – abducted Julie Ferris from her house.'

Shannon was too shocked to speak for a second. Finbar looked at him in disbelief.

'Correct me if I'm wrong,' he said slowly, 'but wasn't there a police patrol car parked right outside her front door?'

'There was, yes. Julie told them she was in for the night and that her friend might come over but she didn't know, she was just going to call her. When the lights in the house were turned off a couple of minutes later the two officers assumed the friend wasn't coming and that Julie had gone to bed. But when her dog started barking and kept it up, they got suspicious and went to investigate. Julie didn't answer the door, so they forced an entry. The alarm wasn't on and the back door to the yard was open. Croft must have gone down the alley behind the house, climbed over the wall and bided his time, waiting for an opportunity. We don't know how long he was hiding there.'

'Why did Julie open the back door?' Shannon asked.

'To get a mop and bucket – her dog had been sick. The alley at the back of her house was checked regularly, but—'

'Not regularly enough,' Finbar finished. He shook his head in disgust.

'We think Croft managed to hide in the next door yard after it got dark,' Casey went on, 'and used a ladder that was there to climb the wall into Julie's yard. Julie's neighbours are on holiday in Spain, so their house is empty. He unlocked and unbolted Julie's alley door, got her out of the alley and pushed her into a car – a car he stole and later abandoned after—' He stopped and glanced away.

'After *what*?' Shannon had tears in her eyes. 'Tell me.'

Casey looked at her again. 'Julie's body was found dumped outside St George's Hall.'

Shannon gasped. She felt Finbar's hands on her shoulders.

'She'd been strangled.'

Jevko's tormentors had played the radio and smoked while they gave him shocks. Sometimes they talked about their hopes for this son's career or that daughter's marriage. They bore no animosity towards him and his pleas for mercy, his agony, did not touch them. To them this was a job like any other – nothing personal. It was some people's fate to be tortured, others to do the torturing.

His arms were strung up behind his back and leashed to a hook in the ceiling, forcing him to stand on tiptoe while they gave him the electric shocks. His body poured sweat and his heart pounded so hard he thought he would go into cardiac arrest any second. But if that meant death, the end of all agony, it was fine by him. Jevko knew he did stupid things during the torture sessions, such as calling out to his dead grandmother. That made them laugh. They told him lots of people shouted for their mothers or grandmothers.

Somebody knocked at the door to the torture room, but his captors did not answer it. Why not? Wasn't it time for their break? They were sweating too, looked like they needed one. The knocking grew louder. He writhed, sobbed, tried not to move his pain-racked body. He prayed, even though he no longer believed anyone was listening. The pain in his arms and shoulders was unbearable, but of course he had to bear it.

Jevko jerked awake in the darkness, drenched in sweat. He sat up, his heart thudding, the nightmare's horror still vivid in his mind. Somebody was knocking at the front door, shouting his name. Mariam sat up and reached for him. He put his arms

80

around her and held her close, to try and comfort himself as much as her. She was trembling.

'Who is that?' she whispered. 'What can they want at this time of night?'

It was two-thirty in the morning. Time for murderers and torturers to come calling. Jevko got out of bed. 'I'll see who it is. Don't worry.' They had nothing to worry about here. Did they? 'Look after Shamila if she wakes.' As she would if this knocking went on for much longer. Shock and fear made him feel sick. He pulled on a sweater and jeans because he wanted to be fully dressed when he answered the door. Jevko could suddenly feel every scar aching, forcing him to remember. No, he told himself. Stop. This country is different, those things don't happen here.

He went down the narrow hall and paused. 'Who's there?'

'Are you Jevko Arib? This is the police. Open the door, please.'

The police? Terror seized him. Had someone reported him, said he was an illegal immigrant as well as an illegal gang-master? But who? The man he had had an argument with a few days ago, the lazy bastard who wouldn't do his share of work but still wanted more pay, the one he had sacked? The man had threatened to get back at him, then slouched off and disappeared.

Jevko unlocked the door and opened it, keeping the chain on. Three police officers stood there.

'Come on now.' The one who spoke looked angry. 'Get this door open.'

Jevko obeyed and they crowded inside, huge in the small space. Mariam appeared, a sleepy Shamila in her arms. Mariam's dark eyes were wide with fear.

'Are you Jevko Arib?'

He nodded, then realised they were waiting for him to speak. 'Yes. I am.'

'Jevko Arib, I am arresting you on suspicion of—'

'Murder?' he gasped, unable to believe the words. 'What murder?'

81

'Of the murder of Jenny Fong on—'

'I don't know this woman! I haven't murdered anyone. This is a terrible mistake.'

'Isn't it always?' They turned him around and clicked handcuffs on him. Jevko was too shocked to resist.

'Murder?' he repeated, stunned. He shook his head. 'No. *No.* You are mistaken. Please believe me – I am innocent.'

Mariam started to wail.

Chapter Eight

Think like the animal you want to track.

Richard Croft had known Julie would not stay away from home for long because of her soppy dog. That animal had ruled her life. He had also known she would not stay away from her favourite local, the Star & Garter. He had watched her from across the crowded bar, her and her stupid mate, the little scrubber from art college who fancied herself as the next Tracey Emin. They had not spotted him, of course; he looked different without his moustache, and he had covered the grey in his hair with a chestnut-brown rinse from Boots, after giving it a clumsy trim with the scissors he'd bought. Simple but effective. His face and frame looked thinner too; he must have dropped a good few kilos during the past twelve months.

He had gone back to Julie's house, knowing the cop car was waiting for her outside the pub. Slipped down the alley, found the ladder in the neighbour's back yard. Waited, crouched in the cold darkness. He hadn't had to wait long. When Julie came home and switched on the lights he could see into the kitchen and down the hall. He had watched her lock the front door then make a phone call. Obviously she was in for the night and the police were leaving her to it. The stupid barking hound might have ruined everything, but he had got out in time, safely down the alley and into the stolen car. She was gagged by the cloth and half-unconscious from his punches. It had been easy to tie her up and bundle her into the boot.

He thought of that last look of terror in Julie's eyes. He was still shaking, still hyper. He wished he could have kept the stolen Audi, but of course that was too risky. Richard remembered the stupid young guy he had seen while walking along the street, watched as this moron in a baseball cap had got out of the car, left the engine running, and dashed into a nearby house, yelling someone's name. He had grabbed his chance. Driving away, he had glanced in the rear-view mirror and seen the guy come out of the house, stand there open-mouthed with shock and then rage. That had made him laugh.

He liked the idea of dumping her body outside St George's Hall, near the spot where the other dead woman had lain. That would freak Shannon Flinder, another victim dumped in the same place as her murdered mate. Shannon Flinder was the next score he had to settle. He patted the black book in his inside jacket pocket, the book which he could see contained a lot of useful addresses – one in particular. Helpful, the receptionist leaving it in that unlocked drawer. He hadn't had to search any further. He now knew that Shannon Flinder had moved, and to where. She would be stunned at Julie's death, might wonder if she was next. And she would be right. Richard had wondered whether or not to dump Julie's body in Shannon Flinder's office, then decided against it. Luck had been with him tonight, and he did not want to push that luck any further.

'Shall I dance for you now, Steve?'

Who the hell was Steve? Richard relaxed as he realised the skinny, dark-haired Eastern European girl with her false smile was talking to him. Steve Kane, his new alias. He liked the name Kane.

He nodded. 'Go on.'

He did not consider her face or figure good enough for the VIP area of this lap-dancing club where he had come to chill after his night's work. The place even had a masseuse; the head and neck massage he had treated himself to had helped him relax, although not much.

Most women were messed-up individuals and not classy. They had always given him more stress than he could handle. Now, with this head injury, he would have to take extra care of himself for the rest of his life. Surgeons had removed the bullet and told him he was lucky to have survived, lucky that the bullet had not gone into some part of the brain that could have caused his death or turned him into a vegetable. Richard was not the same man though; he would never be the same again. He had asked the neurologist how long the tiredness and headaches would last, but the guy had simply shrugged and said he couldn't tell and that everyone was different. He gave the impression he didn't give a damn either.

The girl was talking to him again in her stilted English, holding out her hand for more of his money. Richard hated her smile, wished he could wipe it off her stupid face. He looked down at his hands; they were still shaking slightly, and his fingers ached. It was not nothing to strangle somebody. He imagined the candle he had lit in that dark church burning down and expiring with a wisp of smoke.

'Dance,' he said to the girl. 'On the end of a rope, you whore. What's wrong?' He laughed at her shocked expression. 'That's what you are, isn't it? A whore.'

He got up and headed for the exit. He had had enough of this place now, wanted to be alone with his thoughts. Richard wondered again if he should get out of Liverpool, for a while anyway. Go to Lime Street and take a night train to London Euston or somewhere. But Lime Street station was patrolled by police, and they would probably have stepped up their patrols after his escape. Besides, what about Shannon Flinder? He had the advantage now. He imagined Shannon with a rope or his hands around her smooth, slender neck, those dark-blue eyes staring up at him in terror rather than the contempt he so vividly recalled. She wouldn't be so bloody arrogant then. He looked at the half-naked dancer, wanting to shove or hit her as she cringed away from him. He got out of the club and leaned against the wall, breathing cold night air. A police van turned into the street and cruised past.

Richard pulled his jacket around him and forced himself to walk slowly, keeping close to the wall. He tried to look like he knew where he was going. A second later he stopped and swore. He had left his carrier bag in the cloakroom of that club, the bag with the trousers and change of underwear. He did not want to go back and claim it now, not after the way that bouncer had looked at him.

All he possessed in the world now were the clothes he had on, the address book he had nicked from Shannon Flinder's office, and the consultant's wallet in his jacket pocket. The money wouldn't last long – he would have to get more somehow. He imagined Spain, the blue skies and sunshine. Freedom. He had been there several times on holiday in the past and had loved it, even knew a few words and phrases of Spanish. But he needed a passport to fly there, and how the hell was he going to get hold of one? He might be a convicted murderer, but he had no contacts, no clue about how to get stuff like that. Maybe he could steal one, but he'd have to be lucky enough to find a man around his age who resembled him to some extent and who happened to have his passport on him. Most people only carried their passports when travelling, and it would not be a great idea for him to hang around some airport looking for a suitable victim. Even if he did manage to steal a passport he would have to fly out, escape before it was reported stolen. How could he do that?

Depression closed in on him like sea mist cutting off hot sun. Killing Julie had been the most incredible stress relief, stress which had been building for a long time. This bad feeling he had now was a reaction, he thought. Not remorse, never that. Richard was not sorry he had murdered her. He just felt total desolation, pitied himself for being alone and friendless in the world, for never having had chances other people took for granted.

He walked back to the miserable B & B where the owner, a young overweight woman named Mrs Appleby, was still up.

She had on a red dressing gown and strange coloured things twisted into her dark-brown hair, presumably to make it curl. Richard's head was throbbing again and he felt hot and sweaty. He needed to lie down. He felt too tired and depressed to try to charm Mrs Appleby. Where was Mr Appleby, he wondered? Out with his mates? In prison, on night shift, doing a stint on an oil rig?

'Evening, Mr Kane.' Her eyes had a preoccupied look. 'Leaving in the morning, are you?'

Richard nodded, and even that hurt. 'After breakfast.'

'Would you like the Continental or a Full English?'

He winced. 'Tea and a bit of toast, that'll do me.'

'Right. OK, that's twenty you owe me, please.' She held out one hand.

'Won't it do in the morning?'

'Sorry. I used to do things the polite way, but there were too many people who left without paying. You get cynical after a while.'

'I suppose.' Richard pulled out the wallet and paid her.

'Thanks. Goodnight now.' She disappeared into her sitting room and he climbed the stairs to his room. He opened a can of Coke and took three more painkillers. He wondered if he was taking too many, but he did need them. Richard undressed, got into the lumpy bed and switched off the lamp. He heard the doorbell go and Mrs Appleby's voice again from downstairs, followed by male and then female laughter. So she could be friendly to some people.

Sleep was impossible and he lay there listening to the sounds of the house, doors closing and toilets flushing, more voices downstairs and drunken shouts from the street. People made so much noise without realising. His mind was full of vivid, clashing images from past and present. Julie's face as he killed her, the look in her eyes, Shannon Flinder's contemptuous courtroom gaze. Yvonne coming home unexpectedly that day and screaming at him to leave her daughter alone, that he was a liar, scum, filthy rapist bastard, to get out, get out, that she was going to tell the police and make sure he went down for years. Calling Julie 'babe', telling her she was sorry, so sorry.

Next came a child, a boy of about five with big, dark, frightened eyes staring up at him. The boy wore a white shirt and a pair of grey shorts, long grey socks and polished black shoes. His skinny, mottled legs had goose pimples, and his forehead was bleeding. The boy was him. Richard groaned and turned over.

He fell asleep at last, woke briefly. He dreamed that he was crying, bawling his heart out. For himself, his life, because it seemed he was fated to become the man he was. He had never had a chance, only knew fear, anger, hatred, distrust.

When he woke to dull daylight and rain drumming against the windows he was shocked to find that his face was wet, drenched with warm tears, the pillow damp. He groaned and raised himself on one elbow, looked around the depressing room. He wondered if he had shouted or cried out during his sleep, and if anyone had heard him.

Richard felt deeply ashamed, as if he had lost control of another bodily function.

'When the world was young ... the croak of the raven was not heard, the bird of death did not utter the cry of death, the lion did not devour, the wolf did not rend the lamb.'

'Excuse me, Mr Arib?' Cindy Nightingale glanced at her colleague, a thirty-something man with a beard, wearing jeans and an olive-green sweater, and leaned across the table. 'Can we get on?' Jevko ignored her.

'The dove did not mourn.' He rocked back and forth, his arms folded. *'There was no widow, no sickness, no old age, no lamentation.'* The duty solicitor sitting next to him placed one hand on his shoulder and shot an alarmed glance at Cindy.

'Think we need a break.'

'Well, I know I do. Mr Arib, what are you talking about?'

'I'm quoting from a poem.' Jevko sat still and looked at her. 'It's called the *Epic of Gilgamesh*. My father loved it.'

'Where is your father now?'

'Dead. He was murdered by the Taliban in Afghanistan some years ago. When the Taliban had control. He did nothing wrong. An enemy lied, denounced him. He was a doctor, a very good man. Kind. He liked to laugh.'

Inspector Nightingale seemed about to snap some remark, but glanced at the whirring tape recorder on the desk and bit her lip. She picked up a pen and studied her notes.

'Jevko?' It was Jevko one minute, Mr Arib the next. 'Quoting poetry won't help you now, I'm afraid.' She paused. 'What did you do with the murder weapon you used to kill Jenny Fong?'

Tears came into his eyes. 'I didn't kill that woman, I didn't even know her. How many more times must I tell you?' He thought of Mariam and the baby. What must Mariam be going through now, having to cope without him? What would she do if they put him in prison? 'My wife – my baby – you must help them.'

'Let's not discuss your wife just now, OK?' Cindy rubbed her eyes. 'Although your lack of cooperation won't make things any easier for her. Right, let's go over this again. Two witnesses have placed you at the crime scene – one who saw you there shortly after Ms Fong was stabbed, thought you were acting suspiciously and took the number of your vehicle – and someone else who reported you standing at the crime scene some ten hours later, in a state of considerable distress. He alerted a police officer and you ran off. Why did you go back there, Jevko?' Classic murderer's behaviour, she thought, satisfied if exhausted.

'I thought—' Jevko paused, blinking back tears. 'I hoped that maybe what I'd seen that morning was not real. A bad dream.'

'Is that right? If you're as innocent as you claim, why didn't you contact the police immediately you discovered Ms Fong's body?'

'I was in shock. Frightened. I didn't know what to do.'

'And an illegal gangmaster doesn't want contact with the police, does he?' Cindy's colleague broke in. 'Neither does an illegal asylum seeker. You're in big trouble, Jevko, you know that, don't you?' He sat back. 'You may well get your wish to stay in the UK, although it won't happen quite the way you hoped.'

Jevko knew what he meant. He would go to prison for a few years, then get deported. His fear increased.

'Did you make a lot of money exploiting vulnerable people? There's laws against that kind of thing, you know.'

'I knew it was wrong.' Jevko twisted his hands together. 'I was ashamed. I wasn't going to keep on doing it. I had to take care of my wife and child. I wanted to find a proper job, but things were very difficult.'

'Let's get back to Ms Fong's murder.' Cindy stared at him. 'You say you never knew her?'

'No. I never saw her before. I only found out her name when I saw the news about the murder.'

'If you never knew her, why did you stab her more than twenty times?'

'I *didn't*. I didn't kill her! I never hurt anyone in my life. I'm not a murderer.'

There was a knock at the door. Cindy got up and went out. Her colleague murmured something into the tape recorder about how Inspector Nightingale was leaving the interview room.

'Can I see my wife?' Jevko wiped his eyes on his sleeve. He felt dirty, exhausted. 'I must speak to her.' He wondered why the solicitor was with him; the man sat there looking bored, wrote something down occasionally, hardly spoke. He glanced up at the window he could not see out of and realised it was daylight, if you could describe that grey gloom as light. He thought of the sunshine and stark blue skies of his native country, the mountains, the dust. Cindy came back. Her eyes were bright, her shoulders straighter.

'OK, Mr Arib.' She sat down again and smiled at him. Jevko flinched. Torturers often smiled, although this woman did not look like a torturer. Just a bitch. His scars ached, his whole body ached. He pulled up his T-shirt and sweater and scratched his chest. Cindy's smile disappeared and her colleague's eyes widened in shock.

'What are those marks?'

'Torture,' Jevko replied. 'The Taliban beat me and gave me electric shocks. And they were going to dip me in the acid bath, but for some reason that didn't happen.' He pulled his sweater down. 'I was very lucky.'

They were silent. The tape recorder clicked and the bearded man took out the two tapes and replaced them with new ones, asked Jevko to pick one tape which would be sealed and kept as a copy. Jevko did not understand this bizarre ritual, but he complied. When the new tapes started, Cindy resumed speaking.

'We've just had the results of some tests. Shoe prints in Ms Fong's blood exactly match those of your trainers, Mr Arib, and the DNA sample you provided matches with DNA found at the crime scene, on and around Ms Fong's body.' She grimaced. 'Made you sick, did it, the sight of her afterwards?'

'Yes, the sight of her made me sick.' Jevko shook his head again, despairing. 'When I discovered her body. I didn't kill her! Why don't you talk to that person I told you was hiding behind the column?' he asked. 'Maybe they know something. Maybe that person was the murderer.'

'Oh yes, the mystery witness.' Cindy smirked and glanced at the tape recorder.

'I'm not lying,' Jevko persisted. 'I *did* see someone there. Watching me. That was another reason I ran away. I was afraid.' He jumped up, panicking, terrified at what might be going to happen to him. To Mariam and Shamila. 'I'm innocent,' he shouted. 'I never killed anybody.' He started to cry again. 'I never hurt anyone, never. Let me go.'

He ran to the door. They might not have electric shocks and an acid bath down the corridor, but he still had to get out of here. Cindy's colleague leapt up and dragged him back. Cindy opened the door and shouted. Two uniformed police officers rushed in, grabbed hold of him and handcuffed him.

Jevko was shaking, crying, struggling with them, tears pouring down his face. Cindy watched as they pulled him back and slammed him against the wall. Her eyes were full of contempt and something else. Jevko realised with a shock that the woman was happy. Like it was Christmas or her birthday.

'Lock him up,' Cindy snapped.

Chapter Nine

'Last night I dreamed I was trying to fit my key in the front door while a shadow lurked behind. No need to guess whose shadow.' Shannon looked at DI Casey. 'Recaptured within twenty-four to forty-eight hours, you said. Not happening, is it?'

He shifted in his chair. 'We're doing everything we can.'

'Not enough. Not when Julie Ferris gets abducted from her home while a police patrol car sits out front, murdered and then her body dumped – outside St George's Hall! Croft's got a sick sense of humour, hasn't he? Maybe he murdered Jenny too.'

'There's no evidence to show that. Not so far, anyway. Besides, they've arrested a man for the murder of your friend.'

'Yes, I heard.' Shannon nodded. 'And wasn't *that* remarkably quick and easy?'

Casey looked startled. 'Are you saying you don't think they've got the right man?'

'Maybe they have, I don't know. It just all seems too neat and obvious.' Especially with Cindy Nightingale in charge of the investigation. Shannon wondered why this Jevko Arib had murdered Jenny – if he had. She shivered. Of course neat and obvious did not necessarily mean not true. She didn't know what to think.

'Look – getting back to Julie. Those officers in the patrol car thought she was in for the night. And when the lights went out they assumed she'd gone to bed. There was nothing to indicate she was in any danger. It was only when her dog kept on barking that they got suspicious and went to investigate.'

'Wonder if Croft intends me to be his next victim?' Shannon picked up the thick plastic pen and pencil holder on her desk. Inside the clear plastic sloshed a virulently blue, oily sea on which floated tiny ships and an oversized pink dolphin. 'God, I—' She stopped. What? Couldn't believe Julie was dead? She had barely got her head around Jenny's murder, and now this had happened. She could not feel anything at the moment. Except fear.

Finbar had been furious last night, calling the police morons and a lot of other things; he had not wanted her to come to work today. Shannon thought how much she had liked Julie Ferris, how she had been glad to act for her, help nail Croft for assault and attempted rape. Now all her efforts had been tragically wasted.

John Casey was shaking his head, seemed as shocked as if he had discovered Julie's body himself. 'This is terrible. Of course we'll step up the surveillance outside your place now. Or wherever you tell us you're going to be.'

'Oh great. I feel better already.' Shannon put the pen and pencil holder down and took a sip of hot, sweet espresso. It was two in the afternoon but she hadn't managed breakfast or lunch. 'Do you think that will make any difference? Julie had more protection than I did,' she pointed out, 'and look what's happened.' She banged the cup back on the saucer and stood up. 'How can it be so bloody difficult to recapture Croft, when all he's got are his own violent impulses and whatever he can steal? I still can't believe he was allowed to escape in the first place. Those guards listening to his whinges about his headaches. Taking his handcuffs off, fetching him snacks and cups of fucking coffee!'

DI Casey stood up too. 'I can understand you're upset.'

'Oh really?' Shannon thought of her dead father-in-law, of Rob pointing the gun at her head as she crouched sobbing with terror in the dark bedroom. 'Has anyone ever wanted to murder you?'

'Not that I know of.' Casey's eyes were troubled as he gazed at her. 'Look, I promise you, I'm doing everything—'

'Oh, save it, will you? It seems Croft can go anywhere he likes and murder whoever he wants and leave you lot clueless. I thought the criminal mind one step ahead of the plodding cops was supposed to be a Hollywood myth.'

There was a knock at the door and Helena the receptionist looked in. She gave John Casey her most seductive smile, which he ignored, before turning to Shannon.

'Sorry to interrupt. Finbar just phoned – I told him you were busy, and he said he'd call back later. And there's someone in reception who'd like to see you.' She rolled her eyes. 'A Mr Dennis Ferris – Julie Ferris' father.'

'Oh my God.' Shannon's heart thudded. 'I don't need this now. Wonder what he wants? I didn't know Julie had a father – that is, I mean, not one who was around much. Her parents were divorced. All right, Helena,' she sighed. 'I'll see Mr Ferris. Tell him I'll be a couple of minutes.'

'Sure.' Helena shook back her long, dark hair and bestowed another languishing look on John Casey before she went out and shut the door.

Shannon hesitated. 'I really don't feel like doing this.'

'You OK?' Casey moved closer. 'You look a bit ... you must be knackered after last night.' He yawned. 'As am I.'

'I'm fine.' Shannon went to the door. Casey followed as she walked down the hall to reception. Julie's father Dennis was tall and sandy-haired, with big hands and red-rimmed pale eyes. He wore a crumpled black suit and had a black coat draped over one arm.

'Shannon Flinder, right?' His voice was hoarse.

'Yes. Mr Ferris, I'm shocked about Julie's death. And terribly sorry. I liked her very much; she was a lovely girl.'

Dennis stabbed one finger at her. 'You helped get that f ... that bastard who killed her mother banged up, right?'

'That's correct, Mr Ferris.'

'Julie liked you. Said you were all right. The bloody useless cops let that psycho escape and now he's murdered her as well. Murdered my Julie.'

'I know. Mr Ferris, I'm so —'

'Sorry's nice, love. And you sound like you mean it. But sorry won't do it.' His voice rose. 'Sorry's no fucking good. It won't bring my Julie back. She was a good kid. I wasn't much of a dad to her, I know that.'

And now it was too late. Shannon thought she could not take this, could not take any more. She felt like crying, wanted to run off somewhere. John Casey stood close behind her.

'I had to identify my daughter,' Dennis went on. 'Couldn't believe it. Never seen anything like it, couldn't believe that was my little girl lying there in that morgue. This should never have happened, and I want answers. Who let Croft escape, who let him do that to my little girl?'

'It's terrible. Tragic.' Shannon took a breath and clasped her hands. 'But what exactly can I do for you, Mr Ferris?'

'The cops let that bag of shite escape. They knew he might go after Julie. They've screwed up big time, letting that scum murder her when there was a bloody patrol car sat outside her house! What were they doing, what kind of bloody protection's that supposed to be? You tell me that.' He was shouting now.

Casey stepped forward. 'Mr Ferris—'

'Just shut it, will you, mate, if you don't mind? I'm not talking to you.' He turned back to Shannon. 'This is going to take a lot more than an apology from the Chief Constable, love, I can tell you that. Not that the likes of them ever apologise for anything unless someone forces them to.'

Shannon imagined Finbar's rage if Croft got her next. She had a feeling he would do a lot more than just rage. 'I don't understand. What can I do about that, Mr Ferris?'

'My daughter's dead. My life's fucked – business gone down the bog as well lately. It all started falling apart when that shit murdered my ex-wife. Yvonne and me were still mates, it was a big shock. I couldn't cope, couldn't get me head round it. Now I've lost Julie. What am I supposed to do, eh? Who's going to help me?'

Shannon thought she could see where this was leading.

'I'm Julie's dad – her only surviving relative,' Dennis shouted. 'It's the cops' fault Croft got out and killed her. They did sod all, they didn't protect my Julie and I'm not letting them get away with it. I want you to sue them for me.' He stepped close to Shannon, breathing hard, his face flushed. 'Money won't bring her back, but that's not the point. You take the Chief Con and his merry men for every penny they've got, girl.'

He was right, of course. The State had failed in its duty to protect a citizen, failed big style in this case, and Dennis Ferris was entitled to compensation for his daughter's murder. But Shannon did not feel like getting it for him. The man had neglected his daughter, never been there for her, never made Julie feel loved. Why should he benefit financially from her death? Shannon did not want to set eyes on him again.

'I'm sorry, Mr Ferris, but I can't represent you,' she said, coolly polite. 'My caseload is very heavy and I can't take on any new clients. I'm sorry for your loss. It's tragic. But I'm afraid there's nothing I can do for you.' She stepped back, almost colliding with Casey. 'I'd like you to leave now, please.'

'Eh?' Dennis looked astonished. 'Now hang on a mo. What the bloody hell's up with you, girl?'

'You heard what Ms Flinder said.' Casey's voice was sharp.

'You'll have to find someone else to get you your money.' Tears came into Shannon's eyes. 'Please leave now,' she repeated. 'And don't come back.'

She ran into her office, slammed the door and burst out crying.

'How dare you barge into my office and interrogate me, Flinder!' Cindy Nightingale glared at her. 'We've nicked someone for Jenny Fong's murder, and pretty damn quick that was.'

'Yes. A bit too quick.'

'Jeez. Can't win, can I? What the hell more d'you want?'

'The truth would be good.'

'I should have you thrown out.' So why didn't she? Was she perhaps slightly nervous after all that maybe scumsucking lawyer Shannon Flinder really did have friends in high places?

Bullshit, Cindy thought. She slid off her desk, grabbed a file and made for the door. 'The truth is what we've got – not that you'd know anything about truth.'

'This Jevko Arib. Who is he?'

'An illegal asylum seeker. Comes from Afghanistan. He's been earning his living as an illegal gangmaster, exploiting and endangering poor sods with crap pay and dodgy working conditions. He says the Taliban murdered his family and tortured him. That could be a load of old toffee, for all we know.' Cindy did not want to mention the torture marks on Jevko's body. 'We've got no means of verifying his story. For all we know, he could have been a member of the bloody Taliban.'

'What was his motive for— ' Shannon paused '— for murdering Jenny?'

'Motive?' Cindy looked at her scornfully. 'As you may have gathered from what I just told you, we're not dealing with a spotless moral character here. Arib could have murdered other people, could have a history of violence going way back. We don't know. DNA puts him at the crime scene, his trainer footprint in her blood. Her blood's also on his socks and jeans. And two witnesses clocked him at the crime scene.'

'Two?' Shannon followed her down the corridor.

'The first was anonymous – someone phoned the police, said he was acting suspiciously and gave his van number.'

'Did you follow that up?'

'It was made from some call box in the city centre. It's not really important.'

'But it could be. If you could trace that call and there was CCTV near the spot you might be able to find out who made it.'

'We're looking into it,' Cindy lied. Interfering bitch. 'The second witness was some old guy who clocked Arib staring at the flowers and crying, then running off after he spoke to him. The guy reported this and has ID'd Arib now. That's helpful too, of course, but the DNA gives us more than enough. Arib even threw up over his handiwork.' Cindy grinned, preening herself. 'This sticks better than a lump of Juicy Fruit to your

Jimmy Choo. So now, if you've *quite* finished trying to tell me how to do my job, I do have a suspect to interview.'

'Would that be another bleedingly obvious, pop-up suspect?'

'Now look.' Cindy stopped and glared at her. 'The bleeding obvious is often bleedingly, obviously *true*. However much you may not like that. Your mate was probably just in the wrong place at the wrong time. Shit happens, as they say.' Deal with it, Cindy felt like adding.

'Was there any other evidence at the scene?'

'Well...' Cindy looked shifty. 'There were several other footprints in her blood, all from the same pair of shoes. Could have been some passer-by who didn't want to get involved. We're looking into it.'

'What about Richard Croft?' Shannon asked. 'They might be his footprints. Are you going to ignore the possibility that he murdered Jenny? It's a hell of a coincidence that this happens while he's on the loose. And now he's wanted for murdering Julie Ferris – he dumped her body at more or less the same spot where Jenny was discovered!'

'Yeah, I heard about that. I don't think Croft murdered Jenny Fong – certainly not when he could have had you.' Cindy looked at Shannon, her eyes narrowed. 'Could have been *you* stiffed out with more than twenty stab wounds. It's fate, kismet, shit luck. Call it what you like.'

'Maybe Croft wanted to get me that night but couldn't,' Shannon argued, trying to stay calm. 'Maybe he killed Jenny as a warning, like I said before. He's got motive. I don't see any motive where Jevko Arib is concerned.'

'Since when did a psycho need a *motive*? Killing's their thing and they just go ahead and do it when they get the chance.'

'And Croft got his chance when you lot let him escape!'

Why didn't she want to believe Jevko Arib had murdered Jenny? Cindy was right, the bleeding obvious was often just that. There seemed to be enough evidence to link him with her murder. Because Croft's on the loose, Shannon thought. Because he could have dumped poor Julie's body at the same spot where Jenny had been found. And because I don't trust Cindy Nightingale.

'Right,' Cindy said. 'Goodbye.'

'Wait. This doesn't make sense. The vast majority of murder victims are killed by someone they know. Croft might not have known Jenny, but if he followed us that night he must have guessed she was a friend of mine.'

'Jeez, Ms Criminal Law Solicitor, thank goodness for all your superior knowledge and penetrating insight. Don't know what I'd do without it. For the last time, Flinder – finding a suspect's DNA at a crime scene and having that suspect clocked acting suspiciously by two different witnesses – even if one is anonymous – makes perfect bloody sense to me. It would to you as well if I wasn't heading this investigation.'

Shannon was silent. She couldn't argue with that.

'And when said suspect has dodgy occupation and dodgy past that can't be checked out, it makes even more sense. If you can't accept that, it's your problem. Now piss off. I've been up all night and I'm knackered and I don't need you chewing my ear.'

'It's just—'

'There's no pleasing you, is there?' Cindy laughed, but her eyes were full of fury. 'First it's all, oh, this bitch shouldn't investigate my bestest friendy's murder, she doesn't care, she won't do a proper job – and the minute I get someone arrested and charged, that's no bloody good either. Now haven't you got better things to do, like trying to save yourself from a psycho? Oh dear,' Cindy sneered, 'you've gone all pale. Shall I get one of my minions to bring you a nice glass of chlorinated tap water? Have to save the bottled stuff for important guests, I'm afraid.'

'You're too kind.' Shannon brushed her clammy hands over her black suit. 'Please don't go to any trouble on my account.' This is pointless, she thought. She turned and walked off. This time Cindy followed her.

'Now that I've got your mate's murder sorted, I can get back to concentrating on the really important issues.'

'You mean with your therapist?' Shannon walked faster.

'I *mean*, with the murder you had commissioned and then waltzed away from. Bernie the Bogeyman, remember? Dear ol' Daddy-in-law? Don't think I'm giving up on that – ever. Even if I do keep quiet about it until I've got what I need to nail you.'

She's obsessed, Shannon thought. She was sweating now. How did I ever have the shit luck to come across this mad bitch? 'I hope your therapist gets paid a *lot*.'

'What kind of plant would you like in the interview room when I interrogate you? Venus Fly Trap? Love Lies Bleeding? Forget-me-not?' Cindy laughed again. 'You'll miss Finbar Linnell when you're banged up, won't you? Have to put up with some rather more rough and ready caresses in the nick, if you get my meaning.'

'What would you know about unwelcome caresses? There's no such thing as far as you're concerned – but unfortunately for you no one's that desperate.'

'*Fuck* you.' Cindy stopped laughing. 'Make the most of being free to walk out of here, won't you? Because next time I see you you'll be in handcuffs. Or stretched out on a morgue slab, if Croft gets you first.' She watched Shannon walk away. 'Good luck with saving your life,' she called. 'You're going to need it.'

She had her murder suspect and didn't care if he was the right man or not. Cindy just wanted to carry on with her personal vendetta. She was as vengeful as ever. My God, Shannon thought. What am I going to do?

Jevko Arib's presence at the murder scene did not prove he had killed Jenny, despite the incriminating DNA. His unclever behaviour – getting his footprints in Jenny's blood as well as on his clothes, lifting the coat off her face, throwing up – suggested shock and disorientation rather than a ruthless killer gloating over his victim. And who did the mystery footprints belong to? Were they really from some passer-by who had freaked and run off? Or did they belong to Richard Croft?

Shannon walked out of the police station and paused on the steps to look at the beautiful pink and mauve evening sky. It

101

was later than she had thought. She felt frightened again. She had taken a cab here and now she would have to walk out of the car park and down the street to look for another. What if Croft was around, suppose he had followed her? He might have stolen another car. He seemed to have nerve and luck enough to do anything. Julie's murder would probably give him even more confidence. God's sake, she thought, why can't they just *get* him? Shannon thought of Jenny dying, her blood pooling around her on the frozen ground. She went down the steps, then stopped and gasped as a tall figure came towards her out of the gloom.

'Hey Gorgeous. Only me.'

She ran to Finbar and hugged him. 'What are you doing here?'

'Khalida told me where you were so I thought I'd come and get you. You should have called me.'

'I know. Sorry.'

'Did you talk to that Nightingale bitch?'

'I certainly did. There's only one thing she gives a toss about – and it isn't who murdered Jenny.'

He frowned. 'Stay away from her in future.'

'I intend to. She's loopy.'

'Let's go home.' Finbar glanced up at the building. 'This isn't my favourite kind of place to be.' He kissed her. 'You OK?'

'Not really.'

'Didn't think so. Listen …' He stroked her face. 'She's not going to get you,' he whispered. 'Neither is Croft. It's going to be OK.'

Shannon stared up at him. 'I hope you're right.'

Chapter Ten

'I need to speak to Shannon Flinder. Now. Or make an appointment to see her – today, preferably.'

'I'm sorry, Mrs Brennan, but Ms Flinder isn't able to talk to you. She can't see you either,' the snotty-sounding receptionist informed Wanda. 'But if you'd like to leave a message—'

'I won't bother, thanks. It'd be unrepeatable.'

Wanda crashed the phone down, her face burning and her heart racing. She was starting to think Shannon Flinder was a bitch. Why wouldn't the woman help her and Alex, even if she was busy? It wasn't as if she had to give her services for free. And Shannon still refused to say anything about Jenny Fong, even something gushy, like what a lovely person the murdered woman had been. OK, not everyone was gagging to talk to the press about murdered friends and other horrible experiences. But not even one comment, for God's sake! Well, if that was the way Shannon Flinder wanted to play it, fine. Wanda might be able to make life very difficult for her, should she choose to do so.

Wanda knew she was being unreasonable, but she didn't care. That inspector in charge of the investigation into Fong's murder had proved unexpectedly friendly and helpful. So why did Shannon Flinder have to act so precious? It was as if she considered herself some kind of local celeb instead of a bog-standard criminal law solicitor with a dodgy past and a dodgy partner, the enigmatic-sounding Finbar Linnell. Inspector Nightingale had implied there was more slush than Snow

White about Shannon Flinder, and if Wanda dug deep enough, who knew what she might find? It was all right for Shannon, Wanda thought. She didn't live in some manky rented flat, have to worry about money or the future, and her partner wasn't lying in a coma from which no one knew if he would ever wake.

She shoved the bunch of damp tissues back in her cardigan pocket, took another slug of coffee and popped an extra strength Locket into her mouth. She had a cold and sore throat now, on top of everything else. Of course all this terrible, unrelenting stress would take its toll on her immune system. Wanda hoped she wouldn't get some serious illness. She felt even more tired and depressed today because last night she had had a horrible dream in which the doctors were trying and failing to resuscitate Alex. After that a nightmare in which the blonde Russian doctor came smiling up to her and told her they were going to switch off his life support and there was nothing she could do because she was alone and nobody cared. Wanda had started screaming at the doctor. When she woke up her screams were just gasps.

She sighed and relaxed her tense body. Why couldn't she dream about beautiful things? A crystal path that led to a secluded garden? Sunshine, a forest, fawns nuzzling her hand? The end of all suffering.

'Wanda?' Jane appeared, tearful and red-eyed, fidgeting with a tissue. She wore jeans and a black sweater today, and her brown hair was loose and untidy. Jane usually took care to dress like some high-powered executive rather than a sad bastard's put-upon secretary who should really be called Office Manager and paid twice as much. 'Rod wants to see you.'

'OK.' What did the tosser want now? Wanda got to her feet, sighing. She eyed Jane. 'What's up?' She didn't care, she was simply curious to know what someone who did not have her problems could find to get this upset about.

Jane sniffed. 'Our cat died.'

'Your...?'

'I feel a bit stupid getting so emotional about it. But me and my mum and dad just got back from the vet's and ... well, I didn't realise it would be so horrible. We've had Posy more than ten years. She went off her food, then we discovered she had this growth. The vet said she could have chemotherapy, but—'

'Chemotherapy? For a cat?'

'Yes, of course. Why not?' Jane looked surprised. 'But the vet said it would be kindest to put her to sleep.' She blew her nose. 'I suppose it's for the best. We didn't want her to suffer any more. Posy was one of the family. We're going to miss her terribly. She had a good life though.'

All this fuss over a cat? Wanda could not believe what she was hearing. She felt the laughter start in her stomach and well up into her Locket-soothed throat, an unstoppable force. She bit her lips, her shoulders shaking, and turned away to fiddle with some papers on her desk. But Jane had noticed.

'Well, I'm so glad my misery amuses you,' she snapped, crimson faced. 'I know you've got a lot on your plate and you could do with a laugh. Thanks very much, Wanda.'

Wanda swung round. 'Jane, wait. I'm sorry, I didn't mean—'

'Don't bother.' Jane walked away.

She had lost a friend now, and possibly gained an enemy. Wanda glanced around to see a few people looking at her disapprovingly. She put her hands on her hips, feeling the solid fat. She could still taste the chips she had eaten for lunch, feel the greasy coating on the roof of her mouth.

'Good stuff, Wand,' Rod grinned as she came into his office. His white shirt and black waistcoat, the loosened, striped tie, all looked like the parody of some harassed editor in a sitcom. He pointed to the text he was reading.

'Where d'you get all this in-depth insight about the Jenny Fong murder? Come on,' he smirked. 'Reveal your sources to Uncle Roddy.'

You must be joking, Wanda thought. She intended to keep Inspector Cindy Nightingale all to herself. She would not be

105

working on this rag for ever. If Alex – *when* Alex – woke from his coma, who knew what kind of state he would be in? He might never be able to work again. If she had to support him as well as herself, make a good life for them both – she would need to earn a hell of a lot more money than this chinless wonder considered it appropriate to pay.

'It's a police officer,' she said. 'But he's paranoid about not having his name revealed – not to anyone. Sorry, Rod. I can't risk it.'

'Hmph. What are you giving him to make him cough?' Rod looked her over, taking in the baggy jeans and shapeless maroon cardigan with its bulging pockets, her dried-out, candy floss hair, and Wanda guessed he was thinking it couldn't possibly be sex. She blushed. OK, she didn't exactly look her most glamorous these days. But who in her situation would have the time or inclination to even think about glamour?

'My source implies there's something dodgy about Shannon Flinder,' she said, indulging her resentment about Shannon. *My source*, la-di-da.

'Yeah?' Rod raised his eyebrows. 'Like what?'

'He wouldn't specify. He said he'll tell me more next time.' She had to keep Rod interested, keep him dangling. In the meantime she would do some digging.

'Hmm. Flinder was questioned about her dad-in-law's car bomb murder. But so was everyone who knew that fucker. And then there's her psycho ex.'

'I know. She refuses to talk to me about Jenny Fong, won't even comment on how nice her friend was. She won't say *anything*. I'm not saying that's suspicious, in fact I guess it's to be expected. But I nevertheless get the impression that there's something Flinder's desperate to keep secret – about herself, or someone else maybe.'

'Well, you know what they say.' Rod looked thoughtful. 'The only way two people can keep a secret is if one of them's dead. Get digging, Wand.' He frowned. 'Is Flinder talking to anyone?'

'Not that I know of. Except the police, of course. I thought I could also check out her partner – Finbar Linnell. He's got a dodgy past – present too, I bet. I wouldn't be surprised if that pair have got a lot to hide.'

'Yeah. Could be good. The sexy blonde criminal lawyer and her criminal lover. Shame the police arrested Fong's killer so quickly. I thought that story would run for longer. Find out more about that guy who killed her. We could do something on illegal gangmasters too; that's a hot political potato at the minute. And if your paranoid cop contact can give you more info, who knows what that might lead to? OK, Wand.' Rod nodded. 'Dismissed.'

'What?'

'I said, dismissed. Bugger off. Vamoose, skedaddle.'

She flushed again. 'I don't like it when you talk to me that way. It's disrespectful.'

'A thousand apologies, madam.' He laughed. 'Oh, how's ... er...?'

'Alex? My husband's name is Alex.'

'Yeah. 'Course. Sorry. How is he?'

'Alex had a fit yesterday evening.' Wanda twisted her hands together. 'It was awful, I was terrified.' She knew Rod did not want to hear this, but she could not stop herself. 'It's weird,' she went on. 'When the doctors and nurses are kind to Alex and me, it makes me want to cry. Crazy, isn't it, when someone being nice to you makes you cry? Should be the other way round.'

'Yeah. Er, Wand.' Rod coughed and fiddled with his tie. 'Take the rest of the afternoon off, why don't you? Chill – go and get a cappucino or a couple of glasses of vino down your neck. Have a stroll around town with a mate, buy a new top, get your hair tinted. Fun stuff, you know?'

'Thanks, Rod.' What was with the sudden care and consideration? 'But I've got no mates left, I can't afford clothes, and I'm allergic to hair dye. Right.' Wanda tried to smile. 'I'll get back to work, shall I? Star reporter on the case and all that.'

Rod said nothing, only stared at her.

*

Shannon felt safe down here in the Bridewell, the cells beneath Dale Street Magistrates' Court. Especially at this time of day when it was quiet, the holding cell along the corridor hosed down and emptied of shouting, swearing drunks. Dawn, the Group 4 guard who was manning the desk, gave her a sympathetic smile as she finished her call and closed the last file – Colin Mills, a shoplifter, was looking at a custodial sentence and the fact that he was being treated for depression wouldn't help him this time.

'Why can't all my cases be ordinary and non-threatening?' Shannon sighed. 'Most of them are, of course. Some solicitors go through their entire careers without anyone even calling them the C- word, never mind—'

'Never mind getting a psycho after them.' Dawn came around the desk, jingling the chain around her waist on which hung the bunch of keys. 'Want me to lock you in one of them cells?'

'Yeah, great. I'll take you up on that.'

'I hope they catch that fella soon.'

'So do I, Dawnie darling.' Gossip travelled fast, Shannon thought.

'Must be hell for you right now.'

'I have had more fun times in my life. If you give me a minute I'll try to remember some of them.'

'Be careful, Shannon.'

'Don't worry, I will. See ya.'

Another guard unlocked the inner door then the black mesh cage door to let her out. What should she do now? Shannon wondered as she ran up the stairs. Get a sandwich and some coffee? Call Finbar? DI Casey hadn't called her with any good news about Croft. What if he stayed on the run for weeks, months, longer? He was more dangerous than ever now. She turned left along the corridor that led to the Lawyers' Room.

All the times she had walked this quiet corridor and thought nothing of it. Now, however, she was frightened, glancing back continually, looking into the various rooms she passed, up the steep staircase that spiralled to her right. She remembered the

108

time she had gone into the Lawyers' Room and found her coat slashed to pieces. Rob had done that, although she had not known at the time. He had also turned out to be the sender of some nasty anonymous letters. Shannon refused to have any contact with him now. She wished she could forget Rob existed, because the trauma of everything that had happened still hurt – too much sometimes.

She thought of how great, how kind and loving Rob had been before everything fell apart. The happiness she had believed would last a lifetime. But things happened over which you had no control, went more hideously wrong than you could ever have imagined. Shannon did not hate Rob, despite what he had done to her. She missed the man he had been, even though she loved Finbar now. She hoped things would not go hideously wrong with him.

Her footsteps slowed as she reached the Lawyers' Room, and her heart started to pound. Croft couldn't get into this building, could he? There was CCTV at the entrance and the security personnel had been briefed with his description and told to watch out for him. He might have altered his appearance. Why didn't I ask someone to walk this way with me, Shannon wondered? Because she didn't want to appear frightened? Finbar was right, this was about being sensible, not proving how brave she was. Or how stupid.

Had this Jevko Arib murdered Jenny? And how was she going to resolve her doubts about that? She couldn't exactly count on Cindy Nightingale's help. Of all the bloody people to head the inquiry into Jenny's murder! And deeply ironic that people refused to believe the one thing Cindy was right about – that Shannon Flinder *had* had her father-in-law murdered.

Shannon remembered her boastful, arrogant father-in-law, so arrogant he'd thought he could go on abusing and murdering young girls without ever getting caught. And when Shannon had found out about him, he had tried to kill her. I had to do it, she thought, cold sweat breaking out on her body. I had no choice, I was alone. Rob had left me, he told people I was bitter and crazy, no one would listen. What was I supposed to do, wait for that bastard to come and murder me? She had had this argument with herself many times.

She hesitated outside the closed door of the Lawyers' Room then gasped with fright and jumped back as it flew open. But it was only Charlotte Greene of Greene & Co. by the river. Charlotte looked tanned after her autumn break in Barbados, and had had more blonde highlights put in her long hair.

'Oh, hi Shannon.' She nodded absently. 'How's tricks?'

'Trickier than ever.'

'Good. Good. See you.'

There was no one else in the room. Shannon got her tweed coat and pulled it on, hurried out of the gloomy old building. In the street she blinked at the sunshine. It was a cold, clear day; the smell of the river and a trace of woodsmoke from distant fields mingling with the traffic fumes. She took out her mobile and checked for messages as she walked along Dale Street. There was one from Finbar and another from Helena; she called Helena first.

'That Wanda Brennan's been hassling me again. I tried to give her some names from that list of solicitors you left with me in case she called back, but she wouldn't even listen. She insists on having an appointment with you hey-ess-hey-*pee*.'

'Fuck's sake.' Shannon sighed. 'How many more times? I was thinking again about her husband and wondering if there was some way to help him, even if I could find the time. But it's impossible. I'm really sorry for him – and for her, even if she is a journo – I know she's desperate, but—'

'She got angry and slammed the phone down on me. Not that I minded.'

'She must feel powerless.'

'Can I be rude to her if she calls again? Make that *when*.'

'No, don't,' Shannon warned. 'Certainly not your unique brand of rudeness. It's tragic what happened to her husband. She's got terrible problems.'

'She's not the only one, is she?'

Shannon decided to call Finbar later, from the office. She glanced up and down the street and across the road, searching faces. None of them resembled Richard Croft's. A black cab dropped off a man in a dark overcoat and she got in.

'St George's Hall, please.'

She felt overwhelmed with sadness as she got out of the cab and walked across to the spot where Jenny's body had lain. The striped tapes which had cordoned off the crime scene were gone. The only thing to indicate that something tragic had occurred here were the cellophane-wrapped bunches of flowers at the foot of the stone lion's plinth. The cellophane crackled in the breeze.

Shannon still could not believe Jenny was dead, murdered. She pulled her coat around her and shivered. Tears rolled down her face. I miss you, she thought, staring at the spot where Jenny's body had lain. I wish I could see you now, hear your voice. You were so much fun. Kind. You cared about people. She wiped her eyes. Where are you, where have you gone? I can't believe we just get snuffed out. An elderly couple walking past stopped.

'You all right, love?' the man asked.

'Yes. Thanks.'

They glanced at the flowers and walked on. Shannon looked up at the front of St George's Hall. The hall, opened in 1854 to house an annual music festival which had outgrown nearby St Peter's Church, long since demolished, had been described as having the massiveness of a Roman bath combined with the delicacy of a Greek temple. Shannon climbed the steps and walked to the end of the row of columns. Jevko Arib had apparently told the police he had seen someone hiding here. The distance from the end column to where Jenny's body had lain did not seem far. But would things look different in a cold, pre-dawn light? What time did the Hall's floodlights switch off?

Shannon had racked her brains for other murder suspects – if Jevko Arib was not guilty – but could come up with no one except Richard Croft. And there was nothing to prove he had been anywhere near Jenny. Even if the police believed they had the right man in custody, they still had to build an intimate profile of Jenny and interview everyone she had known. But would they do everything they were supposed to do? Cindy Nightingale had refused to follow up that anonymous phone call implicating Jevko Arib in the murder. And to whom did the mystery bloody footprints belong? That could be something or nothing. Shannon wished she could find out more.

She looked round at the other columns and the expanse of stone flags and cobblestones, past the lions and the war memorial, across the road to the Empire Theatre and the Northwestern Hotel. Traffic sped down Lime Street. Shannon had seen lots of bands at the Empire in her younger days, and had enjoyed a hectic social life until the legal career and then marriage to Rob Flinder had started to take up most of her time and energy. During the past year she and Finbar had been going out and socialising a lot, trying to get back to a normal life after everything that had happened. Now she had to try and pick up her life yet again. I'm tired, Shannon thought, I'm frightened. I don't want to go through anything else, I've had enough.

Surely there must have been people around this area, which was known as Liverpool's cultural quarter, even in the early hours of a freezing morning? But how could she find any of them, let alone talk to them? No one had come forward to say they had witnessed a murder or anything or anyone suspicious. Did the mystery person hiding behind the column exist, or was Jevko Arib lying about that? Had he imagined it? If the person did exist, what had they seen?

What about CCTV, Shannon wondered? There were no cameras directly covering St George's Hall, as far as she could see, but nearby cameras could have picked up something. Surely the police would check that out? Could she get access to footage without Cindy Nightingale finding out? Shannon doubted that. And now that Cindy knew she was unconvinced of Jevko Arib's guilt, she would be even more determined to stop her investigating further. Shannon believed that Cindy had given her what information she had in the hope that she would go away and not bother her again.

She went down the steps. If neither Richard Croft nor Jevko Arib was guilty, this could have been a rare stranger murder, which would be difficult if not impossible for the police to solve without help from the public or some lucky break. But Shannon did not think it was that. She imagined Croft spying on her and Jenny as they drank, laughed, danced. Watching, waiting for a chance to strike. It was pointless to wonder why Croft would bother to murder people when he must have enough to do trying to avoid recapture. That was how a normal person would think, and Croft was not normal.

Shannon stared at the ground as if she might find some clue, some trace of evidence. She pushed her hair away from her face and the wind blew it back into her eyes. There would be a trace, she thought. A trail. Somewhere. There had to be. And she had to pick it up before it went cold.

No crime was perfect.

Chapter Eleven

'It's the new arms race.'

Finbar squinted up at the rotating security camera mounted on its pole at about four metres above street level, spying on the crowds of shoppers in Liverpool city centre. The shopping crowds were thinning out as office workers on their way home began to take their place. He hoped Shannon was all right, but of course hoping was not good enough. The police had failed to stop Croft murdering poor Julie Ferris, and that was it as far as Finbar was concerned. He would not rely on them to protect Shannon. It was time to act.

'Yeah, it's an arms race, all right.' Curtis Bright, his old friend and contact who sold security products over the Internet since he had left the Army, nodded. Curtis did not glance up at the cameras, but looked round at a couple of passing women, who smiled at the tall, good-looking black man. 'There's even more cameras in Manchester, where I live. The whole country's mad for it. *"I've got nothin' to hide,"* he mocked. *"It's great if it helps the police stop crime."* Stupid bastards. Like anyone gives a fuck about your man and woman in the street being safe. What CCTV mostly helps is business.'

'Yeah. Targeting shoplifters, graffiti and property damage, the crimes which bother shopkeepers the most. Creating the illusion of clean, sanitised public spaces, glorified consumption zones to attract investors and lots of shiny happy shoppers.'

'Don't fall off that soapbox, will you, Finbar?'

They crossed Castle Street near the Town Hall; Finbar wondered where exactly the castle had once been. They walked down Water Street towards the Pier Head. The autumn sun was sinking below the horizon and the clear air was cold. He thought of Declan Dowd's corpse buried in the dungeon beneath the Clarence Dock clock tower. Was it still buried? He had heard nothing to indicate it wasn't. But the uncertainty about that was getting to him, playing on his nerves. As was his fear for Shannon's safety.

'Some street cameras will have parabolic microphones incorporated in them soon,' Curtis remarked. 'The Watchers will be able to pick up conversations on the street and in parks, maybe even in shops and restaurants.'

'Terrific.' But Finbar had lost interest in chatting about Big Brother. 'Thanks for coming to meet me,' he said as they reached the bottom of Water Street and paused, waiting to cross busy Strand Street. 'Let's go to my place, okay? I don't think there's any parabolic microphones around there yet.'

Curtis grinned. 'Whatever you say.'

'Away from the cameras, behind closed doors – that's where most of the major crime goes on, isn't it?'

'What crime are you planning then?' Curtis asked when they were seated in Finbar's big, warm living room, drinking coffee and watching the sun go down over the river.

'I wouldn't call this a crime. More of a ... a clean-up operation, you could say.'

Curtis looked at him, his dark eyes serious now. 'Thought you weren't into that sort of stuff any more.'

'I wasn't. I'm not. But needs must, I'm afraid.'

'Be taking a hell of a risk, won't you? I mean, with your past and everything.'

His past? Yes. Curtis might be an old mate, but as far as Finbar's past was concerned, he didn't know the half of it.

'In this case it's more risky to do nothing. But risk is greatly minimised when you hire the best person for the job.'

Curtis stiffened. 'Thanks for the compliment. So what have you got in mind?'

115

'Protection.' Finbar picked up his mug and drank more coffee.

'For you?' Curtis looked puzzled. 'I don't get it. I thought you said—'

'Not for me. For Shannon – my fiancée.' She was not his fiancée, strictly speaking, but Finbar lived in hope. 'She's in danger. I need her to be protected from someone.' He paused. 'Permanently protected. That's what I mean by a clean-up operation.'

'Oh. Right.' Curtis nodded slowly. He was silent for a few seconds.

'Are you up for it? Because if you're not, I don't know who else to ask. Or more to the point, who else I'd want to ask.'

Curtis stared at him. 'I'm up for it.'

'Good.'

'I don't do this for anyone, you know.'

'I know.'

Finbar pushed a particular phrase out of his mind, the words he had spoken when he made his promise to Shannon. Because now he had to break that promise. He hated to do it, but it was necessary.

No more secrets.

'Shannon Flinder speaking. Who is this?'

He remembered her voice from that day she'd come to the house on her Julie rescue mission. And from in court. Richard Croft smiled. 'Guess.'

He heard her gasp, then there was silence. His smile broadened as he sensed her shock and terror. She was right to be terrified.

'Did you get my message?' he asked.

'What message?'

'I think you know. Poor little Julie, eh? That's what you and everyone else are saying, isn't it? Young life cut tragically short by brutal murderer.'

'You should be a journalist,' Shannon said, her voice hardening. 'You've got all the clichés.'

116

His smiled faded. 'Aren't you going to ask what I want then? Tell me to give myself up because this is stupid and I can't stay on the run much longer? Ask me when I'm going to kill you? Don't you want to try and keep me talking in case I hang up before the cops can get a trace on this call?'

'I'm not going to ask you what you want,' Shannon said slowly, 'because I don't care. And you can talk all you like to the other psychos once you're back on A Wing. That's if they want to talk to you. Now fuck off.'

Richard couldn't believe it when she said that. Or when she hung up on him. What the hell did she think she was playing at? He shook the phone, shouted into it, banged the receiver against the glass. He started to dial Shannon's mobile number again, then stopped. She could be trying to trick him, provoking him into phoning back and getting into an argument with her so that the plods could get a trace, and the call would end with this phone box being surrounded. Where was the bitch, he wondered? At court? He had called her office and then her home, but no luck. He couldn't go near the Mags or Crown court, not with the security personnel hanging around and no doubt under instructions to look out for him. He couldn't risk it, even with his altered appearance.

He walked off, shivering with cold, his head throbbing. He did not feel scared, felt safe, in fact, blending in with these crowds of mostly pissed-off looking people in Slater Street. They would be replaced by a more cheerful crowd by tonight, when all the pubs and clubs would be buzzing. Richard was not even bothered by the CCTV which seemed to be everywhere since he had last walked around the city, because he looked different now. Why would they pick him out of all the other anonymous faces? The operators were probably busy doing more interesting things anyway. He thought of a guy he had met in prison, a sad git called Joey, who had been a CCTV operator before he had got caught using his hours of joystick swivelling to spy on women he would later target as his victims.

Richard walked up Bold Street, turned right along Berry Street and carried on until he reached Great George Street and the huge, elaborate arch that signalled the entrance to Chinatown. There was a big old building on the corner which looked as if it was about to collapse; it had once been beautiful and ornate. Shame, he thought. Let it go until it was beyond repair and restoration, then flog the site to yet another grasping property developer who would no doubt erect some monstrosity on it. The city was being changed beyond recognition, ruined by money-grubbing bastards who no one even tried to rein in. And his life had almost been ruined. He would make a new start, Richard thought, but he couldn't change the past. It would be with him always. His eyes filled with tears.

'Get a grip on yourself,' he growled, causing a passing Chinese couple laden with shopping bags to stare at him. He smiled at them. 'All right? Nice day for it.' They averted their eyes and hurried on.

He crossed Upper Parliament Street and reached St James's Place. It was going to take too long to walk the rest of the way, and the headache was getting worse. Richard hailed a black cab and climbed in, flopped on the back seat and closed his eyes for a second. He couldn't really afford cabs because his money was running out, flowing through his fingers like sand or salt, but he could not walk any more for now. The driver glanced at him in the mirror.

'Where to, mate?'

'Verlaine Street.'

He hoped it was true what he had overheard in a pub last night, that this club was still looking for bouncers. If he could find a job, just get cash in hand and no questions asked, that would be better than trying to lift wallets and maybe getting challenged or caught. Besides, Richard hated stealing. He had always liked to earn the money he got. He was proud of himself for never having been on the dole, or income support, as the politically correct chose to label scrounging these days.

Pickwick Street, Dombey Street, Dorrit Street, Dickens Street. Gwendoline, Geraint, Enid, Elaine, Merlin. He recognised them all; the pubs, shops, schools he had attended as a boy, the long rows of Victorian terraced houses that looked

118

small from the outside but had good-sized rooms with high ceilings, and spacious back yards. He recalled the black-and-white photo of his grandmother standing in her back yard wearing an apron – normal dress for housewives in those days – and smiling, shading her eyes against the sun. A dolly tub for washing clothes stood beneath the window. What had happened to that photo? Had Yvonne or Julie torn it up out of spite? Or did the police have it?

Where could he stay tonight? It was unnerving not to know where you were going to sleep. He had spent last night in St George's Hall of all places, dozing in a concert hall on an upper floor. There were loads of places to hide in there. It was stuffy in the concert hall though, so musty that it had made him cough a lot, and he had had to stay past opening time until he could go downstairs and slip out. Before going to St George's Hall he had checked out Shannon Flinder's street, noted the posh apartment block where she lived. It was an old building which had been renovated. Of course lawyers could afford places like that. There was a strong-looking front door, CCTV and an intercom system, so it wouldn't be easy to gain entry. And he couldn't discount the possibility of Flinder having male companionship. He had also seen a police patrol car sitting out front, although it had moved off after a few minutes. They probably drove past every two or three hours throughout the night. He had to think of some way to get Shannon alone.

Richard was surprised to find that the manager of the dark, chilly, stale beer and cigarette-smelling lap-dancing club – no classy joint, this – was a girl in her twenties, tall and thin, who wore a purple leather trouser suit. She had long, straight, blonde hair parted in the middle, dark eye make-up and pale pink glossed lips. He wasn't sure what he had expected; some middle-aged, cigar-smoker in a sharp suit? He wanted to ask the girl – Milena, she called herself – who was in charge, but stopped himself. She didn't ask him any stupid questions about national insurance numbers, past jobs or references, although Richard couldn't resist telling her he'd been a firefighter. Milena was not impressed. She looked him up and down, told him the pay – more than he'd expected – and introduced him to the archetypal, shaven-headed thug in a black suit who she said would show him what to do.

'Come back at seven.' She did not have a Scouse accent. It sounded Eastern European. 'Don't be late.'

After that it was back to the city centre pub to meet his contact of last night, Matty. Matty was going to get him a passport, or so he promised. Richard did not trust him. Matty was young, spotty and white-faced, a chain smoker with trembling hands. But what choice did he have? It had been difficult enough to get the name of someone who could provide passports, and this vampire lookalike seemed to be his best bet. Richard did not have time to mess around.

'Gonna take a couple of days.' Matty gulped lager and sucked on his cigarette. He fiddled with his dirty baseball cap, continually twisting it around on his head, scratched his spots and chewed his chapped lips. Richard could hardly bear to look at him.

'You told me twenty-four hours.'

'Yeah, I know, but I can't always be—'

'Specific?'

'That's it. And I'll need another fifty.'

'What? I've already given you two hundred. What the hell are you playing at?'

'Look, mate. I'm not tryin' to rip you off. I don't operate like that. Take it or leave it, OK? No skin off my nose.'

There would be a lot of skin off his nose, not to mention other parts of his scrawny, track-suited body, if he didn't come up with a decent passport in two days time. Richard had followed Matty home to the nasty bedsit he occupied near Princes Park. He pulled fifty pounds out of the consultant's wallet and handed it to him.

'Cheers, mate.'

'It better be a good one. The photo has to look a lot like me.'

'D'you think I'm stupid or somethin?' Matty looked at him resentfully. 'No worries, OK? I'm sorting it.'

'You better be.'

120

He felt nervous and frightened again. Things might not work out after all. The odds were against him; the police would have upped the ante in their search for him after he had killed Julie. They had probably circulated a picture of him to the local media, and even with the superficial changes he had made to his appearance, he was crazy to remain in the city. But he could not go anywhere without money. He had to hang on for another few days, get the passport and more money, then he would be out of here. He hadn't even got the kick he'd hoped for when he phoned Shannon Flinder. She should have pleaded with him, been terrified. Why wasn't she? Or was it just an act? She was a hard bitch after all, even if she didn't look it.

He thought about Julie again, about the moment when he had killed her. He had been born like this, with these desires. What had happened and what would happen seemed somehow inevitable. Why were people born this way? He had not asked to be burdened with such thoughts and fantasies. He was a victim. Yvonne and Julie had brought their fates on themselves, got what they deserved. And Shannon Flinder would get what she deserved.

Richard picked up his glass of Coke, pulled out the pack of painkillers and swallowed three, trying not to think of the holes they might be burning in his stomach lining and guts. He realised that Matty was looking at him strangely.

'Bit of a headache,' he explained.

'Hell of a headache, I'd say, if you're swallowin' that many.' Matty sniggered. He finished his lager and got up. 'Right. See you, mate.'

'You will.'

Richard managed to find a room in an old house near the club; after paying the deposit he had just over twenty quid left. But he would get paid after his shift tonight, and in cash of course. Honest pay for honest work. He ate some crisps and biscuits, then lay down and took a nap. After that he went back to town – by bus, this time – and started to walk the quiet, narrow streets by the river, near where Shannon Flinder lived.

It was dark now.

*

'I'm no racist, love,' Mr Gerald Elliott of number forty-six told Shannon as she stood shivering on his front doorstep in the street where Jevko Arib and his wife had lived until very recently. 'I don't give a monkey's what colour or creed anyone is, as long as they live and let live. But there's too many of them illegals coming here. They don't want to integrate, they're taking over our culture.'

What culture would that be? Pies, chips, curry, binge drinking, hysterical tabloids, fuckwit minor celebs in the jungle? Shannon glanced up and down the dark street. She hadn't known if it would be any use coming to look around this estate and talk to a few of Jevko's neighbours, but she had hoped she might find out something – anything. None of the few people she had spoken to had been able to tell her anything useful. She had met Gerald Elliott coming home with a bag of mint humbugs and his evening paper.

'So you saw Jevko Arib leave his house at – what time, exactly?'

'Ten past six.'

'How do you know it was...?'

'I'm always up early, love. Don't sleep much these days, not since I retired. I'd been listening to the news and I'd just looked at me watch.' He lifted his wrist and showed her. 'Present from me wife. I hit seventy last month. Three score and ten. But I hope I've got a few more years in me.'

'I'm sure you have. Why don't you like Jevko Arib?' Or was that a stupid question, given what this man had just said to her about illegal asylum seekers?

'He's one of them economic refugees. That's what I think, anyway. I've got nothin' against any poor sod whose been tortured or had to crawl out from under some dictator or fundamentalist nutter. But this fella's takin' the piss. And look what he's done now, got arrested for murdering that poor Chinese girl.'

'How well do you know Jevko Arib?'

Gerald looked shifty. 'We're not exactly mates, love.'

'Did you tell the police you saw him leave the house at ten past six?'

'Police? No police been round to see me, love. Everything I know about this murder I've got from the telly and the papers.'

Shannon was annoyed but not surprised that no one had been to see him. This confirmed that Cindy Nightingale was determined to do nothing that might interfere with her perfect suspect. Gerald Elliott's evidence would not prove that Jevko Arib had not murdered Jenny, but it would introduce an element of doubt, given that her estimated time of death was between three and five a.m. She had to get this information to the police and Jevko's solicitor. She glanced at her watch. And it was time to go home and see Finbar.

'Well, thanks. 'Bye, Mr Elliott.'

'Bye, love.'

She turned and walked down the path. A group of boys across the street were watching her, so Shannon decided not to check her mobile for messages just now. She felt nervous as she walked past, trying to look hard. None of them said or did anything. There were no cabs cruising around here, so she took a short bus ride back to town and found a cab outside the Royal Court Theatre. It was often easier to walk or take cabs around the city rather than drive and have to search for places to park. In the dark back of the cab she took out her mobile.

If Richard Croft called again she would have to try and stay cool enough to keep him talking. She could not get over her shock at hearing his voice. There was no doubt now that it was him who had broken into the Kam Flinder Najeba office, and stolen the address book. She knew Mi-Hae, Khalida, Leon and Helena were all afraid now as well. It wasn't pleasant to know a psycho had your address and phone number. DI Casey said he did not think any of them were at risk, but of course he couldn't be sure.

Shannon called Jevko Arib's solicitor and told him to talk to Gerald Elliott; she was relieved when he said he would alert the police. She had two messages, one from Finbar, asking her to call him, and the other from Anita, the receptionist at Jenny's firm, Steele & Monckton. She would call her back tomorrow, Shannon decided. She had had enough for one day.

123

Her fingers hovered over the phone, brushing the digits on the blue-lit keypad. Some part of her could not believe that if she dialled Jenny's number Jenny would not answer and speak to her. Well, her voicemail would continue to answer for a while. Shannon looked out of the cab window, her eyes blurring. She blinked the tears away and called Finbar on his mobile.

'At last,' he breathed. 'Where are you?'

'In a cab on my way home.' Typical mobile phone conversation. 'I'm almost there.'

'Did that Croft bastard call you again?'

'No. Where are you?'

'At your place.'

'Have you got the wine opened and the dinner on?'

'Not yet, madam. I'll come downstairs and meet you.'

'There's no need to do that.'

'Humour me, all right?'

Fear surged through her again. 'OK.'

'See you in a minute.'

The cab stopped outside her building and she paid the driver and got out, keys at the ready. She glanced up and down the street of Georgian terraces with the dark slits of alley between each building. She ran forward and stuck her key in the door, buzzed the intercom to let Finbar know she was home. She could not wait to see him. She turned the key once, twice, then gasped as she thought she noticed a quick movement to her right, some kind of shadow near an alley.

'Who's that?' she called, like the soppy heroine in some horror movie. And why bloody ask? Did she really want to know? Her fingers trying to twist the key in the lock were suddenly infuriatingly clumsy, like the soppy heroine's would be at such a moment. Inside she heard footsteps coming down the stairs.

'Finbar!'

She caught the darting shadow movement again, now crouched by some area steps. She swore. Was there really somebody, or was it her overworked imagination sending out false messages? She remembered the dream about fitting her key in the door while a shadow lurked behind. She got the door open and almost fell into Finbar's arms.

'So, our Ms Flinder experiences another delightful, stress-free day as a bog standard criminal law solicitor,' he remarked when they were safely inside her living room. He held her close, stroking her hair. 'You're shaking.'

'I thought I saw something – or somebody – just now.'

'What? Where, in the street?'

'Yes, when I was trying to get the damn door open. By some area steps. I don't know, maybe it was just a shadow or ... I don't know.' They went into the dark bedroom and peered out from behind the curtains 'I can't see anyone, can you?' Shannon asked after a minute. 'Not Croft, anyway.' She took a long breath as her heartbeat slowed. 'Maybe I imagined it.'

'And maybe you didn't.' Finbar slid his arms around her waist. 'Better give Inspector Casey another call.'

She groaned. 'I don't want to be the woman who cried wolf.'

'Better to cry wolf than be silent and stoical and end up getting scoffed by the Big Bad One.'

'You're so reassuring. OK, I'll call the Inspector.' She felt like crying. 'I suppose it was really stupid of me to think I could come home, pour myself a glass of wine, have dinner and spend a relaxing evening with you, wasn't it?'

'I'll pour you a glass of wine. And we can relax soon.' Finbar kissed her and moved away. 'Make your call. I've got one to make as well.'

Shannon did not ask who he was calling. Later, after DI Casey had been and gone, assured her he and his 'team' were scouring the area and that he would send patrol cars driving down her street at regular intervals throughout the night, she took a quick shower then stretched out on the sofa to sip the white wine Finbar poured her.

'That's gorgeous,' she sighed. 'Tastes like green apples.'

He sat down and pulled her against him. 'I ordered the pizza. And chicken wings. They said it'll take about half an hour.'

'OK.' She put her wine glass on the coffee table, then leaned her head back and closed her eyes.

'It's going to be all right,' he whispered, kissing her. 'You'll be safe.'

'How do you know?' Shannon kept her eyes closed; she was exhausted. 'Have you lost confidence in the ability of the police to protect me, and got a hit man on Croft's track?' She was not sure she meant that entirely as a joke.

'Yeah, right. *Lost* confidence in the police? Can't lose what I never had, can I? But I'm sure they're pulling out all the stops where you're concerned. And I can tell Inspector Casey's got a soft spot for you. Or should I say a hard spot?'

She laughed. 'Are you jealous?'

'Violently. I'll beat the crap out of the bastard if he gives you another of those lingering calf-like looks when he thinks I won't notice. Listen – how about we go to Ireland this weekend? Fly out tomorrow afternoon and come back Monday?'

'Yes. Can't think why, but I'm desperate to get out of Liverpool for a while.'

'Sorted then.' He stroked her hair and massaged the back of her neck.

'That feels lovely.' Shannon started to relax. She felt him loosen the belt of her robe, then shivered with pleasure as she felt his hands on her breasts.

'All this murder and mayhem,' he whispered. 'I think we should do something life-affirming to counteract it. We've just got time before the pizza arrives.' She laughed again and he kissed her neck, slid one hand over her belly. 'I love you,' he murmured. 'I never stop wanting you, never get enough.'

Shannon shrugged off the robe and put her arms around him. She tasted the wine on his lips and looked into his green eyes.

'I love you too,' she said. 'For ever.'

Chapter Twelve

'Working late, Wand?' Rod paused on his way out, his new brown-fringed suede jacket draped over one arm. 'Don't have to, you know.'

Fringes, she thought. Oh my God. She pointed at the flickering computer screen which was giving her sore eyes and a headache. 'Just working on a story about the Fong murder – and something about Shannon Flinder. I thought I'd finish it and go on to the hospital later instead of driving home and going out again.'

She could not stand the thought of the cold, silent flat with its depressing clutter of unwashed clothes, dirty dishes and piled-up boxes, not until she had no choice but to go back there and spend another sleepless night.

'Up to you. See you.' Rod went off whistling and Wanda guessed he was headed for a city centre bar where students congregated. Rod liked students, especially the female variety. Pathetic bastard, she thought. What must his wife and his twenty-something son and daughter think? She ate a couple more lukewarm chips, took several swigs of Coke and focused on the screen again, scrolled down several paragraphs. After another fifteen minutes typing she gave up and switched off the computer; she was knackered, and the article was practically finished anyway. She got up, collected her stuff and left the building.

In her car driving to the hospital Wanda thought about the article. She was quite proud of it. She had managed to cast aspersions on both Jenny Fong's *'attractive Asian Legal Executive's'* personal life, and Shannon Flinder's past. She had touched on the unsolved murder of Shannon's father-in-law, Bernard, and her failed marriage, as well as the arrest of her ex-husband Rob for murder. Finbar Linnell's dodgy reputation had not gone uncommented on either, although Wanda had been extremely careful to make sure there was nothing libelous. She had also covered the murder of Julie Ferris, and managed to track down the *'distraught, grieving father'*, who was more than happy to express his fury at Shannon kicking him out of her office. Although it was clear to Wanda that Dennis Ferris, while being genuinely upset about his daughter's murder, was still out to get whatever he could for her loss.

Wanda smiled as she imagined Shannon's reaction to the article. She would read it sooner or later – even if she considered *City Inquirer* too lowly a rag for her to grime her manicured nails on, somebody was bound to alert her. Wanda was satisfied with the result because there was plenty of damning implication but nothing Shannon or anyone else could sue her or the paper for. And not Jenny Fong – you could libel the dead all you liked. But all she'd done was ask some honest questions. She would have liked to write more about Finbar Linnell's dodgy past – and present, for all she knew – but that was too risky. What if she could uncover something big that he might be up to? Wouldn't that be fantastic? Goodbye Merseyside, hello Canary Wharf. But there were lots of murders on Merseyside and in the north-west generally, so it was proving difficult to interest any of the big players dahn saff. The story needed something else, some new angle. The other local rags would still be jealous and impressed though.

Alex was no worse. No better either. Wanda spent a couple of hours with him then drove home. She parked her car in a safer street, as usual, and walked the rest of the way. Back at the flat she stood in the cramped kitchen crunching crisps and drinking what remained of last night's Rioja. She wondered again what more she could do to get another step up her particular career ladder and, most important of all, make more money. She wouldn't mind landing a job with a major regional daily. And why shouldn't that be possible? She was good at what she did; she could handle it. No problem.

She experienced some flickers of dangerous hope. Alex might wake up and not be brain damaged; she might get that better job and more money, be able to move out of this dump into a decent house. Her mother, who had not phoned again since she had screamed at her, might suddenly and miraculously start treating her like a person with feelings, someone who actually mattered, even deserved love. The police might find and arrest the man who had attacked Alex.

That made Wanda think of Shannon Flinder again. Once this article showed up in print, not only was there zero chance of Shannon agreeing to take her case, Wanda would have made herself another enemy. Shouldn't she hold back for now, try to talk to Shannon one more time? But what was the point? Shannon didn't want to know. She could try another solicitor, perhaps. Shannon had offered to give her some names. But she wanted Shannon; she had heard good things about her. Wanda decided to try Shannon again. It had to be this evening. Now, actually. She cleared some junk off the living-room sofa, flopped down and reached for the phone.

She didn't have Shannon's mobile number, of course, and had a feeling her home phone number would turn out to be unlisted; it was. Wanda thought for a minute, then called her new mate, Cindy Nightingale, who was at home.

'Whadda *you* want?' Cindy slurred, sounding like she'd sunk a litre of vodka. A television blared in the background.

Great to hear you too! 'Sorry to bother you,' Wanda began, trying to sound upbeat. 'I just wondered if you could do me a favour?'

'Did you now? Well, that depends. If I can and will, don't bloody expect it not to cost you.'

'I know the old free lunch doesn't exist.'

A couple of minutes later Wanda was trying Shannon's home phone number. She was probably there, trying to relax with her boyfriend. Sure enough, a man she presumed was Finbar Linnell picked up after a few rings.

'Hello?' He sounded wary, as well he might, Wanda thought. 'Who's this?'

His voice was calm, deep and pleasant, but contained a 'don't fuck with me' tone, and she felt nervous again. Did she really want to mess with Shannon and him by writing the kind of nasty stuff in the article? But here she was now, speaking to Finbar Linnell, and although she got the urge to crash the phone down and forget the whole thing, something stopped her. *Alex.* She didn't like doing this, it wasn't her, but how else was she going to help Alex get legal protection, plus the compensation she was going to need to help care for him in future? Wanda tried to push thoughts of *The Future* out of her head.

'Hi, good evening, my name's Wanda Brennan. I'm sorry to bother Shannon at home, but I really need to speak to her about her friend, Jenny Fong.'

'Just a second.' Wanda heard Finbar say something to Shannon, but could not make it out because he must have turned away, lowered his voice or covered the phone. Her heart thudded and she held her breath. She could taste the sour, yeasty wine.

'How did you get my number?' Shannon asked. 'It's unlisted.'

'I, er...' Like Wanda would tell her *that* if she didn't want Cindy Nightingale to skin her alive. 'Er ... someone gave it to me.' Always tell a bit of the truth if you could.

'Who?'

'Someone at my office. I don't remember.'

'But how did they—'

'Look. Please. This is really important. I'm sorry to bother you,' Wanda repeated, 'but I need to tell you about a story my editor's made me write.' Would Shannon help her and Alex if she threatened her with the article? It might work. 'It'll go to press soon, tomorrow or the day after, unless—'

'*What* story?' Shannon's voice rose. 'Mrs Brennan—'

'Wanda.'

'I've told you I can't help you, and you just have to accept that. I'm very sorry about your husband, it's tragic what happened to him, and I know your life must be hell right now. But there really isn't anything I can do for him – or you. And this is starting to seem like harassment.'

Wanda blushed. 'I'm not harassing you.'

'I'd call waylaying me in the street, pestering the receptionist at my office and now calling me at home – and refusing to tell me how you got my number – harassment. I think most reasonable people would.'

'Julie Ferris' father is furious with you,' Wanda said quickly. 'He's said some nasty things. And the police might have arrested that illegal asylum seeker for Jenny's murder, but there's still some unresolved questions about her actions that night.'

'What *questions?*'

'Well, it seems odd that she walked that far. Maybe she wasn't going home.'

'You can't expect me to discuss Jenny with you. Or Dennis Ferris. Is this phone call really about trying to get me to help you and your husband?' Shannon asked. 'Or are you just chasing a sick story?'

'No. No way. Look, can't we meet up and talk? That would be really helpful.'

'Helpful to your career, maybe. Your paper. It wouldn't help me or Jenny.'

Wanda sighed. 'I'm sorry you're taking this attitude. A lot of what I've written in the article – for which I would have liked to get your input – is just asking honest questions.'

'Like you give a fuck about honesty. Selling newspapers is all you care about. And you'd better be damn careful what you write about me. Or Jenny Fong.'

'I could get the article stopped if I could tell my editor you'd agreed to talk exclusively to me about Jenny – and yourself too, of course. He'd let me scrap it then. And if you took on Alex's case that would make me even more motivated to fight your corner. I've also got a very helpful police contact.' Wanda paused and took a deep breath. She was shaking, her hand gripping the phone wet with sweat. 'Inspector Cindy Nightingale. I believe you know her?'

Shannon was silent.

Jesus, Wanda thought. I can't believe I'm doing this. She forced a laugh. 'I understand there's quite a history between the two of you.'

'Two versions of every story,' Shannon said slowly, her voice cold.

'Three, I've heard. Yours, theirs – and the truth.'

'Well, you've only heard one version, and it's certainly not the truth. You should be careful who and what you choose to believe.'

'Please help me!' Wanda begged, losing her nerve. 'Help Alex. We've got nobody. *Please.*'

'I'm sorry,' Shannon said at last. 'You just tried to threaten me. I'm telling you one last time, there's nothing I can do for you or your husband.'

'Look, I—'

'Mrs Brennan, I don't want you to contact me again. At home or at my office. If you do, I'll have to notify the police. And let me remind you once again to be very careful about what you write and who you talk to. Goodnight.'

The phone went dead. Wanda swigged the rest of her wine and let the glass drop on the carpet. Nothing ever worked out for her, not one damn fucking thing could go right. She slumped against the sofa cushions and started to sob out her disappointment and hopelessness, quietly at first then louder. What did it matter? Who cared?

No one was listening.

'Don't come back. You're fired.' Milena, wearing a black, lacy mini dress now, flung some money at him. 'Fucking big moron,' she hissed.

She would not have dared to talk to him like that if her hired help hadn't been lurking behind one slim, bare shoulder. Richard was glad he managed to catch the notes she threw at him because he wouldn't have wanted to humiliate himself by having to stoop to pick them up.

'You don't punch a client, not ever.' Milena put her hands on her hips. 'And you don't touch the girls – not during working hours, and not unless you pay.'

'All right, so the night didn't get off to a good start.' Richard tried to sound calm and reasonable, even though he was seething. 'But that guy shouldn't have called me a fat prick. And I was only trying to be friendly to that girl. She got the wrong idea.' What did someone who made a living taking off her kit and gyrating over the laps of glassy-eyed men have to be so sensitive about anyway? Stupid cow.

'Shut up. I'm not interested. Get out.'

He was shaking and on edge, still pumped up after his failure to grab Shannon Flinder earlier as she emerged from the cab and hurried to her front door. The boyfriend had opened it and he had seen him for a split second – tall and broad shouldered, black haired, casually dressed. Looked like he could handle himself.

The timing had been all wrong; he realised that now. He did not think Shannon had spotted him, but she had been nervous, looking around as if she suspected someone was watching her. Richard had wanted to hang around longer in the hope that she would come out again – hopefully alone – or that he could somehow gain entry. But if she had suspected he was hanging around, she might have called the police. He had decided it was best to get away and return later.

'Give me another chance, will you?' he asked Milena. It was against his principles to plead, especially with a woman, but he needed this job; he didn't want to have to risk trying to steal more money. And Richard doubted he could get another no-questions-asked job as soon as tomorrow. 'OK, I might have overreacted a bit. But you don't want Mary Poppins working your doors, do you?'

'*Who*?' Milena glared at him. 'I won't give you another chance, no way. There's plenty more where you come from. And you *are* a fat prick. You creep me out.'

'You...!' Richard stepped forward, his fists clenched. Fucking little tart.

'Hey, mate.' The hired help interposed himself between the two of them. 'You heard what she said.' He shoved Richard hard in the chest. 'Out. Now.'

Richard found himself in the dark narrow street, his head aching again. The music hadn't been too loud where he had stood by the doors, but it had still bothered him a bit. Working in a club wasn't the ideal occupation for someone who suffered headaches, but it wasn't like he could pick and choose. Be an accountant or an IT expert. Or a lawyer. He decided to go back to his manky room and get a few hours kip, then go back to Shannon Flinder's apartment early in the morning and wait for her to emerge – hopefully alone. When she came out to go to work, a bit tired and therefore off her guard, that was when he would strike. He would force her into her car, make her drive somewhere deserted. And then it would be party time.

He would hide her body somewhere, so that at first they would think she had gone missing. He would collect his new passport and take a flight to Spain. After that it would be easy. He would find a job there, bar work maybe. Get pally with the owner, make himself indispensable. Sangria and sunshine, beautiful girls. Sorted. But first he would have the pleasure of killing Shannon Flinder. Would she plead with him? Offer to do anything? Richard smiled at the thought of that.

He shoved his hands in his pockets and started to walk down the dark street, thinking of his bed and the painkillers. He should have brought those with him. Tired, in pain and pissed off, he did not at first notice the footsteps behind him. Suddenly he was surrounded. He stopped, confused. Recognised the ratbag he had punched earlier. The ratbag had brought his mates with him, because ratbags were cowards and that was what cowards did.

'Where d'you think you're goin', mate?'

They crowded around him, shoving up close, stinking of alcohol. Richard looked for a way out, but didn't see one. Before he could think any more he was on the ground, trying to curl up his body to protect himself from their kicks. He heard laughter and swearing, glass shattering. All I need, he thought, panicked. All I bloody well need. They were going to hammer his head in. The perfect end to a perfect night.

One of them tried to drag his hands away from his head. A kick to his lower back made him scream; the pain caused a flash of shock and agony, followed by a wave of nausea. When another foot slammed into his stomach he started to retch. Then he heard a siren, coming nearer and nearer until it almost deafened him. There was a screech of brakes as a car pulled up. More shouts, running feet. Help was coming. But was it too late.

Surrounded by dark figures, Richard passed out.

'Hello? Hello? Can you hear me?'

When he woke up he couldn't think where he was. Bright lights half blinded him, and his eyes were swollen and painful. He tried to turn his head to one side, and groaned. His body was one throbbing, stabbing mass of pain, radiating down from his head and neck. The fingers of his right hand felt like a bunch of bananas. Richard's mouth was dry and he could taste blood on his lips. His ears were ringing. The voice came again.

'Can you tell me your name, please?'

Even in his confused state, Richard knew that would not be a good idea. He realised he was in hospital. The voice belonged to a dark-haired, middle-aged nurse in blue overalls. Her arms were hairy and freckled, and she wore bloodstained latex gloves. A steel, kidney-shaped dish – why were they always that ugly shape? – stood on a nearby trolley. It was filled with bloodied cotton swabs. His blood. He felt sick at the sight.

'Those hooligans who attacked you ran off, but they were caught on CCTV,' the nurse told him. 'An operator who saw what was going on alerted the police. They got there very quickly and called an ambulance. They'll be back to talk to you when you're feeling up to it.'

Caught on CCTV? Great. Richard hoped his face wouldn't be on view, that he would look like nothing except a curled-up human ball getting bounced around. And the police? They were the last people he wanted to talk to. He had to avoid that.

135

'Don't worry, love.' The nurse smiled reassuringly as she saw the panic in his eyes. Richard recoiled as she laid one bloodied latex-gloved hand gently on his shoulder. 'It's all right. You're safe, we'll look after you. You'll be all right now.'

Chapter Thirteen

Temporary, Shannon had said when she refused to move back in with him a year ago. She needed time on her own before she could go back and live with him again, link her fate to his. How much more time?

No pressure, he had sworn. But it was getting more difficult, especially with what was going on now. Finbar stirred in bed, raised himself on one elbow and looked down at Shannon, who was asleep after their lovemaking. He ran one finger along her smooth bare arm, listened to her slow, deep breathing, and kissed her shoulder. She didn't stir, and he smiled.

The two days here had done them both good; they were catching up on sleep as well as sex. For Shannon to be able to go out and about, drive to the town or walk along the nearby beach without having to fear a psycho might be tailing her was a holiday in itself. The location of this isolated old house by the Atlantic hadn't been written down in the bloody Kim Flinder Najeba office address book that Croft had stolen.

He lay there staring across the big bedroom to the three long sash windows that looked out on to the bay and distant hills; the window to his left overlooked the long back lawn. The sun had gone down and it was growing dark, the air still and cold. The sky was a deep violet, pink-tinged around the horizon and the tops of the hills. The smell of fields and the sea, the faint odour of turf fires, drifted in. Finbar loved this place, bequeathed to him by his Auntie Sylvia, the only person in his family who he'd ever got on with. He sometimes thought about coming to live here, but was afraid it might get too quiet after a while.

He leaned over Shannon, wanting her again. He slid back under the quilt, stroking her body, pushing one hand between her thighs. She gave a little sigh and murmur, but did not wake. Finbar decided to leave her to sleep. They had the whole evening, this coming night. He wondered if they had a lifetime.

He got out of bed, pulled on his dark blue robe and walked to the window, picked up the binoculars that lay on top of the chest of drawers and trained them on the calm water. A man stood on a rock fishing, and two others close by in a rowing boat were setting out lobster pots. A light flickered on across the bay. Finbar put the binoculars down, walked silently past the sleeping Shannon and into the adjoining bathroom. It still had the rose-pink walls, gold swans-head taps and other gold fittings that Sylvia had liked so much. A lace curtain was draped over the window which faced on to the back lawn. He took a quick shower and went downstairs to get a drink.

Finbar was beginning to regret his instructions to Curtis, afraid he had acted too hastily. If Curtis did manage to track down Richard Croft, was it such a great idea to kill him after all, even if Curtis could make it look like an accident? One hell of an accident, one hell of a coincidence! The police would suspect him immediately, Finbar thought. They might suspect Shannon too. On the other hand, if he told Curtis to give Croft a beating when he found him – *if* he found him – then dump him in the foyer of the nearest nick, the bastard would still be released from prison one day, even if that was years off. He would be an ever-present menace, just like Shannon's bloody ex, Rob.

Finbar sat at the kitchen table and poured himself a whisky. Suppose Shannon somehow found out what he had done? She might leave him for good this time. He felt nervous and guilty at going behind her back, something which had caused big problems between them in the past, and almost led to a break-up. No more secrets, that was how it was supposed to be. But who would have seen this coming? He sipped the whisky, picked up his mobile and called Curtis Bright.

'How's things?'

'I was just about to phone you.' Curtis sounded excited. 'I've got a result already. I put out some people to look for our mutual friend and one of them got a tip-off that he was working in some lap-dancing club. Very temporary job, because he got turfed out after just a few hours, for punching a punter and touching up one of the girls – being friendly, he called it. The manager said he was a creep and she should know. But by the time my help got there, Mr C had been sacked and vanished off the face of the planet.'

Finbar frowned. 'Are you sure it was *him*? And I don't imagine he was using his real name?'

'No. Called himself Steve Kane. The club's quite near where he used to live. We've been checking the pubs and clubs, keeping an eye out. I presume the cops have too, but you know they can be a bit slow. Mr C matched his photo all right, but he's done away with the tache and his hair's darker and shorter. Dropped a few kilos as well. It was definitely him though, no worries. And there was the weird behaviour.'

Finbar had to smile. 'Isn't weird behaviour a given in places like that?'

'Well, yeah. But apart from the violence and assault part, the manager and the girl he touched up both said he whinged about having a headache. Another coincidence.'

'Where the hell could he have gone after he left that club? Or got kicked out?'

'That's the big question. But I've got some more info for you. Our Steve wants a passport. He's supposed to collect it day after tomorrow – from some spotty little moron he met in a pub.'

'How d'you know that?'

'One of my secret sources. Don't ask. What you don't know they can't torture out of you. But I'll give you a clue. My secret source knows the spotty little moron – he's been blagging about how he's going to make himself a few quid by taking some stupid old bastard for a right ride.'

'Day after tomorrow?' Finbar stood up, pushing his chair back. 'Are you sure about that?'

139

'Sure as I can be. Mr C is supposed to meet his contact in a pub opposite Central Station. One o'clock sharp-ish.'

'Jesus. So you've got him. That is, as long as he turns up at this pub.'

'Fingers crossed, eh? I'll be waiting.'

'That's fantastic. But—'

Finbar sat down again, hesitating. If Croft was after a false passport he obviously intended to get out of the UK. Did that mean he had given up the idea of trying to kill Shannon? Or did he plan to try before he left? What should he do now? Finbar wondered. Tell Curtis he had changed his mind and wanted him to tip off the police instead of doing things the illegal but permanent way? He frowned, fingering the diamond pattern cut into the heavy crystal whisky glass. Fact was, of course, he did not trust the police. They had fucked up big style over Julie Ferris. If they fucked up again and Croft had another lucky escape, it might be impossible to ever find him. And in the meantime Shannon's life could be in danger.

'Yeah?' Curtis asked. 'What is it?'

Finbar glanced up as he heard the stairs creak. 'Sorry.' He lowered his voice. 'I can't talk any more now. I'll call you tomorrow after I get back, OK? To confirm things one way or another. And ... good work.'

'All part of the five-star service. Thanks, mate. See ya.'

Finbar switched off the phone, got up and put it on the dresser next to the fruit bowl, then sat at the table again. Bare feet padded across the hall and down the stone-flagged passage, and Shannon strolled in yawning, wrapped in one of his bathrobes.

'Had a good sleep?' He grinned at her over the rim of his glass. 'I wanted to wake you, but you looked so peaceful I couldn't bring myself to disturb you.'

'You're all heart.' She yawned again and raked her fingers through her wild hair. 'Don't know why I'm so bloody tired.'

'I can think of a few reasons.'

She smiled and blew him a kiss.

'Of course you're tired,' he said. 'Who wouldn't be after what you've gone through – are going through?' Finbar wanted

140

to talk to her, but he had to pick his moment carefully. 'Fancy a drink?' He nodded towards the fridge. 'Some wine?'

'I'll have some wine later. Right now I fancy a cup of tea.' She moved to the sink, splashed water into the kettle and switched it on. Glanced back at him. 'I thought I heard you talking to someone as I came downstairs.'

'You did, yeah.' Shit. 'Me. I often have a good old chat with myself. Helps me get things sorted. But in this case I think I was swearing because I couldn't get the cork out of the Linkwood bottle.'

Shannon didn't bother to point out that it was impossible not to be able to pull the cork out of a malt whisky bottle. 'You're a nut job, Linnell, you know that?'

'Of course. It's why you love me. Insanity *and* refined sexual techniques, what more could any evolved female want?'

'A kind heart. Wit. GSOH. Love.' Shannon came to him and sat on his lap, slipped her arms around his neck. 'Thank you,' she whispered.

His heart beat faster. 'What for, Blue Eyes?'

'You know what for.' She hugged him. 'I love you so much.'

'Well, that sentiment is entirely reciprocated.'

'Why are you talking like the Victorian virgin from the Vicarage?'

'I'm a loony, remember? Want to put some clothes on and take a walk down to the pub, get something to eat?'

'Oooh, yes.' Shannon drew back and smiled. 'I'm starving.'

'Me too. It's the sex.'

'I fancy crab au gratin followed by apple crumble with vanilla ice cream. Then Irish coffee.'

'Why not spoil yourself for once and forget the healthy option?'

'I'm too hopelessly anal to ever forget healthy options.' Shannon's smile faded. 'I can't believe how this weekend's flown. I don't feel like going back tomorrow.'

'Neither do I. You seem a lot more relaxed. Well, you would be.'

'It's so beautiful here. I love this house – this place.'

He looked closely at her. 'Do you?'

'You know I do.'

'We don't have to go back tomorrow. We can stay another few days.'

'It's a lovely idea, but not possible.' She shook her head. 'There's too much to do. You can work from here, but I can't.'

Finbar grimaced. 'You won't be able to work from anywhere if—'

'If I get murdered by Croft? Thanks for that.' Shannon pulled away from him. 'Thanks for concentrating my mind for me.'

'Hey, come on. Don't be like that.'

She didn't just mean work, but also trying to find out more about Jenny Fong's murder. He wished she would give that up, for now at least. Finbar thought of the shit-stirring journo who had phoned Shannon at home on Friday evening and tried to threaten her by implying her new mate Cindy Nightingale would cause more trouble if Shannon did not cooperate with the story she wanted to write. And take on her comatose husband's case. This Wanda Brennan was becoming a serious nuisance. Finbar would have liked to warn her off, but of course he had other much more urgent matters to deal with just now.

It was fantastic that Curtis and his helpers might be able to get Croft the day after tomorrow. But what should he tell Curtis when he phoned him back? Finbar still wasn't sure. He wanted Croft dead, but there had to be zero possibility of comeback. For himself and for Shannon.

'I love you,' he said, pulling her back. 'I'm worried about you. You know that.'

'Yeah, I know.' She relaxed against him and he kissed her, smelling her warm, perfumed body, feeling her heartbeat. Her kissed her harder, opening her mouth, twining her hair around his fingers. She gave a little moan and pushed closer.

'Let's not put on any clothes just yet,' he murmured.

'What clichés?' Wanda felt a shock of insult.

'"*The epitome of respectable, career-minded young woman-hood*".' Cindy Nightingale laughed as she sloshed herself

142

another glass of the restaurant's sour, over-chilled, over-priced house white. "*This distraught, bereaved father,*" she quoted, reading from Wanda's article. 'I mean, fucking hell. Don't you have *any* sense of irony?'

Wanda frowned. Was the writing really that awful? Maybe her new dream of a job on a major regional daily was destined never to be anything more than desperate fantasy. Then again, was Cindy Nightingale a good judge?

'Still.' Cindy laughed again as she shoved the article back at her. 'That'll make Flinder squirm all right. And I don't just mean the fact that you hate to leave clichés unused. I'd like to see her gob when she reads this.'

Wanda swallowed the rest of her wine. She felt sick after the lasagne and chips she had just shovelled down. 'No sign of a murder weapon then?'

Cindy was no longer being very forthcoming about Fong's murder, and Wanda had a feeling Inspector Nightingale regarded this supposedly mutually beneficial alliance purely as a chance to use her as a tool in her mysterious vendetta against Shannon Flinder. Without giving anything back in return.

'No, we haven't found a weapon.' Cindy shrugged. 'We keep telling Mr Arib that it's in his interests to cooperate fully with us now, but he can't seem to get the message. Not even since his wife and kid got moved to a detention centre.'

Wanda knew this was a question Cindy would hate, but she had to ask it anyway. 'Are you sure this Arib guy murdered Fong?'

Cindy did hate it. 'Jesus Christ, don't you start! You sound like Flinder, trying to tell me how to do my job. She's been chewing my ear about that. She thinks it might be Richard Croft, that psycho who escaped, but there's nothing to show he had anything to do with it. Typical of her arrogance that she thinks someone would commit a murder just to get at her.' She drank more wine. 'I can't wait for that bitch to have other more pressing matters to deal with – like how many times a week she can change her knickers in the nick. That's if the psycho doesn't get her first.'

Wanda poured herself the last of the wine and lit a king-size cigarette, ignoring censorious glances from a haughty-looking couple at a nearby table. Cindy's intensity made her nervous. 'Can I ask you something else?'

'Jeez. What now?'

'Why do you hate Shannon Flinder? What's she ever done to you?'

Cindy was silent. She looked around the crowded restaurant, drumming her fingers on the table. She picked up her glass and emptied it.

'Shall I get us another bottle?' Wanda asked helpfully.

'Yeah, why not? Not like I've got some fit bloke waiting at home to lavish his attentions on me.'

Whereas Shannon Flinder had the exceptionally tasty Finbar Linnell lavishing his attentions on her. Tasty according to Cindy; she seemed to have quite a thing for him. Wanda was starting to get the picture. Jealousy was an ugly, shrivelling thing. She signalled to the waiter, who quickly brought them another bottle of sour white. Well, she was not drinking because she appreciated delicate bouquets, year, or variety of grape. Her cigarette smouldered in the ashtray, sending a wreath of smoke spiralling up Cindy's nostrils, but Cindy didn't seem bothered. She poured herself more wine and looked at Wanda, her brown eyes glittering with drink and anger.

'I hate Flinder because that bitch made me look a bloody fool. She had her father-in-law killed by a hit man and just walked away from it trailing fucking fairy dust, got away with the whole damn thing.'

'*What*?' Wanda stared at her, wondering if Cindy was mad. 'Well, I know she – and everyone else who knew him – was questioned. But I thought that was just routine. The police would be bound to talk to her. And of course his victims – the one who survived, that is, the girl who was a student at his school. She managed to stab him in the hand with a penknife, didn't she?' she asked, thinking back to the Bernard Flinder affair. 'While he was trying to assault her in his car. She got out and ran off just before it blew.'

144

'Right. Shannon Flinder had her paedo daddy-in-law stiffed,' Cindy repeated. 'She knows it and she knows I know. The hit man disappeared afterwards, and I'm sure Finbar Linnell had him killed. Or shot the guy himself.'

'Really?' Wanda breathed, not knowing whether to believe Cindy. 'How come none of this came out?'

'Lack of evidence. I had to let Flinder go. I pulled her in myself, I had the bitch. She was tired, freaked. I *know* I would have got a confession out of her if I hadn't been forced to release her. Orders came from on high. I still don't know how that happened.' Cindy went on to repeat the story that had cost her friends, credibility and a promotion. 'No one would listen. Most of them are blokes, of course, and you know what they're like. They take one look at that bitch and start slobbering down their shirt fronts. Being a scum lawyer helped Flinder too. Powerful friends, and all that. Not to mention her bloody criminal boyfriend.'

It was a great story – for a novel. Wanda would have loved to believe Cindy but she could not, in her wildest dreams, imagine that Shannon Flinder would have someone killed. Of course it was politic to pretend to take Cindy seriously. But the woman was obsessed. She stubbed out her cigarette. 'It's just a shame you don't have any evidence.'

'I could get it if they'd give me the time, authority and resources. But even if I could get the evidence, there's no will to arrest Bernie's murderer.'

'Well, he was a paedophile. I suppose most people don't care who killed a monster like that. They probably think whoever it was did society a favour. Why do you think Shannon had him killed?' Wanda asked. 'If she did. Was it to try and stop him murdering more girls?'

'You must be joking. Flinder doesn't give a toss about anyone but herself.'

'Did Bernard Flinder threaten her, maybe? If she found out what he was and tried to expose him, he'd want to shut her up. Wouldn't he?'

'So if that was what happened why didn't she tell the police?'

145

The answer to that question was sitting opposite her, Wanda thought. 'Maybe Shannon couldn't prove anything.' She took a drag on her cigarette. 'Or maybe she tried to tell them and they wouldn't listen. Her ex-husband was a CID detective, wasn't he? If he didn't want to believe her, who would?'

'Crap.' Cindy glared at her. 'Total crap. Are you on her side, or what?'

'Of course not. I'm just trying to be the devil's advocate. Get at the truth.'

'Don't give me that old toffee. You're a hack, remember? What do you care about fucking truth? All I bloody care about is that Shannon Flinder committed murder and got away with it. That's what I am not, no *way*, having.' Cindy thumped the table, startling Wanda. 'And I don't care if it takes me the next ten years to nail the bitch.'

Wanda butted her cigarette. She was bored now, as well as drunk. She didn't think this cop with a grudge was going to help her do anything except maybe land herself in a lot of trouble, like she needed more of that. Even if what Cindy said was true – and Wanda didn't believe it was – imagine becoming notorious as the journalist who helped bring the killer of a murdering paedophile to justice? No thank you. She took another slug of wine and lit a fresh cigarette. Time for a change of subject.

'I went to visit Alex before I came to meet you.' Alex was Wanda's main reason for getting pally with Cindy. Maybe she could get the case moving again, get the man who attacked him arrested. Whether that man was Croft or someone else.

'Alex? Your...? Oh yeah.' Cindy glanced away. 'Must be tough.'

'Remember what I told you – that I think Richard Croft might have done it?'

'Oh God. Not him again. He can't have committed every bloody crime on Merseyside before he got caught.'

And was allowed to escape. 'No. But—'

'Look. If they didn't find any evidence to show he attacked your husband, then there isn't any, believe me.'

146

'Well, if the police could get whoever put Alex in a coma, it might help me cope better.' Wanda stared at her. 'I tried to persuade Shannon Flinder to take his case – help bring his attacker to justice, help me get compensation for him, prevent the hospital from switching off Alex's life support, should they try to do that – but she wasn't interested.'

'She wouldn't be.' Cindy snorted. 'Bringing criminals to justice isn't her thing. She helps them avoid it. Thought you'd have got your head round that.'

'What I want most is acknowledgement.' Wanda's eyes flooded with tears, but she didn't care. 'It's like no one gives a damn about what happened. People think I'm a nuisance for wanting justice.' She puffed on her cigarette. 'They'd bloody well care if it was someone they loved. I feel so alone.'

'Yeah. Well.' Cindy finished her wine and glanced at her watch. 'Got to shove off now, I'm afraid.' She picked up her bag.

'You will help me?' Wanda rose, reached across the table and grabbed her arm. 'It would mean so much.'

'Hey, get off.' Cindy pulled away, her eyes narrowed. 'Listen, I'll ask around for you, OK? I said I'd do that, and I will. I'll check out your husband's case, find out what's going on.'

'Promise?'

'Jesus. *Yeah*. And you'll keep up the pressure on Flinder?'

'Yes. But I can't accuse her in print of murder, can I? Not without losing my job and the paper being whacked with a libel action.' Rod might laugh about would-be libel suitors needing strong nerves and deep pockets, but that didn't mean he wanted to take any risks.

'I don't expect you to accuse her in print.' Cindy looked angry again. 'Not until I've nailed her, anyway. Your job is to keep up the needling and speculation. That'll freak Flinder, make life harder for her. It might even provoke her into doing something stupid – stupid for her, that is.' She threw some money on the table and fished car keys out of her jacket pocket. 'OK. See ya.'

147

'You're driving?' Wanda gasped. 'After all that wine?' She wasn't particularly concerned for Cindy, but if the woman killed herself – or someone else – on her way home, she would no longer be able to check out Alex's case.

'Hey, no worries,' Cindy laughed. 'I do everything better when I'm pissed.' She turned and left, weaving between the tables.

Wanda sat down again and furtively burned her left wrist with the cigarette, trying to stifle her gasps of pain. The shock and agony made her feel sick and faint, and she had to stay sitting there for another few minutes before she could pay the bill, get out and breathe some fresh air. She walked along Lark Lane to the main road and waited for a bus back to town. Sharp pains shot through her wrist, and the cut on her arm was hurting again as well. In the harsh light of the bus shelter the burn mark looked even more horrible. But despite the pain, it gave her a kind of relief. She would put a plaster on it when she got home. Or were you not supposed to do that with burn marks? Wanda's mobile rang, and she sighed. If it was her mother she would hang up.

'Mrs Brennan? Wanda? This is Jennifer from Intensive Care.'

Oh God. Wanda's mouth went dry and her heart started thumping. They wouldn't call at this time unless it was bad news.

'I'm afraid Alex has had another seizure. And now his breathing's altered – he seems to have taken a turn for the worse. I'm sorry. We thought you might want to come in and be with him.'

She would not need financial help to look after Alex, because he wasn't going to make it. He was going to die, and she would be all alone. The man who had murdered him would get away with it. She had no friends, no one to care whether she lived or died.

Traffic raced past. Wanda looked up at the sky, at the few stars glittering between clouds. Pinpoints of light, light she could never reach because she was trapped down here for ever in the dark.

148

'Wanda? Are you there, love? I said Alex is deteriorating.'

Wanda knew they often said 'deteriorating' when the person was already dead, in an effort to avoid the loved one freaking more on their way to hospital. He's dead, she thought. My darling Alex is dead.

'On my way,' she gasped.

'You're a good influence on me.' Shannon slipped her hand in Finbar's as their plane came in to land at Manchester. 'Or a bad one.'

'If you mean getting you to take this whole Monday morning off work, I'd say that was definitely good.' He leaned across and kissed her. 'So,' he murmured. 'You'll think about what I said to you last night?'

'About moving back in with you and getting married? Of course I will.'

However much she loved Finbar, the idea of marriage scared her. Shannon thought she was ready to live with him again, in fact she wanted that now. But *marriage*. They loved one another, that was the main thing. She had never wanted anyone so much and could not imagine that she ever would again. Maybe she felt nervous because of all the tedious, patronising bullshit you heard about marriage. Like how you were supposed to *work* at it. Was that meant to be a selling point? Who wanted to work all day then come home and work some more?

'What are you smiling at?'

'Nothing.'

'I don't want to pressure you,' he joked as the aircraft touched down and screamed along the runway, 'but when can I expect an answer?'

'Soon.'

She had not heard from DI Casey all weekend, so Croft must still be on the loose. Finbar was right, they should have stayed longer. Shannon was getting more disillusioned with being a criminal law solicitor, wondering what good she actually did herself or anybody else. And look what her brilliant career had led to now.

149

She had a feeling Finbar might like to live in that house in Ireland, and it worried her. It was a beautiful place and she loved it – but to live there? The weather had been good this weekend, sunny if cold. But imagine sitting in that huge drawing room on a day of gusting wind and rain, the hills and bay obscured by low, thick cloud, wondering what the hell you were going to do with yourself for the next fourteen or so waking hours?

Shannon had also gone off the idea of having children. She did not see it as the be-all and end-all, like some people. She could only think of the non-freedom, the all-consuming time and energy children cost. Even stupid things, like not being able to have a lie-in any more. And if being a parent was so bloody wonderful, why did most parents seem to do nothing but whinge?

'You're quiet,' Finbar remarked as they walked into the Arrivals Hall. 'What are you thinking? Back to reality and all that?'

'Sort of. But—' Shannon stopped and turned to him, pulling her coat around her. 'I've got to be honest with you,' she blurted.

'You do? Fuck. Well, go on.'

'I love you like crazy.' She stared up at him. 'I want to be with you all the time. I'll move back in with you. But I'm not sure about marriage, that scares me. And I don't care about having kids, it's not an issue for me any more. I don't give a fuck about my bloody biological clock, I don't feel it ticking, I just don't care.'

Finbar took her hand and lifted it to his lips. 'I'm cool with that.'

'Are you?'

His green eyes bored into hers. 'I want you. Forever. Whatever.'

'But suppose some day you want an heir to leave all your riches to?'

'I'll buy one over the Internet.'

She laughed. 'Be serious.'

150

'Look. This doesn't matter. You know what I think – if we have kids that's fine, if we don't that's fine too. It's like I said. I just want you.' He kissed her hand again. 'Why didn't you tell me all this last night over dinner? Or back home beside the fire?'

'I needed to think. After you popped your Big Question.'

'OK. Right. Well, let's not stand in the middle of the bloody airport having this conversation. You love me. I love you. You'll live with me again. That's good enough for—'

'Finbar Linnell?'

In the split second before he turned round Finbar slipped his mobile into her coat pocket, almost as though he had been expecting what Shannon saw to her shock was a reception committee of four men.

'Police.' They flashed their ID and quickly surrounded her and Finbar, cutting them off from the noisy crowd. One of the officers, a youngish, bearded man in jeans and a leather jacket, started to speak; Shannon heard the words 'arresting', 'murder' and 'Declan Dowd'.

Declan *Dowd*? The man who had got into Finbar's apartment that terrible day, more than a year ago now, and who Finbar had killed in self-defence? She could not believe what she was hearing. Finbar seemed as stunned as she was. He kept staring at her as they grabbed him and clicked on handcuffs. No, she thought. Please. Not this, not now. How can they arrest him? What evidence do they have?

'Leave him alone,' she gasped. 'He hasn't murdered anybody.'

'Stand back, please.'

'Where are you taking him?' She shook off a restraining hand on her arm as they tried to separate her and Finbar. He was ashen-faced, fighting shock. Shannon's mind started to race. Had they found Dowd's body? Where had Finbar dumped it that night? What was there to link him to Dowd? There couldn't be anything. People turned to stare as Finbar was hustled through the Arrivals Hall and outside. Shannon pushed after them through the revolving doors.

A sharp, cold wind hit her. They hurried him to a waiting car. Finbar turned and looked at her one last time, his eyes a brilliant green against the expanse of grey paving, square buildings and low cloud.

'I love you,' she called. 'It'll be all right. Don't worry.'

Don't *worry*? There were lots of extremely good reasons to bloody worry.

Finbar grimaced. 'Told you we should have stayed longer.'

Chapter Fourteen

'He didn't die,' Wanda whispered to herself, her tears dripping on to the damp pillow. 'It's all right.'

For now, anyway. So why was she having almost the same reaction she would have had if Alex had died last night, that bloody awful night, the worst in a long time? Or reacting the way she assumed she would have if it had happened? Crying, despairing, in a state of collapse.

She rolled over and looked at the clock. Almost lunchtime. There was no way she could have dragged herself up and gone into work this morning. And no one could phone to ask where she was or what the hell she thought she was playing at, because Wanda had unplugged the phone last night and switched off her mobile after she got back from the hospital. The curtains were closed and the bedroom smelled of unwashed clothes and stale cigarettes. The inside of her mouth was thick with the sour taste of last night's disgusting wine and Cindy Nightingale's hollow promises to help her and Alex. Wanda could not crawl out from beneath this warm quilt, get showered and dressed and face the callously indifferent world, not today. Maybe never again. She was wiped. Wasted.

The golden glow through the dark-brown curtains meant it was sunny outside; she glimpsed a sliver of blue sky. Down in the hall she could hear children laughing and shouting, one of them no doubt the little cow with the doll. The cut on her arm and burn mark on her wrist stung and throbbed. There was an empty wine bottle on the bedside table and another on the floor. The silence in the room frightened Wanda, made her think of waking up in a dank, dark vault full of mouldering stiffs, like Shakespeare's Juliet. I could really let myself go, she thought, and start screaming. But who would hear and come to my rescue?

She turned her head and groaned at the pain, closed her eyes again. She wished she was dead, freed from all burdens, from the terrible suffering of loving a man she could not help. Wanda was not dead though, and her body was insisting it needed paracetamol, bubbly water and lots of caffeine. She would have to get out of bed after all.

A few minutes later she slid slowly from under the quilt, groaning, and stumbled naked to the door, holding on to it for support as the room suddenly seemed to tilt. Saliva rushed into her dry mouth and nausea overwhelmed her. She wanted to die. What was the point in being alive when you felt this terrible?

'Best feeling in the world, being sick,' her grandad used to say. Didn't he mean once you'd *been* sick? By the time she was standing trembling in the sunlit kitchen, wrapped in her dressing gown and sipping strong, sweet coffee after having gulped two paracetamol with a glass of Coke followed by another of fizzy water, Wanda was starting to feel less like death warmed up. Physically, anyway. Mentally, she knew that was it. After last night she could not take any more. But did she have a choice?

The fear loomed large in her mind again, that it would not be long before the doctors would want to switch off Alex's life support. And if she refused permission – as she would – that they would do it anyway. They might use last night's seizure as an excuse. The bitch Russian doctor had been there again, with her cold comments and supercilious shrugs. Wanda felt the doctor despised her for refusing to face what she obviously regarded as the inevitable. Another doctor, accompanied by a nurse, had approached her as she sat crying by Alex's bed, and started to talk about counselling; Wanda had instantly and indignantly rejected that. She needed practical help, not some interfering do-gooder telling her how she ought to feel. She needed justice for Alex.

Shannon Flinder wasn't going to help her, Wanda knew that now, so she would have to look for another solicitor. She wished she had written down the names Shannon and then her receptionist had tried to give her. Dare she phone Shannon's office one more time, make it clear that she only wanted those names? Recommendations would be better than nothing.

She gulped more coffee and nibbled on a stale, pink-iced cake she found in the breadbin. Winced as she thought of last night. Drinking so much, staggering around the streets, at one point sitting on a wall and howling, raging, cursing God's master plan and her and Alex's place in it. She was lucky she hadn't been arrested for being pissed and out of control. That thought made her laugh.

'Look at yourself in the mirror,' she said, walking into the hall. 'See what a bad girl looks like. Bad girl, naughty Wanda.'

How could she laugh when Alex was...? She went back to the kitchen, rummaged in a drawer, chose a knife and slashed her right forearm, gasping, then breathing deeply as blood welled and dripped. What was it with the slicing? Was she becoming one of those self-harming nutters? She should stop it before next summer, or she would have to keep her arms covered during the hot weather.

'Never mind next bloody summer,' she whispered. 'You've got this autumn and winter to get through first.'

She plugged her phone back in and set her mobile to recharge. She called the hospital; Alex was stable. Then she called Rod, knowing he was not going to be happy with her latest absence.

'Don't bother,' he interrupted as she launched into her excuses. 'It's clear your desk time, Wand. Your bottom is grass, love.'

She gasped. 'What?'

'Come on, it can't be that much of a surprise. You write good stuff sometimes, but it's not brilliant. You're not indispensable.'

'But Rod—'

'How can I put this so you'll understand? You're sacked. You've pulled this little stunt once too often.'

'You can't just sack me.'

'Oh, I can, Wand. Very much so.'

'But—'

'Yeah, butts. Everybody's got one.'

'Rod, I promise you, this will never happen again.'

'Got that right. Look, Wand, I don't want a debate. Pop in, collect your gear and pop off again. Story ends there.' He hung up.

Wanda listened to the dial tone, her face wet with tears. Rod couldn't do this to her, he just couldn't. If she lost her job she was finished. She had to get down there now, persuade him to change his mind. There might just be a chance he would. Lethargy changed to frantic activity as she stumbled into the shower and stumbled out again, trying to dry herself while she searched for a bra and clean knickers, jeans and a top. The underwear draped on the radiator was still damp, so she microwaved a black bra and fraying pair of black knickers dry. The clothes she had worn yesterday lay on the floor by the bed and she picked up the turquoise sweater and sniffed, wondering if it was wearable for just one more day. It would bloody have to be. But no. A big, damp, dark red wine stain covered the front. She did not have another clean one, or not one she could even be bothered to look for.

'No,' she groaned. '*No.*'

It was all too much. Wanda decided to go back to bed.

'Yes, you can talk to our mystery man today.' The dark-haired, blue-overalled nurse led the two detectives down the corridor. 'I hope you can get something out of him, because we've had no luck so far. Poor guy's still really confused; he can't remember a thing.'

'Not even his name?' One of the detectives stared at her bottom and small waist, just visible beneath the top and trousers, and thought he'd like to try and make her forget hers one of these nights.

'No. Nothing.'

'Don't suppose he could be that escaped con, Richard Croft,' the other one commented. 'That'd be too good to be true. Have you heard of him?' he asked the nurse.

'You mean the guy in that photo that's being circulated? Looks so ordinary, doesn't he?' She shook her head. 'Not sure I'd recognise him if I saw him in the flesh. Anyway – our mystery man, when he was feeling a bit better, asked us to bring his clothes and leave them for him to look through. He thought that might help him remember something. His clothes are all he's got, I'm afraid. His attackers must have stolen his wallet, assuming he was carrying one. No other personal belongings were found on him when he was brought in.'

'Shame.'

'Yeah.' She stopped, turned to them and pointed. 'He's in this side ward.' She lowered her voice. 'He seems very nervous most of the time – can't relax at all. It must be terrifying to wake up in hospital after being attacked, and not remember who you are. So I don't have to tell you to be very gentle with him, OK?'

Why was she telling them then? 'Sure. Of course.'

'Good. In here.' They followed her into the side ward.

'Oh my God.' She stopped again, staring at the empty bed with its sheets flung back, the crumpled white gown on the floor. 'He's gone.'

'Why did you murder Declan Dowd?'

'Don't answer that,' Roy Gardner, Shannon's barrister friend whose help she had enlisted to try and get Finbar out of this nightmare, snapped.

'I'm happy to answer.' Finbar was trying to remain calm, although he still could not absorb the shock of being arrested, spending the night in a cell and sitting through hours of interrogation. One minute he thought Dowd was buried in the clock tower, next he was being arrested at the airport and accused of the little bastard's murder. How had it happened?

Had there been something on the news about the discovery of a body in the old Clarence Dock clock tower? Had he missed

157

it? Finbar supposed that was possible. And he had just been away for the weekend. Or had the the police found the body but were keeping it quiet? He was frightened for Shannon as much as himself – how could he protect her from Croft when he was stuck in here? And of course he could not contact Curtis either.

'I didn't murder Dowd.' How many more times would he have to repeat that? He glanced at Roy. 'No further comment.'

They had given him a Special Warning in accordance with PACE, the Police and Criminal Evidence Act, but of course it was still best to say nothing, despite the guff about how what you did not say might harm your defence. If the police believed he had murdered Dowd, let them bloody well prove it. But Finbar was starting to fear that they just might stick this on him. He took a long breath, and slowly wiped his sweating palms along his jeans.

How long would they hold him? He had to get out of here soon. He could not even have a proper talk with Roy Gardner, because they both suspected the police interview rooms were bugged.

'Dowd wanted to kill you, didn't he?' the bearded detective who had handcuffed him asked. 'Because he believed you'd murdered his brother Lenny.'

Finbar wanted to protest that he didn't know what the fuck they were on about, but stuck to the phrase Roy had strongly recommended. 'No comment.'

'We've got someone who says Dowd wanted to get revenge on you. He thought you'd killed his brother because Lenny Dowd shot your wife and baby daughter some years ago in the Republic of Ireland when they accidentally came across him and his men unloading arms at a secret location – obviously not secret enough.'

Pain coursed through Finbar as he thought of his daughter, Roiseann, dead for six years now. He heard her baby laughter, recalled watching her as she slept, feeling total, unconditional love and knowing he would do anything to protect her, die for her if need be. But he hadn't protected her. He hadn't been there to stop those bastards murdering her and her mother.

158

A piece of him had died with Roiseann. He broke out in another sweat. 'No . . . comment.'

'Still miss your baby girl, do you? And your wife? Terrible thing to lose a child, and like that. Your baby didn't make her first birthday, did she?'

Roy laid one hand on Finbar's shoulder. 'Stick to relevant questions, please. Not that I've heard many that fit that description so far.' He glanced at his Rolex.

'I didn't kill either of those men.' Finbar took another long breath. 'I don't know what you're talking about.'

'OK, let me ask you something else. DNA found on Dowd's corpse matches the sample you provided us with – under protest. Don't try to tell us you never knew him or had contact with him – close, physical contact – because we know that's not true.'

'Yes, I had close physical contact with him.' Finbar looked at the detective. 'Dowd was involved with the gang who kidnapped me and tried to force me to help them blow up that shopping mall. The close physical contact happened when they beat me up and he shoved a gun in my mouth. After that he disappeared – I don't know where he went, I never saw him again.'

'Dowd helped beat you up? That's how you account for your DNA being on the murder weapon then?'

'Yes. That's how I account for it.' Finbar had kept Dowd's gun after he shot him in self-defence, and when he was kidnapped the terrorists had got it off him. The police had taken it later, bagged it as evidence after he had helped them with their sting operation and the gang members had either been captured or killed in a shoot-out.

'Are you going to tell me exactly what you've got on me?' Finbar felt Roy's grip on his shoulder tighten.

'Well, I'd say that's quite a lot already, wouldn't you?'

'No! I've explained how my DNA could have got on the gun that killed Dowd. You know I was kidnapped by that gang, you know what happened. It's all very clear. You've got sod all. On whose say-so did you pull me in here?' Finbar suddenly

159

wondered if this could be anything to do with that Nightingale bitch. Was she trying to make more trouble for him and Shannon?

The detective leaned back, adjusted his tie and glanced at his colleague. 'I take it you know Dennis King?'

Finbar tried to think. 'Should I?'

'Given that he was a member of Iain Blick's group of Real IRA breakaways who grabbed you and tried to enlist your help with their plan to blow up that mall, yeah, I'd say you should know him.'

'That was all more than a year ago, and I've been trying to forget about it. But OK. So?'

'So once we'd discovered and identified Dowd's body – and you've got a couple of very nosey and persistent local historians to thank for that, by the way – we went to have a little chat with Dennis King. He's got plenty of time to chat, where he is. He told us you'd murdered Dowd, and that one of the reasons Blick – the leader of the gang, unfortunately deceased – was able to get your help was by letting you know he knew you'd murdered Dowd. He said he heard you admit to Blick that you'd killed Dowd.'

'That's bullshit. He's lying.' Finbar tried to remember Dennis King. Fair-haired, slightly built, in his forties? 'The way they got my help, as you put it, was by threatening to gang rape and then murder Shannon Flinder, my girlfriend. After which they said they'd murder me. I believed them. Then Special Branch stepped in and threatened to fit me up with a load of crap if I didn't help them with their sting.' Finbar glared at the men sitting opposite him. 'Don't tell me you don't already know this.'

'How do you explain your DNA being on Dowd's corpse?'

'I've just told you! He was beating me, I was trying to defend myself.'

There was a knock at the door. The detective got up and went outside, started to talk in a low voice to someone in the corridor. Finbar turned to Roy.

'Make sure Shannon's OK, will you? Let her know I'm OK.' Even if he wasn't.

Roy nodded. 'I'll call her. She'll be waiting to know when she can see you.'

It freaked Finbar that he could not contact Curtis. If Curtis killed Richard Croft but something went wrong and it got traced back to him, what then? What if the police tried to blame Shannon as well? Jesus, he thought, stop it. Don't jump ahead of yourself. First he had to get himself out of this place. And Shannon had to stay safe. But how was that supposed to happen?

The detective came back. Smiling. Roy Gardner looked at him inquiringly.

'Good news. The custody extension's just been granted.' The detective sat down again and leaned his elbows on the table. 'You've got another twelve hours to explain yourself to us. Yeah.' He held up one hand. 'I know you think you've already done that.'

'This is bullshit. You've got *nothing*.'

'Would you like some tea or coffee? Something to eat?'

'Shove it.'

'Don't be like that. You'll need some food and a hot drink. It could be a long night for you, Mr Linnell.'

Chapter Fifteen

'Roy, you've got to help him!' Shannon gripped the phone as she stared out at the grey river. 'Finbar hasn't murdered Dowd.' She was not lying, she told herself, because self-defence was not murder. 'I can't stand him being in there. The police might hurt him, they might—'

'Come on, Shannon. They won't do anything physical to him, certainly not these days. You know that.'

'Do I?'

'Yes, you do. Look, I realise this is terribly upsetting for you both, but please try to calm yourself. I'm doing all I can.' Roy did not say that it might help if he could be sure Finbar had told him everything. Then again, perhaps that would not help. It might make things a lot more difficult.

'They authorised a search of Finbar's apartment. They just left.' She glanced around the trashed living room. 'I can't believe they'd arrest him and do all this stuff on the word of some con who's banged up for kidnapping, murder and conspiracy to commit terrorist acts – you name it.' But she could believe it. It was typical of their luck – all of it bad.

'Problem is Finbar's DNA is on Dowd's corpse and on the murder weapon, despite his explanation. That lends credibility to this Dennis King's allegation.'

Roy liked Finbar Linnell, despite rumours of the man's dubious past, and he could understand why Shannon was charmed by him – fatally charmed, in his opinion. Most women would be. Nothing had ever been proved against Linnell, but

Roy still did not think Shannon was doing herself or her career any good at all by associating with him.

'But the police know that Dowd was involved with that gang who kidnapped Finbar. They beat him, kept him locked up. At one point they hit him with a gun, shoved it in his mouth. So of course his DNA would be on that gun and on Dowd. After that Dowd disappeared. Finbar never saw him again.' Shannon felt sick with apprehension and fear. She couldn't believe this was happening, not on top of everything else.

'It's this Dennis King's word against Finbar, I'm afraid. And the police won't accept Finbar's version.' Roy did not entirely blame them.

'They'll have to bloody well accept Finbar's version.' Shannon blinked back tears. 'They can't prove he murdered Dowd, and that's that. How much longer do you think they'll hold him?' she asked, afraid of the answer.

'I don't know.'

'Can't the police see that this King is just trying to get himself a shorter sentence? He's made the whole thing up. This is stupid, he's having a laugh with them.'

'Well, the police are not seeing the funny side.' Roy wondered again if Finbar was guilty; possibly, he thought. He didn't know exactly what had happened or why, and he didn't want to. How much did Shannon know about her enigmatic lover? Not anything like as much as she ought to know, Roy bet. He would do what he could for Finbar, of course, that was his job. But he was more worried about Shannon.

'They won't let you see him,' he warned. 'Not yet, anyway. You being his partner, they think you might—'

'What? Sneak him a gun concealed in my home-baked lime coconut cake?'

'I was about to say, jeopardise their investigation.' Roy listened to her sniffs. 'Shannon – why don't you come and have dinner with me and Rosemary later? You haven't seen my dear wife in quite a while. She's been asking about you.'

'Thanks, Roy, but ... I'm just not in the mood.' Shannon felt guilty. Roy was not stupid and she was sure he guessed he didn't have the full picture about his client. And she knew that although Roy had met Finbar several times and liked him, he was doing this for her rather than Finbar.

'It's just a quiet dinner. We don't expect you to be life and soul.'

'I know. I just don't fancy going anywhere. Thanks anyway.'

'Have you got someone to be with you this evening?'

'Yes,' she lied. 'A friend's coming over.' Shannon did not want anyone with her. Except Finbar. More tears filled her eyes as she thought of him locked in a cell, separated from her, facing ... what? She couldn't believe they would charge him with murder. And it infuriated her to think of Finbar locked up while Richard Croft was still on the loose.

'Did you manage to talk to Carl Mactire?' she asked. 'The DCI who forced Finbar to participate in the sting operation against Blick and his gang? He promised Finbar he'd be left alone after that.'

'Yes, I did talk to him, as you suggested. Just caught him in time – he's leaving the day after tomorrow to do six months in Bosnia.'

'Bosnia?'

'Yes. Help show the locals how to police in the good old Brit democratic manner.'

Another time Shannon would have laughed at that. 'So what did he say?'

'Mactire said that as far as Special Branch were concerned Dowd was officially missing and there was no information about him. But now that his body's been discovered, and circumstances point to a suspect—'

'You said it. *Circumstances.*'

'Point to perhaps Finbar being the murderer, things have changed. There's absolutely nothing Mactire or anyone else can do for him.'

'So he used Finbar – put his life in danger – and now he's leaving him to rot.' Shannon's voice was bitter. 'I suppose I should have expected that.'

'I'm sorry. Look, I'll talk to you again tomorrow. First thing, after I've seen Finbar again.' Roy paused. 'I know it's easy for me to say, but try not to worry too much.' He would not dream of saying it to Shannon, but he wondered if Finbar Linnell being sent down for murder wouldn't be a good thing because it would force Shannon to make a new life for herself. Then again, she did love the man. And she had had more than enough misery and trauma over the past couple of years.

'OK. Roy, thanks for everything you're doing. I – Finbar and I – really appreciate it.'

'No problem. I'm your friend, Shannon. I'll do anything I can to help you. Take care of yourself, won't you? I'll speak to you again soon. Goodnight.'

''Night, Roy.' Shannon noticed Roy had not said he was Finbar's friend. She put the phone down and switched on some lamps in the darkening living room. If it had not been for Finbar's arrest she would have started moving her stuff back here; they would be together right now. She wiped her eyes, feeling desolate. As she rooted in her bag for another tissue her fingers brushed Finbar's mobile phone, and she took it out and looked at it. The phone was switched off but she couldn't switch it on and check the numbers or messages because she could not remember the pin code. She held it in her hand, wondering what secrets might be locked inside. Why had Finbar been so quick to give it to her the second he heard the police officer speak his name? It was almost as if he had been expecting to get arrested. She frowned, staring at it, then sighed and dropped it back in her bag. No use. And she couldn't ask Finbar now. Shannon did not know when the police would allow her to see or speak to Finbar, but she did know that when-ever that happened they would have no privacy.

She missed him terribly, felt more vulnerable without him there. She took another look around the big living room and the other rooms in the apartment, picking up books, clothes, scat-tered papers. Where to begin? It was hopeless; she was too tired and dispirited to tackle the chaos now. In Finbar's bedroom drawer she found the photo of his murdered baby daughter Roiseann, nine months old at the time of her death. She touched one finger to the child's laughing face.

165

'Poor baby,' she whispered.

The police had taken Finbar's laptop and some files and papers relating to his air cargo business. She wondered if they had ransacked his offices as well. They would not find anything, certainly no evidence that he had killed Declan Dowd. She went back into the living room and looked at the shiny wood floor. There had been hardly any blood from Dowd's body, and Finbar had had a new floor laid more than a year ago as a precaution. If the police carried out luminol tests to look for hidden bloodstains they would find nothing. Shannon shuddered, remembering the day she had come back here to find Dowd holding Finbar at gunpoint, about to kill him.

There was nothing more she could do here, not tonight. Best to go home and lock herself in until tomorrow morning. She could not even legally carry some weapon with which to try and defend herself should Croft get to her. She took the panic alarm out of her pocket and looked at it contemptuously. In the hall she hesitated by the closed front door, afraid to go back out there.

Shannon thought of Bernard Flinder again, of Rob. Father and then son had tried to destroy her, but had ended up destroying themselves. She could not let someone else succeed now, not a twisted fuck like Croft. She wondered where Croft was. And where was another hit man when she needed him! The hall phone rang, startling her. She hesitated, then grabbed the receiver.

'Thought you might be here tidying up the mess,' Cindy Nightingale laughed. She sounded like she'd been drinking. 'So your boyfriend's been caught at last. You're next. I'll have you. It won't be long now.'

Shannon hung up and started to cry. What if Finbar was charged with murder, kept in custody, put on trial? What if Croft never got recaptured? And what if he did? Would she just carry on, try to cope after all the crap that had happened? Why did she get all this trouble? What had she ever done to attract it? Should she give up the law? But what else would she do? She swore, shook her head. What was the point of thinking about the future when you couldn't be sure you had one? She almost cried out in shock as the doorbell rang several times. Loud knocking followed.

'Finbar? Are you there? It's Curtis. Open up, mate, will you? I haven't heard from you for two days. I've been trying to call you. Come on, we need to talk.'

Who the hell was Curtis? Finbar had never mentioned him. Shannon crept closer and looked through the peephole. A tall, good-looking black man in jeans and a long coat stood there, an anxious expression on his face. He didn't look like a murderer, but who could tell? Anyway, what was a murderer supposed to look like? Most of them looked frighteningly ordinary, the kind of person you'd exchange a friendly word with in a shop or on a train or aircraft. At least this guy wasn't Croft. She opened the door.

'Oh.' The man looked startled. 'Er ... hi. My name's Curtis Bright. I'm an old friend of Finbar's, although we don't meet up that often' He held out his hand. 'And you would be – Shannon, right?'

She shook hands with him. 'Right.'

'Pleased to meet you.' He glanced over her shoulder and down the hall. 'Is Finbar here? I need to talk to him.'

She shook her head, unable to speak for a second.

'What's up?' he asked, seeing her tears. 'What's happened?'

Shannon tried to pull herself together. 'What did you – what do you want to talk to Finbar about?'

Curtis looked down. Up. Anywhere but in her eyes. 'Just business.'

'What business?'

He hesitated. 'I suppose you could say it concerns a cargo.'

'Must be an important cargo. You sounded pretty urgent just now. How come you've heard of me but I don't know a thing about you?'

'Finbar ... mentioned you. Once when we were having a drink. Said you were his girlfriend. Well, his partner. And that you were a solicitor. Criminal law.'

'Is that why you're being so cagey with me now?'

'I'm not. Look – what's happened?' Curtis repeated. 'Where is Finbar?'

'Just a second.' Shannon had not been there when the police searched the apartment and she wondered if they might have planted a probe or some other kind of bug somewhere. She was not going to take any chances. She went back inside, switched off the lights and came out again, double-locking the front door behind her. Curtis waited.

'Finbar's been arrested,' she said at last, dropping the keys into her bag.

'*What*?' His brown eyes widened in shock. 'What the fuck for?'

'Murder. But he didn't do it.'

'Jesus Christ.' Curtis turned away, took a breath. '*Shit.*' He turned back to her. 'When did this happen?'

'Yesterday.' Shannon started to go downstairs. 'I'm trying to get him out, but so far I haven't succeeded. Whatever your business is with Finbar, it'll have to wait. And you obviously don't want to tell me what it's about. So thank you and good-night.'

She had a feeling this was no ordinary business deal. Finbar must have had good reason not to have mentioned this Curtis Bright to her. What had he – they – been up to? Shannon had to admit to herself that at that moment she did not give a toss as long as whatever it was did not come to the attention of the police, and no innocent person got hurt. Yes, Ms Criminal Law Solicitor, she thought, your moral compass is getting well skewed. But I never looked for all this shit to happen.

'Hey, hold up.' Curtis ran after her. 'Where are you going now?'

'Home,' she snapped. 'I fancy a cosy evening by the fire wondering what the hell I can do to stop my life and Finbar's falling apart.'

'But you're not—' Curtis grabbed her arm. 'I mean, shouldn't you be careful? You're not safe, there's a psycho after you.'

'Now what would you know about that?' Shannon pulled her arm free. 'And what possible business could it be of yours?'

'Can we talk?' he asked. 'Go somewhere?'

'Why should I go anywhere with you? How do I know *you're* not a psycho?'

'Because I'm not wearing my dear old late mother's clothing. I love animals. And I've got warm, friendly eyes. Look. All my lights are on and I'm definitely at home. What more proof could you want?'

'Well, none, of course,' Shannon answered sarcastically. She looked at him, considering. She was wary of him, but did not feel threatened. Was he really a friend of Finbar's? She wanted to find out more. She wouldn't let him into her apartment, but a pub should be safe enough. 'All right,' she sighed. 'A quick drink and that's it.'

'I run a security firm,' Curtis explained when they were seated in a dark, panelled pub with thick red carpets, walls lined with photographs of First World War battleships and quiet, mostly elderly male drinkers. 'And I sell security products online. I used to be in the SAS ... it's true,' he grinned as Shannon rolled her eyes and shook her head.

'Whatever.'

'Finbar and me are old mates, like I said, though we don't see each other that often. I'm abroad a lot.'

'I bet you are. Looking for more security products to sell, right?' Shannon wondered if he was an arms dealer.

Curtis laughed. 'Amongst other things. Finbar and I have done some business together now and then over the years.' He glanced up at a photo on the wall.

'It's all right.' She sipped her gin and tonic. 'I'm not going to ask what.' She knew about Finbar's past, that he had been into drugs and arms deals, things he definitely was not into any more. Or at least she hoped not. She was not going to mention any of this to Mr Bright, of course.

'Finbar contacted me last week.' Curtis picked up his glass of sparkling mineral water and looked distastefully at it. 'We met. He told me you were in danger from this moron named Richard Croft who'd escaped from jail.' He paused. 'Had any more news about him?'

169

'Well, I'm waiting for an inspector to call and tell me Croft's back inside – hopefully for at least the next thirty years without parole – and that I can have my life back, but no joy as yet, I'm afraid.'

'That's tough. Finbar said he was very worried, that he didn't trust the police to protect you. He asked me to keep an eye on you. That is, until Croft's put back inside.'

Shannon put down her glass. 'Keep an eye on me?'

'Yeah. Just some ... discreet surveillance.'

'So why didn't Finbar tell me about that?'

'He thought it might make you more alarmed.'

'Wouldn't it make me feel more safe to know someone was watching over me?'

'Finbar thought it might freak you more to realise he considered extra protection necessary. He didn't want to make a big deal about it.'

Shannon could understand that. 'Problem is, we don't know if or when Croft will be recaptured. It could be tomorrow, or a month from now. Maybe longer. And although I'm sure Finbar's paying you well for your trouble, it sounds like you've got a busy life and there must be other stuff you have to get on with. Did he specify a time limit?'

'Not exactly.' Curtis eyed the array of gleaming bottles behind the bar, none of which contained mineral water. 'He said we'd continue to evaluate the situation.'

'I see.' Shannon picked up her drink and finished it. 'And what were – what *are* – you supposed to do if by chance you come across Croft? If you catch him attacking me?'

'Well, in that case I'd—'

'Evaluate the situation?'

Curtis started to laugh. 'I like you. Fancy another of those?' He pointed to her glass. 'Or shall we go and have some dinner?'

'No.' Shannon felt angry. 'You did say you were a friend of Finbar's?'

'Yeah. Why, what...? Oh hey, come on,' Curtis pleaded, dismayed to see her expression turn cold enough to freeze vodka. 'I only meant it in the sense that if you have dinner with me I'll be keeping an eye on you, won't I? Doing my job.'

'Will you pay for the meal? Will I? Or will you charge it to Finbar? That's if the police let him out to pay you.'

'Bloody hell. Listen, forget it, OK?'

'I will.' Shannon thought. 'Is keeping an eye on me all Finbar asked you to do?'

'Getting a right grilling, aren't I?' Curtis sighed. 'What d'you mean?'

'I think you know.' She stared at her empty glass. 'I'm just wondering. I realise you have to keep evaluating situations and all, but I can't believe you and Finbar didn't talk about what you'd do if you managed to locate Croft before the police did. Finbar doesn't trust them to protect me. Even if they do recapture Croft, he'll be released one day. Why were you desperate to talk to Finbar?' she asked, her suspicions deepening.

'I wouldn't say *desperate*. I just hadn't heard from him in a while and—'

'Have you seen Croft?' Shannon's heart thudded. 'Do you know where he is?'

'No, I don't.' Curtis looked uneasy. 'If you don't want another drink, why don't I see you safely home?' He started to get up.

'Wait.' Shannon grabbed his arm. 'Sit down. Finbar's not here,' she said quietly as Curtis sighed again and sank down beside her. 'He can't be here, and I don't know how long he'll be detained. You must realise his arrest changes everything.'

'That's a given!'

'You're dealing with me now. I want the truth.' Shannon lowered her voice to a whisper. 'Did Finbar tell you to kill Croft?'

Curtis groaned and looked away. 'Not guilty, Your Honour.'

'So he did.' Shannon went cold. 'For God's sake,' she hissed. 'What d'you think I'm going to do? There's no way I'll tell the police, if that's what you're afraid of.' It occurred to her that maybe she should be more afraid for herself if Curtis thought she might get him into trouble. 'I love Finbar,' she said. 'He's in big trouble and I want to do anything I can to help him, not make things worse. Tell me what's going on. Please.'

Finbar had broken his promise about no more secrets. She did not know how she was going to deal with that. But it would have to wait for now.

'All right.' Curtis nodded. 'Like you say, Finbar's arrest changes everything. He said he wanted Croft out of the way – permanently. At least that's what he told me at first. But then he started to have doubts. He wasn't sure what he wanted. That's why I needed to talk to him urgently.'

Shannon got a flash of relief. 'Really?'

'Yeah.' Curtis glanced round the pub again before turning back to her. 'A contact of mine found out Croft's been trying to get hold of a passport. He's calling himself Steve Kane. I don't know where he is right now, but I do know he's got an appointment to collect that passport tomorrow lunchtime in town, in a pub called The Grapes opposite Central Station.'

Shannon gasped. 'But that's fantastic.' She paused. 'Or is it? Are you sure this Kane really is Richard Croft?'

'Oh yeah. There's no doubt.'

'But how can you and your contacts find out all this when the police...?' Her voice trailed off.

Curtis looked at her pityingly. 'Ways and means. Don't ask. I phoned Finbar and told him. He said he'd let me know what he wanted me to do. But he didn't get the chance, as we know. And now...' Curtis shrugged. 'I don't think it'd be a great idea to go ahead with the permanent solution, not in the circumstances. Not for me or Finbar – or even you. But if I do nothing you're still at risk.'

So Finbar had decided to have Croft killed, but changed his mind. Or had doubts. Why? Because it was going behind her back, breaking his promise? Did he think she would not want him to have even a lowlife that like killed? Was he afraid something might go wrong? Croft's death would look extremely convenient, could get both of them into trouble – more trouble. But what had Finbar wanted to do? Get Curtis to give Croft a beating, dump him on the doorstep of the nearest police station?

172

'Don't do anything,' she said. 'I've got an idea. I'm going to tell the inspector in charge of the hunt for Croft that I've had an anonymous tip-off to say Croft will be in that pub tomorrow lunchtime.'

Curtis raised his eyebrows. 'Sure that's a good idea?'

'It's perfect. The information's being handed to them on a gold plate. What can go wrong? Even the police can't mess that up. They can stake out the pub and arrest Croft the minute he turns up. Sorted.'

'Yeah? Well. Let's hope.'

'I'm so relieved Finbar didn't tell you to go through with ... you know. He's in enough trouble as it is. I've got him one of the best barristers I know and I'm trying everything I can to get him released.' Shannon glanced away, tears in her eyes. 'But I seem to be running out of options.' She sniffed hard. 'Sorry.'

'No problem. This must be a very upsetting time for you.'

'I've had better.'

Curtis nudged her. 'Listen, about before. I wasn't hitting on you when I asked you to have dinner with me. Well.' He grinned. 'Not really.'

'It's OK.' Shannon wiped her eyes. 'Forget it.'

'Sure you don't want another drink?'

An idea occurred to her. It was not without risk, and it was something which would normally be violently against her so-called principles. If she got caught she would be in bigger trouble than in Cindy Nightingale's wildest fantasies. Shannon put thoughts of skewed moral compasses out of her head, because this was very much not the time to worry about such things. My God, she thought. Could it work?

'What is it?' Curtis was staring at her. 'Your eyes are glittering.'

'Must be all the crying.'

'Don't think so. It's like the light just went back on.'

'I've got an idea but I'm not sure it'll work. It scares the hell out of me just thinking about it.'

'I'm intrigued.'

173

Shannon wondered how far she could trust Curtis Bright. She could imagine how he and Finbar were friends; they were the same types, had the same humour. Curtis almost certainly had a 'past' himself. Would he be willing, able, to do what she had in mind? 'How much has Finbar paid you to keep an eye on me?'

He smiled. 'Let's just say if the cops do their job – for once – and Croft gets nicked tomorrow lunchtime I'll owe Finbar some money back.'

'Maybe you won't.' Shannon got out her mobile. First she had to call Inspector Casey and tell him about her mystery tip-off. 'I have to phone someone. Then I'll accept your kind offer of another gin-and-tonic with slice but no ice, and tell you my idea. I might have a job for you.'

'*You* might?'

'Yes. That's if you can do it. If you're up for it.'

'I'm always up for a challenge. Can't wait to hear this.' Curtis was not smiling now. 'You're not like any woman I ever met. I hope Finbar realises how lucky he is.'

'Oh, I think he does.' Shannon switched on her mobile and saw that there was one message. It was from Roy Gardner. She hadn't expected to hear from him again tonight.

'I'm sorry, Shannon. I just heard. The police have charged Finbar with the murder of Declan Dowd.'

Chapter Sixteen

'God damn freaking headache.'

Richard Croft rolled over on the hard, narrow bed with its dingy sheets. The thin, worn curtains didn't do much of a job at keeping out the powerful orange street light, and it was almost as bright as day. The back of his throat was sore and his ears felt weird, as if they wouldn't pop back to normal after flying long haul with a bad cold.

The rented room was a cockroach-ridden tip in a dilapidated, cockroach-ridden monument to depressing Victorian architecture, but he would get kicked out of here in a couple of days if he couldn't come up with next week's rent. And how the hell was he supposed to pay rent when he couldn't even afford bread or teabags? The bastards who had beat him up had taken his money. Thank God they hadn't done him as much damage as he – and the doctors – had originally thought. But the way things were at the moment, Richard did not know what he could do. He was supposed to meet this Matty tomorrow to collect his new passport. That was not just a document, it was the key to a new life. And to think Shannon Flinder was still living her life.

He had stayed in hospital as long as he dared, enjoying being fed, medicated and looked after. He had pretended to be more injured and confused than he was – not difficult! – and had milked the memory loss thing for all it was worth. Of course it couldn't last; he could never really relax because he was terrified some copper would walk up to his bedside and recognise him, despite his altered appearance. When he had heard that nurse talking about how they considered he was up to seeing the police, he knew it was time to get out very quickly. Asking for his clothes to look over had been a good trick. The odds might be stacked against him, but he hadn't lost it. He was a player.

Richard sat up slowly, groaning, and swallowed another couple of painkillers. The water he drank with them tasted like it had come out of a swimming pool instead of the tap. He struggled against the feelings of hopelessness and depression that threatened to overwhelm him. What the hell could he do now? He had no money, no prospect of getting any. Things were almost bad enough to consider turning himself in. But no. Not that. Whatever happened, he would not go back to jail. Richard knew that if he did that he would die there.

Shannon Flinder was the cause of all his trouble. She had her posh, period des-res, all the money she got paid for standing in courtrooms talking bullshit and telling lies that destroyed men's lives. What was the bitch doing now? Sleeping? Getting fucked by some bloke she considered good enough to crawl into her bed? Richard lay down again, his head whirling. Street light slanted across the ceiling with its moulded cornices and flaking paint. Maybe Shannon Flinder was alone and terrified, cowering behind the locked, chained door of her apartment, wondering when he was going to make his next move? It made him feel better to imagine that. He was messing with her mind even while he lay here in pain. He imagined her terror, her pleas for mercy he was never going to show.

'Yeah,' he whispered. 'I'm coming for you. Can't disappoint you now, can I?'

He had nothing left to lose.

'I thought a detained person's supposed to be allowed eight hours uninterrupted sleep.'

Finbar sat up, blinking as the cell light snapped on. Cindy Nightingale stood grinning in the doorway. Her long brown hair shone, she wore too much sticky pink lip gloss and her black trouser suit was a size ten squeezed on to a size twelve body. From where he sat Finbar could smell stale cigarettes, in-your-face perfume that she probably thought was irresistible, and dragon breath alcohol fumes. Christ, he thought, if I had a match to strike she'd go up like a beacon. O beautiful thought.

'So you can sleep, can you, Mister Finn MacCool?' Cindy sniggered and put one hand on her round hip. 'Don't think I could if I'd just been charged with a murder I thought was all done and dusted yonks ago. Bit of a shock, eh? Not to mention how worried you must be about the danger your beautiful lay-dee could be in.'

Finbar assumed she was referring to the danger Shannon faced from Croft. But he was not going to discuss Shannon with this bitch, period. He might be panicked, despairing, missing Shannon like he couldn't believe and terrified for her safety, but he was not going to reveal that. He swung his legs to the floor.

'This unauthorised and unclever little dead-of-night social call's going to go on my Custody Record.' He kept his voice calm. 'If you contravene PACE it won't invalidate the murder charge, but it could cause big trouble for you.'

'PACE? Oh, the Police and Criminal Evidence Act. Yeah, I remember that.' Cindy sniggered again. 'Bloody hell. It's obvious you're shagging a solicitor. Although not any more now, eh? Not again for at least another decade. Hope your last was a good one. But hey, don't worry.' She lodged one mani-cured fingernail against her sticky lips. 'No one's going to find out about my visit. It'll be our little secret.'

'Don't think so. Apart from the people who must have seen you and let you in here, I'll be informing my barrister first thing in the morning.'

'Inform all you like, Mister MacCool. Won't do you any freaking good. Or *feckin'* good – isn't that what you colourful Irish characters like to say?'

Finbar thought how much he would enjoy beating her until she resembled a lump of steak mince. 'So what's the reason for the visit? I'd like to get back to sleep, if you don't mind. You look like you could do with a few hours yourself.'

177

'Ahhh, gee, thanks for the concern. That's *really* sweet. I am quite tired, now you come to mention it.' Cindy glanced back then walked unsteadily into the cell. 'I heard you'd been charged,' she breathed. 'I know it's late and all, but I just had to pop down here and get a look at you, all locked up and absolutely nowhere to go. I wanted to have a pure, unadulterated—'

'Wow, big word. D'you know what it means?'

'A pure, unadulterated *gloat*. I also wanted to get a last look at your handsome face and tasty, fit body before all that yumminess gets kicked in by some very pissed off people who think you've been having a right laugh with them for far too long.'

'You mean some lowlife you term colleagues?'

'You're finished.' Cindy came closer. 'You're going away for a long, *long* time. And let me leave you with this thought: I'm going to destroy your precious girlfriend. Once and for all. That's if that psycho Croft doesn't get to her first. And it's a distinct possibility he will. She's in big trouble. And there's *nothing* you can do to help her. Hey, I wonder if you'd be allowed out to attend her funeral?'

Finbar stood up. Cindy was close enough to touch now. He wanted to grab a fistful of that shiny hair and smash her across her grinning face. Tell her she was the one who was going to be destroyed.

'I can't help Shannon,' Cindy went on. 'But maybe I could help you. If you'd be sensible. If you'd be —' she tilted her head back and gazed into his eyes '—really, *really* nice to me.'

He glanced up at the angled security camera. 'What, be really nice to you right here? On tape?'

She followed his glance and sniggered again. 'Oh, dear. You must think I'm very stupid. You don't think that thing's switched on, do you? God's sake. A good mate of mine just very kindly turned it off, all for sweet little me.'

Shit, Finbar thought, his hope of her being caught on tape behaving very badly crushed. 'I didn't realise you had any mates. So how d'you reckon you can help me?' he asked. 'Prove my innocence?'

She wagged her finger. 'You're such a joker.'

If the camera really was switched off he could tell the bitch exactly what he thought of her. But what good would that do? It wasn't like he could back up insults or threats with anything more concrete. Finbar stepped back and sat down again, trying to suppress the chilling thought that he might have to look at cell walls for the next ten to fifteen years. Be without Shannon all that time. Maybe for ever, because if he got sent to prison he would tell her they were finished. He had done that once before, for her protection, so she might not believe him at first. It would take some doing because he loved her and she loved him, and he knew she would stay loyal. But he did not want Shannon ruining the best years of her life hanging around waiting for him to get out of prison.

'Thanks for dropping by.' He looked at Cindy. 'It's been great. But I'll say goodnight now, if you don't mind.'

His calm, measured words had more effect than any insults or threats he might come out with. Cindy blushed, knowing he didn't want her, never had and never would, not even now when she thought she had the upper hand at last. She flinched at the contempt in his eyes.

'OK,' she hissed. 'Go back to bloody sleep. You'll have plenty of time for it where you're going. Dream about your girlfriend. Dreaming's all you'll get to do from now on.'

She stormed out and slammed the door. A drunk in a cell further along the corridor started yelling obscenities. Keys jangled and bolts were drawn, classic nightmare sounds which reinforced the fact that his freedom had been taken away and might not be restored to him for a long time. The light snapped off.

Finbar lay down and closed his eyes. But he didn't sleep.

Wanda's fountain pen dripped black ink as she held it poised over her diary. She put the pen down and thought. She could not write 'got job back' because that would sound like good news and she only recorded disappointment, death and disaster. That was not normal, of course, in fact most people would

179

regard it as downright unbalanced, but she couldn't get rid of her childhood habit now. Somewhere, tucked away in one of those boxes dumped around the flat, were other diaries with entries such as 'Mum slapped my legs', 'lost the race', and 'didn't win Milky Way'. And of course 'Dad left'.

Wanda remembered how she had longed to win that Milky Way for tidiness and obedience, how she had spent the entire day in class breathless with hope and anticipation, making a huge effort, and her agony when the teacher had announced the winner – a smug, blonde bitch named Amanda, who had thick golden plaits you just longed to pull until she screamed. Wanda had bought herself a Milky Way at the sweet shop after she got out of school, but it had not compensated, just tasted of gooey, cloying disappointment and failure. The next day she had stolen Amanda's packet of crisps.

She thought for another minute, staring at the date – Thursday 8th October – then tightened her lips and wrote 'Dim Bim started today'. 'Dim Bim' was a pleonasm of course, because bimbos were by definition dim. Wanda would not have had a clue what a pleonasm was until that morning when, stung by Cindy Nightingale's mockery of her writing technique, she had started reading a book on grammar and common style faults, and how to improve them. The bim in question was the exotically named Serafina Condorado, who Rod had met in one of his favourite bars and tried his tired old line of chat on. He was not acting sleazy with Serafina, but taking the earnest approach. Must be lurve. Serafina had a degree in something silly, and in an effort to impress the slim, dark-haired twenty-something – bit old for him, Wanda thought sarcastically – Rod had lost his head and offered Serafina a job: Wanda's job. She had got there to find Serafina at her desk looking depressingly bright-eyed and eager to start her career as a journalist.

What was it with sad bastards like Rod? He must be losing brain cells faster than hair follicles if he seriously imagined that sparky, sexy Serafina would ever consider him shaggable. She was using him, Wanda thought, and good luck to her. Rod had realised, however, that Serafina couldn't hack it as star reporter after just one day, so had accepted Wanda's desperate pleas and promises to use her police contact to get more info on Shannon Flinder and Finbar Linnell, and given her her job back. For now, anyway. Things were going to get more interesting now that Finbar had been charged with murder. But Wanda would have to put up with Serafina tagging along after her like an irritating puppy who kept wetting the carpet. And this irritating puppy would take over her job.

She picked up the phone and dialled. Shannon Flinder answered after just one ring, sounding breathless and desperate to hear from someone in particular.

'Hi, it's Wanda,' Wanda said, as if they were mates. 'I heard your partner Finbar's been charged with murder. Must be awful for you. How are you coping with—'

'*Fuck – off.*' Crash. Dial tone. Oh well. If Shannon wouldn't cooperate she would have to take the consequences of her stupid arrogance. Cindy was right, who did Shannon think she was? Most people had the sense to be more polite to journalists these days. Wanda got that cold feeling again. How much longer would she remain a journalist? She was on borrowed time. Every bloody area of her life now was on borrowed time. She wrote in her diary:

"Sentence of Execution".

Chapter Seventeen

'I'm afraid Croft – alias Steve Kane – didn't show.'

'Shannon gasped. *'Fuck*. I don't believe…!'

But of course she did believe it. Everything else had gone wrong, so why not this? It would have been too good to be true for Croft to have been caught and be on his way back to prison.

Alone in senior partner Mi-Hae Kam's office-cum-conference room, she looked down into Exchange Street East, wondering if Croft was somewhere out there now, just waiting for the chance to grab her. Finbar of course was still locked up.

'Maybe this Steve Kane wasn't Croft after all.' Curtis Bright might not be as on the case as he made out. He might be a bloody liar and con artist. Shannon hoped that was not true. She stared out at the rain.

'Well, your anonymous tip-off was correct in that a Steve Kane was supposed to meet with someone named Matty Rice in The Grapes around one o'clock to collect a passport,' DI Casey said. 'Rice is known to us, he's a petty criminal. We pulled him in. He admitted he'd stolen a passport from some tourist, and was about to sell it. He recognised the picture of Croft we showed him, said it was definitely him, except that he's lost some weight, shaved off his moustache and his hair's darker and shorter. Rice has got no reason to lie to us – he knows it's in his interest to cooperate. Your tip-off was right. The man he was there to meet was definitely Croft.'

So maybe Curtis wasn't a bullshit artist after all. It now remained to be seen if he could pull off the other thing he had promised. Shannon raked one hand through her hair and picked up her cup of coffee. She had waited all morning for this call, desperate for good news, and the shock and letdown was horrible now.

'I wonder why Croft didn't show? Are you certain he didn't?' She asked before Casey could reply. 'He could have spotted your men first and done a runner.'

'Look, I realise you're upset.' Casey sounded annoyed. 'So am I. But my team and I aren't some bunch of wankers who went blundering into that pub shouting, "'ello 'ello 'ello, wot's goin' on 'ere then?" Take my word for it.'

'When someone says "take my word for it" or "believe me", it's like Reichsmarshal Goering and that culture word – I reach for my gun.'

Shannon wished she had one now. She imagined pointing it in Croft's ugly face, letting him know what it was like to be frightened for a change.

'Thanks for your confidence,' Casey grumbled.

'Do you expect me to have any, after what's happened? First you let that bastard escape, now you can't catch him.'

'You still haven't got any idea who gave you that tip-off?'

'None whatsoever. I told you.' She felt herself blush. 'Like I said, it was an amazing phone call out of the blue just as I was leaving the Mags Court. Must have been a well-wisher. It's good to know there are people who wish me well, even if I don't always know who they are. It provides a welcome balance, helps me keep things in perspective – know what I mean?'

Casey sighed. 'You're sure you didn't recognise the caller's voice? A man, you said?'

'Again, as I told you. I've got no clue.'

'You see, I find that hard to believe.'

'Are you saying you think I'm lying? That I know who it was but won't tell you?' Shannon's blush deepened, but she felt furious. 'Why the hell wouldn't I, if I knew?'

'An amazing phone call out of the blue,' Casey repeated. He sighed again. 'Shannon, can I give you what really is just some friendly advice?'

'I'm always looking for friendly advice.' She started to pace the room.

'If you, or anyone you know, has some information about the past, present or possibly future whereabouts of Richard Croft, I strongly suggest you don't keep it to yourselves. Because if somebody was thinking of taking the law into their own hands—'

'What?' Thank goodness Finbar had not done anything about Croft. Casey couldn't possibly know what she had discussed with Curtis. Could he? Could she really trust Curtis? If not, it was too late now. 'Who exactly is *somebody* supposed to be?' she snapped. 'Me? Do you think I've got some mad scheme to find Croft and recapture him all by myself? You can't be that stupid. And if you're referring to Finbar Linnell, my partner, the law's taken *him* into *its* hands. Wrongly, as it happens.'

'I heard about him being arrested.' Casey paused. 'I just wonder who the hell gave you that very timely and accurate tip-off.'

'You and me both.' Shannon was starting to sweat. 'But hey, don't worry. I won't try to defend myself against a murderer, or anything. I mean, he might get hurt, and we have to think of the criminal's rights, don't we?

'Calm down, OK? I wasn't—'

'Don't tell me to calm down! I'll calm down when you and your precious team have put Croft back in prison so that I don't have to feel terrified for my life every minute of every day. You've got no idea what I'm going through.'

'I have. Shannon, please—'

'Get stuffed.' She hung up, trembling with rage and fright. Her mobile rang again and she switched the phone off. Mi-Hae Kam walked in, shrugging off her raincoat. She dumped her bag and a bundle of files on her desk and smoothed her long, shiny, damp, black hair.

'Bloody weather.' She glanced at Shannon. 'You look upset,' she remarked. 'More upset, that is.'

'Bloody police.' Shannon turned away and stared out of the window again. 'One of them in particular.' Casey was not

184

stupid. It unnerved her to think that what he suspected might actually have happened. Oh Curtis, she thought. When are you going to deliver? I've got to get Finbar out. The waiting was driving her mad.

'I'm glad you're here,' Mi-Hae said. 'I've been wanting to have a chat. Shannon, why don't you take some time off?'

Shannon turned, surprised. 'I just did.'

'I'm not talking about a weekend. Something a bit more long term is what I had in mind.'

'I see.' She had been expecting this. 'My work's OK. Isn't it?'

'It's fine.' Mi-Hae smiled. 'No worries there. Except that I think you could be overdoing things. You've got a lot to cope with at the moment.'

'You're so right. That's why coming to work is a holiday.'

Mi-Hae looked at her, considering. 'I'm going to get myself some tea. Can I bring you anything?'

'No thanks, I just had coffee.'

'OK. Sit down, why don't you? I'll be back in a minute.'

She knew what was coming, Shannon thought. Stressed out, tired, in a dangerous situation, publicity not good for firm's image, possible risk to colleagues, especially after break-in. Stay away until it's all over – or stay away permanently. She considered Mi-Hae and Khalida friends as well as business partners, and they had stuck by her and given her a lot of support during past crises. But had their sticking and supporting powers become exhausted? They had never talked to her about her relationship with Finbar, or not much. But now that he had been arrested and charged with murder, did they believe he was guilty? And wouldn't it look very bad for one of their partners to be having a relationship with a known criminal?

'Let me save you time and trouble,' she said as Mi-Hae came back with her tea and sat at the polished oval table they used for meetings. 'You want to get shut of me, right? It's OK, I don't blame you. I don't see who else is going to want one of Liverpool's most notorious solicitors in their firm, so I guess

I'll have to set up as a one-woman operation in some high street in the sticks.'

'Shannon – I don't want to get shut of you, as you put it. Neither does Khalida. We were just wondering how best to help you, that's all. And OK, yes, ourselves. Your life could be at risk from Richard Croft. He broke in here and stole our office address book – he knows where everybody who works here lives! I'm not saying we're at risk too, and neither are the police, but who knows what a monster like Richard Croft might do? I know it's very frightening for you, you're most at risk. But it's not exactly pleasant for us either.'

'No.' Shannon felt guilty and selfish for not having given that any thought. She had been so preoccupied with her own terror. And now with Finbar's arrest.

'It's chaotic here,' Mi-Hae went on. 'Don't think I'm blaming you, this isn't your fault, but Helena tells me there's been a lot of calls from journalists asking about you and wanting interviews. It's interfering with the work, the daily routine. People who need to call us for good reasons can't get through.'

Wanda bloody Brennan, Shannon thought. She had lost all sympathy for her.

'You've done great, continuing to manage your caseload. I do appreciate that. But I'm afraid there's another matter – the most delicate one.' Mi-Hae took a sip of tea. 'You can guess what that is, I think.'

'It's not great publicity for the Kam Flinder Najeba firm for one partner to be the partner of a man who just got arrested and charged with murder.' Shannon paused. 'Even if he's not guilty.'

'Guilty or not … yes, this is really awkward. Shannon, your relationships are your own business. Or they would be normally. But you can see in this case … it's not just this murder charge. Finbar Linnell does have something of a repu-tation. I know nothing was ever proved against him.' Until now, Mi-Hae thought. 'And he's a got a perfectly legitimate business and everything. But this latest thing doesn't help. Most of all it doesn't help *you*.'

186

'Would it be less awkward if Finbar got released and the charge dropped?' If only she could snap her fingers and make that happen, Shannon thought.

'Maybe. But people might still think there was no smoke without fire. There could be a lot of unpleasant gossip – about Finbar and therefore you. There's been enough talk about you in the past – again, not that it was your fault – and now that could start again.'

Shannon felt angry. 'Well, if we all had to regulate our lives in accordance with how people might or might not *gossip*—'

'Come on, Shannon. You're not that disingenuous. This is a law firm and one of the partners is having a relationship with a murder suspect. You can see how that looks. I know things are pretty tough for you now, and that's not your fault. Richard Croft should never have been allowed to escape. But I also have to think about this firm. Its reputation, the security of the people who work here.' She reached across the table and held Shannon's hand. 'I do *not* want to get rid of you, please understand that. You do great work, you're a very good solicitor and we don't want to lose you. But I do think it would be a good idea if you took some time off, stayed away until this is all over.'

'You mean until the police have recaptured Croft and the local media lose interest in me and my chequered life?'

'Exactly. We'll divide your caseload between ourselves – or try to. Hopefully this won't be for too long.' Mi-Hae smiled and let go of her hand. Her smile faded. 'You should also stay away until ... well, until the other situation is resolved. One way or another.'

Shannon's face was reddened and tearstained. She stared at Mi-Hae. 'Finbar?'

'Look, I know this is none of my business, but ... Shannon, I really like Finbar. He's kind, great fun, and it's obvious he really loves you. I can see how you fell for him. But given his past, his reputation, and what's happened now ... think of the effect on your career, not to say your personal life, of continuing to have a relationship with a man who's been charged with

187

and might be found guilty of murder? I'm saying this to you as your friend,' she said as Shannon got up, grim faced. 'Think about it, Shannon, please. Think of yourself, your own interests. What will you do if Finbar gets sent to prison?'

'I don't know what I'll do, Mi-Hae,' Shannon said slowly. 'I haven't a clue.'

'That chicken curry was shite,' Dennis King complained as he stacked his tray. 'Scran like that must be a violation of some section of the Human Rights Act.'

'Well, you'd know, Dennis.' The young, easy-going warder, a new guy and one of the few screws Dennis had any respect for, smiled. 'You spend enough time with your gob buried in those law books.'

'Got to make sure I know my rights, haven't I?'

'Isn't it a bit late for that now that you're stuck in here?'

'Doesn't mean I can't try to get out sooner rather than later though, eh?' Dennis yawned and stretched. 'Right. I fancy a game of pool then a spot of telly.'

Dennis did not have a small television set in his cell, unlike some other jammy sods, because he had not qualified for that luxury under the Incentives and Earned Privileges Scheme. He also wanted to phone his wife, because he was worried. Megan was a crap letter writer so he didn't expect much communication from her that way, plus he hated the thought of whatever she wrote being looked over by some snotty little censor before he got to read it.

Megan had not visited him last month, and every time he spoke to her on the phone she sounded like she couldn't be bothered. Nothing was wrong, she said, she was just tired a lot, and fed up. As if she thought he wasn't fed up, stuck in here being told what to eat, wear and do every bloody minute of every day. Dennis did not want to jump to obvious conclusions, but he had a nasty feeling Megan might have found herself some male companionship to help her through the chill, dark, autumnal evenings. She didn't like being on her own, never had. It scared her.

188

'Sorry, Dennis.' Colin, the screw, shook his head. 'Early lock-up, I'm afraid. No Association tonight, due to staff shortages.'

Dennis looked at him in dismay. 'But it's only half bloody six.'

'Association' as it was known, when prisoners met to watch television, play pool or snooker, talk to one another, take showers and make phone calls, was a privilege not a right. And this privilege was being denied more and more often lately.

'Sorry,' Colin repeated, shrugging. 'Nothing I can do about it, mate. Question of supply and demand, isn't it? Prison warder's not most people's dream job.'

Dennis had been given a Category A rating and locked in this high-security jail more than a year ago, having been moved there from a local Merseyside prison after he had been sentenced. He did not want to think about the years he had left to serve – even after being the model con and earning every possible bloody privilege going – because it panicked the hell out of him. The only star on his horizon was his statement about how Finbar Linnell had murdered Declan Dowd.

Dennis did not know if that was true, of course, and he didn't care. He was sure the other two gang members in prison – not this prison, but which one he didn't know – would not contradict him if the police spoke to them as well, because they too hated Linnell and would have liked to kill him when they had the chance. Blick, their leader, had been shot dead after they had kidnapped Linnell and tried to blow up that shopping mall. If it hadn't been for Linnell they would have got away. All along the bastard had been in on a sting. In the end Finbar Linnell had escaped from Blick at the last minute, shooting him dead in the process and being allowed to call it self-defence.

When the police came to tell him Declan Dowd's body had been discovered more than a year after his family had reported him missing, and did he know anything about the circumstances of Dowd's death, Dennis seized his chance and stuck the blame on Finbar Linnell. He hinted he knew more about Linnell than he did, hoping he could cut a deal. They wouldn't release him – he wasn't stupid enough to think that – but he might be able to get himself transferred somewhere where the regime was more relaxed, be granted more privileges and get some time shaved off his sentence. That was the best he could hope for, and he would go for it.

Dennis walked slowly back to his cell. He felt restless, did not fancy hitting any law books this evening. He was getting bored with them anyway. It had kept him going for a while, and he had even thought about trying to do a law degree, not being unaware of the irony of that. But he was not motivated enough. He would start that thriller he'd got from the library. Might even try a bit of writing himself. Some prisons – not this one – had creative writing courses run by real bestselling authors, some of them women. Be good to get on one of those. The woman or the course? Dennis laughed to himself, then thought of Megan again. The last time he'd seen her she had had her hair done, blonde highlights, her nails manicured, and had lost so much weight that she could fit into a pair of size ten jeans for the first time in years. She said the weight loss had happened because she didn't cook big meals any more, just nibbled sand-wiches, fresh fruit and salad. She didn't drink much either, just the occasional glass of wine.

Dennis was sitting on his bed contemplating the thriller – the book had a sexy, dark-haired heroine on the cover that the blurb said had just got out of jail, lucky her – when Colin appeared in the doorway. Smiling as usual. The sight of that smile reassured Dennis. Not many people smiled in here, certainly not with warmth and friendliness. They only smiled when they did you down.

'Here comes the turnkey.' Colin held up his keys. 'All set for the night, mate?'

'No. I fancy going down the pub.'

'Well, you can do that in your imagination.' Colin glanced at the sexy heroine on the book cover. 'Do a lot of things in your imagination.'

Dennis sighed. Colin stepped back and glanced along the landing then walked into the cell, partially closing the door. His big teeth looked a bit yellow against his pale skin and frizzy red hair. He was tall and scrawny, his uniform loose on him. He took a sealed envelope from his inside pocket and tore it open.

'What's that?'

It occurred to Dennis, not without great dismay, that Colin might be going to offer him drugs, and he was one of the few people in here who would not appreciate that offer. The thought of it made him feel sick, especially with all that was at stake for him now. Any con could be picked at random and made to give a urine sample, and it would be just his luck to get pounced on. So how could he decline without giving Colin the hump?

'Hey listen, mate, sorry, but I'm not cool with—' He cringed and ducked to one side as Colin suddenly upended the envelope over his head. A tiny cloud of what he could only think looked like hair cuttings floated over him. But they were not hair cuttings. 'What the hell are you doing? What is this?' Dennis brushed his shoulders and scratched a finger, drawing blood. 'Oww. What are these things?'

'A chopped-up tiger's whiskers, mate. Razor sharp, they are, like little needles or piranha teeth. Some poor bastard eats them mixed in with their food – like that chicken curry you just managed to stuff two helpings of even though you said it was shite – and a couple of days later they die in agony and the doctors aren't any the wiser. The whiskers perforate – that means pierce – their way through your guts. No cure. Just death.'

'*What*?' Dennis' heart started to pound.

'Somebody once thought of trying to kill Hitler that way,' Colin went on, 'only they didn't have a tiger handy.' His smile did not seem friendly any more; Dennis was seeing him in a whole new light. 'Better than Miss Marple, isn't it?' He nodded at the book. 'You don't need thrillers, mate, not when you've got the real thing in here.'

Dennis was dry mouthed, his heart racing. He felt himself turn pale with shock. 'What's going on?' He tried to laugh, but only managed a humiliating croak. 'You're bullshitting me. Where would you get tiger's whiskers anyway?'

'Mate of mine's a keeper at Chester Zoo. If you don't believe what I'm telling you about what those things can do, look it up in one of your sodding library books.' Colin stepped closer. 'Point is though, this is a message. The message is that you're surrounded by some very pissed-off people – Finbar Linnell and some mates of his. And if you don't unpiss them off quick sharp, Dennis, you are fucked. They're powerful people, and you're nothing. You'll be dead long before any tiger's whiskers get the chance to work their way through your stinking guts.' Colin laughed.

'What does he ... do they ... want?' Of course Dennis knew. He should have known his little scheme wouldn't work. Nothing ever bloody did work out for him. He hadn't been thinking – why didn't he ever bloody think? He trembled, his breath coming in gasps.

'What do you fucking think Finbar Linnell and his mates want, you moron?' Colin opened the cell door and checked the landing again, then stepped back inside and grabbed Dennis by the hair. He shoved him against the wall.

'Finbar Linnell,' he hissed. 'It's your word against his, nothing more. And you lied. You're one miserable, lying little bastard.'

'I ... I ... please don't...!'

'Don't what? Kill you? If you don't want to die, Dennis, tell the cops you lied. Tell them *now*.'

Chapter Eighteen

Matty Rice weaved his way along the pavement towards the house in Princes Park where he had his flat, swearing and dropping his chips as he went. He was still in shock after being grilled for hours by the filth about that old bloke he had been supposed to meet earlier today in the pub, the moron who he now knew was an escaped psycho who had murdered two women. It made Matty shake with fear to think of it, even now after he'd had a skinful. He would bloody well let the cops know if he saw the bastard again. But he hoped he wouldn't see him.

He'd been lucky, Matty thought; the cops were so wound up about this psycho – Croft, his real name was – that they hadn't even thought to search his flat. If they had found his prized possession, the revolver he'd bought a couple of weeks ago from some Romanian guy he'd met in a dockside bar, he'd be locked up now and looking at a five-year stretch. Matty had boasted about the revolver to the psycho – it made him shiver to think of that. As it was, he had been charged with stealing a passport and bailed to appear in court next Monday. Matty had also been thick enough – and frightened enough – to admit he'd been going to sell the passport to this Croft. He had stolen it from an old American guy, a tourist who'd been walking around the Albert Dock with his wife.

The police had promised he wouldn't be in too much trouble because he had cooperated with them about Croft. What had they called it? Mitigating circumstances? No, something else he couldn't remember. But Matty felt sure he was still looking at a stretch of some kind as this wasn't the first time he'd been done for theft, amongst other things. It was no use not turning up at court, as he'd done once before, because then he would be in even bigger trouble. He could do a runner, but where would he go? And suppose he turned up at court and got let off because of the mitigating circumstances or whatever? He would have scuppered himself for nothing. He had to think about it. But not tonight, he was too knackered. And ratarsed. He had to get rid of the revolver as well.

'Yep,' he muttered, giving up on the chips and tossing the greasy parcel in a nearby rubbish bin, 'a good night's sleep, that's what you need.'

Matty supposed he also had to consider himself lucky that this Croft hadn't done anything to him, given the fact that he'd screwed him out of two hundred and fifty quid and had intended to screw him for more. You never knew who you might be dealing with. He hadn't asked for enough either. Someone he had got talking to in a bar the other night had told him you could charge eight hundred quid for a passport.

He rooted in his jeans and jacket pockets, looking for his cigarettes. And his keys, because he was home sweet home. He lit a cigarette and let himself in, went up the stairs on hands and knees. The bloody landing light wasn't working again. He had to get out of this dump. He stuck the key in the door, stumbled in and snapped on the light. His mobile rang and he pulled the phone from his jacket pocket.

'Matty? It's me, Debbie.' His sister. 'I've had the baby.'

He frowned and blinked, swaying. 'You *wha*'?'

'I said, I've had the baby. What's up, have you been on the piss again?' Debbie's voice was high, excited, and she was laughing. 'It's a little boy. He's gorgeous. I might name him after you and ask you to be godfather if you stay off the pints long enough to stand up in church and promise to save him from the Devil.'

'Godfather?' Matty started to laugh. 'How'd you know I won't stick a horse's head in his cot?'

'You daft sod. Oh Matty, he's lovely, he really is. Uncle Matty!'

Matty could not imagine himself as someone's uncle. It sounded old, boring and responsible, and he was none of those things. Well, boring, maybe. He laughed again and took a drag on his cigarette.

'So how...?' He was about to ask Debbie how she was and what was an uncle supposed to do, and what should he get the baby for a Christening present when time suddenly seemed to freeze and he was stuck there like a statue, unable to get the words out. Matty dropped his cigarette. He heard heavy breathing, an animal grunt that sounded like the animal was in pain.

What the fuck was happening? He realised he'd been hit on the back of the head. When he was hit a second time Matty staggered forward, his legs giving way. He fell, arms flung out, and bashed his head against a sharp corner of the smoked-glass coffee table. A tattered copy of *Loaded* slid off and fell on him. He lay there, face against the carpet, stunned and disoriented.

He became conscious of a malignant presence. Someone was moving around the flat, going from room to room, opening cupboards and drawers, throwing things on the floor. Matty could hear Debbie's voice from a long way off, calling to him, asking what was wrong. He could hear a baby screaming, his newborn nephew. Blood flowed, trickled into his eyes. He blinked, unable to focus. A dark shadow came closer, grew bigger. Matty groaned in panic when he realised it was Croft the psycho standing over him.

'You little shit.' Croft trod on the mobile, crushing it, cutting off Debbie's frantic voice and the baby's wails. His eyes looked blank, not angry. Matty would have preferred anger. On the carpet lay what looked like a chair leg, one end of it covered with blood. Croft must have hit him with that. Matty closed his eyes and opened them again, trying to blink away the blood.

He saw that Croft had hold of his stash of cash, at least five hundred quid, and the revolver. Shit. Why hadn't he hidden them properly, instead of leaving them in that drawer? There was nothing else of any value in the flat, Croft must know that now. So what was the bastard waiting for? Why didn't he piss off? Matty started to shake with terror, his powerless limbs twitching. Would Debbie call the police? He prayed that she would. Matty hadn't prayed since infant school. How long would it take them to get here?

Who was going to save him from the Devil?

Cindy Nightingale glanced over her shoulder, expecting to see some glam girl or a thinner, prettier, younger woman behind her, then looked back across the bar. No, there did not seem to be anyone else at whom the tall, dark, well-dressed, gorgeous-looking man could be smiling – not unless he was a Granny Grabber. As if wanting to dispel her remaining doubts, the man smiled at her again and raised his glass in a salute. Cindy was sure she had never met him, because how could any warm-blooded hetero female forget a face and body like that? Her heart beat faster and she felt herself flush.

His smile was warm, friendly and admiring, as opposed to the nasty smirks some of her colleagues had been pissing her off with since about four this afternoon. Cindy did not know what *that* was all about. When she had asked what was going on, the smirks had turned to laughter. Some bullshit joke or piece of gossip about her must be doing the rounds – it wouldn't be the first time. Just before she left work she had received a message to say that the Super wanted to see her first thing in the morning. No reason given. Cindy had the uneasy feeling that it wasn't to discuss a promotion. But what had she done? Or not done? Nothing she could think of.

'Hi. I'm Ewan.'

She jumped. The guy was by her side now and looked even more tasty close up. He held out his hand and she hesitated then took it. She even managed a smile. It was hard not to smile at him.

'Mind if I come and chat to you?'

'Not at all.' Cindy was still smarting over Finbar Linnell's controlled and contemptuous rejection of her, and this Ewan was definitely what the doctor had ordered to soothe wounded female pride. Linnell was going to get what was coming to him anyway. And about bloody time.

'You're not waiting for somebody?'

'I'm always waiting for *somebody*.'

He laughed. 'Want to tell me your name?

'Cindy. Cindy Nightingale.'

He looked into her eyes. 'Pleased to meet you, Cindy.'

She smirked. 'Charmed, I'm sure.'

Of course the second she told him she was a cop, that might scupper the beautiful friendship thing. And Cindy was still suspicious. She wasn't bad looking, but this guy could take his pick, and why would he pick her? He might have a wife, girl-friend, several girlfriends. Kids, dog, guinea pig. God knew what. This seemed too good to be true.

'You haven't seen me before, have you?' she asked. 'You don't know me?'

'No. But I'd certainly like to.'

She couldn't stop herself. 'Why?'

He laughed. 'I can see you're bursting with self-confidence. No reason, really. Just that you seem like an attractive, sexy, interesting-looking woman with whom a lot of men might want to form a deep and lasting attachment. I'm sure you've got an evil sense of humour as well.'

'And you've obviously got all the chat, you smooth git. Still,' Cindy sighed, 'that makes a refreshing change from the kind of inarticulate, unreconstructed morons I'm forced to deal with on a daily basis.'

'That's a shame. What d'you do, Cindy?'

Here it comes, she thought. Oh well. 'I'm a police officer,' she said, watching his expression. 'A CID inspector, to be precise.'

'Oh.'

'Yes. *Oh.*' Cindy leaned one elbow on the bar and pointed at the door. 'This is where you suddenly remember an urgent appointment and piss off for ever. It's OK.' Well, no, it wasn't. 'I understand. Won't be the first time.'

She didn't see any point in lying; if this was going to go anywhere he would have to know what she did, and it might as well be sooner rather than later. Besides, men's reactions when she told them about her brilliant career were usually a good gauge of honourable – or dishonourable – intent.

'It's fine.' Ewan shrugged. 'An inspector? I'm impressed.' He smiled. 'I can't remember any urgent appointments. Can I say something unreconstructed?'

'Yeah, go on. Spoil yourself.'

'You don't look like a police officer. Or how I imagined a lady police officer would look.'

'A *lady* police officer? Groan groan.' Cindy laughed. 'So what do you think I look like then? A librarian?

'Definitely not that.'

'Rocket scientist? Owner of a dating agency?'

'Some sort of businesswoman. High polish, high maintenance.'

'High polish?' She batted her eyelashes at him. 'That'll do me.' Cindy was glad she'd had her hair cut and conditioned and her nails done. She was wearing her favourite slimming black trouser suit again. She finished her vodka-and-tonic.

'If I can ask a delicate question, are you attached?'

'Only to my job.' She sighed again. 'All work and no play, that's me in a nutshell.'

'Time you bust out of it then.' Ewan looked at her glass. 'Another drink?'

'As long as you don't plan to give it a kick with some cunning chemical concoction that'll make me lose my inhibitions and short-term memory.' He looked a bit offended, and she hoped she hadn't gone too far.

'Being a police officer, I suppose you hear a lot of bad stories and get cynical.'

'Well, let's say you get careful. Realistic.'

'Yes. But don't lose perspective because in your work you mostly come across the sad and bad people. Speaking of which, it's not exactly flattering to feel that the only way you can get someone to lose their inhibitions is to drug them.'

'You're so right.' Cindy really liked this guy, although it was all happening very quickly. Ewan signalled to the girl behind the bar and ordered two large vodka-and-tonics with slice but no ice.

'So tell me about you.' Cindy took a big swig of her drink to help steady her nerves. 'All I know is your first name.' And that I want to shag you.

'Why not let me tell you over dinner? My treat. Your favourite restaurant.'

Over a fab champagne dinner at an Albert Dock restaurant – the kind of place Shannon Flinder probably went to a lot, Cindy thought resentfully as she took her seat at the table – Ewan told her he was a 39-year-old businessman, owner of an import-export company who lived on the Isle of Man but wanted to relocate back to Liverpool for business and family reasons. The 'family reasons' consisted of his newly widowed mother and a twelve-year-old son who lived with Ewan's ex-wife. His ex was remarried now and Ewan wanted to see more of Greg, his son. It all sounded pretty plausible and Cindy was becoming more attracted to him by the minute. That did not mean she wasn't going to check him out as soon as she got to work tomorrow morning.

Work. The only thing to nag and needle her on this otherwise magical evening. What the hell did the Super want to see her about? She hadn't done anything wrong, had she? Or nothing he could have found out about. No one knew she was feeding bits of info to that journalist, Wanda Brennan.

Why had those bastards been laughing at her this afternoon? OK, as a female inspector she was a target for lots of men with jealous grudges and various-sized chips on their padded shoulders. Although some of the women were worse; it was as if they wanted to drag her back down to their level as she tried to smash her way through the old glass ceiling. But what the hell could this be about? As Ewan signalled to a waiter to order a second bottle of champagne, the answer hit her. It was so obvious that Cindy couldn't think why it had not occurred to her sooner.

Shannon Flinder, of course. Who else? The bitch had tried to interfere in the Jenny Fong murder inquiry from the word go, sticking her bloody oar in and trying to tell the police – Cindy in particular – how to do their job. Whinging and whining about scene of crime shit, bloody footprints and the like, chewing people's ears about so-called leads that in her almighty opinion should be checked out *now*. Labelling Jevko Arib a bleedingly obvious pop-up suspect, as if they didn't have more than enough evidence to convict him. Had Flinder interfered some more? Cindy wondered. Perhaps she'd got something somebody had overlooked, batted her eyelashes and flashed her tits at some senior officer? That would be typical.

Cindy got a hot flush of enraged panic, followed by a cold one. Calm down, for Christ's sake, she told herself. Flinder can't do anything. What the hell would she find out anyway? I've made sure it's access *no* areas, as far as she's concerned. I bet she's tried to drop me in it though. But how? Whatever it was, she had to talk her way out of it. She clenched one hand under the table, plucking at the fabric of her trousers. Didn't Shannon Flinder have enough to worry about, with her precious boyfriend locked up facing a murder charge, and a psycho after her?

The pop of the champagne cork jolted her back to the here and now. Ewan was staring at her. 'Something wrong? You seem very tense all of a sudden.'

'No. Nothing's wrong.' Cindy managed a twisted smile. 'Well, OK. I did just think of a problem I've got at work. Or might have.' He poured fresh champagne into her glass; she picked the glass up and swallowed half. 'I won't bore you with it.'

'Please. I'm interested. Really,' he persisted as she looked disbelieving. 'Go on.'

'I can't name names, of course, or go into case details. But there's this solicitor who hates me.' Ewan refilled her glass and she drank more champagne. This stuff was all right, if a bit overrated; it could do with a shot of vodka to give it a kick. 'She's got some stupid grudge against me. She's always trying to make trouble, interfere in any investigation I'm involved in. She's been doing that for some time.' Cindy frowned. 'Something weird happened this afternoon, and I'm worried. I'm sure she's behind it. Being a lawyer, she's got some powerful friends.' Roy Gardner, for one, the barrister who Shannon had got to come rushing to Finbar Linnell's aid. 'She's a hell of a flirt too. Twists men around her little finger, as they say. You can't believe it until you see it happening.' Cindy put down her glass. She was dying for a cigarette, but Ewan didn't smoke and she didn't want to repel him. 'She just does it for fun – to use them. And they fall for it, believe she really likes them. They get let down big style. Sha—' Cindy stopped. *No names, stoopid.* 'She only cares about herself and what she wants.'

'Sounds like bad news.' Ewan smiled. 'Want me to kill her for you?'

'Yes, please.' Cindy laughed, 'That would be fantastic. Friends for life. I'll buy you dinner next time.' She blushed, cursing herself. How did she know he would want there to be a next time? But Ewan didn't seem to mind.

'You're not exactly powerless yourself though, are you?' He ate the last gamba wrapped in prosciutto and pushed his plate away. 'Can't you cause any trouble for her? I'd imagine there must be quite a few ways in which a Detective Inspector could make life difficult for a solicitor.' He paused. 'If not impossible.'

Cindy hesitated. She would have loved to launch into a rant about Shannon Flinder, but that would be highly unclever. She didn't want to put this guy off. She realised she very much wanted there to be a next time. She felt amazingly comfortable with Ewan Morrison. Comfortable, but at the same time bloody excited. She smiled at him across the table, thinking of what she'd like to do to him and have him do to her. Cindy had a great feeling of promise about to be thrillingly fulfilled.

'You're right,' she nodded. 'There's a lot I can do to make her life difficult. And believe me, I am certainly working on that.'

'Good for you. Think you can get a result soon?'

'I already got one actually, although that wasn't down to me.' Cindy meant Finbar Linnell's arrest for murder. 'And I've got other ways to shaft her. She's in for a big shock,' she said, thinking of the article Wanda Brennan had written.

'Glad to hear it.' Ewan reached across the table and took her hand. An electric thrill shot through Cindy. Bloody hell, she thought, if he makes me feel like this by just holding my hand...! 'Fancy a pudding?' he asked. He stroked her fingers and played with her smooth, shiny nails. 'I noticed earlier they had lemon tart on the menu. I've got a thing about lemon tart. If it's not up to standard I trash the place.'

'I'm like that about Crême Brulèe if the caramel layer isn't cracky enough.'

They did not have everything in common, but why should they? Ewan liked classical music, Mozart in particular, and classical music bored the hell out of Cindy. Ditto golf, cricket and reading. He liked literary fiction, thrillers and crime novels.

'And now I've met my very own, real live detective.' He kept hold of her hand. 'Don't suppose you need to unwind with a crime novel while you soak in perfumed bubbles after a long, mad day?'

Cindy liked the idea of soaking in perfumed bubbles with him. 'Unwind is the last thing crime novels would make me do,' she laughed. 'I'd probably go crazy at all the stuff the authors got wrong. I bet most of them are Miss Marple types who've never set foot in a prison or police station.' She paused. 'Or lawyer's office.'

When Ewan asked her back to his five-star waterfront hotel for a nightcap it seemed the most natural thing in the world, not tacky at all. Especially as Cindy had downed two large cognacs after they had finished the champagne. She was also drunk with happiness, happiness she had not felt in a long time. What incredible luck to meet someone like Ewan, even more incredible to think he fancied her too. They walked back to his hotel and stopped several times to kiss deeply and passionately. It felt wonderful, a hell of a lot better than Cindy's last kiss, an anonymous, drunken, desperate snog and grope at a New Year party – the only one she'd got invited to – which had left her feeling violated and so lonely. The difference between that and this brought tears to her eyes. Ewan looked at her in the darkness, stroking her hair, her face, her lips.

'You're gorgeous,' he whispered.

'So are you.'

'I have to go back tomorrow, but I'll phone you. I'll be in Liverpool again next week. Once I've bought a place and moved back we can see more of each other. Would you like that?'

'I would bloody love that.'

'Stay with me tonight?'

'Oh, yes.' The most natural thing. She thought of how even her mother would like Ewan, and her mother never liked anyone Cindy went out with, saying her daughter only picked riff-raff because she thought she couldn't do any better. Cindy was done with riff-raff now though, well and truly.

In the big, subtly lit hotel room she bounced giggling on the king-size bed, popped into the luxurious red marble bathroom for a much-needed pee while Ewan poured them more cognac, then stared out at the river lights while she drank it. He took off his jacket and wrapped his arms around her, murmuring how beautiful and sexy she was and how he couldn't believe his luck. Cindy wanted to say she couldn't believe hers either, but she wasn't quite drunk enough for that – although she was starting to feel a bit dizzy. She would have one hell of a hangover in the morning.

She felt momentary unease at the thought of Ewan seeing her naked in the unforgiving morning light, pale, sick and hungover, eyeliner and mascara encrusted around bloodshot eyes. Cindy dismissed her fears. It didn't matter, nothing mattered. This was bigger than wrinkles and encrusted mascara. This man cared about her, she could tell.

Ewan laid her on the bed and started to gently pull off her clothes. Cindy's dizziness increased until it seemed as if the room was revolving, and she hoped she was not going to have to spoil the romantic ambiance by dashing to the bathroom to throw up. Damn, she thought, why don't you fucking drink less? Cindy sometimes worried about her drinking, if not enough to do anything about it. She gasped as she felt Ewan's hands and mouth on her breasts, his tongue circling her hardened nipples.

'I feel a bit weird,' she muttered, trying and failing to raise her head.

'Well, you look fantastic.' He slid off her knickers and tossed them on the floor. She was naked now. Her eyelids felt as if weights from old-fashioned scales were pressing them shut. Her whole body felt weighed down.

'Have you got a...?' She was about to say, have you got a condom, even though it was a bit bloody late now to ask that vital question. She didn't have one – she had long since given up carrying them around. But surely it would be OK with Ewan. Now it seemed that her lips wouldn't move, or her voice work. She couldn't finish the sentence.

Cindy passed out.

She woke gasping and groaning to depressing grey light, dry-mouthed and sweating in the overheated room. Her head was still spinning. She tried to sit up then slumped back against the pillow. Her head wasn't just spinning, it was splitting. But when her mouth filled with saliva and she knew she would have to throw up, Cindy had to move. She crawled out of bed and staggered into the bathroom. It was only when she had flushed the toilet a couple of times and was hunched over the double sink rinsing her mouth with cold water, wiping her streaming eyes and thinking what a horrific sight she looked, that she realised Ewan was not there.

She staggered back into the bedroom, the headache so awful that she could hardly bear to stand. She collapsed into bed again, wrapping herself in the quilt. Did she have any paracetamol in her bag? She felt too ill to get up again and go to the dressing table where it lay. The green dial of the bedside radio clock said 06.21. Could she face going into work today? And where the hell was Ewan? Had she even shagged him? She couldn't remember a bloody thing. Cindy broke out in a sweat and started to feel sick again. Oh God. Someone pounded on the door.

'Police. Open up.'

'*What*?' She sat up again, gasping with shock. What was going on? Where was Ewan? The *police*? Cindy tried not to panic, tried to tell herself there must be some simple explanation why he was not in bed with her. Well, yeah. Her handsome hero had done a runner. How simple did it have to be?

Maybe Ewan had got bored when she passed out. That hadn't been the most romantic thing she could have done. Or had he had to leave early and not wanted to wake her? She couldn't remember him saying he had to leave early, but what in fact did she actually remember? She looked for a note on the bedside table, but there was nothing, not even a business card. What the bloody hell did the police want? The knocking came again, louder and more insistent.

'Open up. Now, please. Come on.'

'Jesus Chr...!' Cindy glanced frantically around looking for a robe or her clothes, but there was nothing. Ewan's clothes were gone. 'Where are my fucking *clothes*?' She couldn't even see her shoes. The quilt was too heavy, so she tried to pull off the bottom sheet and wrap that around her naked body. Before she could do it the door was unlocked by a nervous, blonde, hotel girl in a black suit, and three uniforms burst in.

'What the hell is this?'

To her horror Cindy recognised one of them – Lola Hanlon, a sergeant she hadn't seen in a while because Lola had transferred out. Lola hated her guts because Cindy had once stolen a boyfriend of hers. Lola stopped and stared, then a grin spread over her face.

'Well, look who's here. Inspector Nightingale. What a surprise. We had a report of a disturbance in this room,' she said. 'Drugs being used.'

'*Drugs*? That's crazy.' Cindy managed to cover her breasts with the sheet. What the hell had happened to her clothes? Had

205

Ewan packed them by mistake? But how could he have done that? She couldn't believe he would have deliberately taken them. How was she supposed to get out of here, go home wearing nothing but a damn sheet? She sweated with humiliation and horror. 'You've got the wrong room.'

'Wrong room?' Lola strolled to the other end of the junior suite and stood looking down at the scattered white powder and red-striped straws on the coffee table. The grin didn't leave her face. 'I think not.'

Cindy stared in shock, one hand clamped to her sweating forehead, the other holding the sheet above tit level. She had been so desperate to make it to the bathroom in time, so busy wondering where the hell Ewan could have got to that she hadn't even noticed that stuff lying there. She didn't do drugs, she wasn't that stupid. She had smoked a bit of skunk in her younger days, but that was it. Alcohol was her poison of choice. And my God, had it poisoned her last night. Cindy still did not understand though; she never got so drunk that she passed out.

New horror dawned. Had Ewan spiked her cognac? Actually done what she had joked about in the pub? No. It couldn't be. Had she fallen for that? The first decent – or seemingly decent – bloke who'd talked to her, and she literally fell into his arms because she was so pathetically needy and desperate? No, Cindy thought again. I'm not that stupid. If I am, someone can shoot me right now.

'This is all a terrible mistake,' she whispered. 'It was him, not me. I don't do drugs, I never have.' Tears rolled down her ravaged face. 'I don't understand!' But she did, of course she did. She just could not bring herself to believe it.

'All seems pretty damn clear to me, Inspector.' Lola was rummaging in Cindy's bag now. She drew out a tiny, clear plastic sachet full of white powder, and held it up. 'Oh dear. We have been a naughty girl, haven't we?'

'That's not mine,' Cindy sobbed. 'He must have planted it.'

'Jeez, such an original excuse. How did you think that one up?' Lola paused. 'Who's *he*?'

'This bloke I met last night in the pub. We had dinner then came back here. This is his room. His drugs. Oh God!'

'Chopping the Charlie with blokes you meet in pubs? What an exciting life you lead, Inspector Nightingale.' Lola laid the sachet on the dressing table and walked to the bed. She was laughing now. 'I've got more bad news. Should you feel you need it in these already humiliating and unfortunate circumstances.'

Cindy wiped her eyes, smudging mascara, and stared at her. 'What are you on about?'

'A mate phoned me last night to tell me something that gave me a right laugh. It's been giving a lot of people a right laugh. You know that camera in Mr Linnell's cell? The camera your one remaining little mate Terence said he'd switch off while you had your fun?' Lola stooped until their faces were almost touching. 'Well, hon,' she whispered. 'Terence isn't your mate and he didn't switch it off. There he was on another boring shift, and you hip-hopped along and made Christmas come early. You were a little too stupid there. But hey, fame at last. And no one thinks you don't *fully* deserve it.'

Cindy had to be sick again. This time she did not make it to the bathroom.

Chapter Nineteen

He experienced another of those moments when time just stopped. They were happening more often. Detached, terrified, disembodied, suspended in a grey, silent, misty miasma, cut off from everything and everybody. It was like he imagined drowning might be. He was drenched with sweat, struggling to breathe. Then it all changed and he was overwhelmed with light, noise, smells, everything coming at him at once.

He had chosen this corner of the café because it faced the beige wall, but he couldn't bear even that after a few minutes. He had to get out, go and lie in his darkened room and close himself off from all the terrible stimuli.

He could take a cab now he had the cash he'd nicked from that miserable lowlife Matty. What had he done? Was the little shit dead, or ... what? Richard could not think, did not want to know. It was done and that was that. He had to look forward, not back.

The cab driver thought he was pissed or on some good gear. Richard could still think clearly enough not to give the exact address. He climbed slowly out, leaving the door swinging, and walked off, the driver shouting and swearing after him. He groaned at the brightness of the afternoon sun, cringed in agony as a couple of shrieking gobshite kids ran past kicking a football. He reached his door and opened it, climbed the stairs and locked himself in. He drew the curtains and collapsed on the bed.

Julie's dead, staring eyes gave him a shock, then Shannon Flinder's face morphed on to his personal cinema screen. Her features were distorted, her dark-blue eyes and bright gold hair zig-zagging across his retinas. Richard raised himself on one elbow and reached for the bottle of water. He took three painkillers.

He could not think about Spain any more for now, or about getting his hands on a passport, or anything much really. He did not know where to go next or what to do. He had no energy to plan, could not even organise his thoughts into any kind of logical pattern. He had a feeling that time was running out. But he somehow knew he was not going back to jail.

He thought of Shannon Flinder, allowed the fat worm of hate and destruction that lay curled inside him to swell and grow as he gave it more nourishment. She had to die. She would die. He would kill her if it was the last thing he did.

'The last thing,' he muttered, his eyes closed.

Rest, sleep. Feel better. Go out again later. When it was dark. Richard tried to slow and deepen his breathing, let his aching head and body relax. He slid one hand beneath the lumpy pillow, felt the cold thing that lay there pressing against his cheek.

The gun.

'Matty Rice was hit with a chair leg,' DI Casey told a stunned Shannon, 'then strangled with the belt of his jeans. Croft's prints, his DNA, are all over Rice's flat. There's no doubt Croft killed him.'

Shannon nodded, trying to take in this latest horror. 'You didn't think this Matty Rice would be at risk from Croft?'

'No. Rice told us he only met Croft in pubs, that Croft had never been to his place and didn't know where he lived. Croft must have followed him.'

'My God. Another victim. Not just of Croft, but of the system's incompetence.' She felt like saying police incompetence. 'Well, thank you for letting me know. It's what I really needed to hear.' She slumped back on the sofa.

'What did you do today?' Casey glanced round her living room. 'Now that you're taking time off work?'

'What did I do today?' Shannon sat up again. 'Well, I watched my back every minute I was out, of course. Tried to speak to my partner, but the police wouldn't allow that. I avoided contact with anyone in case I put them as well as myself at risk from Croft. A friend asked me to have lunch, but I said better not. I even wondered if it was safe to get my hair and nails done.'

Her hair and nails looked great, Casey thought, as did the tight blue jeans and sexy purple top, but of course it wouldn't be appropriate to say that. And it was obvious Shannon was not enjoying her forced leave of absence from work. 'I like your place,' he said, looking around the big living room again. 'It's very nice.'

'Thank you.' She sipped her tea.

'D'you think you might get away for a few days?'

'What, you mean on holiday?'

'Not holiday, exactly. Just ... stay with a friend or relative. Someone who doesn't live in Liverpool, of course.'

'I might. Or not. It depends.'

Casey guessed she would not go anywhere while Finbar Linnell was banged up. Which meant she might not be going anywhere for a very long time. He was still wondering who had given her the tip-off about Croft meeting Matty Rice in that pub.

Shannon looked at him again. 'I don't suppose you've got any good news for me?' she asked, knowing the answer. 'In regard to my biggest and most immediate problem?'

'Sorry.' Casey shook his head. 'Still no sign of Croft. He could be holed up somewhere. In some bedsit, maybe. We're looking.'

Shannon's other big problem was Finbar, of course. He was about to be moved to a local prison and put on remand. She had not yet been allowed to see him, and she was trying to psych herself up, prepare herself for the horror of seeing someone she loved in prison, rather than clients towards whom she usually felt no more than mild pity and sometimes a desire to help. It was going to be tough. Especially now that it looked like her brilliant plan had failed. What was Curtis Bright up to?

210

The failure of her plan was bad enough. But what if Curtis had told somebody about their conversation the other night? What if he tried to blackmail her? She had risked everything – her career, her life. Shannon wondered if Casey was still suspicious about the anonymous tip-off.

She put down her cup. 'Why would Croft want to kill Matty Rice? And why am I even asking that? It's not like he ever needs a *reason*.'

Casey shrugged. 'Maybe Rice tried to rip him off. About the passport. Actually,' he began, 'I've got something else to tell you.'

'Oh God,' Shannon groaned. 'Go on then, make my day. Although I've got a feeling it won't.'

'We found some cartridges scattered on the floor in Rice's flat. From a revolver.'

'I didn't think you meant a fountain pen.'

'But there was no gun. So—'

'So Croft's got this gun?'

'Probably.'

'Terrific.' Shannon got up and walked to the window. 'OK. Well, if I'm forced to choose, I suppose I'd prefer a quick bullet as opposed to manual strangulation.' She turned. 'Thanks for dropping by. And for keeping up the concern and protection.'

Casey got up too. 'Thanks for the tea.'

'You're more than welcome.'

He looked at her, his expression hopeless, as if he wanted to repeat how he was doing all he could, and a lot of other people were doing all they could. But what was the point? He nodded to her.

'Take care.'

'I'm getting sick of that irritating admonition.'

'Yeah, you must be. Sorry.' He walked out.

Shannon looked at her watch. Six-thirty. She should barricade herself in for the night now, and make something to eat. But she wasn't hungry. She did not know what she wanted to do, apart from things she couldn't. Try and find

211

out where Richard Croft might be hiding? If the police couldn't, what chance did she have? Her mobile rang and she snatched it up.

'Hello. Meet me in our favourite pub in ten minutes,' Curtis said. 'Or can I come to your place? I've got something to share with you, and given the sensitive nature of it, complete privacy really would be best.'

'Is this a joke? Because I'm not in the mood.'

'Oh, you will be. For this, definitely.'

'All right,' Shannon sighed. 'My place. Ten bloody minutes.'

It was twenty before Curtis arrived. He spent another few minutes checking her apartment for bugs, although he said bugs were very much yesterday's technology.

'Clean,' he announced at last, smiling as Shannon drew the living-room curtains. 'You lucky girl. And you very sensibly don't have a great big mirror over your beautiful, ornate marble fireplace that somebody could use to beam – and I won't blind you with technie stuff here – *beams* on to.'

'Oh, thanks. I love it when people keep things simple for me. I presume you're talking about those directional parabolic microphone things?'

He stared at her. 'Want to give up the legal career and come and work for me?'

'Well, I'm certainly thinking about giving up the legal career.'

Curtis followed her into the kitchen and watched as she poured herself a glass of white wine and took a bag of crisps out of a cupboard. 'You look tired,' he commented. 'Pissed off. Another long, hard, mad day?'

'If you count going to the hairdresser and getting a mani-cure.' Shannon took a gulp of wine. 'But yes. Psycho still on the loose. He just murdered someone else to give himself more practice. My fiancé's still locked up on a murder charge because my brilliant plan to get him freed didn't work.' She got a slight shock as she realised she had referred to Finbar as her fiancé.

'Didn't work?' Curtis looked puzzled. 'I don't get it. I told you I could do it and I did. I know someone who's got a contact in that prison and he bribed that screw to threaten our Dennis. It was even easier than I thought it would be – I feel like I don't deserve to keep Finbar's money.'

Shannon stared at him. 'Are you sure it worked?'

'Yeah, 'course. I expected a result any time now.'

'Well, there's none that I can see.'

'Maybe you just need to be a bit patient.'

'I don't think patience is a virtue. Anyway, go on.' She crunched a crisp and sipped her wine. 'Put me in a good mood, like you promised on the phone.'

He grinned. 'You shouldn't say things like that. Might give me the wrong idea.'

'Just get on with it.'

'There you go again, you torturer. OK. This is going to be good. You might want to put those crisps down. I hope they're not your evening meal, by the way.'

'What's it to you?'

'I'm concerned, that's all.'

'Well, don't be.' She took her wine and the crisps and trailed after him back to the living room. Curtis took a brown A4 envelope from his briefcase and held it out to her. 'Go on,' he urged as she hesitated. 'Open it. It doesn't contain a snake.'

'What a relief.' Shannon took the envelope, opened it and pulled out some colour photos. She gasped.

'I don't ... oh my *God*. Oh my *God*,' she repeated.

Curtis laughed, enjoying her reaction. 'Told you it'd be good, didn't I? It's a cold night,' he said. 'You might want to burn those in your lovely fireplace when you've finished looking at them.'

'That's not a real fire. I'll have to use my mini shredder.' Shannon looked at him, stunned, her eyes shining. 'How – where the hell did you get these?'

'Took them myself, once she'd passed out. I thought it might be difficult to hit on her, but she was instantly – well, almost – felled by my fatal charm.'

'Literally felled.' Shannon looked at the photograph of a naked and unconscious Cindy Nightingale sprawled on the bed, pink gloss smeared across her drooling, half open mouth. 'She looks like she drank a vat of brandy. Or did you...?' She glanced at Curtis, alarmed.

He shrugged. 'All right, I did slip her a little something to help her on her way. But don't worry, I knew what I was doing. There was no danger.'

'Did you ... did you have sex with her?'

'Come on.' He stopped smiling. 'Give me some credit for good taste, won't you? She's not my type and anyway, I'm not that desperate. Why?' he asked. 'Would you be jealous if I had?'

'*No.*' Shannon gasped again as she looked at another photo. 'Drugs? Did she have them on her?'

'The Colombia's finest was courtesy of Uncle Curtis.'

'Bloody hell.' Shannon looked at him. She felt scared now. 'I didn't ask you to do this. Why did you?'

'Call it a bonus. Finbar told me Nightingale was making life tough for you again. Or trying to. I did it for him. And you. What's wrong?' Curtis asked. 'Don't you like icing on your cake?'

'But Nightingale must realise this was a fit-up.'

'Not necessarily. Picking up strange blokes in bars and going back with them to their hotel rooms can be very risky, as every good mother warns her darling daughter. I took her money and credit cards just for good measure. And before you ask, I've destroyed the credit cards.'

'But why would you leave the Charlie in her bag?'

'It's a big bag, untidy. Maybe I was in a hurry to leave and didn't find it. It doesn't matter. No one's going to believe it didn't belong to naughty Cindy herself.'

'She could ID you. And she's bound to think I'm behind it.' Shannon flung the photographs down, panicking. 'You're mad! I wish you hadn't done this. I'm in enough trouble. I don't need any more.'

'Calm down, OK? It's all right. You've got nothing to worry about, I promise you.' Curtis stooped and picked up the photographs. 'I took care of everything. I put latex gloves on once she'd passed out, and wiped her and the suite clean of my prints. My prints and DNA aren't on any police database anyway.'

'You do surprise me.'

'I left the hotel the back way to avoid the CCTV at the entrance. I'd given a false name and address and paid cash in advance for the room. After I left I called the cops from a phone box and told them there was a disturbance in that room and that drugs were being used. They did the rest. It's all right,' he repeated. 'Nightingale's caught, hungover, busted with a load of Charlie. She can accuse all she likes, but no one's going to listen. You're fine, Shannon, you're cool. She's the one whose got the explaining to do.' He laughed. 'She's *fucked*.'

Shannon thought of Cindy's unauthorised visit to Finbar in the early hours of this morning. Finbar had told Roy Gardner about it, and Roy's junior had managed to get hold of the tape of the camera Cindy had so wrongly assumed was switched off. What she had done would get her suspended, maybe even sacked eventually, and it was enough to get her taken off the Jenny Fong case. But how would that help Finbar? And Cindy could still make trouble for her, Shannon thought. Or try to. But as Curtis said, who would listen to her now? If Cindy had been caught in a hotel room in possession of cocaine she was looking at a jail stretch. And the courts would come down hard on a police officer disgracing herself and the force in this way. Shannon's heart started to lighten. One burden was gone, at least.

'That bitch is finished,' Curtis went on. 'Ruined, history, all washed up.' His eyes darkened as he looked at her. 'I know you wanted this.'

'What you did was brutal. You didn't have to take her clothes as well as—'

'You feel sorry for her? Come *on*. Tell me you wanted this,' he repeated.

'OK.' Shannon stared at him. 'I did want it,' she whispered. This was almost too fantastic to believe; enemies being vanquished only happened in fairy tales. 'I'm not sorry for her. She had it coming.'

'Thank God for that, you're human after all.' Curtis relaxed. He moved closer and pushed the photographs at her. 'Those are all that's left. I destroyed the negatives.'

'You did?'

'What? You think I might try and blackmail you or something?'

'That possibility had occurred to me.'

'You've got a really low opinion of me, haven't you? Although you must have trusted me a bit to tell me about your plan and get me to help. Give me a break, will you, Shannon? I know you're scared. But like I said, it's all cool. And Finbar – I promise you, it's sorted. Everything's going to be fine. Oh, and – I'll keep on looking for Croft.'

'Don't do anything if you find him. If anything happens to Croft it'll look too obvious. Just tell me and I'll tell the police I had another amazing, anonymous tip-off. I don't care what they think.'

'OK, will do. Right, I'll be off.'

Shannon hesitated. 'Thanks for … everything.'

'No problem.' Curtis gave her a quick kiss on the cheek and ruffled her hair. 'Take care, Gorgeous. And give my regards to Finbar.'

She saw him to the door then went back into the living room and sat down, finished her glass of wine. She looked through the photographs again. Cindy Nightingale was not a pretty sight. How must she be feeling now? Furious, ashamed, humiliated? Betrayed?

'Didn't work out the way you planned, did it?' she whispered, gazing at the shocking images. 'You're going where you wanted to stick me. Tough.'

She would feed the photographs to her mini shredder. In the meantime she should think about feeding herself. Shannon thought of Finbar again and felt anguished. Was Curtis right, had her plan really worked? When would she see him again? She could not bear the thought of him being found guilty of murder, but if that happened she would have to deal with it somehow. One thing was for sure, she would not give up on him. Even if that meant losing her job and having to set up as a one-woman operation somewhere else.

She got up, went to the kitchen and opened the fridge. There was a small piece of cheddar, half a dozen eggs, butter, six bars of the Belgian chocolate she stocked up on whenever she went to London, two lemons and a pack of wild Irish smoked salmon. The salmon, she decided, since that did not involve cooking. She would do some toast to go with it. She was laying the slices of bread under the hot grill when she heard someone at the door.

She turned and listened, her heart thumping. How had whoever it was got into the building? Why didn't they ring the bell? My God, she thought, is it Croft? She hadn't double-locked or chained the door after Curtis left. She rushed into the hall, but it was too late. The door was opening.

Finbar stood there wearing the jeans, navy sweater and black jacket he had been wearing when he was arrested. That seemed like such a long time ago now. He was pale and gaunt, his black hair limp around his narrow face. He held out his arms and she ran to him. His clothes smelled of staleness, disinfectant, nasty institution food.

'They dropped the charge, told me I was free to go. But that's all they told me.' He hugged her to him, kissing her neck and burying his face in her hair. He was shaking. 'D'you know what happened? I don't get it.'

Shannon took his keys, locked the door and put the chain on. She turned back to him and smiled. 'I perverted the course of injustice for you, darling.'

'What?' He frowned. 'Still don't get it. But never mind that now. Come here.' He grabbed her and pulled her against him. 'Christ, you smell good. You smell like you. I've missed you like I can't believe. I thought that was it, thought I was finished. I was frantic about you, for your safety. Especially after what that Nightingale bitch said to me.'

217

'I missed you too.' Shannon had tears in her eyes. She remembered the photographs. 'You'll never guess – I've got something amazing to show you.'

Finbar laughed. 'Got that right.' He pulled up her sweater and unzipped her jeans.

'No, I mean—'

'I love you so much. I thought I'd never hold you again.' He stroked her back and undid her bra. He paused, sniffing. 'What the hell's burning?'

Shannon gasped with laughter. 'Toast.' She sprinted to the kitchen and pulled out the grill pan, tossed the two slices of charcoal into the sink. Finbar followed.

'Bloody hell.' He stared down at her, his green eyes wet. 'Look at you. Burnt toast, hair all messed up, your clothes falling off. Can't leave you on your lonesome for five minutes, can I?'

'No.' She slid her arms around him. 'So you'd better not do it again.'

He held her tight. 'That's a given.'

Chapter Twenty

'So I'm not off the hook, Alex.'

Wanda could barely stand the creepy hissing sound of the machine that helped Alex draw those laboured breaths. Her hand tightened on the warm, wrapped, sweaty cheeseburger she had bought for her lunch but would not of course eat in here.

'Rod didn't like me much before,' she went on, 'but now he hates me. Still. What with the Jenny Fong murder, Shannon Flinder and Finbar Linnell, and now the shocking case of Inspector Nightingale naked, drunk and busted with a load of cocaine in some hotel room, he won't sack me yet. There's too much to do. And Serafina's not what you'd call up to speed. *Speed*, ha-ha. She's quite sweet though.' Wanda smiled down at him. 'I suppose I should hate her because she's going to get my job. But I can't. She's really nice to me, Alex. She suggests words and phrases for articles that are better than the ones I come up with, and she brings me cups of tea and coffee. She says Rod's a wanker. And she asks about you a lot. I posted and e-mailed some more job applications, by the way. No luck yet though. I suppose it's a bit soon to expect to hear from anyone.'

Hiss hiss. Sigh. Something bleeped. Wanda got up and stood over Alex. His eyes were not quite closed and she could see slits of white – or yellow, really. His skin had a yellowish tinge too, made more obvious by the whiteness of the sheets and pillow. His limp dark hair was growing longer, as were his nails. Incredible how his hair and nails kept growing. Or was it? Wanda had heard that nails and hair kept growing for several months after death. The thought of that happening while you mouldered in a coffin was creepy, and gave her the feeling that she might not be able to take her next breath.

She had taken to coming here even more often, sitting by Alex's bed and talking to him as if he were conscious and able to respond to what she said. It helped somehow. She walked to the window and looked out at the beautiful blue sky. Even in here with the odours of disinfectant, stale urine, formaldehyde and the chips and cabbagey-smelling lunch now being served to those who could sit up and eat, she could smell wood smoke, leaves and distant fields. It made her remember cold, clear autumn days during her childhood. Although why she should get sentimental about *that* ... maybe because childhood was carefree, or supposed to be.

Why? Because children did not have to worry about paying bills and holding down jobs? Wanda could not remember feeling happy as a child, but she supposed she must have done sometimes. It had all seemed like worry worry worry. Does this or that person like me, how can I please my mother, why didn't she like that birthday present, why doesn't my dad want me? It's no good coming second or third in games, I've got to be first. Nothing but stress, anxiety, being conscious of always trying and failing to please. She thought of something else and turned back to Alex.

'It's funny. Well, not really. Rod told me to get on to my special police contact and find out more about Cindy Nightingale.' She giggled. 'Of course I didn't tell him she was it! I don't care. I'll just make up the stuff I write. Other people blag their way through life, why shouldn't I?'

A radical thought for her. If only Alex would sit up, nod, smile, agree. He had been the only person who had ever encouraged her in any way, and she missed that terribly now. Wanda thought about Shannon Flinder. Shannon must be grieving about her friend. The police had not yet released Jenny Fong's body, so the funeral had to wait. And Finbar Linnell was suddenly and mysteriously free now; Wanda knew there was no way she would find out how *that* had happened. So at least Shannon had something to be glad about. And she must be delighted about the shocking downfall of Cindy Nightingale.

That was the thing about life, Wanda thought as she looked at the blue sky again and felt the sun's weak warmth on her face – good stuff as well as bad happened. But for her there was no good to balance the unrelenting bad. She felt the crease between her brows deepen as she frowned. The crease hadn't been there at all, then one day she had noticed a tiny, faint line, and now it seemed deeper every time she looked. She had lines around her eyes and mouth too, had to put blusher lower on her cheeks to avoid the crows feet – that was when she bothered with make-up. Age was not so much creeping up on her as whacking her in the kisser. She put the smelly cheeseburger in her pocket. A nurse came in to check on Alex.

'Hi Wanda, all right? You're staying here longer than usual. Got the afternoon off, have you?'

'No. Actually, I should be getting back now.' Well, not quite yet. She had to try and see Cindy Nightingale, who wasn't answering her mobile or home phone. Wanda had guessed something was up when she had tried to phone Cindy at work and been told she wasn't available and was not likely to be. She had not spoken to Cindy since that night in the restaurant.

Wanda did not ask the nurse any stupid, hopeful questions because she had given up doing that; it made everything seem even more heartbreaking. She kissed Alex, smoothed her hand across his forehead, and squeezed his hand. She let her hand linger in his, unable to resist hoping and praying that she might feel some answering pressure. She had imagined it many times, Alex squeezing her hand in response, opening his eyes, recognising her. Asking where he was, what had happened. Her relief, the tears and joy, knowing everything was going to be all right.

'Bye for now, love,' she whispered. 'See you later. I love you. I'm always thinking of you, Alex.' The nurse patted her shoulder. Along the corridor waiting for the lift, Wanda had a bit of a cry. Then she wiped her eyes and took a big breath. She had things to do.

Cindy Nightingale's house was a smooth, redbrick 1930s semi in a long, wide, tree-lined street in Crosby, the kind of place Wanda would have loved for herself and Alex. She rang the bell several times. Cindy had to be in, because where would she go? Plus her black Audi was parked in the drive. Wanda stooped, pushed open the porch letterbox and yelled inside.

'Cindy? *Cindy*? It's me, Wanda Brennan. Are you there? How are you doing?' Like she gave a toss about how Cindy was doing. But she had to pretend. Had Cindy managed to find out anything about Alex's case, like she had promised? 'Let me in, will you? Please. I want to talk to you.'

She waited, glancing around. And shivering; it was cold, despite the sunshine. Come on, she thought. A minute later Cindy opened the front door and porch door.

'Fuck's sake, don't yell at me like that. And what's to talk about?'

Her voice was slurred and she was smoking a cigarette. The smell of booze hit Wanda full on. Cindy's hair looked greasy and her features were blotched and reddened from what must have been a lot of crying. Her feet were bare and she was wrapped in a grubby cotton bathrobe in a shade Wanda could only describe as virulent peach.

'Well,' she began, 'I thought—'

'What's to talk about when I've been fucked over big style?' Cindy puffed on her cigarette. 'What do you want anyway?' she demanded, blowing smoke in Wanda's face. 'An exclusive interview?'

'I heard what happened.'

'Yeah, I bet you did, Ms Ace Reporter. Our Girl Wanda.'

'And I wanted to come and see how you were doing.' Wonder no longer, Wanda. Cindy didn't do anything by halves. When she hated someone she hated them. When she fell apart she did that in spectacular fashion too. It must feel even worse to know that what had happened was all her own incandescently stupid fault.

I don't think even I could have been that thick, Wanda thought, remembering the regional news coverage about the drunken police officer who had visited a suspect in his cell in the early hours of the morning to proposition and then attempt to intimidate him, and followed up that episode by getting herself involved in a drug bust. It was all supposed to be confidential, but of course some little mole thought it was too good not to be shared with the public. And although this bit wasn't on telly or in the papers, there was a rumour that the suspect had been Finbar Linnell. Wanda could not feel much sympathy for Cindy, although she could empathise with the drinking, smoking and lack of attention to personal appearance. Most of all, the feeling of powerlessness.

'Can I come in?' She pulled her parka around her. 'It's freezing out here.'

'Yeah, why not indeedy? Be my guest.' Cindy stepped back and flung out one arm in a grandiose gesture. 'Not as if I've got a houseful of rellies and friends all wanting to keep vigil with me and attend my next court appearance to provide warm, caring support. Yes, you come on in, Wand. Join me for a drink. I was about to crack open another bottle of Bombay Sapphire.'

Wanda was creeped out by the scary, Laura Ashley-like décor, plus the fluffy toy tigers, puppies and bears lying around, most of them the expensive World Wildlife Fund variety. So Cindy had a soppy side. How chilling. She shoved two baby brown bears out of the way, sat on the flowered sofa and lit a cigarette. The spacious sitting room stank of smoke and the central heating was on overdrive. Cindy went to the sideboard and unscrewed the pretty blue glass bottle of Bombay Sapphire.

'D'you want ice?' she asked, sloshing gin and tonic into two glasses. Her tone implied that the fetching of it would constitute a great bore and nuisance.

'No thanks. I hate ice.' Wanda took the glass and nodded her thanks. The drink was very strong, but she liked it that way. 'I once had a craving for ice.'

'Did you really, well, isn't that fucking fascinating?' Cindy slumped in an armchair, glass and fresh cigarette in hand.

'Crushed ice, mostly.' The combination of gin, full sugar tonic and cigarette was delicious. 'Any drink I had, even water, had to be crammed with it. Alex would wrap ice cubes in a tea towel or freezer bag and bash them with a rolling pin for me. Once he did it at midnight and the neighbours complained.' Wanda laughed, but she felt nervous and she knew she was babbling. 'The craving turned out to be a symptom of iron-deficiency anaemia, caused by heavy periods,' she went on. 'I read that people with anaemia can get cravings for ice or dirt – don't know what kind of dirt!' She laughed again. 'Anyway, three months on iron tablets and I was fine again. I've hated ice ever since.'

Cindy was glaring at her. 'Wow, that's one hell of a story.'

Wanda blushed. 'Sorry.'

'And guess what? I've got a story too. About how my life, my whole fucking *life*, is in ruins. Beats your sodding heavy periods! Jesus Christ.' She tossed back her drink and got to her feet. 'I was fitted up. And no bloody prizes for guessing who's behind it.' She made for the sideboard again.

'You don't mean...?' She's paranoid, Wanda thought. Obsessed. She can't possibly blame Shannon Flinder for *this*.

'Flinder, yes, of course. Who else would do something like this to me?' Cindy replenished her drink and sat down again. 'And now they've released her frigging boyfriend, can you believe it?'

'Well, if he's innocent ... how did that ...?'

'That *fecker's* not bloody innocent, no way. Neither is she.' Cindy butted her cigarette in a white and gold china Merseyside Police ashtray, obviously wishing she was stubbing it out on Shannon Flinder's bare skin. 'That bitch,' she spat. 'She's *fucked* me.'

Wanda knew this was not the time to point out that if you wanted to pick up strange men in pubs, get pissed and accompany them back to their hotel rooms, most people would regard that as practically begging to end up a victim of some kind of crime.

'Nobody believes me,' Cindy went on. 'I haven't had one phone call or visit. Nobody gives a toss, they're all laughing

224

their heads off. Even my mother and brother say it serves me right.' She was crying now. She swigged more gin and tonic and lit another cigarette. 'I'm ruined. Finished. I'm looking at a stretch for this, and it won't be a short one. The bastards want to make an example of me.'

Wanda did not blame them. 'It's terrible,' she murmured.

'Imagine what it'll be like for me, a police officer, in jail?' Cindy's voice rose in panic. 'I can't do it, it just can't happen. It should be Shannon Flinder who's going to jail, not me. I wish I could get my hands on that bitch, I'd kill her right now.' Cindy looked at Wanda, sniffing and wiping her tears on her sleeve. 'You've got to help me.'

Wanda got a shock. 'What?'

'Give my side of the story. Prove Flinder fitted me up.'

'But how could I possibly prove that?' Especially when it was all crap.

'There's got to be a way.' Cindy smoked furiously. 'Look, you owe me. I tried to help you. Actually, that's what I'd spent the day doing just before I went out for a much-needed drink and got talking to that ... that *bastard*.' She sniffed and wiped her eyes again. 'I really liked him. I thought he was – oh, fuck it. Anyway, I'd just been going through your Alex's case file, talking to people and seeing if I could get things moving again. Nothing's been done for a while, as you know. I thought, well, I can check out this stuff and do what I can, but what Wanda also needs is a good solicitor. I phoned a few I know, but none of them were interested. Then Shannon Flinder turned up to chew my ear about her precious murdered mate, and I mentioned you to her.'

'What?' Wanda nearly dropped her cigarette.

'Yes. I pleaded for you, not that it did any good. I said if she was so concerned about justice, why not try to help the living rather than the dead? Especially as Fong's murderer had been charged and was in custody. But you know what she said?' Cindy glanced away. 'I shouldn't tell you really. It wasn't exactly sensitive.'

Wanda's heart thumped and she was sweating. 'Tell me. I want to know.'

225

'OK, but don't say I didn't warn you. Our Blessed Lady of the Mags Court said she'd heard of animal rights, but vegetable rights was taking it too far and she didn't give a shit about Alex Brennan. And she said you were a fat slag stalker who she was going to get put away so you couldn't hassle her any more.'

Wanda's face burned. 'I never hassled her! And how could she say such a terrible thing about Alex?' Her instinct told her Cindy might be lying, but she still could not prevent her eyes filling with tears. For a second she felt she couldn't breathe. 'She surely didn't call poor Alex ... how can you say that?'

'Hey, *I* didn't say it, you moron,' Cindy cried, enraged. 'Flinder did. What's wrong with you, you big thick?'

'I don't believe you.'

'Why the hell would I lie?'

'Because you want me to help you. Get me on your side. You must think I'm stupid. Well, you do – you just called me thick.'

'It's true. I swear. Look.' Cindy lowered her voice and tried to smile. The smile looked more like a grimace of pain. 'You can appreciate that I'm very upset right now. I can still help you, but you've got to return the favour. I took Alex's file with me when I cleared my desk. Brought it home.'

'Where is it?' Wanda jumped up. 'I want to see it. There might be something.'

'There are several things. Leads not followed, witness statements that seem to have been ignored. One witness describes having heard Alex beg his attacker not to hurt him and the attacker said it served him right for interfering that afternoon.'

Wanda gasped. 'That means it *was* Richard Croft who did it! Alex and me ran into him – I told you all about that.'

'Yeah, I know you did So you see, I am trying to help you.' Cindy was crimson faced. 'Now listen. I want you to write a piece giving my side of the story, and shafting Shannon Flinder—'

'Who is this witness? How come I don't know about this? Tell me more about the witness,' Wanda persisted.

'That doesn't matter right now.'

'Of course it bloody matters!'

She was feeling the gin she had drunk. And how could Cindy stand the heating this high, even if it was cold outside? Wanda tried to control her hurt and outrage at Shannon Flinder calling Alex a vegetable. It probably was true, now she came to think of it. What did Shannon care about her? She might act nice sometimes, but really she didn't give a toss.

'I'll talk to your paper exclusively,' Cindy was saying. 'Your editor will love it. And I don't give a fuck, I'll talk to the press, so what? What have I got left to lose?' She started crying again. 'Nothing but my freedom, and I'm not going to bloody well lose that. I won't go to jail, I can't. I'll do anything. Maybe I could get Flinder to confess she set me up—'

'Tell me about the witness!'

'Fuck the stupid witness! Christ's sake, we're talking about *me*.'

'Where's Alex's file?' Wanda glanced around. 'You shouldn't have brought it home. You can let me see it. Then you can go back to the police station, hand it in and tell them you took it by mistake.'

Cindy wiped her eyes and glared at her. 'In your dreams, lard woman.'

'Have you really got it?'

'Of course I have.'

'Show me then.'

'Not until you've done what I want. That's the deal. Take it or shove it. Don't think you've got much choice in the matter, do you? Now get your bloody pen and notepad out.'

Wanda glanced around the room again. It was a mess, with scattered newspapers and magazines, biscuit and crisp packets and empty glasses. Almost as bad as her own place. There was no desk where Alex's file might be. She ran out and into the hall, looked in the kitchen and living room.

'Hey.' Cindy followed, pulling her robe tighter around her. 'What the fuck d'you think you're doing? *Hey*!' She yelled as Wanda shoved past her and headed for the stairs. 'You can't go up there. Stop. Come back. This is my house, you bitch.'

Wanda stumbled upstairs, sweating and panting. She didn't know if Alex's file was here, but she wasn't leaving this house until she knew for sure. Cindy rushed after her, swearing, and Wanda tripped and cried out in panic as Cindy grabbed hold of the hood of her parka and dragged her back. She clutched at the banister.

'Get off,' she shouted, trying to wrench herself free. 'I just want to see the—'

'Out. Of. My. House. Bitch. *Now*.' Cindy grasped a handful of Wanda's hair and yanked her head back. Wanda kicked out again, clinging to the banister, and caught Cindy on the leg. Cindy screamed and let go of her hair. She still had hold of the parka, trying to pull Wanda back.

'Stop it, you'll make me fall!' Wanda kicked out again, twisted around and pushed Cindy in the face, desperate to free herself so that she could search for Alex's file. She caught the belt of Cindy's robe in her other hand, and tugged. The belt slithered loose and suddenly she was free. Cindy was falling.

It happened in slow motion, like a dream sequence. Cindy falling backwards, her arms flung out, hair flying, the robe billowing around her bare legs. Mouth open, her eyes filled with shock, knowing what was going to happen and that she was too late to stop it. She screamed, and the scream jolted Wanda out of her trance. Cindy crashed to the bottom of the stairs, arms and legs splayed, the robe bunched up over her hips. Her head was twisted to one side, her hair over her face.

Wanda gasped and clapped both hands to her mouth. 'I didn't do anything,' she whimpered, trembling with fright. 'It's not my fault, I didn't ... oh, my God! Cindy?' she called, her voice shaking. 'Are you...?'

All right? Don't think so. Cindy had to be seriously injured. Or ...? No, please God, no. The stairs were carpeted and not that steep. But had Cindy hit her head on the solid banister? Wanda was shaking all over and pouring sweat, her heart doing great big thumps. Her legs shook so much that she could barely get to the bottom of the stairs.

This wasn't real, it couldn't have happened, she would wake up from the nightmare any second. She gave a cry of horror as the fingers of one of Cindy's outstretched hands suddenly moved and flexed, and a little sigh or moan escaped her, followed by a choking sound.

Wanda could not bear it. If Cindy was alive, and it seemed she was, she had to call an ambulance right now. Every second was vital. But she could not move. She could only crouch on the bottom stair, both hands clasped to her mouth. The ghastly sound must be air escaping from Cindy's lungs, she thought. It stopped after about a minute. Then there was silence. The silence was worse.

Wanda forced herself to get to her feet. She felt sick and faint as she stood over Cindy, bent and flicked the long strands of brown hair off her face.

'Cindy? It was an accident, you know that. It wasn't my fault,' she repeated. 'I didn't do anything.'

The silence into which she stammered the words seemed disbelieving, condemning. Cindy could not hear her anyway. There was no blood that Wanda could see. Cindy's eyes were open, staring into nothing. Or something.

'Oh God, no! Oh God.'

No more gin, cigarettes, desperation, picking up dodgy men in pubs, plotting revenge on enemies real or imagined. Cindy Nightingale was dead. Wanda burst into loud, panicked sobs.

'It's not fair,' she wailed, like a child. 'It's not my fault. I didn't *do* anything!'

229

Chapter Twenty-One

'Don't go.' Finbar hooked one arm around Shannon's waist, pulling her back as she tried to get out of bed. 'Stay here with me.'

'I can't.' God, she thought, not this again. 'I have to meet Khalida at the Mags Court. Just to have a chat, keep in touch.'

'Why can't she come here?'

'I can't stay in this bloody apartment all the time. I'll be fine, don't worry.'

'But I do.'

Finbar's relief and joy at being released and having the murder charge dropped had turned to despondency, if not depression this past couple of days. He hardly went to his office in India Buildings or at the airport, leaving most of the work to his managers. He postponed or cancelled appointments, hung around his or her apartment most of the day and was too restless to read, listen to music or even watch crap television.

'Cancel Khalida.'

'No.'

'You don't have to meet her. You don't have to work ever again.'

'Why, because I've got this generous rich guy who wants to take care of me?'

'If you like to put it that way. What's the problem?'

Shannon laughed, but she was not amused. 'Don't wind me up at this hour of the morning, you torturer.'

'I'm not. You're not exactly poor yourself.'

'I would be if I didn't work. And I don't think my retired parents in the Lake District would be delighted if their only daughter, that inconvenient child they never planned on having, turned up on their doorstep and threw herself on their mercy.'

'You wouldn't be poor because you've got me. What are you worried about? I love you, you know that. This isn't some economic power balance thing. Last night you told me you were fed up with being a criminal law solicitor.'

'I tell you a lot of things. Now let me go, I have to get ready.' She tried to struggle out of his grasp. 'Look – the way you feel now – you'll get over it. It's just a reaction to what happened.'

His expression was grim. 'Not to mention what might still happen.'

She stopped struggling. 'What's that supposed to mean?'

'Croft's still on the loose – after killing again. You could be next. I don't want to let you out of my sight for one second.'

'That's called suffocation, isn't it? Sorry,' Shannon said as he sighed, let go of her and lay back in bed. She pulled on her robe, walked to the window and peered through the blinds. There was misty golden light over the river and the pilot boat was out, surging upstream. She turned. 'Like some coffee?'

'Thank you, no. Bit early for me.' Finbar lay down, pulling the quilt over himself. 'I'll just go right back to sleep and not stress myself any more about the danger you could be in. You have a good day, darling.'

'Please.' Shannon felt miserable. 'Don't be like that.'

'Like *what*?' He sat up again. 'Don't be pissed off because you're putting yourself at terrible risk?' His eyes were dark with anger.

'Putting myself...? What the hell are you talking about? What did I do, unlock Croft's cell door and shout, "Hey sucker, come and get me"?'

'I meant you could do more to protect yourself.'

'Such as what? Buy a gun? Ask you to have Croft stiffed for me? I didn't need to ask, did I? You planned to do that anyway. Without telling me. When I think what could have happened...!'

'I know you're pissed off about that, and you've every right to be. But I didn't go through with it, did I?'

'You went behind my back. You promised you'd never do that again.'

'And when I promised I meant it. But how could I have seen Croft coming? How could you? I don't know, maybe I'm naïve. When he got put away I didn't expect he'd get the chance to escape on some hospital visit. Anyway—' Finbar paused, looking at her '—I'm not the only one who took the law into my own hands, am I?'

'Don't you dare throw that at me!'

'I'm not—'

'D'you think I enjoyed having to trust someone I hardly knew? Get him to bribe a prison officer to threaten that con who told the police you'd murdered Declan Dowd? D'you think I thought it was all a right laugh? Going against all the principles I've ever had, being terrified that it wouldn't work? I'm not exactly proud of myself for doing it. And what if I'd got caught? You'd be visiting me in prison now!'

'I know that. What you did – it scares the hell out of me to think of it. Shannon, look. Let's just go away today, get out of all this. You can come back when Croft's been caught and put back inside.'

Shannon's heart was racing. 'And when's that supposed to happen? If it does.'

'Of course it'll bloody happen. Sooner or later. What is it with you? You're not stupid, far from it. But you're in danger and you just want to keep on doing your thing.'

'Oh, I get it.' She stepped back. 'This is about me not doing *your* thing.'

'Shannon...' He sat naked on the edge of the bed and leaned forward, calm again. 'We've talked a lot, and you know what I want, it's cards on the table time. You told me this living apart together thing was temporary – that was a year ago. I understood how you felt, that you needed your own space and everything. But I've had enough, especially given what's happened now. It's made me realise all over again – like I needed to! –

232

how much I love you. I love you and I want to protect you. What's wrong with that?'

'I said I'd move back in with you.'

'There's a thirty grand sparkler going to waste in the safe.'

'What?'

'No, I didn't tell you about that, did I? Not after you said marriage was a friendship recognised by the police. It's been there for three months now. I want us to be together properly, to get married. You know I don't care about bloody kids or anything, I just want you. I want to be your husband, spend the rest of my life with you. But at the same time...' He held her gaze. 'I'm not going go on asking indefinitely.'

Shannon got a flash of shock. And fear. 'What is this, an ultimatum?' He said nothing, and her eyes filled with tears. 'Why are you being like this? You know I love you.'

Finbar shrugged and raised his eyebrows. Went on staring at her.

'I don't do ultimatums,' she hissed. 'And sorry about the waste of jewellery. Take it back to the shop or give it to the Sally Army. Throw it in the River bloody Mersey, for all I care.'

She ran out and slammed the door, went into the other bedroom and locked the bathroom door. She threw off her robe and got into the shower, her tears mingling with the steaming water. How could he be so horrible, so unfair? They were both freaked out, but that was no excuse. Finbar was not stupid any more than she was, so why couldn't he see that his behaviour would have the opposite effect to what he intended? Christ, she thought, like I need this crap to start the day. She dried her hair, and put on a tight white trouser suit that made her look more like a soap character than a lawyer.

Maybe a part in a soap could be her next career move. Some producer on a drink driving charge will spot me and make me an offer I can't refuse, Shannon thought, as she smoothed on dark pink, berry-scented lipgloss from a tube. She looked for a tissue, but the box was empty. She swore and wiped her sticky rose-glossed fingertip on her inside trouser leg.

'I'm still a slob,' she muttered to her reflection. 'Isn't it great? Nice to know I haven't lost all my filthy old habits.'

Khalida Najeba looked surprised at the suit, but had more important things on her mind. 'Cindy Nightingale's dead,' she announced, as Shannon walked up to her in the lobby of the Magistrates' Court. 'Leon heard, he just phoned me.'

Shannon stared at her in shock. 'How? What happened?' My God, she thought. . .

'Fell down the stairs in her own house. Looks like an accident. She'd been drinking. Upset about her ruined career and life, no doubt.'

Shannon put the Mars bar she had just bought from the WVS coffee stall in her bag. 'Who found her?'

'The police. Inspector Nightingale did what lots of our lovely clients do, and failed to turn up for a court appearance. Two officers went round to her house. She didn't answer the doorbell, there was unopened post lying in the porch, and a neighbour said she hadn't seen her for a couple of days. The officers broke in and found Cindy crumpled at the foot of the stairs in her dressing gown. She'd been dead for at least a couple of days, and the heating was on full blast, so you can imagine it wasn't pretty.'

'My *God*.' Shannon tried to absorb the shock of it. 'So she . . . what? Broke her neck or something?'

'Yes. She must have tripped and fallen while drunk. Her system was flooded with alcohol, and there were bottles of gin and vodka all over the house. Like I said, she must have been very depressed. And if a couple of days had gone by without anyone visiting, that wouldn't have helped her mood either.'

Shannon felt a pang of sadness. She reminded herself that it was Cindy Nightingale's own fault that she had had no friends. And despite what Curtis had done, Cindy had ruined her own career the minute she walked into Finbar's cell that night.

'A lonely death,' she remarked. 'After a lonely life.'

'It was her own fault she was lonely, Shannon.'

234

'I know. But still.' She hated me, Shannon thought. Wanted to destroy me. And Finbar. She wouldn't have hesitated. Why are you even bothered about this? But it was such a shock.

Khalida grimaced. 'I must admit, my first thought was, whodunnit? I can't think of anyone who liked the woman, can you?'

'No.'

'OK, disliking someone is a long way from murdering them. But you never know. And although it looks like an accident, it's too soon to be certain. The police are doing door-to-door enquries and the forensics team are still checking out Cindy's home – in between trying not to trip over all the empties!'

Shannon shook her head. 'I just can't believe this has happened.'

'Neither can I. Let's get some coffee. I suppose that Mars bar was meant to be breakfast?' Khalida tutted. 'How's Finbar?' she asked once they had reached the stall and ordered coffee. 'Getting over his ordeal?'

'Not really.'

'I'm sorry. Of course it'll take time. And I suppose he's very anxious about your safety right now. As are we. How are you?' she asked, handing Shannon a coffee. 'Heard from that inspector lately – what's his name?'

'Casey. I saw him yesterday. Croft's still on the loose.' Shannon did not feel like telling her about the murder of Matty Rice. She took a sip of coffee. 'Seeing as I'm here, why don't I take some cases for you this morning? That's if Mi-Hae won't mind.'

'Shannon, it's very kind of you and I appreciate it and I'd love to say yes. But you're supposed to be taking leave. I might as well do them myself – you couldn't complete the paperwork back at the office anyway.'

'No. OK.' Shannon paused, looking at her. 'You and Mi-Hae – you do want me back, don't you?'

'Of course we do.' Khalida glanced at her watch. 'Sorry, Shannon. Got to dash.'

'Yes. I know.'

235

'Be careful,' Khalida called as she hurried off. 'I'll phone. See you again soon.'

Shannon was wondering what to do next when her mobile rang.

'It's me,' Finbar said. 'I'm sorry about before.'

'I'm sorry too.'

'Why? It was me acted like a prick. Just the thing you need to start your day. Are we friends again?'

'Much more than friends. Yes, of course. You won't give that sparkler to the Sally Army, will you? Or throw it in the river?'

'Probably not.' He paused. 'I love you.'

'And I love you. Guess what?' she whispered. 'I just heard that Cindy Nightingale's dead. Khalida told me. She was found at the bottom of her stairs with a broken neck, having lain there for a couple of days. Looks like she tripped and fell while trolleyed out of her skull.'

'Jesus.'

Finbar was silent and Shannon knew he was shocked but, like herself, not exactly stunned with grief. He was also probably wondering if Cindy Nightingale's death was an accident. Of course he would not say that over the phone.

'I'll see you soon, OK? We'll talk then.'

'Yeah. And listen, you be careful.'

'Khalida just told me that. Aren't I always?'

'We won't go into that now. See you soon, Blue Eyes.'

Her mobile rang again. 'Hi Shannon. This is Catherine Rose, remember me?'

'Of course.' Shannon smiled. 'My favourite copper.' If there could be such a thing. 'The rose between all those thorns. Haven't seen you in ages. How are you?'

'Oh, you know. Same old. I phoned your office but the receptionist said you were on leave. She gave me your mobile number. I was very sorry to hear about your friend, Jenny Fong. I've now taken over that murder investigation.'

Thank God, Shannon thought. Someone civilised.

'Have you heard about Cindy Nightingale?'

'That she's dead? Yes, I have. Just now, actually.' Shannon hoped she did not sound too pleased; she was already starting to feel nothing but relief about her worst enemy's demise. Worst enemy? Well, no. She thought of her ex, her dead father-in-law, and now Richard Croft. What did I ever do, she wondered, not for the first time, to attract all those enemies? She pulled herself together.

'A tragic accident, I believe?' Now she was starting to sound sarcastic as well as relieved.

'So it seems. Of course it's too soon to tell.'

'You say you're working on Jenny's case now? I know it's a bit soon to ask, but have you possibly come up with anything new?'

'We're following up some stuff that was previously—' Catherine paused, obviously searching for a suitable alternative to the word *ignored*, out of loyalty to her deceased colleague '—that Cindy hadn't got around to checking. It doesn't mean we don't think we've got the right person in custody,' she added. 'We just want to be sure we've covered everything.'

Shannon grimaced. 'Of course.'

'We've got Jevko Arib's footprints – in Jenny's blood – at the scene. We still haven't found out who the others could have belonged to, though. And we haven't found the murder weapon.'

'I thought that escaped con, Richard Croft, might have killed her. He was on the loose at the time. I told Cindy Nightingale, but she ... well, didn't agree. The footprints could be his.'

'Yes, I heard you suspected Richard Croft. We're checking that out, but there's nothing so far to link him to the crime. But of course we can't know yet if those are his footprints. Let's hope he gets recaptured soon. This must be terrible for you.'

'What are those footprints like?'

'Well, they're from a trainer. Some brand called Ikon, which I've never heard of.'

'Me neither.'

'And they probably belong to a smoker because the sole's got markings which look like they were made by treading out fag ends. There's also a drawing pin embedded in the heel. Not much to go on, I know.'

'I believe Jevko Arib said someone was watching him from behind a pillar of St George's Hall – and that he ran away because he thought that person might be the murderer.'

'I know, but he could be lying. Or if not, it could be some passer-by who didn't want to get involved. And there was other unidentified DNA on Jenny's clothes and body.'

'Oh?' Shannon stiffened. 'I didn't know that. But then why should I?'

'We don't know whose it is, not yet anyway. We'll check if it's Croft's. I'll let you know. I'll keep you posted about whatever we find out. Shannon ...' Catherine hesitated. 'I heard there was some history between you and Cindy, that you weren't exactly best mates. She had a habit of rubbing people up the wrong way. So I can understand your lack of confidence in her. But that didn't mean she couldn't do her job.'

'Of course not.' Shannon was glad Catherine could not see her expression.

'And let me assure you, I'm doing everything I can. I'm not going to ignore anything that might cast doubt on Jevko Arib's conviction.'

'I know.'

'OK. I'll speak to you again soon. And watch yourself, Shannon.'

'Do you know, you're the first person to give me that gem of advice.'

'*Not.*' Catherine laughed. 'See you.'

Shannon's mobile rang again. My God, she thought, it's as busy as if I was working. 'Hello?'

'The mad, posh bint with the blonde highlights phoned,' Helena informed her. 'In a right freak. I told her you were on leave, but she wasn't having it. She's desperate to speak to you. I said I'd call you and give you her number, that's if you haven't already got it.'

'Mad posh...? Do you mean Charlotte Greene of Greene & Co. by the river?'

'That's her, yeah. Have you got her mobile number?'

'No, only home and office. And not on me.'

'Well, here's her mobile.'

Charlotte Greene did indeed sound freaked. 'I need to see you, Shannon. Now.'

'What's up? I'm on leave, as I think our receptionist told you?'

'Yes, but please, this is really important. I must see you this minute.'

'But what's up?' Shannon repeated, mystified. 'At least give me a clue.' She and Charlotte were friendly but not that close, and she had no dealings with Greene & Co, or not at present. Even if she had, what could possibly be this urgent?

'I'll tell you when we meet. I can't discuss it over the phone. Will you come now? Please?'

'Oh, all *right*.' She is a mad bint, Shannon thought. Still. What else have I got to do at the moment? She looked around the busy Magistrates' Court lobby. It felt strange to come here but not for work. She might think she was fed up with being a criminal law solicitor but here she was, already missing her job even though she was only supposed to be on leave. She wondered if Khalida and Mi-Hae really did want her back.

'Come to my house,' Charlotte said. 'I'm here now.'

Charlotte and her husband owned one of the few private residences remaining in gorgeous Georgian Rodney Street, the big houses originally built for rich merchants, some of whom had made their fortunes from the slave trade. Most of the houses now served as premises for dentists and various kinds of doctors, and one house, number 59, was now a museum where an internationally famous photographer, Edward Chambre Hardman, had lived and worked. Shannon had once been invited to dinner at Charlotte's house, an evening of boring conversation and pretentious food enlivened only by Finbar whispering in her ear at intervals the things he wanted to do to her when they got home.

'Shannon, please hurry.'

'On my way, all right?' Impatient bitch.

Shannon got into her car and headed for Rodney Street, at a loss to think what Charlotte could want. There was nothing, really nothing that she could imagine. If Charlotte had some big personal news – good or bad – Shannon did not think she would be the first person with whom Charlotte would choose to share it. She switched on the window wipers, swore at the rain and the slowness of the traffic.

'Panicked' was not too strong a word to describe Charlotte's state. And although Shannon did not know Charlotte that well, she did not regard her as the type to get aerated about nothing.

She shook her head as she peered through the rainwashed windscreen at the tail lights of a dark-green Jaguar XJ Exec. 'I don't like this,' she muttered. 'In fact I hate it.'

Something weird was going on. Actually, a lot of weird things were going on. Handsome, smiling Curtis Bright and his chilling tricks, Croft still, unbelievably, on the loose, Cindy Nightingale apparently getting so drunk that she fell down her own stairs and broke her neck. And now this. Shannon had a bad feeling, made worse because she was not sure exactly why she had it.

It was impossible to park in Rodney Street. She cruised past Charlotte's house with its scrubbed steps and shiny blue front door. Charlotte was not at the windows watching out for her, as Shannon might have expected. She carried on down the street past a restaurant and the abandoned dark-grey church of St Andrew's, it's strange, pyramid-shaped grave standing out amongst the crumbling stones in the disused cemetery. She found a pay-and-display parking spot around the corner in Pilgrim Street.

She sat in the car because she did not want to get out, walk back to Rodney Street and ring Charlotte's doorbell. Instinct was urging her not to do that, and Shannon listened to her instinct a lot more these days. She picked up her mobile and called Charlotte's mobile; it was switched off. Then she tried Greene & Co.

'Hi, it's Shannon Flinder. Is Charlotte Greene around, please?'

'No, she isn't.' The receptionist sounded harassed, as if a lot of people had been asking her that question. 'I expected her

240

back from court more than an hour ago, but there's no sign of her. Her mobile's switched off. She was supposed to be back by now because she's got an important meeting. I can't think what's going on; this is totally unlike Charlotte.'

'Have you tried her home number?'

'Yes, she doesn't answer. But I wouldn't expect her to be home at this time.'

'Charlotte just called me and asked me to go to her house. She said she wanted to talk to me and that it was very urgent.'

'Why would she call you? Sorry, I don't mean that to sound rude. I just don't understand.'

'Neither do I. She wouldn't say what it was about, only that she'd tell me when I got there. OK, thank you. I'll try her again at home.'

Why wouldn't Charlotte answer her home phone if she was supposed to be at home? Shannon started to feel frightened. She dialled Charlotte's number and waited. The phone rang ten times and someone picked up on the eleventh ring. Did Charlotte have the kind of phone where you could see which number was calling?

'Charlotte, are you there? It's Shannon.'

No answer, just the faint sound of what she gussed might be an indrawn breath. The silence lengthened. Somebody was there, listening but not speaking. Two men in suits walked past the car, and rain drummed on the roof.

'*Charlotte*? For God's sake, what are you playing at?'

Another sound, like a gasp. Charlotte spoke at last. 'Shannon. I—' She was almost crying. 'Where are you? You are coming?'

It was as if someone had handed her the phone. Somebody's there with her, Shannon thought, chilled. Her heart started to race. Somebody Charlotte did not want to be there. She was in big trouble. But who was it, what was going on? Charlotte doesn't want to see me, Shannon thought. Somebody else does though. Somebody who was prepared to waylay Charlotte, force her to go back to her house and make that call to lure Shannon there, thinking she would not suspect she was putting

241

herself in danger. Shannon could think of only one person who would do that: Croft.

'Oh my God.' She mouthed the words.

He had not been able to get to her up to now; not at her apartment or Finbar's, and not at the office. He must have been hanging around the Crown Court or Magistrates' Court – he was probably arrogant or desperate enough to risk that, and his appearance was altered now – and could have seen her talking to various people, Charlotte Green among them. Had he picked Charlotte because she was female, on her own in a convenient place at a convenient moment? Whatever the reason, Richard Croft was in Charlotte's house now. Waiting.

What should I say, Shannon wondered? Do? She couldn't walk up the steps and ring the bell. But Charlotte's life might depend on what she said or did during the next few minutes. If she said she was not coming after all, would Croft let Charlotte go? Or would he kill her? Shannon felt terrified. And her terror was nothing to what Charlotte must be feeling at this moment.

'I can't find a parking space,' she lied. 'It's chocka around here. You wouldn't know anywhere I could sneak in, would you? Preferably gratis.'

'Sorry, not at this time of day.' Charlotte spoke slowly, like she was trying to keep a hold on herself. 'Do you know Pilgrim Street? It's just around the corner. There's a pay-and-display there.'

'Right. OK. See you in a few minutes.'

Shannon hung up and called DI Casey. He answered immediately.

'It's Shannon Flinder. I think I've found Croft.'

'I see.' He kept his voice calm. 'Are you in any immediate danger?'

'No.' Shannon glanced round. 'At least I don't think so. He's got somebody I know and he's holding her in her house. I need your help. But please be careful, please get him this time. Don't let anyone mess up.'

Including myself, she prayed.

Chapter Twenty-Two

'What do you want with me?'

Wanda stared in shock at the two young plainclothes police officers who in her opinion looked more like the crims they were supposed to catch. She could not get the horrific sight and sounds of Cindy Nightingale's violent death out of her head. As if she didn't have enough horrific sights and sounds to contend with in her existence. And what the hell now?

'We're sorry to bother you, Mrs—'

'It's lunchtime,' Wanda interrupted, as if that was a valid excuse in the country with the longest working hours in Europe. 'I'm just off to visit my husband. He's in hospital, he's in a coma.'

'Yes, we know. This won't take long.'

Cops always came in pairs and they always said it wouldn't take long. What wouldn't? An arrest ... being accused of murder? Wanda trembled with fright. Of course she had not said a word to anybody about what had happened, and she did not intend to. She wanted it all to just go away. Like so many things.

'We need to talk to you about Inspector Cindy Nightingale. I believe you knew her?'

'Yes, that was terrible, wasn't it?' Serafina, standing by her desk in tight jeans and a flowery top, flashed them her bright smile. 'That police officer's death, falling down her stairs like that. But gosh.' She turned. 'I didn't realise *you* knew the lady, Wanda. Was she one of your contacts? I'm well impressed. Are you OK? You've gone a bit pale. Can I get you a tea or coffee or something?'

'No thanks. I'm fine.' Wanda was not exactly grateful to Serafina for drawing attention to her sudden pallor. She looked at the two officers and prepared to try and brazen it out. She knew she didn't have to go to the police station with them, should they ask – you only had to do that if they arrested you. And she had nothing to worry about, did she? It had been reported that Cindy Nightingale's death was almost certainly accidental.

Well, it was. Wanda felt a sudden, stupid bubble of nervous laughter rise and almost escape. One of the detectives glanced around the big, noisy, open-plan office in which most people were taking no trouble to conceal their curiosity.

'Somewhere more private we can go, please?'

Wanda led them into Rod's office and shut the door. He had gone out for one of his long lunches, this time combined with some obscure local writer's book launch at a small art gallery. He wouldn't be back for hours.

'Why do you want to talk to me about Cindy Nightingale?'

'I already said – because you knew her. We're talking to everybody who knew her.'

Wanda flushed. 'Well, I didn't.'

'Then can you explain why she would have written your name and phone number – home as well as office – in her address book?'

Shit. 'OK. I meant – when I say I didn't know her, I mean I didn't know her in the sense that we weren't friends or anything. I barely knew her.'

The officers exchanged glances. 'Where were you on Monday the seventh of October, the day of Inspector Nightingale's death?'

'I was either here working, or spending time with my husband at the hospital. Oh, and I'm sure I went to the supermarket.' She shrugged. 'Those three things are just about all I do these days.'

'Where were you Monday lunchtime, early afternoon?'

'Let me think. I was here, then I spent my lunch break with Alex – my husband. I was with him for about an hour. I'm sure the Intensive Care staff can confirm that. Most of them know me. I mean, they would by now.'

'What time did you leave the hospital?'

'I don't know. I think it was about one-thirty, two o'clock.'

'What did you do after that?'

'Came back here to write up a story.'

'You came straight back here?'

'That's right.'

Another exchange of glances. Wanda was sweating. She wished they would go the fuck away and leave her in peace. 'A neighbour who lives opposite Inspector Nightingale thinks she saw a red- or auburn-haired woman in her late forties ring Inspector Nightingale's doorbell at about two that afternoon.'

'Well, how many redheads are out there?' Wanda slid her hands inside her sweater sleeves. 'That wasn't me.' She flushed. 'And I haven't hit my mid-forties yet, never mind *late*.' Although the way she looked these days she could understand how some casual observer might take her for several years older than she was.

'So you didn't go to Inspector Nightingale's house on the afternoon of her death?'

'No. Nor at any other time.'

'What exactly was your association with her?'

Wanda thought the detective sarcastically emphasised *association*. 'I was writing a piece about the murder of that legal executive, Jenny Fong. I phoned the person in charge of the investigation into her death, and that turned out to be Inspector Nightingale. We spoke on the phone a few times – oh, and we met once for a drink.' Wanda paused. 'I was a bit shocked by her behaviour on that occasion, because she drank almost two bottles of wine then said she was going to drive home. I don't know if she does – did – that kind of thing on a regular basis. As I said, I barely knew the woman. And to be honest, I didn't want to. It was just work.'

245

The detective who was writing looked up from his notebook. 'Would you be willing to give a DNA sample?'

Wanda got a shock. 'What for?'

'There's other DNA in Inspector Nightingale's house besides hers, some of it unidentified. We just need to eliminate—'

'But I thought her death was an accident. Are you saying it wasn't?'

'We're not saying anything at the moment. It's a question of elimination. So, would you be prepared to give a sample?'

'No way.'

'Can I ask why, Mrs Brennan?'

'Because I'm not stupid, that's why.' Wanda flushed again. 'I know the government and police want to get every citizen's DNA registered on a national database. I also know that the chances of my DNA matching a crime scene sample is not only possible, but a lot more likely than me winning the lottery. I even heard of someone being accused of providing false details and being wrongly imprisoned because their fingerprints looked like someone else's. These things happen, and I'm entitled to protect myself. If I'm not legally obliged to give a sample, there's no way I'll agree to it.'

The detective snapped his notebook shut. 'That's clear enough.'

The sarcastic one grimaced. 'Maybe you, as a journalist and therefore guardian of our democratic order, might want to write an article about the erosion of civil liberties.'

'Thanks for the tip.'

'And thanks for your no-holds-barred cooperation, Mrs Brennan. Don't go anywhere foreign and exotic, will you? We might want to talk to you again.'

'I don't see why. I've told you all I know.'

Wanda thought they looked as if they were not too sure about that. When they had left, she went back to her desk. She was trembling, and felt cold and sick.

'God, that fair-haired one was sexy.' Serafina looked wistful, tapping her shell-pink, acrylic nails on the desk. 'How about a feature on a day in the life of a CID detective? I think that'd be

246

brilliant. I could—' She broke off. 'Wanda, are you okay? You look really—'

'*Shut up.*' Wanda clapped one hand over her mouth and rushed for the loo; it was a long rush and she almost didn't make it. Damn those spongy brownies. Damn her nerves. And damn the bloody police, hounding her over the accidental death of that bitch Cindy Nightingale when they couldn't even catch the bastard who had put Alex in a coma. It was enough to make anyone sick to their stomach. She rinsed her hands, wiped her chilled, sweaty brow, and was sipping cold water when the door swung open and Serafina walked in. She stood there watching her.

'Sorry, Wanda.'

There was such kindness and concern in Serafina's dark eyes, kindness like Wanda had not experienced in a long time, that it was too much for her. She burst into loud, gulping sobs. Serafina stepped forward and put her arms around her.

'It's all horrible for you, Wanda, I know.' Her voice was wobbly. 'But you'll get through this, you really will. Things won't always be this bad.'

At the centre of Wanda's grey haze of hopelessness and misery was a dark knot of fear. Would the police be back? Ask her again for a DNA sample? She couldn't do that, because it would prove she had lied, place her in Cindy Nightingale's house. She remembered the greasy glasses on the sitting-room coffee table, the glass from which she had drunk her gin and tonic. She had been too freaked to think of rinsing and wiping it before she left the house. Her DNA might even be on Cindy's body, because they had struggled before Cindy fell. And who was this damned interfering neighbour who had nothing to do but gawp out of her bloody windows? But was that actually true? Sometimes the police said things to try and trick people. She sobbed against Serafina's shoulder.

'Things won't always be this bad,' Serafina repeated, hugging her.

'No.' Wanda sniffed, then broke into another wail. 'They'll get worse.'

*

247

'Do you know why heroic acts get publicity?' DI Casey asked Shannon. 'Because they're *rare*. There's no way I'm letting you stand on the step and ring that doorbell. Croft's got a gun, remember?'

'But it's my fault Charlotte's in this situation. Croft picked on her because she knows me. He's using her to lure me.'

'It is not your fault. It's Croft's fault. And the fault of—' He stopped. The morons who let him escape. Yes. 'Look, I've scrambled the armed response team. Let them deal with this.'

'There isn't time. If you don't act soon, Croft will realise something's up. I don't want some terrible, long-drawn-out siege which ends with him murdering Charlotte. He'll kill her if you don't do something *now*. He doesn't care, does he? He's got nothing to lose. He's probably decided there's no way he's going back to jail.'

'I'm not letting you ring the bell and walk into that house, so forget it.'

'Croft won't shoot me on the doorstep. He'll have some murderous fantasy he wants to act out first. Maybe he's not even there any more.'

'Let's let the armed response team find that out. They'll be here any minute.'

He was right. Shannon could not believe the speed with which they arrived and surrounded the house, other police officers cordoning off the area. She had never seen Rodney Street so quiet, not even after leaving nearby clubs at three a.m. The rain had stopped and she could smell the river. She sweated with fear for Charlotte. If anything happened to her, she would never forgive herself. Charlotte had two young children. From her hiding place down some area steps across the street she could see Charlotte's drawing-room windows. She remembered the large room in which she and Finbar had sat one summer evening, trying to make polite conversation over pre-dinner drinks. The walls were painted a cold, eggshell blue and the ornate ceiling a brilliant white. A whistle blew and she heard shouts, running feet.

'Oh God!' she whispered. 'Charlotte!' Casey put a hand on her shoulder.

248

Dark figures kicked the door in and crowded inside. She heard shouts, but no guns being fired. She waited, trembling. 'OK,' Casey said at last, in response to a signal. 'We can go in.'

Shannon walked across the street and into the house, her heart pounding and her legs shaking. Dark figures with guns milled around the downstairs rooms, shouting to one another. She went into the drawing room.

Charlotte Greene lay on the floor beside the polished telephone table, her hands tied behind her back. Her shoes were missing and her black tights had been ripped off. Her clothing was dishevelled and a cloth gag was crammed into her mouth. The highlights in her hair gleamed. She had blood on her forehead, trickling down one side of her face. Her eyes were closed.

'Charlotte!' Shannon ran forward and knelt beside her. 'Oh my God, what's he...?' She gently pulled out the gag. 'Charlotte, speak to me, come on. What happened?' She shrugged off a hand on her shoulder.

Charlotte opened her eyes and focussed on her, dazed. 'He tried to rape me,' she whispered. 'Couldn't finish the job.' She started to cry.

'Was it Croft?' Shannon asked before realising Charlotte would not know him.

'Don't know his name. He waylaid me as I was getting into my car – must have followed me from court. He had a gun, said he'd kill me. I believed him. He made me drive back here and phone you. He said he was going to kill you, that you and him...' She closed her eyes again, gave a sigh. 'Has he gone?'

Shannon glanced up to see John Casey standing there.

'Oh, yeah.' He nodded. 'Long gone.'

Chapter Twenty-Three

Was it his sixth sense kicking in to warn him of danger? Richard did not know why he had suddenly lost his nerve and fled the woman's big posh house. But Shannon Flinder was taking just that bit too long arriving, despite her excuses about congested traffic and parking spaces.

Had she suspected something and alerted the police? Richard had reached a point where he no longer believed she would turn up. Then came the ping of alarm going off in his head, telling him to get out *now*. He had got out the back, through a gate in the wall. He had been going to kill the terrified woman lying bound, gagged and struggling at his feet in her drawing room, but changed his mind and decided she wasn't worth the time and hassle after all. She was one rubbish ride as well – or would have been. Ugly cow, he thought.

Where was Shannon Flinder now? What had she done, where had she gone after getting that phone call from the woman, the phone call he had forced her at gunpoint to make? She obviously hadn't been a sufficiently convincing actress. Of course he should have picked someone else, someone much closer to Shannon, but that option had not come up. This bitch had told the truth when she had said she didn't know Shannon that well. So his brilliant plan had failed. What now?

He hurried on down the grey, sloping street. It had started to rain again, and his hair and the back of his neck felt cold and wet. Traffic fumes irritated his nostrils and the back of his throat. The gun was in his jacket pocket. He was feeling terrible again, the daylight too bright despite the rain and low thick cloud. His head ached, his whole body ached like he had arthritis. The pain behind his eyes was getting harder and sharper, concentrating itself. He felt weak, sick and tired. He should be in hospital, of course, but that was just one more unavailable option. He went into the next best thing to a hospital, a cool, dark pub near the bombed-out church which had been kept as a memorial to the 1941 May Blitz, and ordered a large brandy and fizzy mineral water. The black-haired, middle-aged barmaid gave him a funny look, or so he imagined, then glanced towards the door as a siren blared past.

'Wonder what's going on out there?' she said to no one in particular.

'Murder and mayhem in the mean city,' Richard joked, passing her the cash for his drinks. But his wit was wasted on her and she handed him his change, unsmiling. The siren was heading up the hill, he thought – towards Rodney Street? The woman couldn't have freed herself, or not yet, surely? Or had someone else freed her? He had to find out what was happening. He had to be careful though. He drank the brandy, swallowed two paracetamol with the fizzy water, even though he knew that wasn't the wisest thing to do, then braved the rain and daylight again. He walked back up the hill.

'You can't go this way,' a bossy policewoman informed him and a few other pedestrians as he attempted to cross Leece Street. 'Rodney Street's been cordoned off.'

'What?' Bewildered glances all round. 'Why's that, love?' a senior citizen in flat cap and glasses asked. He was carrying a shopping bag. 'What's going on? Some terrorist gone beserk with a sub-machine gun?'

'Nothing like that, sir.'

'Is one of them chinless royals in town then? You should have told me, I'd have brought me flags.'

People sniggered and the policewoman smiled. 'Just move on, sir, please.' She shooed them away. 'Everyone. All right, thank you.'

So polite. Shannon Flinder must have called the police; he had been right. Richard obeyed and started to walk back down Leece Street. It amused him, despite his pain and frustration, that PC Plodette had no idea that she was turning away the main man in the drama. He was glad he had listened to his instinct. It was as if somebody was watching over him, although he couldn't think who that might be. Not his parents. And certainly not Yvonne or Julie.

He reached St Luke's Place and stood at the foot of the steps of the bombed-out church, listening to the cry of the nearby *Echo* seller. The brandy warmed him and made him feel light-headed. Richard stood there thinking. He was safe; he could blend in with the crowds. But Shannon Flinder wasn't safe. Because he was going to find her.

Today.

'I can't stand this any longer.' Shannon sat huddled on a sofa in Finbar's living room, a glass of white wine on the low table in front of her. 'It's got to be over – today!'

'Well, it's just gone four in the afternoon, so I suppose there's still a slight chance of that.' Finbar put down his phone, shifted close and hugged her. 'But I wouldn't hold your breath.' He lifted a strand of hair off her forehead, smoothed it back and kissed her. 'Right, I've made the reser-vations. The flight to Cork's at seven this evening. We're get-ting out of here, and that's that. If it was me being hunted by a psycho you'd want me to get away.' He paused. 'Wouldn't you?'

'Of course. That's if you didn't kill him first.'

'Don't start that again.'

'I'm not starting anything.' She got up and walked to the windows. 'Croft must be around here.' She sipped her wine and looked out at the river. 'Somewhere close. They've got to get him this time, surely.' She turned. 'My God, poor Charlotte! Croft didn't stop at slapping her around, he tried to rape her. Luckily he couldn't perform. Not that that makes her ordeal any less horrific.'

'Sexual dysfucktion usually goes with his kind of territory, doesn't it?' Finbar got up and came towards her. 'OK, Charlotte won't be feeling lucky right now, but it could have been a hell of a lot worse. Croft could have murdered her. And you, if you hadn't suspected something was up and called the police.' He wrapped his arms around Shannon. 'I hope you're not blaming yourself for any of this.'

She was silent for a few seconds. 'It happened because of me.'

'Jesus. I knew it.'

Hot tears stung her eyes. This ordeal had happened to Charlotte Greene, but she was terrified and in shock herself. What if she had gone into that house and found Croft waiting? Would she be dead now, like Yvonne and Julie? Matty Rice? Another statistic on a police file?

'I hate him,' she burst out. 'Who does he think he is?'

Finbar grimaced. 'God?'

'I wish he was dead.' She turned and looked up at Finbar. 'You won't do anything now, will you? The police might have let you go, but that doesn't mean they'll leave you alone from now on. I told Curtis not to do anything.'

'Yeah, I've had a word with Curtis too. Don't worry, OK? At least not about that. I promise,' he said, holding her tight. 'You've got my word as a gentleman.'

'Is that what you are?'

'Very much so, and certainly where you're concerned.' He ruffled her hair. 'She's always insulting me, how do I stand it? Must be love.'

Shannon wiped her eyes. 'If you'd like to get that sparkler out of the fridge ...' She laughed. 'I mean the *safe* ... I'll try it on for size.'

'Hang about.' Finbar held her at arm's length and stared at her. 'You don't have to get engaged, that is, re-engaged to me just because you're grateful I'm being masterful and whisking you away for a while.'

'It's not gratitude, you idiot. I've been thinking.'

'You've got more than enough to think about right now.'

'Does this mean you've gone off the idea?'

He laughed. 'Jesus. I can't win, can I? *What do bloody women want?*'

'Bastard.'

'That's good. That's the Shannon I've come to know and adore. How about we discuss our particular issues at a more relaxed and convenient time? Like when we're in Ireland, sitting by the fire in that isolated, romantic house and watching the lights come on across the bay?'

'You're right.' Shannon hugged him. 'I love you so much.'

'You better.' Finbar glanced at his watch. 'We'd better leave for the airport soon. I'll pack a bag and make a few calls, and you'll just have time to fill your twenty suitcases with yoga gear, lingerie, day cream, night cream, body cream, anti-gravity eye cream—'

'Bastard,' she laughed again. 'Given the hard, cold fact that you're pushing forty, mister, you could use a few licks of anti-gravity cream yourself.'

'Forty's nothing. Sixty's the new forty. Besides, I'm a man. The older I get the more craggy, gravelly and irresistable I become.'

'You wish. I'm afraid that's just a sad old Hollywood myth, *darling.*'

'What?' He stared at her in mock dismay. 'You mean all those gorgeous young actresses don't actually fancy Sean Connery or Harrison Ford?'

'They fancy the money they get paid for pretending to. Right.' Shannon turned. 'I'll go back to my place and pack a few things.'

'I'll come with you.' Finbar picked up his keys. 'I wonder how long they'll keep Charlotte in hospital.'

'Overnight, the nurse I spoke to said. She'll probably be out by lunchtime tomorrow. But it's going to take her a long time to get over what's happened.' Shannon looked at him, troubled. 'I don't really know what to do. I can imagine I'm not Charlotte's favourite person right now, even though she said she didn't blame me—'

'Why should she blame you?'

'Yes, I know. I'd like to send her flowers or something, but I don't know. Her husband's furious. He might see that as adding insult to injury.'

Finbar gripped her shoulders. '*This – is – not – your – fault.*'

'It doesn't make me feel any better about what happened. Not right now, anyway.'

Finbar sighed and kissed her hand. 'Let's go and get your stuff. I hope you're not taking any work with you to Ireland.'

'You must be joking. And I'm on leave, aren't I? If Mi-Hae doesn't want me around she can damn well get on with it all herself, and good luck with that.'

Finbar looked thoughtful. 'D'you think Nightingale's death *was* an accident?'

Shannon shrugged. 'It must be. I know she drank a lot, but maybe she had more of a problem than anyone realised. And after she got caught on tape going into your cell ... not to mention what Curtis did ... even if it turns out not to be accidental, I've got loads of credible alibis to prove I was nowhere near her or her bloody house on the day she died. They can't even think I had any motive to kill her since her own colleagues laughed at her when she tried to tell them I'd had my dear departed F-in-L stiffed.'

Finbar said nothing, just raised his eyebrows. Shannon knew what he was thinking; that that had to be just about the only thing Cindy Nightingale ever got right. They looked at one another for a few seconds without speaking. Finbar knew how she felt; that she did not want to refer to or revisit that old nightmare.

'Let's hope this Inspector Rose makes some progress with Jenny's investigation,' he said at last. 'That's if this Arib guy really is innocent. God knows how they'll ever find out who that unidentified DNA or bloody footprints belong to.'

Shannon nodded. 'Images of needles and haystacks do spring to mind.'

'Come on,' he said. 'Let's get going.'

'You don't have to come in with me,' Shannon protested as Finbar parked his car across the street from her apartment building and got out with her. 'I'll be ten, fifteen minutes tops.' She glanced up and down the quiet street.

'I'll come in anyway.' He looked at the black Jaguar XJ. 'Maybe I should get a different car.'

'Why?

'This one attracts attention sometimes – the wrong kind.' He ran his hand along the smooth side of the car where the scratch had been. 'I get the Buddhists' point about possessions being a burden.'

'Lots of people would like to have your burdens.' Shannon frowned. 'Well, maybe not.' They crossed the street. In the hall she unlocked her post box and felt inside nervously, as if a poisonous spider might crawl on to her hand and bite it. It felt spooky going into her apartment when she had not been there for a couple of days.

She did not know many of her neighbours, although the musical tastes of one or two of them were irritatingly audible at times, and the few she occasionally came across collecting their post in the hall barely acknowledged her. Shannon had got this place when she had moved out of Finbar's apartment more than a year ago. Now I'm ready to leave, she thought, walking through the silent, high-ceilinged rooms. In the sitting room she checked the answering machine for messages; there was one from a friend asking if she was going to attend some solicitors' dinner – which she wasn't – and two where the caller, who did not give his or her name, apparently liked the sound of silence

'Shit,' she sighed. 'I hate that. Why do people wait for the bleep if they don't want to leave any message? Or—' She looked at Finbar. 'Maybe it was Croft. I've applied to have my home phone number changed, but it hasn't gone through yet. I was on to them about that yesterday.'

'Croft'll be banged up again before it's changed.' But Finbar looked worried too. Shannon took her keys and double-locked the front door, even though she wasn't going to be here long.

'Have I got time for a quick shower? I feel filthy.'

256

He smiled. 'Yeah, you look it.' He glanced at his watch, then put his arms around her, kissed her and nuzzled her neck. 'Mind if I join you?'

'I'd love that. You can scrub my back,' Shannon whispered, hugging him, loving the feel of his arms around her. He was gorgeous, so sexy and comforting. He slid off her jacket, pulled her cream silk shirt free from her jeans and unhooked her bra. His fingers circled her hardening nipples.

Half an hour later she sat wrapped in a big, soft towel, blow-drying her hair and feeling more relaxed than she had in days. She was looking forward to going to Ireland; sometimes the best thing to do was just run away. Finbar came in drying himself, his wet black hair spiky and shiny. He bent and kissed her smooth shoulders.

'All right?'

Shannon smiled at him in the mirror. 'Fantastic.'

'Good.' He turned and started to pull on his clothes. 'Can you be ready soon? I don't think the airline will regard the post-coital bliss of two of their passengers as a valid reason to delay take-off.'

'Don't worry, I've packed my anti-gravity cream.' Shannon became aware of a car alarm whining in the street, and realised the noise had been going on for some time. 'Why doesn't someone switch that thing off?' She glanced towards the window. 'I don't know why people bother with those things, it's not like anyone ever takes any notice.'

'I'm taking notice.' Finbar strolled to the window, pulling on his sweater and zipping his jeans. He gasped. '*Shit.*'

Shannon looked at him, startled. 'What is it?'

'It's only my bloody car, that's what! Some fucking bastard's smashed the windscreen and headlights.'

'Oh my God.' She got to her feet.

'I'll be back in a minute.' He grabbed his jacket off the bed and his keys off the dressing table. 'You finish getting ready. We'll have to take a cab to the airport. Christ, if I get whoever did this I'll beat the fucking crap out of them.'

'Was there anything valuable in the car?'

257

'Not that I can think of. I usually remember not to leave briefcases full of US dollars lying on the back seat.'

'I know *that*.'

'Back in a minute,' he repeated, rushing out. The front door slammed. Shannon put on jeans and a dark-green zip-up cardigan, closed her bag and put it ready in the hall. She ran into the sitting room and looked out of the window. Finbar was down in the street talking on his mobile as he inspected the damage to his car, a couple of older men standing aimlessly by, one of them pointing at she could not think what. She had thought this street was safe. Well, relatively. Finbar was talking to the men now. He glanced at the building then up at her windows. Shannon waved.

He was gesturing, shouting something, but she could not make it out. She undid the catch, pushed it up and leaned out. A couple of cars drove past, followed by a big furniture van, making it impossible to hear. She ducked back in and glanced at the clock on the mantelpiece. Should she call a cab now? But she didn't know how long it would take Finbar to make arrangements for the car. She decided to go down and ask him.

She took her keys and went out, checking the landing before she stepped outside and double-locked her front door. As usual she did not take the lift; she disliked lifts and it was only a couple of flights of stairs anyway. At the bottom of the first flight she paused. Someone was coming up. One of her indifferent neighbours, no doubt, home early. She was fed up with smiling and saying hello and getting nothing but a grunt or suspicious glance in return. They seemed full of mindless animosity. Jenny had once talked about moving into one of these apartments, then changed her mind

She didn't want to encounter this person, but what did it matter? Shannon forced herself to go on. She saw the top of a man's head, dry, reddish-brown hair with greying roots. Powerful shoulders encased in a cheap black leather jacket. Baggy jeans, dirty old shoes. Not to be snotty, but he did not look like he lived here. He looked like ... no, she thought. *No.*

The keys felt warm, clenched in her hand. The man raised his head and she saw his pale, pouchy face, and those wary but otherwise expressionless dark eyes, eyes that had haunted her dreams. He looked ill, exhausted, older than the last time she had seen him. Shannon heard his voice before he spoke: '*Most women have problems, they're not classy. They're all messed up. She gave me more pressure than I was supposed to have. I couldn't take it.*' He thought that was a good excuse for murder.

Shannon saw that he was carrying a gun, the revolver she knew he had stolen from another of his victims, a young man whose life he had casually snuffed out.

Richard Croft.

Chapter Twenty-Four

'Wanda?' It was 'Wanda' now, not Mrs Brennan. 'Why didn't you tell us you left a message on Inspector Nightingale's mobile phone the day she died? Asking where she was and could you see her urgently?'

'I didn't!' *Shit.* 'Did I? I don't remember.'

She was not lying. She forgot a lot of things lately, because she had so much on her mind. Wanda had been here before – there was the fair-haired detective whom Serafina fancied, but this time with a different colleague, a forty-something brown-haired woman in a grey trouser suit, the three of them standing in the corridor having this fraught, disjointed conversation-cum-interrogation. Wanda sensed their hostility, or thought she did. To say Cindy Nightingale had not been popular with her colleagues would have been a spectacular understatement, but she was still a cop, still one of them even in death. And it seemed they were no longer sure Cindy's death was an accident. Serafina came out and stood there looking anxious, pretty in her pink V-necked top and tight jeans.

'Everything all right, Wanda?'

Why does she like me? Wanda couldn't understand it. And why did she like Serafina, even if she was an irritating puppy who was going to steal her job any day? The female detective gave Serafina a hard look.

'Leave us, would you, please? This is private.'

Serafina shrank back, blushing, and disappeared. The woman turned to Wanda again.

'Will you come down to the police station for a formal inter-view?'

'No, I bloody well won't.'

'Why not? It'd be easier.'

'Yeah, I'm sure. For you. Get me on your territory. God knows what you'd do then. Probably try to pressure me into signing a handwritten statement or something.' Being rude was not going to help, but Wanda was too panicked to think straight. 'I know my rights.' She did not like her own loud, aggressive tone, but if she didn't stand up for herself, who would? 'I don't have to go anywhere with you unless you arrest me for some-thing.'

Shit again. Don't tempt them. Why hadn't she remembered that bloody voicemail message and thought up some excuse to account for it? She could have avoided this. What was wrong with her? Well, what *wasn't* wrong?

'If you'll excuse me,' Wanda turned, hoping she could somehow just magic this pair away, 'I have to go and visit my husband.'

'Hold on a sec, Wanda.' The woman blocked her path. She had a perma-tanned complexion and bright red lipstick. 'You can't just walk off and refuse to talk to us. Whether you like it or not, you've got some explaining to do. And yes, actually you will have to make a statement. Not necessarily handwritten.'

'You can come back here some other time then. When it's convenient for me.'

'Why did you want to meet Inspector Nightingale that day?'

'It didn't have to be that particular day.'

'You said it was urgent. What was urgent?'

'Look.' Wanda sighed. 'I'd forgotten all about that, I really had. Otherwise I would have told you. But I've got so much on my plate with my husband and everything ... now I think about it, yes, I did want to see her. To get a story. About what had happened to her, her career being in ruins. It was a long shot and it didn't work out. She wasn't interested, or she would have called me back.' She shrugged. 'Next thing I hear, the woman's dead.'

261

'And you're certain you didn't go to Inspector Nightingale's house on the day she died?'

'I think I would have remembered if I had, given what happened.'

'You just told us you're having a lot of trouble remembering things.'

'Well, I—'

'The overweight, red-haired woman Inspector Nightingale's neighbour says she saw ringing her doorbell and peering through her letterbox and shouting – that wasn't you? Would you be willing to let her see you?'

'No, I bloody wouldn't. People are notoriously bad at remembering faces, research proves that. They think they remember things even when they don't.' Overweight, indeed. OK, so she was, but still.

'Why are you so defensive?'

'Most people get defensive when they think they might be being accused of something. This is the second time the police have hassled me. I don't like it, who would? Who wouldn't be bloody defensive?' Wanda did not want to say what she thought they might be accusing her of. Her face burned.

'Wanda, we're going to require a DNA sample from you. No messing this time.'

'And I suppose you're going to tell me we can do things the easy way or the hard way.'

'You obviously watch a lot of telly.'

'If only I had the time. Look, why are you harassing me? It's Shannon Flinder you should be going after. She's a criminal law solicitor; she knew Cindy Nightingale.'

'Why should we be going after her?' They exchanged glances.

'Because she had a motive to kill Cindy Nightingale. She—'

'Excuse me, but who said anything about Inspector Nightingale being killed?'

'Well, if you're demanding statements and DNA samples, it sounds like you don't think it was an accident any more.' Wanda sweated with fear. Be careful, she told herself. 'She –

Cindy Nightingale, that is – told me she knew for sure that Shannon Flinder had had her father-in-law murdered. That paedophile headmaster who was in the news, oh, well over a year ago now. She said Shannon Flinder was terrified that one day she'd get found out, and that she was prepared to do anything to stop Cindy Nightingale or anyone else getting evidence to prove her guilt. When Cindy got caught in that hotel room in possession of cocaine – she believed she'd been fitted up and that Shannon Flinder was behind it. Maybe her boyfriend too, that Finbar Linnell. He's got a dodgy past, I believe.' Wanda rushed on, reckless and desperate. 'Shannon Flinder hated Cindy Nightingale. And she hates me too, because I ... well, I—'

'Because you pestered her for a story? That's what you lot do, isn't it? What kind of story?'

'I didn't pester her, I just asked her a couple of times if she'd talk to me about her murdered friend, Jenny Fong. But she took it the wrong way, she blew up at me. I was frightened. That woman's got a temper – she should be careful. Who does she think she is, anyway? Just because she's a solicitor.'

Wanda thought she sensed a subtle shift in their attitude; another possible lead and yes, being police, they probably were not crazy about lawyers. But they were not going to deviate from their particular trail, not right now.

'The DNA sample, Wanda.' The woman's voice was firm. 'No argument.'

The fingerprints on the gin glass would place her in Cindy's home! It would become obvious that she'd lied. And when she said she'd run off in panic, would they believe her? She might be charged with murder. Wanda trembled. Her options were running out, not that she'd had many to start with. She was in such a panic she could not think what to say or do next. Rod pushed his way through the swing doors and came up to them. He wore a black silky waistcoat embroidered with tiny coloured balls. His tie was loose and his balding head shiny. Wanda stared at him, stupidly hoping he might somehow save her from all this.

263

'I'll be right there, Rod,' she called, even though she knew she wouldn't be. Her next stop was the police station, arrest or not. What the hell could she do now? How was she going to fight her way out of this crazy mess? Why hadn't she just told the truth from the start? You stupid bitch, she thought.

'Right *where*, Wand?' Rod brushed a hairy hand across his forehead. 'Don't know what you're on about, but I've come to tell you not to bother coming back. Take all the time you want gabbing to your new mates, whoever they are. Those last two pieces you wrote were shit – I couldn't even make sense of them. You're sacked, Wand.'

'Rod, no! You can't do this, not now. These people aren't my mates, they're the police.'

He laughed. 'Oh dear. Been a naughty girl, have we? Look, Wand, this time I mean it. And don't even bother trying to argue with me, because I'm not bloody interested.' He turned and disappeared. Wanda stared after him, trembling, her eyes filled with tears.

'Hmm.' The lady detective smirked. 'Doesn't seem to be your day, does it, Wanda? Still. Never mind, eh? You'll have plenty of time to come down to the police station with us now. Won't you?'

Richard could not believe he was face to face with Shannon Flinder at last. He took in every detail of her appearance as she stood there stunned with terror. He had to act fast; by the time the boyfriend had clocked the damage to his flash car and phoned a garage, he would be back for his other piece of expensive, high-maintenance property. Richard gestured with the gun and she gasped and shrank away, one hand grasping the banister.

'Up the stairs,' he hissed. 'Now.'

For a second he wondered if she would be able to move; she seemed paralysed with shock. This was what she had dreaded, of course, the moment which must have caused her nightmares. And now it had arrived.

'Move,' he repeated. He was sweating and frightened himself. He had taken a hell of a risk coming back here and

264

hanging around after what had happened today, hoping his luck would change for the better. He hadn't seen any cop cars cruising past in the time he had been here, and he wondered if they were still patrolling past her place or if all the available resources were being concentrated on the hunt for his good self. They had to be combing the city. They wouldn't guess he'd be cocky enough to turn up at Shannon Flinder's apartment. Maybe they thought he wouldn't even be able to get near.

His head was hurting and the sensory torture thing was starting to get worse. He had to end things. Today. And they were not going to end with him going back to jail.

He stared at Shannon. Why wasn't she doing what he'd told her? He felt a rush of anger. She was poised on the stair, visibly shaking, trying to get her breath, so ashen-faced he thought she might faint. Time seemed to break up and fracture into tiny, shimmering pieces that flew everywhere. Shannon's pale lips moved and he frowned as he tried to follow the words she stammered in not much more than a whisper.

'If you want to kill me you'll have to do it here. I'm not going anywhere with you. I won't do anything. How will killing me help? It'll just make things worse for you. Stop this now.'

He laughed. 'I might have known you'd say something stupid.'

Shannon edged back up the stairs. '*Me* say something stupid? What about you? You're the archetypal sad criminal, the boring old bogeyman who's had a shit life and takes it out on everyone. You're a walking cliché.'

'Don't worry. I won't bore you much longer.' If she thought insults and defiance was going to put him off and make him creep away ashamed, she had that dead wrong. He lunged at her and she screamed and jumped back, stumbled. A shaft of pain flashed through his head as he lunged again and brought her down. Shannon fell, screaming and flailing at the banister for support, her hair over her face. Richard grabbed a handful of hair and jerked her head back, jammed the gun against her right temple.

265

'Want me to kill you here then? I can do that. I'll shoot you in the stomach first. Or in that big gob of yours. Which is it to be? You choose.'

'No. No, please.' She was sobbing, gasping with terror. 'Don't.'

'You're the boring one,' he said. 'Not me. You're just another sad bitch.'

'Why did you kill my friend? Why did you kill Jenny?'

'What are you on about, you stupid cow?' Then he laughed. 'Yeah, I did. I killed her because I bloody felt like.' He had no idea what she was talking about, but let her believe that if it made her even more frightened. She was desperate now, would do anything to hang on to one more minute of precious life. 'Pick up those keys,' he ordered.

Shannon did as he said. She stumbled up the stairs ahead of him. On the landing she glanced around. But there was no escape.

'Unlock the door. Do it. Hurry up.'

Her hands were shaking so much she could barely manage the lock. Down in the hall, or somewhere around, Richard heard what sounded like a buzzer. He didn't have much time. He manhandled Shannon inside her apartment, keeping the gun jammed against her head, slammed the door and pushed her to her knees. Then he kicked her, sending her sprawling. The buzzer went again, and the phone started to ring. Through the living-room window he could hear someone shouting down in the street. It didn't matter. He stood over her, pointing the gun.

'Alone at last.'

All Shannon could think of as she lay winded and terrified, staring up at Richard Croft, was that the next time she left this apartment she might be zipped in a body bag. He must have been hanging around; it must have been him who had smashed Finbar's car windscreen and set the alarm off. His diversionary tactic had worked. And he would have been ready, waiting to rush in when Finbar ran out leaving the door to swing shut. Of course this had to happen just when she had her guard down,

266

thinking about how she was safe with Finbar and about to fly off with him to the house by the ocean. The car alarm in the street stopped, and the phone started to ring again. She could hear Finbar yelling from the street, yelling her name over and over. Of course he hadn't grabbed his set of keys to the apartment when he rushed out because he assumed she would be able to let him back in. Where were the bloody police?

Lying there clutching her stomach, half blinded by tears, Shannon saw Croft's dirty shoes come closer. She tried to roll over and scramble away, get to her feet. No chance. He dragged her back and knelt over her, straddling her chest. She kicked out, gulping for breath, crushed by his weight. The gun was in her face. His dark eyes stared down at her. Even now when he was doing his thing, the thing he liked most in the world, they were expressionless.

'I'd like to do more,' he said. 'But there isn't time.'

Did that mean he wasn't going to rape her? Or try? 'You can't do more,' she panted. 'Charlotte told me you couldn't finish the job. She was laughing about it. You're pathetic.'

She caught a flicker of anger. He grabbed her face, trying to hold her head still. Shannon made one frantic, desperate effort and twisted her head sideways, managed to sink her teeth hard into the soft flesh between his thumb and forefinger, fighting the urge to gag. He shouted in pain, stared in shock at the bright blood, and dropped the gun to clutch at his injured hand. Shannon tried with all her might to shove him off and roll out from beneath him. She brought up one arm, her shaking fingers closing around the gun. She grabbed it by the barrel, hoping it wouldn't go off, and lashed out with it, catching him in his left eye. Croft screamed and toppled sideways. Shannon struggled to her feet, gripping the gun, spitting in horror as she tasted his blood on her lips.

'Get out!' she screamed, levelling the gun at him. It felt so bloody heavy. 'Get *out* of here.'

Croft lunged at her and she ran. He followed her into the living room, blood dripping from his hand on to the shiny floor. 'Come here, you bitch.'

267

'I've got a gun, you stupid bastard, your bloody gun. I'll shoot if you come any nearer. Get away from me, get *out*.'

He took no notice, just kept coming at her. Did he think she wouldn't fire it? That she would just give up and be the victim? Shannon felt the breeze from the open window at her back, ruffling her hair.

'Get out,' she screamed. 'Go away.'

But he wasn't going anywhere. She jumped to one side as he rushed her again and turned, facing the windows. She levelled the gun again and squeezed the trigger. Or tried to. It wouldn't work.

'I'll kill you,' she shouted, dodging him again. 'Get away.'

He laughed. 'Stupid bitch.'

She squeezed the trigger again, harder. Croft had his back to the windows now. The gun went off, a deafening noise and blinding flash that knocked Shannon off her feet and sent pain jolting up her arms and across her shoulders. She landed on the sofa and slid to the floor, the breath knocked out of her; she dropped the gun. She wanted to close her eyes, but stopped herself. She saw Richard Croft's dark bulk outlined against the light of the low sash windows, also lifted off his feet, his arms wide. A spray of blood hit the white wall as he flew backwards and disappeared in a shower of splintering glass. There was a bang. Then silence.

A lot of time seemed to pass. Shannon got to her feet and steadied herself. She was sweating, trembling, drained. She staggered into the hall and pressed the button to open the downstairs front door, then opened her door and flung it wide. Feet pounded up the stairs.

'Shannon! Shannon!'

She stumbled back into the living room and looked out of the shattered window, her feet crunching broken glass. Richard Croft lay on the pavement below, surrounded by horrified passers-by. His jacket was half off one shoulder, the shirt beneath dark with blood where she had winged him. There was a huge dent in the roof of the white van he had landed on and rolled off, its windscreen shattered. She hoped no one had been inside. Croft's eyes were closed. He must be dead, killed by the fall not the bullet.

'Dead,' she whispered, biting her lip. People were staring up at her, pointing and calling. Did they think she had murdered him? In the distance she heard a siren; the cavalry arriving too late, as was their wont. Finbar rushed in and grabbed her, pulled her into his arms. Shannon could not speak, could not answer his urgent questions. She had no idea if she was all right. She couldn't feel anything.

She looked down into the street again, her face against Finbar's shoulder, staring at the dead man on the pavement. She experienced an overwhelming sense of fear and evil, more terrifying than when Croft had been astride her, pointing the gun in her face, and she had thought she would die.

'Shannon, for Christ's sake.' Finbar had tears in his eyes. 'Did he hurt you? Talk to me, please, tell me you're...!'

He broke off, following her shocked gaze. Richard Croft's eyelids were moving, fluttering. He opened his eyes and looked at the grey sky, as if seeing it for the first time. Or the last.

Then he looked at her.

Chapter Twenty-Five

Jevko could hear the radio playing in the small office at the end of the ward, a song about how no one knew what it was like to be the bad man or the sad man. The song brought tears to his eyes just when he had thought he couldn't feel anything else any more. The fat, grey-haired guard, her hips bumpy in the black trousers and her chest bulging through the blue shirt she wore, came back and shrugged at the sight of his untouched lunch tray.

'Not going to eat that?'

More stupid questions. 'No,' he replied. 'You can have it.' He stared at the peeling dirty-white paint on the ceiling. This place was so old, and it stank. Shepherd's pie, they had called the nauseating mess on the scratched plastic tray with accompanying plastic cutlery. There was another mess beside the shepherd's pie, a lump of yellow sponge topped with a glutinous dollop of custard. 'I only eat food.'

'Fussy, aren't we?' The guard took the tray. 'You're not helping yourself by not eating, you know.'

Like she cared. She didn't even call him by his name. She thought he was just another illegal asylum seeker, a bloody criminal. Some of the tattooed, unhinged souls who wandered around this hell called him a terrorist because he came from Afghanistan, alternately laughed at and swore at him, said 'fuzzy-wuzzies' didn't like it up 'em. Yesterday a solemn shrivelled old man had quoted at Jevko what he said was a Rudyard Kipling poem, something about being left for dead on the

Afghan plains, blowing out your brains and going to your God like a soldier. Jevko supposed quotes from poems were preferable to beatings, stabbings or acid baths. Loved ones being hauled away in the dead of night and murdered, their bodies turning up on waste ground or in the backs of dusty trucks.

'I want my wife,' Jevko said. 'I want my baby.'

But he had no hope of seeing Mariam or Shamila at the moment. Social workers, the lawyer, he did not know who exactly, were supposed to be arranging for his wife and child to visit him, but nothing had yet materialised and he did not know if or when it would. Jevko had no hope of anything ever again, despite what his useless lawyer tried to tell him. He could do nothing for Mariam or Shamila, nothing for himself. He wanted to die. The guard shrugged again, took the tray and lumbered off, her keys jangling and jigging over her hips.

Another cough stabbed his chest and tore through his thin, weakened frame. He had developed this chest infection a few days after being transferred to this prison on remand, and the antibiotics the doctor had prescribed him did not seem to be having much effect. Jevko did not care.

Nothing would happen now. It was all just wait, wait, wait. He was sick to his stomach. To his heart.

Jevko wanted to die.

Richard had always believed there was a place deep inside him that nothing and no one could touch, no matter what happened. To know that place existed and that he could retreat to it whenever he needed to had always helped him. But there was nowhere to retreat to now; the ancient, timeless, untouchable place had failed him, vanished for ever the second that doctor had shown him the X-ray – like he could understand that anyway – and explained about his damaged spine and broken vertebra, talked about irreversible nerve damage and spoken that terrible word: *paralysed*. He had gone on to talk about the previous head injury and what treatment they could give for that, but Richard had not listened, had not even tried to take it in. What was the point?

Panic had set in then and the tears had started to roll, soaking his pillow and leaving silvery snail tracks on his skin where they dried. Lying on the pavement outside Shannon Flinder's apartment, looking up into the dark-blue eyes of the woman he had wanted to kill but who had ended up almost killing him – he wished she had succeeded now – Richard had realised his injuries were serious. But he had assumed the numbness in his body was temporary, caused by shock and massive trauma. How far had he fallen, exactly? Lying flat, strapped to that stretcher, had been terrible, paramedics and then doctors asking him could he feel this or that, did he have tingling in his limbs, any feeling at all? He knew what they were thinking then, because he was thinking the same thing himself. Now the horror was confirmed.

Better to have been killed in that fall. Now he was trapped, an active mind trapped in a helpless lump of a body. Richard gathered things were not going to improve. He could not even kill himself. He would never again be able to do another thing for himself as long as he lived, not even change the channel on the television screen angled above him. He lay alone in this room in the spinal injuries unit. He would not stay here long, because there was nothing more they could do for him now.

Richard's panicked mind was crowded with images from his past as well as the nightmare present. He saw himself as a child going to church, making his first communion, hiding under the table from his father, feeling the sting of his mother's hard hands as she slapped his bare legs. He saw his victims and felt their struggles, heard their last breaths and gasps, the pointless pleas for mercy. Their spirits hovered in the room, closing around him. Richard did not feel sorry for what he had done, or feel pity for any of the women, only for himself. He thought of Shannon Flinder, still very much in the material world. She must be laughing her head off now. What she had done to him – shooting him in the shoulder and knocking him off his feet so that he flew backwards through that window – was attempted murder. She would get away with it of course.

272

How much longer would he live? More tears welled and spilled over. There was the head injury too. He had neglected to ask the doctors how much longer he had, and they probably did not know anyway. He wanted to die.

There were no police in his room or outside, although he had seen a few uniforms around. Why bother to guard him now? It wasn't like he was going to run off anywhere. Ever again. Richard wondered if this had been on the news and in the papers. From now on he would know only what people chose to tell him. He had no choices left. That thought made him want to scream, lose consciousness, never again wake up and be forced to confront the horror of what had happened to him.

A nurse walked in, a young woman he hadn't seen before. She looked warily at him, as they all did, and moved around the edges of the room, keeping her distance from the bed as if she feared he might jump up and grab her. None of them felt sorry for him, none had offered him one word of comfort or cheer. Not one word, period. Some sort of social worker or counsellor was supposed to be coming to talk to him. They could shove it. What could anyone say? Richard remembered the words his mother had always snapped at him whenever he cried: '*It's not the end of the world*'.

It was the end of his world now.

'Paralysed from the neck down?' Finbar stared out at the dark river. 'Jesus Christ. I'd rather be dead.'

Shannon turned over, pulling the quilt over her bare shoulders. 'What, do you feel sorry for him or something?'

'Of course I'm not bloody sorry for him.' He went to the bed, sat down and wrapped his arms around her; she was shivering. 'Did you manage to get some sleep? Why don't I get you a hot water bottle?'

'And a cup of tea, yeah, right.'

He held her gently, stroking her arms and back. 'Don't knock it.'

'What time is it?'

'You mean, now?' Finbar smiled down at her but she didn't respond. He shook his sweater sleeve out of the way and

273

glanced at his watch. 'Just gone eight-thirty. How about some supper? Want to watch telly?'

'Lovely. The news, my favourite programme. No thanks. I wish Croft was dead,' she whispered. 'It'll never be over now.' She slid out of his arms, turned away and lay down again, hugging the pillow.

'Come on, Shannon.' He felt another rush of anxiety. She had been like this for the past day or so; lying in bed, not eating, hardly sleeping. 'It is over. Not in your head, of course. Or mine. That'll take time.'

'I'm bloody sick and tired of taking time to get over things. Other people lead quiet, boring lives. Why the hell can't I?'

He leaned over her, smoothing back strands of her hair. 'It'll be quiet from now on, I promise. More quiet than you know what to do with. You'll be raving for a bit of excitement.'

She started to cry. 'I won't.'

Shannon felt more freaked now than when she had thought Richard Croft might kill her. The feeling would not go away; she felt she would never get over this, never again be able to lead a normal life. She had had to bounce back – that stupid phrase – too many times. Now all she could do was try to keep the shattered pieces of her personality superglued together, and that might take what little strength she had left.

She sobbed into the pillow as a worried Finbar held her, kissing her and murmuring how it was going to be all right, she was safe now, they both were, he loved her so much and she loved him and he wasn't going to let anything or anyone hurt her ever again. They were words that Shannon wanted, needed to hear, but she could not believe them or feel comforted.

'Something will hurt me again,' she cried. 'No matter what I do. I can marry you and go and live in that house by the ocean and never leave it again, and something terrible will still happen. I'm not safe, no one is. Jenny wasn't. I loved her, I miss her.'

'Of course you do. It was terrible what happened. It's too much for anyone to take. You feel bad now, of course you do.'

274

Shannon was glad he did not spout bullshit about how she was strong and would get through. He went on holding her and she stopped crying eventually. She lay there, feeling exhausted, her eyes shut against the lamplight, feeling his heartbeat, smelling his sexy, comforting smell. Through the open window she could hear the night sounds of the city and the river. She had not been back to her apartment since Croft had forced his way in and tried to murder her; she felt she could never go back there again, not even to pack stuff in preparation for moving. She felt like she could not cope with anything.

'What am I going to do now?' she whispered, more to herself than him.

'I'll tell you what.' Finbar pulled her into his arms. 'I'm going to get you a hot water bottle, some veggie soup, and chicken sandwiches with the crusts cut off. After that you can have a cup of tea and a few chocolates. We'll watch some telly. Later you're going to pop one of those cute little yellow tablets the doctor prescribed, and have a healing, dreamless and unbroken night's sleep.'

'I love tranqillisers,' Shannon murmured. 'I can understand why people get addicted.'

'Yeah, well.' He smiled and kissed her again. 'You've had two out of the fifteen he gave you, but maybe you won't need the rest.'

'Don't count on it. I'll be back down that surgery to demand a few hundred more.'

'Hmm, worrying. Think I'd better phone that Victim Support counsellor who so kindly offered his services.'

Shannon threw him a startled look. '*Fuck* off.'

'That's her, that's my Shannon.' Finbar got off the bed grinning. 'It's all right, darling, I was just joking about the nasty counsellor man. You relax, OK? I'll be right back with your supper.'

She snuggled down in bed again. 'I'll have a few crisps with the sandwiches,' she called as he went out.

She was surprised to find how hungry she was. After wolfing the soup, sandwiches and crisps she lay back in Finbar's arms to sip tea and nibble Neuhaus pralines while they watched an episode from yet another re-run of *Das Boot*.

'I keep thinking the U-boat Captain's about to say something incredibly profound when he stares at his crew,' she murmured, winding the green-and-yellow chocolate box ribbon around one finger, 'something you'd want to make a note of. But when he does finally open his mouth, all he says is "good men", or remarks on the rough weather or how the tinned meat is badly shaved.'

'You're missing the point, you fluffy female. He's strong and silent and cool, isn't he? Like me.'

She smiled. 'Oh yes, just like you, darling.'

'A guy who can convey any thought or emotion he wants just with a gleam of his eyes. That's profound in itself.'

'You're so right. Thank you for pointing it out to me.'

'You're more than welcome.'

Shannon felt so sleepy she did not need a tranquilliser.

'Darling Alex, can't you hear me at all?'

Obviously not. Desperate for some response, Wanda squeezed his hand again, tears running down her face and dripping off her chin. She had been here all night.

'So anyway,' she resumed, blotting her tears. 'As I said, I'm sure I'll love the new job.'

There was no new job, of course. No new nothing. Only old nightmares, real and imagined. And the police interrogating her, asking her why she had lied about being in Cindy Nightingale's house the day Cindy fell down her own stairs. *'Why did you lie to us, Wanda? Why?'*

She had finally admitted she had been to Cindy's house that day, and said Cindy had been alive when she left, but they didn't believe that. She had even tried again, in her panic, to shove blame on to Shannon Flinder. Anything to make the police leave her alone! Wanda couldn't tell Alex all this bad stuff, of course, just in case any of it should penetrate his dark sleep and panic him. Although she was starting to think nothing would ever again penetrate his brain. She could not tell him she

276

was still shaking with terror after her latest run-in with the police, and thought she might be arrested and charged with murder any time. But there was nothing to prove she had killed Cindy – especially as she hadn't! There were only her prints on that damn gin glass and her admission that she had panicked and run off when Cindy fell downstairs, drunk. But she had lied, that was the problem. That was what looked so suspicious. Of all the unbelievable, terrible things to happen, like there wasn't enough shit going on in her life! And what was she supposed to do now, without a job? She wouldn't even be able to afford the nasty flat in that nasty old house, surrounded by those moron neighbours with their mindless animosity.

Panic shimmered over her in waves, like a fever. Events and memories began to intrude, things Wanda had pushed deep down into her dark subconscious, locked away and intended never to resurrect. She was losing control over everything. She suddenly felt she could not stay here any longer, even if she did have the whole day free now. She would go back to the flat and get some sleep. Then try to think what to do next. Wanda realised that a nurse and the consultant had come into the room and were standing by Alex's bed. The consultant was tall and dark haired, wearing a dark suit. He looked relaxed and confident.

'Good morning, Mrs Brennan. Could I have a word, please?'

Wanda wondered what she had done to deserve a visit from the man himself. She got up and followed him outside. Her legs felt weak and she could not stop trembling. She had a moment of blank-out, where she could not be sure that what seemed to be happening was real. It was as if she was outside herself, an independent witness shaking her head sorrowfully over the traumatic events that kept hitting this poor bloody woman, and thinking, thank God it wasn't her. It felt cold in the corridor. The nurse touched her arm.

'All right, Wanda?'

She nodded, then shook her head. 'No. Not really.' She bit her lip as more tears welled up. 'Sorry. I'm a bit tired, I—'

'Yes, of course. It's OK, don't worry.' The consultant was looking at her with pity. 'Mrs Brennan, we were thinking—'

277

'No!' Wanda backed away, horrified. She knew what was coming – it was what she had dreaded. 'You're not doing it,' she shouted. 'No way.'

He looked startled. 'Not ...?'

'You're not switching off Alex's life support. Don't you dare. You can't do that, I won't let you. You'll have to kill me first. Don't you touch one hair of his head except to help him.' She was sobbing now. 'Oh God, Alex! I love him so much. You can't do this. I won't let him go, I can't!'

'Wanda.' The nurse reached for her but Wanda dodged out of the way and rushed back into Alex's room. She ran to the bed and cradled him in her arms, her tears dripping on to his forehead.

'Leave him alone,' she shouted 'Don't touch him, don't hurt him. He'll live, he's got to live. I won't let you touch him. Go away!'

She would stay here for as long as it took.

Chapter Twenty-Seven

'India Buildings was designed by an architect named Herbert Rowse and inspired by his travels in the US of A,' Paula, Finbar's office manager intoned as Shannon tapped her fingers on the desk. 'It was originally built for the Blue Funnel shipping line in the nineteen twenties and early thirties, and designed so that it could be converted to a warehouse in case it proved impossible to let as office space.'

'Very impressive, but can you save that spiel for Finbar's clients?' Shannon moved to the windows and looked down into Water Street. 'I've got other things to think about at the minute.'

'I'm sure you have.' Paula looked at her. 'How *are* you now, Shannon?'

'Terrific,' Shannon muttered, wishing the girl would shut up.

'Is it good to be back at work? How are your colleagues treating you?'

'Welcomed with open arms, that's what I am.' That wasn't quite true, at least not as far as Mi-Hae Kam was concerned. Khalida and Leon were delighted that she was back though. Shannon turned. 'How long d'you think Finbar will be?

'Hard to say.' Paula looked at the closed office door. 'This very important meeting's run on longer than I expected. And I think he wants to take those two boring bastards to lunch. Well, he doesn't want to, of course, but hey. You know how it is.'

'I won't hang about then. I just thought I'd drop in to see if he was available.'

Shannon was still freaked after a phone call from Cathy Rose to tell her that Wanda Brennan was being questioned by the police about Cindy Nightingale's death, and had tried to cast suspicion on her, saying she would have had a motive to kill Cindy. And Wanda had been in Cindy's house that day.

'She broke down eventually,' Cathy said, 'and admitted she'd been to see Cindy Nightingale the day she died. But she swears Cindy was alive when she left. She kept saying you could have killed her because you wanted to stop Cindy proving you'd had your father-in-law murdered.'

'That all sounds very fanciful.' Shannon had tried to keep the fear out of her voice. 'A lot of journalists go on to become crime novelists, don't they? Maybe that should be Mrs Brennan's next career move.'

'She's not a journalist any more – she got the sack. For being late and taking too much time off to spend with her husband, apparently. Seems a bit harsh.'

'Forgive me for not bursting with sympathy at the moment. Are you saying you think Wanda Brennan killed Cindy Nightingale? I thought her death was supposed to be an accident.'

'We've got no proof either way. But it is suspicious that Wanda Brennan lied.'

'Why would she kill Cindy – if she did?'

'Well, that's the thing. She's got no motive, not that we can see.'

Shannon sweated. 'Neither have I. I've also got more than enough alibis to prove I never went anywhere near her house that day.'

'Don't worry, Shannon, I'm not accusing *you*. I just thought it was weird what she said about Cindy Nightingale telling her she believed you'd had your father-in-law murdered.'

'Cindy Nightingale never liked me, Cathy. From the second we met I just knew she had it in for me. I don't know why, it was just one of those things. She questioned me after Bernard

Flinder was murdered, and I know she would have liked to nail me for that – or anything! Simply because she took a dislike to me. When she had to let it go because – of course – there was no evidence, she was pissed off and she has been ever since. I've heard she also often took against colleagues for no particular reason.'

'Mm. She could be somewhat ... intense, shall we say?'

Cathy Rose seemed to think either Wanda or Cindy – or both of them – talked a lot of rubbish. Shannon had to hope she didn't change her mind. Was the Bernard Flinder business never going to go away and leave her in peace? After that she had rushed here to tell Finbar. But he was caught up in this damn meeting.

'So how do you do it?' Paula was asking.

Shannon started. 'Do what?'

'Go on looking great, despite the awful things that happen to you?'

'Sheer bloody mindedness.' The phone rang.

'Oh, bugger,' Paula sighed. 'Then again, it might actually be someone I want to talk to.'

'I'll leave you to it.' Shannon backed away.

'What's up with that stoopid ol' be-atch now?' she heard Paula demand as she walked out. 'I mean, I can understand she's pissed off about the other night in that club, but it's not my fault if her bloke suddenly gets the hots for me, is it? I didn't give him any encouragement.' Shannon rolled her eyes

She went back to the office, buying a cheese roll on the way. It felt strange being back at work, like nothing had ever happened. She did not know how things would work out, if she would stay with this firm much longer. She would wait and see how it went. In the meantime, she supposed it was good to get back to work and strive for a feeling of normality. Although at the moment she could not summon up much enthusiasm. Her morning in court, representing a shoplifter who claimed innocence, a clubber who had got into a fight and bitten off someone's earlobe, insisting she had done it in self-defence, and a woman who was facing jail for not being able to pay her television licence, had bored the hell out of her.

'DI Casey called round,' Helena informed her. 'He wanted a chat.'

'I've got nothing to say to him. It's enough to know I'm no longer at risk from an escaped psycho.'

'Yes.' Helena smoothed her long dark hair and smiled. 'At least not that particular psycho any more, anyway.'

'I can always rely on you to come up with the appropriate comforting words, can't I?

'All part of the service.'

Shannon made herself a cup of coffee and ate the cheese roll. She had a tape of a police interview to listen to, paperwork to catch up on and a letter to write for a client who wanted a solicitor's letter sent to their neighbour threatening legal action if they did not desist from what they claimed was aggressive behaviour and criminal damage. But her immediate priority was Wanda Brennan. The woman might be going through hell what with her husband in a coma and everything, but that did not excuse her talking bullshit to the police about how Shannon could have murdered Cindy bloody Nightingale. Shannon started to dial the number of the newspaper office, then remembered Cathy Rose had told her Wanda had been sacked. She did not know Wanda's mobile or home phone number, or her address. Where was the woman now? At the hospital, probably, spending time with her husband.

'Damn,' Shannon whispered. She had no desire to go barging in while Wanda Brennan sat holding her husband's hand, wishing he would open his eyes, sit up and start talking to her. Or just open his eyes. But Wanda had tried to cast suspicion on her, and Shannon decided she could not let that go.

A tiny envelope on her PC screen told her she had e-mail; the mail was from Anita, the secretary at her and Jenny's old firm, Steele & Monckton. Shannon clicked on it and started to read.

'What the...?' She stared. Then she called Anita.

'Shannon, hi.'

'How are you?'

'Not great. Still missing you. And Jenny, of course. It's horrible without her around. I'm not having such a good day.'

'Me neither. We'll have to get together soon, OK? Go out for a drink or meal or something.'

'I'd like that.'

'Anita ... I was just looking at your e-mail, scrolling down that list of Jenny's old clients you sent me.'

'Oh yes. I know you wanted as much info as possible about what she was working on before she died, in case it could be relevant to the murder inquiry. But then they arrested that man and I didn't think about it any more. Then I came across this draft e-mail I'd done but forgotten about, so I just clicked it to you.'

'There's a name here – Wanda Brennan. Know anything about her?'

'She's a journalist on some local paper. She was a client of ours – briefly. Very briefly, actually. Her husband got attacked and—'

'Yes, I know about him. Wanda Brennan was a client of yours? When? How long ago?'

'I dunno. Couple of months. I remember she was always complaining because she thought we weren't doing enough for her husband, although quite what she thought we could do I'm not sure. I don't know why Gavin agreed to take her on in the first place. Well, I do actually.' Anita lowered her voice. 'Because he's a money-grubbing little bastard. Anyway, he saw her just the one time then shoved her on to Jenny.'

'Wanda Brennan knew Jenny?' Shannon's voice rose in shock. 'How come I didn't know?'

Because no one bloody well told you, she thought. Including Wanda herself, those times when she pestered me. Why didn't she tell me she'd met Jenny, had dealings with her? Shannon could barely take in what Anita was saying.

'So Wanda Brennan dumped us – it must have been a day or so after Jenny's murder. The day she phoned to dump us she demanded to speak to Jenny, but of course—'Anita's voice wavered '—Jenny wasn't here any more. So I put her on to Gavin. He didn't want to take the call, naturally.'

'Did the police ask for a list of people Jenny was dealing with?'

'Yes, and I gave it to them. But I've heard nothing more. Not that I'd necessarily expect to.'

Shannon talked a bit more to Anita then said goodbye and phoned Inspector Rose, who promised to get back to her. Five minutes later she did.

'Yes, Shannon, Wanda Brennan was checked out along with everyone else on that list. She admitted she'd known Jenny and been a client of Steele & Monckton, if only briefly. She spent that night – the night of Jenny's murder, that is – at the hospital with her husband.'

'What, the whole night?'

'Yes. The day staff found her asleep in a chair beside his bed when they came on duty. Brennan's alibi for the night of Jenny's murder is solid, if that's what you're worried about.'

'Oh. Well.' Shannon relaxed. 'I didn't really think ...' She laughed shakily. 'OK, I suppose I did for a minute. I just thought it was strange that Wanda never mentioned she'd known Jenny. Not to me, anyway.'

'I'll ask her about that when we talk to her again.'

'Which hospital is her husband in, d'you know?'

'The Royal.'

The dark horse with red hair, Shannon thought as she hung up. Well, Wanda Brennan owes me a few answers now. She drank the rest of her coffee, took her bag and car keys and drove up the hill to the Royal Liverpool hospital. She followed the signs for the Intensive Care unit and pressed the buzzer outside the closed and locked doors.

'I'm looking for Wanda Brennan,' she said when the intercom crackled. 'Would she be here?'

'Who are you, please?'

'My name's Shannon Flinder, I'm a solicitor.'

'Oh. Well, actually we've got something of a situation going on here. Does Wanda know you?'

'She does.'

'Could you talk to her? She's in a bit of a state. One of our counsellors tried, but she told him to ... anyway, come in.'

The buzzer went and Shannon pushed open the door and walked inside. A situation? What did that mean exactly? A young nurse with a flushed face and long brown plait came to greet her.

'Hi. It's this way.'

'Look, what's happening? I don't know if I can—' Shannon stopped as they came to a room outside which were standing several nurses, a doctor and a security guard.

'We don't want to call the police if we can avoid that,' the nurse explained. 'It might make things worse for her. But if Wanda keeps refusing to come out, we've got no choice. There don't seem to be any relatives or friends we can phone, or not any who could get here quickly. If you could talk to her and persuade her to come out, that'd be great. She's got this idea that we want to switch off her husband's life support, but that's not true. The consultant just wanted to have a word with her about her husband's condition and tell her he thought it would be a good idea if she talked to a counsellor because all this is so much trauma for her. A nurse tried the other day, and got nowhere, so they asked him to talk to her. Wanda just freaked, she didn't give him a chance to explain. She immediately thought the worst and panicked. We were getting worried about her, thinking she was at the end of her tether, and this confirms it.'

Shannon looked into the room. Wanda Brennan stood by her husband's bed clutching his hand, her other hand stroking his brown hair. She was crimson faced, sobbing and shaking. Shannon felt scared at the sight of her. And sorry. This was not a moment to start upbraiding Wanda for pestering her, writing crap about her and Jenny, and trying to get her accused of murder. She walked in.

'Hi, Wanda.' Shannon kept her voice gentle. 'Having a bad day? One of many, I imagine.'

Wanda stared. 'What the hell are you doing here?'

'I came to find you. I thought it was time we had a talk.'

'About what?' Wanda kept running her fingers through her husband's hair.

'Well – about how I can help you.'

'You don't want to help me, you never did. And you said ... you said—'

'What?'

'You called Alex a vegetable!'

'I didn't! That's rubbish. I'd never say that, not about anyone. Who said I did?'

'Cindy Nightingale.'

'I might have known. Wanda, she's a ... she was a trouble-maker. She was lying.'

'I didn't kill Cindy Nightingale,' Wanda shouted. 'She fell. I didn't touch her.'

Shannon glanced round at the nurses and doctor, who were all listening.

'She said she had Alex's file, that there was some witness statement in it that I hadn't known about. I wanted to see it, but she wouldn't let me. I ran around looking for it, ran upstairs and she followed. She was trying to drag me back – we struggled. But I didn't push her, I swear. I was just trying to get free as I thought she'd make me fall. Then she fell. It was terrible. Oh God. I didn't do anything to her, I swear!'

Shannon had the urge to turn and walk away from this, leave Wanda to the hospital security staff. Or the police, who wanted to talk to her some more anyway. She did not know if Wanda was telling the truth about not pushing Cindy, but thought she probably was; she could not imagine her as a murderer. She glanced back at the nurses and doctor again. 'Let's forget Cindy Nightingale for now. Listen, the hospital staff don't want to switch off Alex's life support. You panicked, jumped to the wrong conclusion before the consultant had a chance to explain.'

'No,' Wanda wailed. 'They've wanted to do it for ages.'

'That's not true. Look, you can't stay here like this. The nurses have to check Alex, do things for him. You're stopping them helping him.'

'Stopping them killing him!'

'No. They can't switch off his life support, just like that. Not even if they wanted to, and they don't, I promise. They can't do it without your permission.'

'Is that true?'

'Of course it's true.'

'Really?'

'Yes.' Shannon suddenly felt very tired. She glanced at the tubes, the filling catheter bag, the machines poor Alex Brennan was hooked up to, and suppressed a shiver. 'Please, Wanda, let the nurses help Alex. That's all they want to do, help him.'

'We need to change Alex's feeding tube, Wanda,' one of them called. 'It's long overdue.'

'See? Come on.' Shannon held out one hand. 'Let them do their job. No wonder you're upset,' she said, looking round again. 'This is too much for anyone to cope with. And it's been going on for so long now.'

'No one helps me,' Wanda moaned. 'Nobody cares.'

'The hospital staff care. I care. The consultant only wanted to suggest that you talk to somebody.' Like that would help, Shannon thought. 'Everyone knows how hard this is for you. How alone you must feel.' Wanda was staring at her again and Shannon wondered if she believed or was even listening to a word she spoke. 'Come on,' she repeated. 'Let's go and sit down somewhere. Take a break. We'll talk.'

Wanda let go of Alex. She bent and kissed him, smoothed her tears off his pale forehead. 'I love you,' she whispered. She came around the bed and put her warm, clammy hand in Shannon's, like a trusting little girl. They walked out of the unit, down the corridor and into a visitors' room, where Wanda collapsed into a chair and started crying again.

'I'll get her a cup of tea.' The nurse hurried off.

Shannon put one arm around Wanda's shaking shoulders. She could not even begin to imagine how she would feel if it was Finbar lying in there. She did not know what to say to Wanda now, how to comfort her. How could you comfort somebody who had to deal with that? She also did not want to

287

make any promises she might not be able to keep. Wanda raised her head and looked at her, her bloodshot eyes streaming.

'Will you help me?'

Shannon hesitated. 'How?'

'Protect Alex. Don't let them switch off his life support.'

'Wanda, I told you, they're not going to do that.'

'All right, maybe not now. But in future.'

'It's still a long-drawn-out legal process before it could happen. We're talking months. Maybe even years.'

'So...?' Terrible hope flickered across Wanda's features. 'During that time Alex might wake up?'

'I suppose it's possible.' If not probable. Shannon got the impression the doctors and nurses did not rate that chance very highly.

'I want the police to arrest that man who hurt Alex – Richard Croft.'

'Richard...? Didn't you know?' Shannon looked at her, startled. She told Wanda what had happened to Croft. 'But you can't be sure he attacked Alex, can you?' she finished. Any more than she could be sure Croft had murdered Jenny. No evidence had come to light.

'No. But it's all a hell of coincidence.'

The nurse came back with a mug of tea which Wanda took and drank in gulps despite its steaming heat. She rooted in her bag, pulled out a pack of king-size cigarettes and lit one, difficult for her to do because her hands were trembling so much.

'No smoking in here, Wanda, love.' The nurse pointed at the notice.

'Oh, shit.' Wanda got to her feet and glanced around. Shannon stood up too.

'Don't suppose you could give her a lift home?' the nurse asked. 'Or if not, we could phone a cab. Didn't you say your car was at the garage, Wanda?'

'Yes. It's OK,' Wanda said. 'I can get the bus.'

'I'll give you a lift home.' And that would be it, Shannon thought. She didn't want anything more to do with Wanda Brennan.

288

'Thanks. That's very nice of you.' Wanda re-lit her cigarette the minute they got outside. 'Can I smoke in your car?' she asked. 'If I keep the window open?'

'Yes.' Shannon pulled her keys out of her coat pocket. Who was she to deny Wanda her nicotine fix in the circumstances? They got in and she started the engine. 'Where do you live, Wanda?'

The boarded-up windows of knackered houses and groups of menacing-looking, loitering youths would be enough to depress anyone without Wanda's problems, Shannon thought fifteen minutes later as she turned into the street and stopped outside the house number Wanda told her.

'Thanks very much for the lift, it was really kind of you. Come in for a minute?'

'Well – I don't really have time.' Or inclination.

'Oh, just for a minute. I'm still a bit upset, and it'd help to have someone ...'

'All right.' And that was *definitely* it, Shannon thought. The police could decide whatever had happened in Cindy Nightingale's house the day she died; Shannon still believed it was an accident. Wanda had probably freaked and run off the minute Cindy had fallen, and lied because she had been too frightened to tell the truth. That had not been very clever because it had landed her in a lot of trouble now. And she would not ask Wanda why she had not mentioned knowing Jenny; Wanda had probably forgotten all about that. She looked as if she could barely function on any level at present.

The garden of the old house was a tangled mess, and the narrow hall with its dark, greasy lino reeked of stale cooking. A child playing with a doll gave them a long, measuring stare as they passed. Wanda's flat was a shock.

'Excuse the mess.' She waved her third cigarette in fifteen minutes at a pile of cardboard boxes and dirty washing dumped in the tiny hallway. Shannon caught a glimpse of the kitchen and averted her eyes. Every room of the cramped flat was stuffed with unpacked boxes of clothes, books, crockery, shoes,

289

all kinds of household junk. In the sitting room it was difficult to find a place to sit, and Shannon was not sure she wanted to anyway.

'Hang on, I'll just move these ...' Wanda shifted a heap of old magazines and newspapers. They crashed to the floor and she laughed nervously, puffing smoke. 'Take a pew.' She moved another pile of stale-smelling clothing. Underneath were dirty spoons and forks and a couple of mould-encrusted dinner plates. Shannon gasped.

'Sorry. That is disgusting, isn't it?' Wanda swept them up and disappeared into the kitchen. There was another plate just visible beneath a magazine. A cork popped and something smashed. Shannon winced and closed her eyes, slid further towards the edge of the armchair and checked again that she was not sitting on something horrible. This was the kind of place where you wiped your feet on the way out.

'I'm afraid I've been a bit of a slob these past months,' Wanda apologised, coming back with a bottle of white wine and two dusty glasses that Shannon guessed she had unearthed from one of the boxes. 'Just been rushing between work and the hospital – well, not work any more, of course, not since I got sacked.' She sighed.

'Have you got any job interviews lined up? Oh, not for me, thanks,' Shannon said as Wanda started to pour a second glass of wine.

'You sure?'

'I'm driving.'

'Oh, yeah. Oh well, cheers!' Wanda took a slug of wine then tipped the contents of Shannon's glass into her own, spilling some. 'Shit.' She lit another cigarette and sighed again. 'No, nothing lined up so far. I've sent my CV to a couple of editors, but it's a bit soon to expect to hear from them. They're busy people.'

Shannon felt exhausted. She decided not to go back to the office. She had more or less finished for today anyway. She would call Finbar when she got out of here. She felt like driving back to his apartment, gazing out at the river while she slowly

290

sipped a glass of champagne, then getting into bed with him for the rest of the day, only getting out to fetch more champagne and microwave cartons of gourmet stuff. And that was what she would bloody well do. This woman had already caused her enough trouble and she didn't want to spend one more minute letting Wanda's chill, depressing aura of hopelessness and tragedy suck up what little energy she had left. It was true, some people did seem to suck up your energy. She reached for her bag.

'You seem a lot calmer now. I'd better get going.'

'But you said we could talk.' Wanda frowned and sat up straight. 'You promised you'd help me.'

'We have talked.' Shannon's voice was firm. 'I've had it for today. I'm wiped, wasted, wrecked, you name it. I'm going home.'

'Nice for you that you've got a home to go to.' Wanda's eyes narrowed. 'A real home, I mean, not a shithole like this. And that you've got a man in good health who loves you.'

'Yes.' Shannon felt annoyed now. 'Aren't I the spoilt bitch.'

Wanda blew out a stream of smoke. 'You said it.'

'Now look, I ...!' Shannon paused, gripped by freezing shock as she stared down at Wanda – or rather, Wanda's upturned sole. Dingy grey-blue, the little black logo on one side, *Ikon*. Markings made by treading out burning cig ends. Drawing pin, dirty white, stuck in the heel.

It's coincidence, she thought. It has to be. She had pictured this footprint, thought about it, wondered where it had come from, to whom it belonged. Imagined it walking around Jenny's lifeless body, standing in her blood.

Now she was seeing it for real.

Chapter Twenty-Eight

'Hey, boss!'

'Stop calling me that, will you?' Cathy Rose stared at the night-time CCTV footage of St George's Hall and its environs on the screen in front of her. 'What d'you think this is, Paul, bloody Lynley or Frost or something? We're the reality, not the so-called art imitating it.'

'Sorry, b ... er ...' The DC, Paul King, stood there looking like a spare part.

'Well, get on with it. I'm due to appear on *Crimewatch* this evening.'

He gaped. 'Are you?'

'*No.* What's up?'

'They've managed to pinpoint the location of that anonymous phone call made the night of Jenny Fong's murder – the call which placed Jekvo Arib at the scene, gave his van number and said he was acting suspiciously. It was made from a booth just outside Lime Street station.'

Cathy frowned. 'And why's it taken this long?' Cindy Nightingale burying it probably, she thought.

'Don't know. There's a camera nearby which would have caught on film anyone who used that phone booth that night.'

'Great,' Cathy sighed. 'How I love scrolling through aeons of CCTV footage!'

It was all she seemed to do lately. She did not like CCTV much herself, believing it gave many people a false sense of security, and that better street lighting would do more to discourage crime. But it did help sometimes. Not much luck with the Jenny Fong murder though. If the case didn't break soon she would have to go on to other stuff. And there was lots of other stuff. She got up from the desk and stretched, glancing around the office.

'Bring it on then.' She smoothed her hair and pulled down the sleeves of her jacket. 'Let's take a look.'

Paul King got his smart-arse look. 'I already did.'

'Wow.' Cathy stared at him. 'Showing initiative, whatever next? So, yes, and ...?'

'A face you'll recognise.' Paul grinned. 'Making a call at exactly the right time. And very near the Fong murder scene.'

'Really?' Cathy got a thrill that took away her tiredness. 'Set it up.'

A minute later she was staring at an image of that face as it turned towards the camera and emerged from the phone booth after making a call. 'Well, well. Weird!'

Paul's grin broadened. 'Isn't it just.'

'But what the hell ...?' Cathy slumped back in her chair. 'More explaining needed, I think,' she murmured as Paul replayed the image. 'A lot more. Better pull this person in again right now.'

'Shall I tell *Crimewatch* you can't make it?' Paul asked.

'Wiped and wrecked, are you?' Wanda downed her glass of wine, poured more and lit another cigarette. She slid further down the sofa, balancing the glass on her round stomach. 'Well, so am I. Desperate to forget about poor, fat, tragic, unemployed me? So am I. Want to drive home to your posh apartment and sexy boyfriend? So do I. What's up?' she demanded. 'You look like you've just had some very bad news.'

Shannon perched on the edge of the soft, lumpy, armchair, trembling with shock, trying to still the wild thoughts zipping around her brain. She averted her eyes from Wanda's dusty, upturned trainer, the whirls and grooves, the drawing pin stuck in the heel. It's coincidence, she told herself again, it has to be.

Lots of people get drawing pins stuck in the soles of their shoes, and until very recently Wanda Brennan had worked in an environment where there must have been squillions of the things lying around. She smokes – again, so do lots of people. This is mad, it doesn't mean anything.

'What's up?' Wanda repeated, staring at her. She laughed.

Shannon suddenly wondered if Cindy Nightingale's death was an accident. Wanda had been at her house that day. If she was innocent, if she hadn't done anything, why run off and keep quiet? Even if she had been frightened, surely she would have realised it was best to tell the truth? Wanda seemed different now, not so hapless and helpless any more. And if that trainer of hers was the mystery footprint that the police were trying to identify, it placed her at Jenny's murder scene. What had she been doing there? Christ, Shannon thought. Freezing fear gripped her. She got to her feet. Her legs were shaking.

'Nothing's up,' she said. 'I'm going home now.'

'Oh, don't go yet. Just when we're having such a nice chat. And aren't we going to talk about how you can help Alex and me?'

'Some other time.' She had to get out of here. 'See you, Wanda.'

'Wait.' Wanda jumped up, frighteningly agile all of a sudden, and darted around the back of the sofa, reaching the sitting-room door before Shannon could get there. 'I've got something to show you.'

'Forget it.' Shannon's mouth was dry. She gripped her bag. 'It'll keep.'

'No, it won't.' Wanda ran out.

She had to call Cathy Rose. Shannon headed for Wanda's front door, desperate to escape. But Wanda stood in the tiny hall blocking her exit.

'Don't go yet, Shannon.'

She smiled and held up the knife.

'Why didn't you tell me Shannon had been here?'

'I'm telling you now, aren't I?' Paula's mascaraed lashes were downcast and she thought it might be a good idea to close her copy of *All About Soap* that she had been engrossed in until this unwelcome interruption.

'Yeah, after I've just got back from lunch with those two boring bastards.' Finbar grabbed the magazine and flung it across the room. 'You should have told me before.'

'Well, you were talking to them as you walked out. And I was on the phone.'

'You're always on the bloody phone.'

'Shannon said not to bother you. She said she'd just popped in on the spur of the moment, it wasn't a big deal and she'd see you later. So don't go taking it out on me, OK, Mister Big Boss Man? It's not my fault you had to sit through lunch with two boring bastards and pick up the tab afterwards.'

'If that's another of your bloody mates,' Finbar said as he pointed at the ringing phone, 'tell them to call you back on your mobile or at home. And home's where you'll be spending lots of time soon if you don't buck up your ideas quick-sharp'

Paula looked up at him, hurt. 'Charming. Classy.'

He strode into his office and slammed the door, sat at his desk and leaned back sighing. The truth was he hated to let Shannon out of his sight, even though Croft was no longer a danger to her. She seemed better and more relaxed, able to cope again, but he was not sure she really was all right. How could she be yet? He thought about her all the time, had to stop himself calling her too often. But he wouldn't stop himself now. Finbar got up again, went to the door and opened it. He looked out at Paula.

'Sorry.'

She gave him the middle finger, keeping her eyes on the PC screen. 'I forgive you, thousands wouldn't. But yeah, I should have told you before. Just didn't think.'

'You can tell your mates you work for a bastard.'

'They already know that. Now if you'll excuse me I'm trying to type some letters.'

He went back into his office and shut the door, dialled Shannon's mobile number. There was no answer, so he called the Kam Flinder Najeba office.

'Shannon's not here, sorry,' Helena informed him. 'I don't know where she went. But she should have been back by now because she's got an appointment with a client in just under ten minutes. The client's already arrived.'

'Ask her to call me when she gets in, will you? Thanks, Helena.'

He tried Shannon's mobile again, then left a message on her voicemail. 'Call me, Shannon, please. Soon as you can.'

He flipped his phone closed, stood up and stared out of the window at the slow-moving traffic down in Water Street.

Got that bad feeling.

'This is stupid,' Shannon said after what seemed an eternity of silence and stillness. 'Just let me walk out of here now, Wanda, OK? If you put that knife down and let me go, I promise you I'll forget this.' Well, maybe not. 'I won't say anything to anybody.' She paused, searching Wanda's pale, impassive face for some spark of response, waiting and hoping for the realisation to dawn on the woman that she was actually standing here menacing somebody with a Sabatier carving knife.

'Look, I know you've been – are – under a hell of a strain,' she went on, trying to keep her voice steady. Her head was all over the place and she was talking on auto-pilot. 'Too much for anyone to take.'

'Kind words.' Wanda gripped the knife handle more tightly. 'Useless words. I've heard so many – too bloody many.'

'Yes, I know. Look. Come on.' Shannon tried to fight back a wave of debilitating panic. She jumped as she felt a movement in her bag and realised it was her mobile shuddering in silent ring mode. She didn't dare even attempt to answer it. 'No!' she gasped as Wanda moved towards her. 'Wanda, don't, for Christ's sake ...!'

'Get back in the sitting room.' Wanda pointed. 'Go on. Put your bag down and sit in the armchair again. I just want to talk.'

'OK, but you must realise we can't really have much of a conversation at knifepoint.' Shannon stumbled back into the sitting room, keeping her eyes on the gleaming blade. What had it carved? Juicy roast chicken, lamb, pork crackling? Human flesh?

'Yes.' Wanda nodded and laughed, following her stare. 'This is it. The murder weapon.'

'The . . .?' Shannon felt faint.

'Sit in the armchair,' Wanda repeated. 'Throw your bag in the corner of the sofa – the furthest corner away from you. That's right.' She shut the door and edged back around the sofa, reached down and opened Shannon's bag with one hand. 'Hmm.' She pulled out Shannon's mobile. 'Bet that was lover boy who just called. Imagine if he could see you now, eh?

'Wanda – I realise you've got a horrendous case of acceptance overload, and I don't blame you. But this is stupid, you can't—'

'Shut up, all right? Just shut the fuck up.' Wanda dropped the mobile. 'I followed you two that night,' she said, her voice toneless now. 'You and your precious Jenny.'

Shannon gasped. *'What?'*

'You heard. Had a good time, did you? Drinking, laughing, clubbing. Fong could do that, she could just go out and enjoy herself without a care in the world the day after she'd told me it didn't look like the police were going to arrest the bastard who had hurt Alex, and there was nothing they could do. Don't!' she screamed as Shannon half rose. 'Fuck off and die, that was Fong's attitude. The next day I was walking around after I'd been to see Alex – I told the staff I was just popping down to the canteen for a bite to eat, but for some reason I carried on walking out of the hospital – I didn't even know where I was going. I found myself outside her office building. I wanted to go in and talk to her again – her or her little bastard boss – but I knew it was pointless. Then I saw her come out – she must have been working late. Not on Alex's case, of course. I followed her to that bar where she met you. I knew who you were, I'd heard of you. Seen your picture in the paper once or

297

twice.' She held up the knife, turning the blade. 'I'd started carrying this around in case I ever came across the man who hurt Alex. It's sharp enough, you know. I'll prove it. I know you lawyers are big on proof. Or what looks like it.'

Shannon watched in horror as Wanda pushed up her sweater sleeve to reveal a forearm covered in scabbed gashes, and carved a long, deep cut with the knife. Blood flowed, dripped down.

'See?' Wanda held up her arm. Drops of blood fell on Shannon's bag. 'I followed you both on your big night out,' she resumed. 'Were you celebrating something?'

'No,' Shannon whispered.

'I watched you eat, drink, saw blokes try to chat you up. They were only interested in you, weren't they? I thought Fong seemed a bit jealous, although she played the good sport. Suppose she was used to doing that. Cinderella out clubbing with her ugly sister. That's a familiar scenario, isn't it?'

'Jenny isn't – wasn't ugly.'

'Maybe she didn't love you as much as you think. I was in a daze about Alex, wondering what the hell I could do next. I felt so angry, so bloody powerless.' She shook her head. 'I thought killing her would help me. But it didn't.'

Shannon was wondering if she could make a rush for the door, get out and down the stairs before Wanda caught her. Her mobile and car keys were in her bag, but she would have to leave them. She was fitter than Wanda, could run a lot faster. I knew Jevko Arib was innocent, she thought. I so knew it.

'I wasn't sure if I'd do anything.' Wanda looked at her again. 'To Fong, I mean. But then I thought, who does she think she is? She knows about Alex, knows some bastard put him in hospital, in a coma. She can laugh and have fun while she knows he's lying there, knows I'm at the end of my tether, dreading every minute of every day that he'll die and leave me all alone. She knows all that and she doesn't fucking care.' Wanda started to cry. 'Some stupid old fat cow with mad hair,' she sobbed. 'That's what Fong thought I was.'

'No.' Shannon shook her head. 'Never. Jenny wasn't like that.'

'Not to you, maybe. When you and she said goodnight to one another I followed her. Even then I wasn't sure I'd do anything. I just kept walking after her, at a distance, all the way to St George's Hall. She passed a few people, so I couldn't do anything with them near. She couldn't find a cab – if she had it might have saved her life.' Wanda wiped her eyes on her sleeve. 'I caught up with her once she was alone again, no one around. I told her I didn't like her, didn't like her indifference. She got a big shock, started gabbling rubbish. Then she started acting the stupid little girl trying to be brave, and told me to get lost. When I showed her the knife she started crying and begging me not to hurt her, made all kinds of promises we both knew would never materialise. Like you before – that struck a nasty chord with me. I didn't believe Fong, of course. And by then I was really angry. I just lost it.'

'You murdered her. You murdered Jenny.'

'If you want to call it murder. When she was lying there in all that blood and I realised she was dead, that it was me who'd actually killed her, stabbed her all those times, I couldn't believe it. I thought, Christ, what have I done? What about Alex? I can't let them catch me and put me away for years, Alex needs me. I ran and hid behind one of those stone pillars. It was all floodlit, but I was safe there. I stayed for a bit, wondering what to do. Then that guy – the one who's been arrested for Fong's murder – crashed his van. He found her. I watched – I could tell he was terrified when he found her. She must have been a nasty sight, because he threw up. I wasn't too freaked to get his van number though because I thought that could be my chance to put him in the frame. I didn't care. He was nobody, nothing to me. And I had to think of Alex.'

Shannon took a breath. 'You haven't helped Alex at all though, have you?'

'Well, no one knows I killed Fong – except you now.' Wanda smiled through her tears, a chilling smile. 'I went back to the hospital, slipped in through some side door. No one noticed. I sat by Alex's bed again and when the day staff came on duty they assumed I'd been there all night. And now the police might be pestering me about that Nightingale bitch, but they can't prove a thing. That's because I didn't bloody do anything to her, the drunken cow. They pester me for something I didn't do. Irony, eh?'

'Life's full of it.' Shannon stared at the knife. 'Wanda, let me go. I won't say anything to anyone about this.' Of course she would call Cathy Rose the minute she got the chance. If she got it.

'Well, letting you go means I'd have to trust you, doesn't it? And I'm afraid I don't. Trust you, that is.'

'Look. Think, will you? For once. That nurse at the hospital knows I gave you a lift home, remember? Her colleagues must know too. If I end up dead right after driving you home, isn't it going to look a bit bloody obvious who might have done it?'

'Not necessarily. You're a lawyer, you've probably got lots of enemies waiting and hoping for a chance to waylay you.'

'The police will search this place. What do you want, my blood spattered all over your walls? I don't think so.'

'There won't be any blood. We'll go for a drive in your pretty car.' Wanda rummaged in Shannon's bag again and pulled out the keys. 'Come on.' She pointed the knife. 'We'll go now.'

'Forget it.' Shannon shook her head. If Wanda, in her freaked unpredictability, suddenly decided to start stabbing her while she was trying to keep control of a moving car, she would stand less chance of escape than she did now.

'Do what I tell you!' Wanda screamed. 'Or I'll kill you right now.'

'You're going to do it anyway.' She's overweight, Shannon thought, out of condition. She's drunk nearly a whole bottle of wine. It's got to be now or never. But Wanda had the knife. She readied herself, her heart pounding. Wanda's menacing bulk edged closer. She's strong though, Shannon thought. Strong and mad. She dodged sideways as Wanda lunged at her, stabbing into air. There wasn't much room to move. A grime and mould-encrusted plate cracked as Shannon stood on it.

'Sorry about the Wedgwood,' she shouted, dodging the knife again. She grabbed a couple of forks and flung them; one hit Wanda on her left shoulder, the other dropped to the floor.

'Fucking bitch,' Wanda screamed. 'I'm going to stick you the way I did your precious mate. You know what? She deserved everything she got, every cut. I loved doing it.' She made another lunge as Shannon stumbled over a couple of sweaters on the floor and almost fell back on the sofa. 'I loved terrifying her, I loved hurting her. I loved killing her!'

Shannon grabbed the wine bottle and flung it, spilling what remained. It missed Wanda's big head and smashed against the wall. Wanda laughed and shook back her hair, her eyes wild. She ran forward again, slashing at air, and the knife caught Shannon on her upper right arm. She felt a stinging sensation, then warmth and wetness.

'No,' she screamed. Wanda struck out again, gasping and grunting with fury. She was intent on her purpose now, not even thinking about the police coming here, searching her filthy pit of a flat, measuring blood spatter patterns on walls. There was no chance of appealing to her reason; she had none left. Shannon tried to stop her mind blanking out with panic. She had to keep moving, keep thinking.

Everything was a blur except for the tip of the knife, now smeared with her blood, a few black shreds of fibre from her jacket clinging to it. Shannon had a vision of Jenny that freezing night, trying to fight, shield herself from death. Wanda jabbed the knife at her again, missing her face by centimetres. She managed to grab Wanda's forearm and twist hard.

'Get off me, you bitch.' Wanda screamed again. Shannon guessed it wasn't so much her twist of Wanda's arm that hurt as the gashes Wanda had given herself. She tried desperately to hang on and twisted harder, trying to force Wanda to drop the knife. If she let go she was finished. Shannon kicked her, making her stumble. She kicked again and pushed Wanda to the floor. They were both shouting, grunting, screaming. Shannon wondered if anyone would hear and phone the police; of course she could not count on that. She might be dead any second. One stab to her heart, lung, neck, a major artery in her arm or thigh, and it would be over. They rolled on the floor amongst broken glass, dirty clothes, cracked dinner plates and old magazines. Wanda was biting and spitting now, like a cornered wild animal. Shannon gave a huge wrench to her arm and cried out in horror at the sickening crack that resulted. Wanda let go of the knife and started to howl.

'You broke my arm! You fucking bitch, you broke my...!'

Shannon struggled to her feet, gasping and sobbing, and kicked the knife beneath the sofa where Wanda could not reach it. She grabbed her bag and ran out of the flat, stumbled down the stairs. In the hall she rummaged in her bag for the mobile. Lipgloss, wallet, Moleskin notebook, pens and car keys fell out.

'Shit, shit, shit.'

'Did she do something to you?' The little girl in the hall pointed up the stairs. She came forward and started to pick up the fallen objects. 'She's weird,' she said, pointing again. 'Bad news, my mum says.'

'Your mum's right. Go back inside, go to her now.' Shannon ran out.

In the street she stopped and took big, gulping breaths, trying to get herself together. She called Cathy Rose, praying she would answer. Cathy did, but at first all Shannon could do was cry.

'Shannon, what on earth's the matter? What's happened?'

'Wanda Brennan. She murdered Jenny – she just tried to kill me. Her footprints – it's her footprints that were at the crime scene, the ones you couldn't identify. The knife's under the sofa. I kicked it there. Get over here quick. Her place – now.'

'Jeez ... on our way!'

When the police burst into her flat Wanda Brennan was still lying on the floor, still wailing like some lost spirit from Celtic mythology, her broken arm limp and useless by her side. The knife was retrieved from under the sofa, bagged and tagged. Cathy Rose stepped forward.

'Wanda Brennan, I am arresting you for ...'

Wanda took no notice, just kept on wailing and screaming. In between her wails Shannon heard her repeat one name. Over and over again.

'*Alex. Alex. Alex!*'

Chapter Twenty-Nine

'Great news, Jevko! They've dropped the murder charge.'

'What?' Jevko opened his eyes to find his solicitor standing at the bedside. She was smiling, holding back her long blonde hair as she leaned over the bed. He had never seen her smile before, or not at him. The nurse finished changing the saline drip and went away. Jevko knew he had allowed himself to become very ill because he did not care any more and wanted to die. But some force was ruthlessly dragging him back, tugging on the thread that kept him anchored in this world.

'They've dropped the murder charge,' she repeated. 'The police have arrested someone else for Jenny Fong's murder. They've got evidence. There's no doubt.'

Jevko closed his eyes again. 'I don't believe it,' he whispered. 'I've been telling them all along that I'm innocent. Why would they suddenly start to believe me now?'

'I told you. They've arrested someone else.'

'Who?'

'Some woman. She knew the victim, she's ... well ... she's very disturbed, to put it mildly. She's confessed and they've got other evidence as well – they don't just have to rely on her confession. You're in the clear.'

Jevko let the information sink in. Slowly. When he opened his eyes again the solicitor was glancing at her watch. Of course she had a lot of other clients to visit.

'But this doesn't mean I'm free now. Does it?'

'Well, no. There's your illegal alien status and the gang-master thing. Pretty serious, I'm afraid; both those things are hot political issues that the powers-that-be want to crack down on.' She cocked her head to one side, the smile gone now. 'Of course they don't carry as heavy a sentence as murder but—'

Jevko was too tired for this. 'How long?'

'Er. Well. You could be looking at three to possibly five years.' She was glancing through papers now. Lawyers always had so many papers, documents of all kinds. And cheap biros that didn't work. 'I'm not sure though, we'll have to see. But I'm doing my very best for you. And at least you're not facing the murder thing any more.'

'Yes. Wonderful not to be charged with a crime I didn't commit.'

He supposed this was not the worst thing that had happened to him. Jevko nevertheless felt the tears start. The last time he had cried was when he had seen Mariam and Shamila, that terrible visit a few days ago. They were living in some detention centre now. Doing time, just like he was. Mariam did not say much about what their life there was like. He got the feeling she did not want to worry him more.

'What will happen now?'

'Well, the first thing is for you to get better. Jevko, try not to be upset.' She handed him a couple of tissues from her handbag; they smelled of perfume and leather, the outdoors. 'You'll continue to be kept on remand.'

'What about my wife and daughter?'

'They won't deport Mariam and Shamila, certainly not while you're—'

'Deport them? No!' Jevko struggled to sit up. Pain stabbed his chest, making it difficult to breathe. 'They can't do that, they can't separate us. Don't try to tell me my country is safe now, it's not. Not for women or children. My wife and daughter can't go back there, they have no family any more. There is nothing for them. And I was imprisoned, I was tortured. They might be persecuted!'

'Exactly – that's what we're claiming. Okay, there's a new government in your country now, but I'm still sure they won't be sent back, seeing as they've no longer got family there. Like I said, Jevko, I'm doing all I can. Try to calm down, all right?'

He lay back on the pillows, sniffing, swallowing tears. She said goodbye to him and walked out, turned to throw him one last pitying smile. He supposed she was right, that at least he wasn't facing the murder charge any more.

Appeals. Years in prison. Separation from the two people he loved most in all the world. That was what he faced now.

Despite everything he had been through, Jevko felt that this was just the beginning.

'Why did you murder Jenny, Wanda? Did you blame her?'

They kept asking questions even though she had bowed her head, compressed her lips, silently suffered the pain from her broken, strapped arm and retreated to the space deep inside herself. If she didn't stay silent she would descend into screaming, gibbering madness. Of course the police, shrinks and lawyers thought she was mad anyway. Some impatient doctor had given her an injection after she refused to stop strug-gling and kicking out, screaming for Alex. She was quiet now. They had locked her in this cool blue cell and brought her out from time to time to ask her more stupid questions.

Wanda knew there had been stuff about her on television and in the papers; one of the policemen had made some remark about how she was quite a celeb now. Her mother had disowned her, weeping through one interview after another about how she had done her best and did not deserve the dis-grace and humiliation being heaped on her in widowed old age by her selfish psycho daughter who had been nothing but trouble from the minute she was born. The policewoman, the spiteful one who didn't like her, had shown her the tabloid article on the quiet. It had had the opposite effect to the one she intended though, because Wanda had felt nothing but relief that she wouldn't have to face the evil, rancid old bag paying her a visit in here, or giving her that demented, shrivelling glare from across a courtroom when her trial began. Court. Christ!

They were going to put her away for years, that was a given. So why couldn't they just get the fuck on and do it, instead of subjecting her to all this humiliation and the nightmare of a trial? Justice being seen to be done, Wanda supposed. But how could you see justice being done when there was no justice? And what would happen to Alex now? They wouldn't let her see him.

Why had she suddenly remembered Jenny Fong when she thought she had done such a good job of shoving that thing so deep into her subconscious that she could never again resurrect it? Wanda had almost managed to persuade herself that it had never happened, that it was all just one more bad dream. She did not feel guilty or shocked now. Just completely bewildered. And if she couldn't figure herself out, how could any police officer, lawyer or psychiatrist hope to? Fuck the lot of them, she thought. They had found her diaries, of course, the detritus of her life recorded in thick black ink. They were not interested in the truth, they would just think what they wanted to think, bend and twist everything to fit their half-arsed theories.

She sat still, staring at the blue tiled wall, thinking how easy it would be to hose down should she suddenly decide to bash out her brains on it. They had taken everything away from her – shoes, pens, lighter, anything she could have used to harm herself. The tension was building again, her broken arm hurting, her mind through the painkillers and tranquillisers a miasma of unresolved thoughts and chaotic emotions. Wanda could not cry, could not think straight. All she could do was sit and look at the wall.

She sighed as she heard footsteps along the corridor. She had been caught, locked up, she was finished now and she knew it, thank you very much. If only they would leave her in peace instead of getting her out, marching her around, parading her like some circus exhibit. They were the pathetic ones, not her. Stupid, self-important bastards. They were a lot sadder than she could ever be. Was it time for another meal, she wondered? She couldn't smell food. She was hungry again, was putting on more weight.

The door was unlocked and a police officer and some plain-clothes person – social worker, counsellor, solicitor? – came in. The plain-clothes person was a thin, fifty-something woman with short grey hair and lined brown eyes behind small round glasses. She wore a long denim skirt, a blue sweater and black boots. Her bag was stuffed with yellow plastic files. She introduced herself and Wanda immediately forgot her name.

'Wanda?' The woman sat next to her and smiled, made a movement to take her hand then seemed to change her mind. 'It's about your husband,' she said. 'Alex.'

Wanda could not be bothered to retort that she might be a murderer but she wasn't stupid, thank you very much, and she did know her own husband's name. She caught her breath and chewed her lip as something welled deep inside her, the beginnings of crying, maybe even a scream. As if public opprobrium and the prospect of decades in jail wasn't bad enough, they were going to take away from her the only important thing in her life, the only person who mattered, the person she would always love. Alex.

'Alex,' she whispered. 'He's not ... oh, please, he's not...?'

'Not what? Wanda.' The woman grasped her hand now and squeezed it. 'It's all right,' she said. 'I promise you. Better than all right. I've got great news for you.' She was smiling now. 'Alex regained consciousness. Just a few hours ago. He's not brain-damaged; he remembers things. He's asking for you.'

Wanda stared at her, stunned. Then she started to scream.

Chapter Thirty

'There's something about death and funerals,' Finbar murmured as he hooked his thumb in Shannon's red lace panties and slid them down over her hips, 'that always makes me horny. Of course I realise it's inappropriate, not to say in extremely bad taste.'

The sun was setting over the river and the bedroom was bathed in soft golden light. They could smell the sea and the sharp, clear autumn air.

'Not necessarily inappropriate or distasteful. You want to affirm life.' Shannon slipped her arms around his neck. 'Did you know "horny" comes from the Egyptian fertility god Amon, who's represented by a man with a ram's head?'

'Jesus.' He grinned as he tossed her panties on the floor. 'You're a walking bloody encyclopaedia since you started reading that esoteric blockbuster.'

'An esoteric encyclopaedia.' She gasped as he flicked his tongue over her nipples.

It had been one hell of a day. Again. Jenny's funeral; Shannon had been relieved that it could take place at last, but at the same time she had dreaded it. It had been as harrowing as she had expected. It was bad enough when the loved one had reached a good age and experienced a swift, painless death, but when it was someone only in their early thirties who had been murdered . . . she shuddered and closed her eyes.

Shannon's head swam with exhaustion, sadness, desire and the champagne she and Finbar had drunk when they got home, as a toast and a tribute to Jenny's memory. Champagne had been Jenny's favourite drink. She gave a little sob.

'Hey, what's this?' Finbar stopped what he was doing and stared down at her. 'I don't mean to be an insensitive bastard, but don't you think you've done enough crying for one day?'

'Jenny should be drinking champagne and making love with someone she's crazy about. She should have the rest of her life to look forward to. But she's dead, murdered. Lying in that fucking grave.'

Finbar nodded. He stroked her face and touched one finger to her lips. 'She was your best friend. A great person. You'll always miss her. The only positive thing is that at least you've got closure. Wanda Brennan's locked up, and that poor bastard who had the bad luck to be in the wrong place at the wrong time – well, he won't go free of course, not yet, but he's got one less thing he'll have to deal with now.'

Shannon shifted on the bed and stretched. 'I don't know anything any more.'

'What do you mean?'

'Richard Croft, for one thing. There was Rob, his bloody father – they hated me too. Why, what did I ever do? I can't get my head round it. Is it just bad luck?'

'You've certainly had enough of that.' Finbar's voice was gentle.

'And why did that Brennan bitch have to murder Jenny? OK, I know she's confessed and said she blamed Jenny and every-thing, however irrational that was. But lots of people have terrible problems and they don't go hurting or murdering anyone. I didn't like Brennan. I thought she was weird, but I never even suspected she'd be capable of murder. She's got no criminal record, nothing. She seemed so hopeless.'

'It was a one-off,' Finbar said. 'She flipped. It happens, doesn't it? Bloody ironic, her husband waking from his coma – without brain damage or anything, like the doctors feared he'd have – to find his devoted wife's committed murder. Christ almighty.' He sat up and reached for the champagne bottle. 'That won't exactly aid his recovery. What a nightmare. I hope he gets shut of her. Still.' He refilled their glasses. 'I don't want to think about that any more. Don't want to think about any of the shit that's happened.' He put the bottle down and leaned over Shannon again, kissing her and stroking her body. 'My only concern is you, Gorgeous'

'Gorgeous will be all right,' she murmured. 'Eventually.'

'How about a good long holiday somewhere beautiful and hot?'

'Make the reservations and I'll pack my anti-gravity cream.'

'You sure?' He grinned. 'What about work?'

'Fuck work. Fuck it for ever and ever and ever.'

Shannon closed her eyes as fear and the bitter pain of Jenny's loss swept over her again. Traumatic images clashed in her mind, replayed themselves. Richard Croft about to kill her, Wanda Brennan's footprints in Jenny's blood. The moment passed and she could breathe again.

'After the holiday ...' Finbar wrapped his arms around her, 'you can have a long, safe, quiet, boring existence. With me. If that's what you want, of course.'

'You know I want you. For ever.' She stared into his green eyes. 'But you don't do quiet and boring, and I wouldn't want you to.'

'You want me for ever, do you?'

'That's a given. Get out the sparkler.'

He smiled and kissed her. 'First, another toast.' They sat up and he handed her a glass of champagne. 'To Jenny.'

'To Jenny.' Shannon clinked her glass to his, her eyes wet. She drank the champagne in one go and Finbar took the glass from her and put it back on the bedside table. He kissed her again and stroked her bare shoulders.

'I'll get the sparkler in a minute. Right, Blue Eyes.' But he was not looking at her eyes. 'Where were we?'